The Brain That Couldn't Think

L. J. Dopp

The Brain That Couldn't Think

ISBN 10   0-9890242-1-0
ISBN 13   978-0-9890242-1-1

Edited by Paul Jeffrey Davids

First Printing, First Edition   March, 2017

Yellow Hat Publishing
A Division of Yellow Hat Productions, Inc.
5605 Riggins Court #200
Reno, NV 89502

Back cover photo by Paul Essick
Cover painting, George Clayton Johnson, H. P. Lovecraft, and the
Griffith Observatory paintings; and illustrations for "The Brain That
Couldn't Think" and "Tommy Amos of Mars" by L. J. Dopp

Jacket design and computer imaging by Don Allen
Additional typography by J. Kent Hastings

Foreword © 2013 by Geoge Clayton Johnson

"The Sound of Thunder – The Wrath of God" was previously published
in *October's End* (2016; Horrific Press).

"A Conversation with George Clayton Johnson" © 2011 by L. J. Dopp

Dedicated to George Clayton Johnson ~
friend, teacher, and fellow science fiction fan.

Foreword

I know L. J. Dopp to be an excellent painter. He did a portrait of me that knocks me out every time I look at it. The funny thing about artists is that in addition to drawing and painting they are often adept at writing, directing, acting, or any other pop-culture art form.

They are children of the media who love their parents.

L.J. is also a long-time member of science fiction fandom. "Fandom" is a place where a man can make a name for himself by being himself. It is a well-organized, world-wide society of individualists.

It is also the only leaderless society that I know of. No one or no group is in charge, although each fan has a measure of influence and the egoboo that goes with it.

The issue here is "LIBERTY."

Daffy Duck says, "Nobody tells this little black duck what to do." Daffy speaks for me, and, I believe, for L.J. Dopp as well.

Wanting to make you "laugh, cry, or throw up," L.J. decided to write a book. Since no-one was there to stop him he took matters into his own hands and wrote this one!

Read "The Brain that Couldn't Think" and discover what a fascination with pop-culture, a satirical turn of mind, an ironic sense of humor, and a head full of bright ideas can do to a man.

Sincerely,
George Clayton Johnson
Pacoima, CA
December, 2013

Author's Preface

In grammar school, I loved the comedic stories of James Thurber, Jean Shepherd, and Robert Benchley, and in high school, I had a similar fascination with the satiric, sci-fi writing of Robert Sheckley. But, it was in my '20s, after reading Charles Bukowski and Raymond Chandler, that I started writing.

Most of these stories were written between 1999 and 2003, and in their original drafts, most were rejected by publishers. I'm more into the Elmore Leonard, less-is-more thing, these days, so all of them have been fiercely trimmed and re-written for this volume. In part, I used Ray Bradbury's method of self-editing taught to me by George Clayton Johnson, which is outlined in my 1999 interview with George, published in the back of this book.

At the time these stories were written America was still basking in the healthy market economy left by the Bill Clinton administration and had not yet experienced the economic downfall that came in the wake of the 9/11 attack, nor had waged wars that landed us trillions of dollars in debt. If you take issue with that statement, it's about as political as this book gets – except for "In the Day," a story based on my experiences as a political cartoonist at *The L.A. Free Press* during the 1972 Watergate scandal. There's where I discovered Bukowski's weekly column, and had my first professional cartoons and comic strips published.

For the most part, I decided not to go back and put iPhones in peoples' hands. Let the stories stand as they were written, reflecting a simpler time – wayyy back when. During the intervening decade-and-a-half the way we communicate with each other has changed completely: Facebook, Twitter, and text messaging, have all emerged in the new millennium.

Some of these stories are interlinked. A fictional movie from the titular "Brain" novella appears on a marquee in 1972 with a real film in "In the Day." A future Martian town mentioned in the latter story exists in "Tommy Amos of Mars." The Morbid Opus, a fictional horror-themed boutique, appears in "Daughter of Depravity" and "The Man Who Was Severely Edited" – while, the latter story ties into "In the Day" …And, so on.

George Clayton Johnson was truly a dear friend – and many can say that about him as he made everyone feel special. He was The Pied Piper – literally, at times. We blew our share of reefer over the years, and had long conversations on story ideas and life. He kindly appeared in two of my films, as well as reading all the stories in this book and giving me invaluable feedback. The above-mentioned interview, keyed to his collection, *"All of Us Are Dying and Other Stories,"* has been posted on several sites over the years, but has never seen print until now. If you are a writer yourself, or a fan of George's work, it is a must-read.

He offered to write a foreword for this ten years ago, and asked me several times over the years, "What ever happened to *The Brain that Couldn't Think?"* Well, George, here it is. I hope it measures up. Thank you for your mentoring and friendship!

Brad Linaweaver, sci-fi author and writer-producer of *The Silicon Assassin* web-series among other entertainments, also read these stories when I wrote them, and even threatened to publish a collection in 2012, but it never came together on my end. Brad is a great patron of my art, co-produced my horror parody, *"Crustacean,"* and with Jessie Lilley, publishes my art and writing in their *Mondo Cult* franchise (now mondocult.com). We've had, and will continue to have, big laughs and many creative adventures together – thank you, Brad!

If not for these two men you would not be reading this book at all, and without the collaboration of Paul Jeffrey Davids (producer of *Roswell, The Sci-Fi-Boys,* and 2016's *Marilyn Monroe Declassified),* it would not have been published at this time. Special thanks to Paul, for being such a relentlessly cheerful and versatile collaborator, and for giving me so much creative freedom in the writing and illustrations.

L.J. Dopp
Sherman Oaks, CA
October, 2016

Table of Contents

The Man Who Was Severely Edited

Burton Tolliver was in a good mood for a Tuesday. If he could just get this thing copied without someone seeing him, it would be a perfect crime. *"Clunk – whirrr,"* went the copy machine, *"clunk – whirrr."*

Tolliver was the senior editor of *Dreaded Cutlets*, one of the top horror/fantasy magazines in the country. As such, he had little to fear from anyone in the office, but liked to make a game of it anyway – surreptitiously copying submitted manuscripts, after hours when the office was empty, but only when he'd found something he thought he could use. In this case, although he'd rejected the story and would return it to the author, it contained a perfectly good twist ending that was worth copying for his files at home.

"Not a bad story. Too bad he doesn't know a dash from a semicolon," Tolliver said to himself. "He splits infinitives like Lincoln split rails."

"Then why'd you copy it?" Bob Ratchet asked, peering out of the supply room at him. Tolliver was a master of psychological manipulation, on the order of a Captain Bligh or Hannibal Lector, and had learned long ago that the best defense was a strong offense.

"Are you actually asking me to qualify my movements around my own office? Is that what you're doing, Mr. Ratchet, or do I surmise wrongly?"

"Uh, no… you surmise wrongly, Burton," the managing editor said, smiling his thin, underdog smile.

"What did you say? – Did you just tell me that *I'm wrong!?*"

"Uh, *no* – I mean, I'm not asking you to qualify anything…"

"Please, Bob – I thought you'd gone, that's all. You startled me a little," Tolliver said, turning to leave, "now, goodnight."

"I'll have another batch of stories for you Friday," Ratchet called after him.

"I know you will," the senior editor said, without looking back, "that's your job." Tolliver opened the door, the hallway leered in; suddenly, he wheeled, facing the younger man. "Just why, exactly, is that headline news?"

"It isn't," Ratchet said, "it's just my way of saying goodnight – trying to please you… to curry favor obsequiously. That's what you want everybody to do, isn't it, Burt?" Tolliver took this insubordination rather poorly, staring without blinking, cobra-like.

"The name is Burton – not *Burt*, and you don't have to be redundant about it. I'd really prefer those manuscripts be on my desk tomorrow, Mr. Ratchet – tomorrow morning, in fact. Feel free to work late. And be selective – no vampire stories this month."

"But, Burton – thirty-two more submissions came in over the weekend, alone! I'm almost through last week's arrivals, but I want to do the writers justice – there's just no way I can read…"

"Now, you're arguing with me? It would seem that you harbor a longing to return to your old post at *Gothic Pet Quarterly?*"

"No – not *that!* Anything but that!"

"I'm wrong again, then?"

"Yes – I mean, no," the smaller man said, utterly beaten.

"Then you'll have the manuscripts – the best of the lot, anyway – on my desk at 8:30 a.m., or it's back to pushing marble cat-boxes, agreed?"

"I… uh… uh…"

"I knew you'd see it my way, Bob. Take the work home if you like," Tolliver said, chuckling wickedly, "you have my permission."

The senior editor of *Dreaded Cutlets* turned up King's Road, off the palm tree-lined stretch of billboards and bistros known as the Sunset Strip. He could taste the salt-sea air that had crawled inland all day, hugging the Santa Monica Mountains and their thousand little canyons before melting into twilight fog. The chaparral-covered range spread east from the Pacific, carrying Sunset along its cuffs, rising over Brentwood and Bel Air, and finally becoming the Hollywood Hills. There, Burton Tolliver lived, high above his office on the Strip.

Driving up, past the butterscotch glow of windows set, laughing, in the stone aeries of the great and the near-great, Tolliver wondered into which of those categories he fell? Would time be kind to him? Would his literary fame sustain itself? Would his books and stories still be in print a hundred years hence? – *Fifty* years?

It was into the garage of one of the many, alleged former residences of Errol Flynn that he pulled his Beamer. A vertically split, deco duplex built in the twenties, the house had been home to his last marriage – the ashes of which were strewn from one end to the other. Tolliver parked and just sat for a minute, reasonably happy, yet some inner part of him felt like having a good cry. Was this subconscious remorse for cheating potential contributors out of a fair appraisal of their work, just to punish Ratchet for sarcasm – the venom on which he, himself, thrived?

Hardly: Tolliver enjoyed his reputation as a tyrant, abusing co-workers and contributors alike. It afforded him some comfort, as he was miserable enough to try and make everyone around him more so. Dogs growled and children burst into tears when blasted by his withering glare. Twice divorced, he was childless, morally dissolute, and worst of all – *written out*. In fact, his laurels were about to collapse from all the resting.

Royalties continued to trickle in from his classic, still-in-print novels, however. *Crucible of Pain* and *Stargoat Eulogy* had firmly established him in the horror and sci-fi markets, and his fifth effort, *Time Wastrel*, had even made the New York Times Best-Seller List... in 1987.

Now older, and well-off from years of royalties, the pressure to create fiction for a living had long since evaporated, as had the desire – and eventually, even the ability. Many imitators had cranked-out variations on his earlier works, and he was still respected in the genre, despite the crap he was writing now. But, he resorted to borrowing from his purloined file contents more often – and more carelessly – than ever before, having just enough decency left to realize what he was doing was wrong, but not enough to stop doing it.

"Eureka!" he'd exclaimed when discovering today's find, in another story by that creative but sloppy writer, Justin Dial. It contained exactly the twist Tolliver had been looking for, even though it was the third idea he'd be cribbing from Dial, alone, for his new book – ironically titled, *Spirited Away*. The manuscript for this latest short story collection was due in New York in a few weeks.

It wasn't his fault he'd had to reject Dial's stories, Tolliver thought; they were well conceived, but badly executed. And, like so many green, would-be contributors, Dial didn't proofread his manuscripts carefully enough for Tolliver's taste. *Dreaded Cutlets* had high standards, and its busy editor had a reputation to uphold. At the third error, he'd stop reading a story – unless a clever idea he might be able to use begged continuing.

Tolliver wouldn't admit to himself that he rejected stories just because they'd been chosen for potential plundering – thus, compounding his dark deed. He knew that publication in his magazine was a sought-after achievement, and that being privy to writers' ideas before they hit the marketplace was a moral responsibility. He *was* the marketplace, or a part of it, at least; still, he had little problem justifying his actions.

If he published sloppy writers like Dial, not only would the quality of the publication diminish, but in Dial's case at least, direct *access* could be proved. He would be providing a "smoking gun," as it were, pointing a finger at himself and his new, *Spirited Away* collection. As far as cliché goes, that volume would prove to be the proverbial back-breaking straw of Burton Tolliver's career, just as surely as Justin Dial would become the axiomatic camel with the personal injury suit because of it.

Six months later, *Spirited Away* was out and Tolliver had returned from the East Coast leg of his book tour. Today, he was signing at The Morbid Opus in Encino. Nestled between a Starbucks and The Aroma Therapy Scenter (sic) in a posh, two-story strip-mall, The Morbid Opus was about the most pretentious excuse for a specialized bookstore one could find in L.A. – which is saying a lot.

The short, long-haired owner, Bill Vandermeer, had a small staff composed entirely of darkly dressed Goth-types, some even costumed. Whisper-thin and pale as corpses they slunk silently across the carpeting, the metal from their piercings reflecting purple-and-green light from the neon ceiling bat. Two *Alien* figures hung on wires, salaciously interlocked above the sci-fi section, and there was a blonde guy who looked like a gay, surf vampire playing be-bop dirges on a spinet. Potpourri-scented dead flower arrangements stunk-up a rack by the door, where guest author Burton Tolliver was grabbing a smoke.

"Excuse me, Mr. Tolliver," the pear-shaped man in the Hawaiian shirt said, "I met you at Cin-Con 24, last summer – Bix McLarty, Cincinnati – remember?" Bix held up a paperback. "*SEE?* I found that rare, Blackthorne Press edition of your third Ponston Chanticleer book we were talking about, '*The Antediluvian Quixote*,'– *SEE?*" The affable fan shoved the volume in Tolliver's face, not a doubt in his mind that the famous author remembered their conversation as well as he. "It's the one with the Gunnar Krebs cover – *SEE?* The one with Ponston in that Robin Hood-lookin' hat, ridin' his dinosaur into Princess Gwynwrynn's fairy-castle – *SEE?*"

"Sir," said Tolliver contemptuously, "kindly, allow me to enjoy my cigarette in peace, and take your place in line. Remember, patience is a virtue, and murder, a deadly sin – for, should you happen to obstreperously spray the word, 'see,' in my face one more time, then surely I shall gouge out your eyes with my fountain pen, and you will see no more – *SEE??*"

"Hey… That's not very cool. Screw you, big-shot! I came all the way from the L.A.X. Hilton to see you again, *schmuck* – I coulda gone to Disneyland." With that, the beefy owner of Biff's Driveway Upgrades pushed his way into the store.

Minutes later, Tolliver was back at the table, petulantly signing away. "May I have another glass of chilled mineral water?" he asked the nearest black-clad troglodyte, who shuffled away, mutely nodding. "And, tell that Troll doll with a hyperactive thyroid he's overpaying you."

Suddenly, a young man jumped in front of the signing line, grabbed one of the copies of *Spirited Away* and waved it at Tolliver, yelling, "You have the nerve to put your name on this? – Plagiarist! …*Thief!*"

"Excuse me?" Tolliver said, taken by surprise. "Just who do you think you are?"

"I'm the guy who writes your plots – uncredited, and unpaid!" the man said, as a clerk in a Mummy-costume limped toward him as fast as his bandages would allow. Fear began to tickle at Tolliver's insides, but he continued to act blasé.

"I'll have to ask you to keep your voice down, sir," said the Mummy.

"You don't understand! I'm suing him for ripping off my stories!" Turning back to Tolliver, he added sourly, "…Which all got REJECTED by his magazine, *Dreaded Cutlets!* … That's right, you rat with a tail, I'm Justin Dial – and Kirby Carmichael told me you ripped off his "*Parallel Lives of a Bengal Lancer*" story, too, only you changed the character to a Foreign Legionnaire instead!"

"I've never heard of you, nor laid eyes on you in my life, sir!" the guest author protested. "*Security!*"

"I *am* security," drawled the Mummy, "today, anyway – on Sundays, I'm the floor manager." He made the mistake of laying his hands on Dial.

"Back off, Im-hotep, or you're gonna need real bandages!"

"Call the police!" Tolliver yelled, but the crazed writer was back in his face.

"You took the blind Venusian slave-girl from my '*Hell Tours, Inc.*' story and made her a deaf Martian geisha in your '*Loyal Dynasty*,'" Dial declared. "You turned my city of zombie clowns from '*Jesterday*' into a city of junkie mimes in your story, '*Silent Needle Night!*' You even ripped off the twist ending from my novelet, '*I Scream Sunday!*' You used it to cap the loadstone of your book, – that completely derivative '*Hemlock for the Soul*' piece of junk. God, Tolliver – you even stole the *title!*"

"These seem to be vague concepts you're pointing out; similarities exist in nearly all genre stories…"

"Bullshit! You're just burnt out, that's what it is – I'd feel sorry for you if I had a dime in my pocket. I don't think you really understand how it is out there, today."

By the time the cops showed up, Dial had calmed down, and was telling Tolliver how hard it was for unknown writers to break in – even without getting ripped off by the editors they submit to. Seeing no disturbance, the officers moseyed into the Starbucks next door, against the protests of Vandermeer and his guest author.

"I've suspected you were doing this for a while, Tolliver, but you glommed three of my plot points in this last volume *alone*," Dial said passionately, holding up a copy of *Spirited Away*. The 'senior editor of *Dreaded Cutlets!*' I'm *really* impressed – *Eerie Yarns* and *Boneyard Stomp* are both better magazines, anyway."

"Look, young man, I read thousands of submissions a year. You can't possibly expect me to remember your particular stories – especially if our staff has passed on them? How do you know they even got to me? You can't prove a thing – go ahead and sue if that makes you happy."

"I've got something even better in mind, you shameless thug," Dial said. "I'm gonna jack up your ass bigtime, you just wait an' see! Screw your damn book – an' you, too! Your glory days are over. You're history, Tolliver. In fact, not *even* history, when I get through with you!"

"I simply can't sign under these conditions. I'm leaving."

"Not before signing my Ponston Chanticleer book," Bix McLarty said, leaning the red-faced half of his 240-pound frame on the table, right in front of Tolliver.

The author reluctantly complied.

"Thanks a lot... asshead."

"Not even history, Tolliver, not *even* history!" Dial repeated.

"You realize that once I place the spell on him, it will be irreversible. I can't call it off," the auburn-haired young woman said.

"Why would I want you to call it off? I want him to be miserable for the rest of his life. I want him to lose everything... everything that I don't have!"

"The senior editor of *Dreaded Cutlets* Magazine?" she said, confirming. She was trying to get all the practice she could, anyway, and wanted to impress Justin, who was buying her dinner at Chez Noir.

"Yeah... Burton Tolliver, that son-of-a-bitch. How do you do it, Deborah? Do you use a spell from one of those grimoire repros?"

"No," she said, laughing, as she noted the information on a cocktail napkin. They'd met in the occult store where she worked; her business card read, "*Necessary Evils*, Deborah Craven, Intern/Practitioner."

"Voodoo doll? – I can get you a lock of the bastard's hair if you want."

"Don't make fun of my power – it comes from my mother's side of the family. I don't use anything, I just *think* it. When I was little, my sister was playing with her new puppy in the bathtub – I guess it drowned – anyway, my parents told me I brought it back to life."

"No way!"

"That's what they told me. Mom always said I was special."

"You're freaking *Carrie.*"

"... I'm not telekinetic," she said, "and my mother isn't crazy... just a witch."

"All right, Deborah. So, you can make everything he's written just... disappear?"

"Probably... I'll try." He didn't really believe her, but *what the hey?* They toasted, glasses clinking, spilling just enough Cabernet to blur Tolliver's name on the napkin, leaving only the words, "SENIOR EDITOR OF DREADED CUTLETS MAGAZINE," legible. Neither of them noticed. She knotted her eyebrows, staring at the words remaining on the napkin, thinking hard.

"Done!" She said. "It'll take two weeks, though. The major spells always take two weeks to kick in. God, Justin, this is so mean – this one's on you!"

Two weeks later, Burton Tolliver woke up in a small, hot, one-bedroom apartment in the flatlands of downtown Hollywood. He looked out the window and saw a bum evacuating his bladder in the front yard. Then, he looked more carefully around the room, and saw some of his furniture, and at least *some* of his books – about half – and this was the thing that made him sit down, gasping: all of *his* books were gone – the ones that he'd written, that is!

Every single original novel, collection – even the anthologies he'd edited had vanished – hardcover and paperback alike! In a panic, he opened the file cabinet where his original manuscripts had been kept for the last twenty-five years. It was full of sales records – *vacuum cleaner* sales records, with a version of his name on each one. "Burt Tolliver," the invoices read. Apparently, this Burt Tolliver, with whom he was being horribly confused in a nightmare, was a salesman for the Suck-It-Up Vacuum Company.

His driver's license read Burt Tolliver, too, and its address was on Gardner, not King's Road. He didn't own an '84 Ford Escort, but another glance out the window revealed one sitting in the driveway. He called the office and asked for his secretary. After the third degree and five minutes on hold, the receptionist, a Ms. Bean, *whom Tolliver had hired*, came back on and not only said they'd never heard of him, but that for the last ten years, the senior editor had been a Robert L. Ratchet.

It got worse. Not only did *he* not have any of his books, but the bookstores and public library had none either. His agent and publisher had never heard of him. There was a mere $631 in his checking account, little more than that in his savings, no stock portfolio, and he only had one VISA card – maxed. Tolliver had gone from being halfway to a millionaire, to having less than a couple of grand – literally, overnight.

It was as if every cent he'd ever earned from writing had never existed.

He hoped it was only a bad dream, but as the day wore on it became obvious that something was terribly wrong. The next morning, when things were exactly the same, Tolliver knew it wasn't a dream and felt dreadfully ill. He wept bitterly and stayed in bed shaking for two days, refusing to eat, or clean himself. He'd forgotten all about Justin Dial's threats, and Bob Ratchet had forgotten all about him – along with everyone else in the world who'd ever heard of Burton Tolliver.

If he wanted to be a writer now, he was all alone in it. There would be no favors called in, no more requests for his stories, and absolutely no more resting on laurels. There was one bright thought in his head, though: he was no longer written-out, because this new world had never read, or even heard of, his early books and stories.

Having enough money to live for a while, he would simply rewrite a few short stories and his best-selling novel, *"Time Wastrel,"* from memory, submit them to publishers, and Burton Tolliver would rise again. He found his old manual typewriter: the same one with which he'd begun writing so many years before.

An hour later, the phone rang.

"Tolliver? What the hell are you doing there? Are you drunk again? You're supposed to be in Fresno right now!"

"You have me confused with another Tolliver – someone named, *'Burt.'*"

"Wha...? You're drinking again, aren't you? Well, just so you know, Superior Appliances called. The owner waited all afternoon yesterday for you to take him to lunch. He's a new client, and he's not happy. Some things just can't be done by fax and e-mail, dammit – *'Suck It Up,'* Tolliver!"

"I beg your pardon? Perhaps you don't understand – whoever you are. Let me put it this way: I do not sell... *vacuum cleaners.* Not for you – not for the bloody Queen. For some unknown reason I've been cursed with living in a nightmare, and – although I am loath to end a sentence in a preposition – fortunately, *you* are the part I can hang up on. Good day," he said, and hung up.

"I *reeeally* need a drink after that."

He quickly found a bottle of gin in the cupboard. No wonder he'd been crying in bed for three days – he was an *alcoholic*, and had forgotten to drink. Thank God, that Suck-It-Up person had called and informed him of his condition. After three drinks he almost felt good for the first time in his new life of squalid anonymity.

After two weeks, Tolliver had paid a month's rent and bills, drank-up another $150, and was down to a little over $700 – his total life's savings at the age of fifty-five. But soon, he'd be getting checks in the mail from his submissions. Soon, he'd get a fat advance on the novel, which was half reconstructed. And soon, he'd be back up in the Hills where he belonged.

He'd driven past his old house a dozen times – weeping. The butterscotch windows of the great and the near-great laughed at *him*, now – their stone aeries, cold as dead lawyers.

Two weeks and two days after his rebirth as a nobody, Tolliver thought he'd imagined the doorbell, but kept typing. Moments later, a familiar voice piped in through the open window, "Excuse me? …Burton Tolliver?" It was Bob Ratchet. …At *his* apartment. Now that's what happens when a real pro sends out a classic short story – the editor actually comes to his house with the check. Or, so he thought.

"See, Bob, I tried to tell you I was a great writer – but you wouldn't hear of it… *See? – SEE?* … Pretty good story, huh?"

"Actually, I'm not the editor any more – and I still don't remember you, Tolliver, but that crazy thing you said happened to you? Well, now it's happened to *me*."

"To you…?"

"Everything I've ever written has disappeared from the face of the Earth," Bob said. "Everything… After ten years as senior editor of *Dreaded Cutlets*, nobody even remembers me. The new editor, Cameron Kilgore? His name has even replaced mine in the staff boxes of old issues! … Swears he's never heard of me – it's creepy."

"…Hate to burst your bubble, Bob, but you were *never* senior editor – till two weeks ago. I was the senior editor for ten years; you've been the managing editor for the last four. Prior to that, you worked for a pet magazine."

"Everything I ever wrote is gone – and here I am, telling a complete stranger. I only had two chapters to go on a pre-sold novel. The on-publication payment was going to cover an operation for my youngest boy, Little Elvis, but I guess we can forget that. It'll take me a year just to reconstruct what I had. Now, that's a horror story, Tolliver, to be erased from history."

"What did you say?" Tolliver asked, stunned.

"Huh?"

"*History!* ... Erased from *history!* – That's it, Ratchet! Don't you SEE? That callow upstart, Justin Dial, from whom I was stealing..."

"I finally decided to publish one of Dial's stories last week, for some reason..."

"Small potatoes, now – anyway, Bob – he said he was going to curse me, and that I wouldn't even be *history!* We've got to get hold of Dial. Only he can undo this perverse injustice!"

It didn't take them long to locate the young writer's number.

"Hi... you've reached the answering machine of Justin Dial, and I can't come to the phone, because principal photography actually started on my movie and I'm on location for three weeks! – YA-HOOOO! If you're a burglar, my Rottweiler can't come to the phone either, but he's fuckin' there... BEEP!"

Three weeks later, Justin Dial's doorbell rang. When he answered it, Burton Tolliver, Bob Ratchet and Cameron Kilgore, none of whom he recognized, were standing on his porch.

"I've never heard of any of you guys in my life," Dial said, after letting them in. "And I don't know how you found out about the spell. I had this girlfriend for a while – she and her mom are witches – anyhoo, I had her put this spell on the senior editor of *Dreaded Cutlets*... what's his name...?" He fumbled, grabbing a dog-eared issue. "Here it is in the staff box – *see?* His name is *Garner Hempstead*, not any of your names, and he's still editor!"

"Let me see that, Tolliver said. "God, it does read, 'Garner Hempstead!' And it's *over a year old!!*"

"Last week he was only an assistant editor and today he doesn't remember me," Kilgore said, shaking his head.

"Deborah – the witch I was dating – went to Ireland for the summer. All she said was that the spell takes two weeks to kick in and it can't be reversed. I don't know what else to tell you... except, congratulate me – besides selling that script, I got a story picked up by that new medical sci-fi monthly, *'Phantasthma.'"*

Outside Dial's apartment, the three "severely edited" writers decided that the best thing to do was to just keep writing and sending it out, and to keep in touch with each other. And, of course, to monitor the revolving door editorship of the spellbound magazine. "The fool cursed the position of Senior Editor – not just me," Tolliver told the others. "Now, whoever becomes editor only lasts two weeks, and then their entire body of work disappears."

"Tell me about it," said Kilgore, "you *schmuck!* – No offense – I mean, if what you've told us is *true* – you schmuck."

Since only the writers who'd been "edited" knew what was going on – but none remembered their predecessors – there was little organization among them. Tolliver tried to band them together, partly to appease his appetite for controlling people, but it didn't last. Just as Bob Ratchet had called the magazine and faced off with Kilgore, so had Kilgore tried to go to work when he was "edited," and ended up confronting Hempstead, who of course, didn't remember him, either, and so-on...

For some reason, there was a flaw in the curse. While the work of those writers "edited" by the spell was erased *from the memories* of everyone in the world, those "edited" writers seemed to be immune to the erasure from their memories of the work of those writers "edited" subsequently. Confusing? You bet.

At one point, Tolliver led several of the fallen editors on a crusade to the compound of the magazine's reclusive and oblivious publisher, Wolf J. Farnsback, to try and convince him of the ongoing effect of the spell, and were turned back at the gates.

About two months, or four *Dreaded Cutlets* editors later, Tolliver started getting his stories back from the other magazines – rejected. Those editors all said pretty much the same thing: *Well written. Perfect grammar and pro style, but story ideas unbelievably trite. Done a thousand times before. Try to come up with an ORIGINAL concept.*"

Tolliver's stories had been copied so much that even though noone remembered them, his creative story elements had permeated the genre, nonetheless, by having influenced countless books and stories not "severely edited."

Tolliver was more crushed with each rejection: his screams upon opening the mailbox turned heads and stopped traffic on his street. The same day his rushed-out reconstruction of *Time Wastrel* came back, he got the eviction notice.

Most of the talented editors who were "severely edited" landed on their feet – especially the young ones. Bob Ratchet ironically wound up back at Gothic Pet Quarterly, and under his benevolent guidance it became a bi-monthly. He managed to afford that operation for Little Elvis after all, and the tiny, timorous lad not only learned to walk, but got busted for graffiti tagging along with his "normal" classmates.

Unlike Ebeneezer Scrooge, Burton Tolliver did not repent for his selfish, mean-spirited ways, and wound up on the streets. Despite all the trouble that he'd caused, he still only felt sorry for himself. Too proud to beg, he earned wino money on Hollywood Boulevard by reciting passages from his books and stories – which, of course, nobody had ever heard, or at least, didn't remember reading.

Some say you can still find him out there on the Boulevard of Broken Dreamers, late at night, mumbling lines from *Stargoat Eulogy* or *Pisces Unhinged*. They say he often clutches a bottle of Night Train, or MD 20-20, curled up in the fog beside his star: the blank, terra cotta "Walk-of-Fame" star on which he's neatly printed his name with a felt-marker.

After twelve months and twenty-three erased *Dreaded Cutlets* editors, the frustrated, though now widely published Justin Dial – who lobbied, lied, and eventually *summoned the powers of darkness* to get there – became the twenty-fourth and final senior editor of the magazine. Two weeks later, everything *he'd* ever written vanished from the face of the Earth, too, and the octogenarian publisher, Farnsback, died peacefully in his sleep.

A few months after the magazine folded, its editors' horrors unbeknownst to her, Deborah Craven O'Leary and her husband were celebrating in their Dublin flat.

"I know we could make a go of it, Deb, just think what wonderful tours we could arrange! I make enough at the factory to cover the adverts – and with your… *special skills*, we could level the playin' field. Make the big comp'nies compete with us on our level." He was the reason she'd never returned to the States.

"Honey, I've been saving up my power since I quit the practice and married you. It's time I blew out the pipes, I guess. What do you want me to do?"

"Well, Deb, it's been a hard row to hoe, tryin' to keep up without feckin' *computer skills*. I had a helluva time getting' on at the toy factory because of that, an' I think we could get the edge on the tour competition… if you could just get 'em all to crash like they was never here – so they can't be fixed."

"Huh?"

"You could create a virus…"

"Liam? What about peoples' bank accounts? Air travel? The nukes? What about the nukes, Liam?" Deborah stroked his thick, brown hair.

"The nukes'll be okay, Deb. If we've got no computers to fire 'em, neither will the enemy – right?

Tonight was their first anniversary, and she was a sucker for that brown-eyed, puppy-dog look – having had a thing for puppies since childhood.

"You're so smart. I've always hated computers, myself… But, *what the hey?*"

She squinted, knotting her eyebrows and thinking hard. Then, she said, "Done! Happy anniversary, Honey! …It'll take two weeks, though. The major spells always take two weeks to kick in."

AFTERWORD

Not sure where I got the idea from for this one, but the humorous pulp writing of Ron Goulart was definitely a source of inspiration. I enjoyed inventing the fictional Morbid Opus book boutique in Encino, and wish there was a horror boutique that cared enough to costume their employees for Halloween and special events.

Although Burton Tolliver is a completely fictional character, parallels with Ebeneezer Scrooge and "A Christmas Carol" are intentional – as Scrooge is an icon of bitterness. Elements that may seem reminiscent of actual people and events are merely coincidental. Tolliver is a sadistic little man, whose own unhappiness at being short, lonely, and written-out, compels him to make others miserable by controlling and bullying them – and there are lots of sawed-off bullies out there.

The editor of a leading fantasy and science fiction pulp magazine liked the comic tone of the piece, but couldn't connect with it, "perhaps because the basic idea of an editor practicing this sort of plagiarism seems so preposterous to this editor." So, making someone's literary output magically disappear from the face of the Earth seemed plausible enough, but an editor cribbing ideas from submitted stories could not possibly happen? All humans are fallible – that's what makes us human.

Admittedly, magazine editors are held to a higher standard than Hollywood screenwriters, but I've had scenes from a shopped screenplay of mine appropriated into a major Hollywood film. What did I do about it? The same thing Ib Melchior did when his *"Space Family Robinson"* idea got ripped off as *"Lost in Space"*… nothing. 'Cause, if you sue, the shysters say you'll never work in this town again.

The Sound of Thunder - The Wrath of God

Mr. Darrow had gambled that his kids would be able to get in some trick-or-treating before it rained. He'd been looking forward to this all summer and a little precipitation wasn't going to get in his way. Halloween had always been his favorite holiday, ever since he'd discovered the wealth of sacred and arcane knowledge contained within the pages of *Famous Monsters of Filmland* magazine at the gloriously ripe age of ten.

This wasn't the first time the school and the children's parents had signed-off on a field trip lead by the 52-year-old, lifetime teacher. He'd already introduced his hearing-impaired first-through-third-graders to the great horror star of silent films, Lon Chaney –who had "deaf-mute" parents himself – so they'd been anticipating this night quite a bit.

Some of them wore hearing aids, but Mr. Darrow had received a Cochlear ear implant a few years earlier, which greatly improved his own hearing – the better to shepherd the children, who were giggling and pointing. Sunset-orange jack-o-lanterns grinned back at them from yards and porches along the way, some melting as a result of too-early deployment. The children signed and spoke to each other, inhaling the smell of burning candle-wax and pumpkin rind, eying the colorful costumes passing in the cool evening.

"Can we stay out another hour?" Charlene asked. "Please, Mr. Darrow?" She'd been named after the city where they all lived, Charleston, South Carolina, and was costumed as a Southern belle in a green velvet gown sewn by her mother, using the girl's tutu as a bustle. Charlene was the oldest, at nine.

"I'm sorry, Miss Scarlet," Mr. Darrow replied, smiling, making her read his lips. Bobby wore a pirate outfit, and seconded Charlene's request, but the teacher shook his head, explaining that he was responsible for them, and it was going to pour at any second. He hadn't been trick-and-treating since he was a kid, and this electrical storm had hit a roof sign on a downtown office building the night before.

Their little group of ten had seen only kindness in the two hours it had been out, and as the kids entered the weedy yard of an old, two-story house, their leader made it clear that this would be the last score for the night. Many neighbors had a place in their hearts for Darrow's Kids, and had filled their bags and hollow, plastic pumpkins to overflowing status, happy to see them at their doors. But this house had no decorations, and from the children's experience with old, dark houses, the chances for decent booty looked slim.

As the weathered wooden porch creaked beneath their feet, a light bulb above the door showed it opening slowly. "Hello," an elderly voice called out, as a light went on inside. "No sense burning power if no-one's around," the man said from his seat in an old-fashioned wheelchair. "I have Mars Bars – Milky Ways – but no children came to my door all night."

"Well, here we are," Mr. Darrow said, "and you're our last stop. Maybe the storm has folks staying inside this year. These kids have room for one more treat in their bags, but getting them to go home is the trick."

"Sounds like there's a bunch of you – here you go," he said, holding out a bowl of full-sized candy bars. "Hope there's enough." A thunderbolt ripped the sky a few miles north, and the wind was blowing south. "Hear that?" the man said. "It's gonna be a corker!"

"I just live at the corner house on Garden, up there," Mr. Darrow said, pointing up the street. "Maybe you've seen it? I'm driving them back to school, where their parents will pick 'em up."

"Mister, I'm blind, and I haven't seen anything in twenty years. …Industrial accident. They paid me off pretty good, though," he said, pausing, and the teacher sensed a painful memory glimpsed from behind dark glasses. "I bought the big kind but nobody came, so you can take 'em all." The children grabbed the candy and thanked the man. "Do me one little favor before you go?"

"If we can," Mr. Darrow said.

"Could you please describe your costumes to me? It won't take long. Quickly, now, tell me who you all are this Halloween! It was always my favorite holiday."

The children were only too happy to oblige. Charlene said, "I'm the most famous Southern belle in literature. Brittany is only six – she's The Little Mermaid. We're a special needs class, but we can see okay."

"You hail from Atlanta then, Miss O'Hara?"

"Oh, yes… my family is quite well-known, there."

"I'm Captain America," said Justin, describing his costume, as a louder thunderbolt crashed through the Payne's gray sky overhead.

Three older boys were passing and the one wearing the hockey mask said, "How 'bout this place? Looks like The Addams Family lives here!"

"That's Old Man Sanchez's place – he's blind as a bat!" the zombie said. "And look – it's Darrow's Dummies at his door! Talk about the blind leading the blind. Haw, haw!"

"…Leading the deaf, in this case," said the one wearing the Freddy Kruger glove and slouch hat. "Let's scare hell out of those dummies when they come out the gate!"

Mr. Darrow had heard every word they'd said with his implant and prayed to God the children hadn't; he saw the bullies crouch behind a hedge next door.

Why do some people have to be so mean? he thought, waving off the boys without the children seeing him. He saw the flash peripherally, turning back to the door; it lit up the yard like high noon, as lightning struck an oak tree with a searing *crash!*

"Holy cow, what was that?!" Mr. Sanchez said, and the group wheeled around to see a branch that would crush a Holstein land, flaming, not six feet from where the bullies hid. They fled screaming, but Hockey Mask stopped to look back one more time. *Had this deaf teacher somehow heard them?* he thought instantly, *And brought down the wrath of God?* It burned a lesson into his impressionable, tween-age brain, and even the children who wore no hearing aids could hear the thunderclap that followed.

Dedicated to Ray Bradbury.

AFTERWORD

Inspired by the life of Jim Morrow, a friend of Ray's and Forry's and mine.

The Drawer

He opened the drawer and stared. Expecting to find something else, he had found *that* instead, so he closed the drawer and went back to bed, where he shivered and finally slept.

Later, he awoke, and opened the drawer again... and stared again, hoping to find whatever it was that he'd expected to find the first time. He remembered that time, and it was still the same: instead of containing small objects, bits of folded cloth, and important papers, the drawer held... more of *him*.

It was full of human flesh. Not arms, or legs, or strips of torso flesh... just full. ...Up to an inch-and-a-half from the top – all around – as if someone had poured it in, like pink custard or Spam Jello. Its top was nearly flat, sealed all around at the edges – a three-dimensional, seemingly boneless, rectangular mass of human flesh, covered with a layer of epidermis. It had tiny, evenly dispersed pores and hairs and no sign of elbow or armpit skin – even at the edges – as if it had grown right there, filling out the drawer as it matured.

He touched it with a fingertip and could feel it twice: the flesh-mass in the drawer was soft beneath his finger; and, he could feel his fingertip – hard, *through the flesh within the drawer!* It moved, quivering slightly, but returned to its flat shape in a second. He touched his left arm with his right forefinger – and created the same sensation – feeling through nerves in both arm and finger. How could he actually feel through the flesh-mass in the drawer, when it wasn't even connected to him? Would he still feel its sensations if someone else touched it? He decided he was dreaming.

He pinched his arm, slapped himself in the face, but he did not wake up.

He hit the flesh-mass in the drawer with his fist – *it* did not wake up, either, but it hurt like hell... just *where*, he couldn't rightly say – it just hurt *somewhere*. He rubbed the drawer-flesh; its little hairs stood up and his pain was somewhat relieved.

He shut that drawer, and opened the next one. His eye was closed, for fear of what he might see, but everything got brighter, anyway. In his mind, he saw himself standing there, and remembered shadowy images of a life: *red car... white dotted line on the highway... woman's face smiling... hand swiping an I.D. card… the lab door opening… THE LAB!* That was the most familiar of the images. He was a doctor or scientist of some sort! So why couldn't he remember his name? If his eye was shut while all this was running through his mind, how could see himself standing there?

He opened his eye and blinked in shock. There, in the second metal drawer, recessed in a similar mass of human flesh, identical to that in the first drawer – was his *other eye* – looking up at him! He saw a double image. He moved his head, it followed him. He blinked, *it* blinked. He closed his on-board eye, but could still see himself standing there from the drawer. He shut the drawer and the room darkened.

There was one more drawer in the small, air-cooled cabinet, but he didn't dare open it. Instead, he looked at his thalidomide reflection in the dull shine of the closed drawers. A thick shock of white hair crowned a normal-looking head, except for his one, off-center eye, and the smooth, concave area – grown-over with skin – where his other eye should have been. His mouth was wide, his nose long and pointed – but a *human* nose nonetheless. He was naked, of course, because his bureau was full of more *him*, instead of clothing.

The two doors in the room were painted on the walls – as was the frame around the window; its flat, photographic view of green grass and blue sky had been cut from a magazine and pasted behind the barred window's opening. He poked through the paper sky, but there was another wall behind the window, so even if he could remove the bars, he still couldn't get out. Hungry, he hoped the patch on his side offered some nutritional or medicinal value.

He prayed to God for an answer – for some relief. Why was he here? Why did he remember vague shadowy things? Had he been in an accident? Did he have amnesia?

He played with his tail, sitting back on his haunches – and that was another thing; he wanted to walk on his hands as well as his feet. Walking upright was difficult, to say the least. That's it, he thought – he'd been in a terrible accident, and this was some sort of hospital or sanitarium. But, what about the drawers? He wanted so to open that last one.

All right, God – he thought. *Just don't give me a heart attack, okay?* He bent down and pulled out the bottom drawer, once again with his eye shut, and once again he had the flashes, saw the images in his mind: *children at play... woman dives into a swimming pool... red car... dots on the highway... swiping the I.D. card... lab door opens... his point-of-view, walking to the BIG climate-controlled metal storage cabinet, a larger version of the one in his cage... What does it all mean, God?* He opened his eye and looked in the bottom drawer. He felt his heart, at the same time that he *saw* another one beating in the drawer, in an artery-and-vein connected tangle of liver, kidneys and other working viscera. ...More of his insides, somehow *outside* of his body?

He shut the bottom drawer, and opened the top one again. Its human meatloaf contents almost looked normal; he stroked the smooth skin, feeling it with his fingers, as he felt his fingers with it. Again, he closed his eye and prayed. *Please, God – get me out of this nightmare!* He saw the BIG file drawers in his mind again with its tiny labels – but, they streaked by too quickly to be deciphered. Then, his mind's eye stopped on the one drawer that he knew with certainty to be his.

Please, God, in all your glory, reveal yourself to me! he thought, carefully opening the special drawer in his mind. A rolling, sliding, thunder roared in his round, pink ears. A great brightness shone all around him as the room shifted sideways, knocking him over – and then, the Creator's benign face gazed down at him. Nearly identical to his own, its smile filled the sky.

He scrambled to his feet, calling out, "Here I am, Lord. The best that God and Science can do! I'm all yours – you made me. Now, *please* get me out of here!" Sadly, the only sound the Creator heard him make was a desperate squeaking.

A giant, rubbery hand picked him up, while another jammed a big steel pipe into his neck, pumping in liquid. Darkness lulled over him like high tide on a sand castle.

"That thing is hideous, Steve. It looks like you, but with rat-ears and a tail! And, those *hind legs*? …Back to the drawing board, Frankenstein."

"Lighten up – *he's* only a day old, and most of that was spent sleeping."

"Why the little dollhouse motif? You don't actually think it knows that it's part human, do you? Or, that it knows anything at all, for that matter?"

"He feels through the symbiotic tissue, Dennis – don't you see? There's a… psychic neuro-muscular link with the remote tissue cultures cloned from the same…"

"Whoa! *Psychic* neuro-muscular? Steve, you said it feels through the nerve-endings of the flesh in those little climate-controlled trays… but you didn't say it could move that flesh."

"He sees the specimen trays as drawers in a bureau… and he can move the eye."

"'*He??*' Whatever, Steve – how the hell do *you* know how it sees them? You've got two eyes – both in your head, for one thing."

"I just *know*, that's all."

"You can lose your license over this Dr. Moreau stuff…"

"He's a lab rat, not a primate, for God's sake."

"God has little to do with this… abomination. It's a lab rat clone with your spliced DNA."

"You'd better go now, Dennis. I want to finish up here. I'll meet you later at Jerry's – save me a place."

"You won't show up – you wanna stay here and play with your rat. Last night, that blonde waitress you like asked about you."

"…Liar."

"I'm outta here, Brainiac."

"Laugh all you want, but I'm going to prove you're wrong. He does have human intelligence – the mind of a three-year-old, perhaps, I'd be happy with that – but the way he looks at me! What if he does have a tiny little piece of a soul?

"...A soul? Are you crazy, Steve? You said it yourself – it's a freaking lab rat! Literally, freaking... *A soul*, the man says!"

"Goodnight, Dennis, I'll stop down later." Steve shut the lab door and locked it, crossed to the big metal cabinet across the room. His eyes scanned the labels on the drawers from habit as he reached for *the one...*

He dreamed that his hands shut the lab door and locked it from inside. ...Then, he crossed to the BIG metal cabinet in his big person body and scanned the labels. There it was – HIS label. He opened the drawer – HIS drawer.

The room shifted again, waking him, rolling him off his straw bed. The ceiling slid aside with a roar and a rumble, and the smiling face of the Creator beamed down at him.

"Lord," he squeaked unintelligibly, "thank you, for creating me. Now, please – get me the hell out of here!"

Steve wondered if he would like a bit of cheese.

AFTERWORD

This tale of mixing human and animal DNA didn't work for the editor of a leading fantasy and science fiction pulp in 2000. He wrote in his polite rejection letter, "...I just didn't connect with the horrific central image for this story, alas."

Richard Matheson had liked an article I'd written about the reunion signing of the Charles Beaumont Writers Group (*Cemetery Dance Magazine #33; "The Quest for the Green Hand"*), so I asked him for a blurb on this in 2002 and he wrote, "I can't even get through this gross story much less comment on it. This kind of fiction – even if presented as satire – has always revolted me..."

That prompted Brad Linaweaver to ask for the story that grossed-out Richard Matheson, and he subsequently offered this quote: "Has the power of vintage *Weird Tales*-era Ray Bradbury. The completely fantastic is made disturbingly real with images that will haunt you forever..."

Mr. Matheson later said he was glad that his comment helped get me a good blurb. I got the inspiration for this tale from seeing a real hairless lab rat with a human ear growing on its back on the paranormal TV show, *"Strange Universe,"* in 1996 – and that revolted me enough to write the story.

The Brain That Couldn't Think

Chapter One: Prince of the "B's"

C.B. Remington hadn't had a hit in ten years, if you could call *Leather Werewolves* a hit. At least it hadn't lost money like his last seven pictures.

God Fever on Hell Island almost broke even too; ironically, the fact that the film's title had been misspelled on the video box and one-sheets might have actually helped that particular cinematic dog, but C.B. fired the Taiwanese printer anyway. The *"Gold Fever"* series had been getting very tired, with international sales sagging almost as badly as its three buxom stars, all pushing the big "4-0" now, which is *dig-a-hole* time in Hollywood.

C.B. was older, but fortunately for him he was a producer not an actor, he still had a good head of hair (which he kept subtly dyed) and the eye-and-jowl job from a couple of years ago was holding up nicely. If he didn't take any outdoor meetings, he could continue to pass for forty-five, an acceptable age for a producer.

C.B.'s real name had originally been Bernie Small; not exactly the kind of surname you want to hang on your studio, like "Selznick International," or "Warner Bros." *"ANOTHER SMALL PICTURE"* just didn't have the punch as a slogan that Bernie felt his future studio would require. Even as a young man, Bernie Small was thinking big, and obsessed with two things: making movies and finding a better name.

He would go through a host of aliases before eventually cranking out the gaggle of stink-bombs that would come to be associated with his last and favorite *nom de plume.* Grade "Z," Ed Wood-on-a-bender-bad movies like *Dope Titans of Little Italy, Mayhem A-Go-Go* and *The Disembowler* were typical of the exploitative flotsam one came to expect over the years from Remington Pictures, Ltd.

He'd called himself Brian Huston, Reed Baxley and Trump Chandler variously, in his early acting days. Needless to say, the camera did not love him. Switching to a production assistant role (the entry level position on a movie set), somehow—and this is the first of the *preternatural* occurrences to forever change his life—in the spring of 1968, Bernie Small, then known as Morris Carloff, was mistakenly assigned to *direct* a turkey called *Gourmet Vampires* in Mexico for miniscule Penknife Productions.

Small/Carloff's "bump up" to director was met with disbelief by cast and crew on location, but in Mexico who was to argue? Especially if the producer didn't object. There was a lot to be said for being in the right place at the right time... and for just *wanting* to do it. That's all Ed Wood had going, he'd proved that it didn't take money or great talent to get movies made—you just *made* them happen despite mainstream Hollywood. And mainstream Hollywood had made a movie about Ed Wood.

The thought infuriated Bernie today, even though Wood had preceded him, was much more famous and for the most part, had made better films. Now, at fifty, "C.B. Remington" resented the increased difficulty in getting pictures made, and took the crash of the independent home video market *personally*—in addition to feeling slighted by Hollywood. Why had no-one proposed doing a bio-pic about *him*?

What was so great about Ed Wood, anyway? Any schmuck can put on a dress to get attention. He was nobody's clown, he thought, twitching like Hitler in the bunker. Paranoid? You bet. Our boy got his permanent moniker during that first-and-last, grossly inept attempt at directing, south of the border in '68. The crew found their greatest task on *Gourmet Vampires* was to avoid laughing openly at the fledgling, 18-year-old director as he made every mistake in the book, *whatever the book is*. After a few days the phrase, "Ready when you are, C.B." (which referred to the great DeMille), became at once the buzzword and in-joke of the shoot. Grips had it printed on T-shirts, and Director-Boy even wore one, oblivious to the depth of the crew's blisteringly derisive contempt for him.

The fact that the producer didn't shit-can his hopelessly callow ass the first day on the set, combined with the fact that communications from the home office had been hopelessly garbled in the first place, might have caused another man to consider the possibility of divine or demonic intervention in his life. But Bernie, godless and self-serving to a fault, was actually convinced that he had somehow earned the promotion to director. In any event, the "C.B." stuck, and after shooting a rattlesnake with a Remington .38 in the hundred-degree Mexican desert, "C.B. Remington" rose from the ashes of Morris Carloff—but for some reason, most people still referred to him as Bernie, no matter what he called himself. Following the marginal success of *Gourmet Vampires*, the former P.A. decided that he would make a better *producer* than director and wangled himself a job doing just that on *The Exacerbaters*, a British/Danish/Korean biker flick shot in the Philippines. C.B. Remington was on his way, producing a string of gutbucket, T&A mutant slasher-from-outer-space opuses that truly defined the post-Wood, bottom-of-the-barrel indie programmer throughout the late sixties, seventies, and early eighties.

By '86 he couldn't get U.S. theatrical distribution any more, so he went direct-to-video, selling the cable rights up-front to finance the pictures. By the mid-nineties the premium cable companies and major studios, themselves owned by parent companies and umbrella corporations, had swallowed up the direct-to-video market and pushed the little guys, like Bernie, out of business. It looked bad...

Then, just when it seemed that nothing could save him... when all funds and assets were exhausted... when the chances of getting backing for so much as a *promo trailer* were nil... when Bernie was actually reaching deep, deep into the back of his big, flat middle desk drawer for that old Remington .38 to end it all—he found it.

It being a screenplay, that is.

Submitted a while back by writer/fan, Kip Lothar, it had been optioned by Bernie with his standard "$100-for-five-years-contract, based on its title alone. Intended as both an homage and further sequel to the "brain cycle," Remington Pictures' most popular drive-in series, *The Brain That Couldn't Think* was also the script that hadn't been read.

Beginning with *The Brainmaker* in 1972, a decent hit for its tiny budget, and followed by *Runaway Brain* in '74, C.B. Remington had been on a roll. But 1978's dismal attempt at mining comedy from the series, *Three Brains in the Fountain*, a musical no less, bombed like the Luftwaffe. By 1980, Bernie had climbed back on top with the taut political sci-fi melodrama, *Citizen Brain*, perhaps his finest work—besides the incomparable *Frankenstein Meets the Elephant Man*, of course.

This time he read *The Brain That Couldn't Think*. Within hours he was on the phone to an agent, all thoughts of suicide shelved, certain that, like *Get Shorty's* Harry Zimm, he'd found his *"Driving Miss Daisy."*

"Sandy, I read it two hours ago an' I'm still cryin'—you gotta read this—I'm sending it right over. "

"I don't understand what you want me to do, Mr. Remington, I can't represent you. Your pictures are notoriously non-union, and our office is, of course, a signatory to SAG, AFTRA, the WGA and even IATSE..."

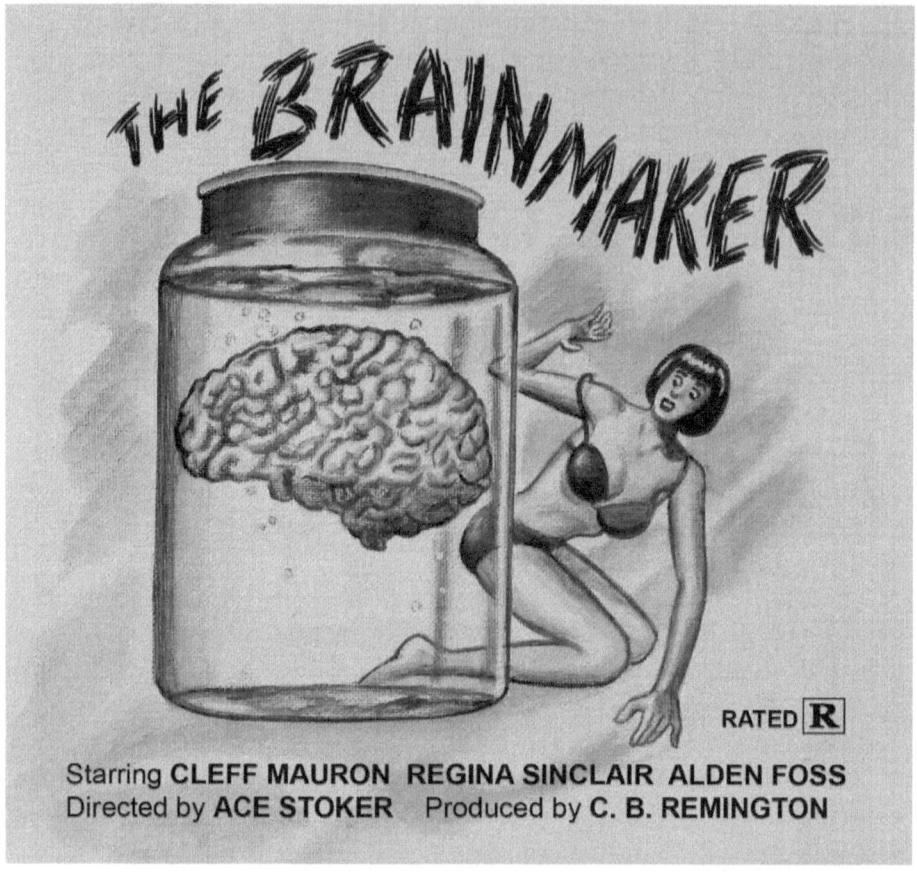

Starring **CLEFF MAURON REGINA SINCLAIR ALDEN FOSS**
Directed by **ACE STOKER**   Produced by **C. B. REMINGTON**

"What the hell business does IATSE have with a talent-and-literary agency? Next you're gonna tell me you're in bed with the Teamsters... Not you personally, I mean..."

"We are contractually linked to every union that works in the entertainment industry, Mr. Remington; the ones that you've been giving the run-around to for twenty-some years."

"I made *Gourmet Vampires* in '68! For *thirty-two* years I've been producing quality entertainment in this town—if you count Mexico, Romania and the Philippines. HBO knows my name and they also know they can hype the shit out of it. Like that *"Roger Corman Presents"* they had, over on that other channel..."

Sandy Arbogast cleared her throat, interrupting Bernie's self-ag-grandizing, "I happen to know Roger Corman. Roger Corman is a friend of mine, and you, Mr. Remington, are no…"

"Yeah, yeah… I heard it before. Look, Ms. Arbogast—it couldn't hurt to take a look at this. It's unique, I'm tellin' you! When is the last time you saw a great horror movie that also made you cry?"

"Well… *The Sixth Sense*, but that's because I didn't sell it…"

"You know what I mean, Sandy—*poignancy!* This script is poign-ant as all hell—it's about a brain, kept alive by medical science—but it can't communicate…"

"That's been done. Dennis Pottter wrote it for the BBC."

"Not just any brain, Sandy—you gotta read this yourself—Are you ready? It's the dyslexic brain of a mentally challenged youth, killed in a traffic accident so horrible, that only his head is left intact. A scientist keeps him alive, but he's just a brain—and no Einstein, either—trapped in a tank…"

"Like *Free Willy*, but with a brain?"

"Sort of…" Bernie paused for a moment, thinking, "It's more like… It's more like… *'Forrest Gump meets Edward Scissorhands'*—but with a Brain."

"*Forrest Gump*, huh?" She paused, drumming her lacquered nails on the speaker-phone, putting all of the tension of the moment on *him*. After a few interminable seconds she pushed a button on the console that caused an electronic "beep" to sound on the line. "I've got another call—I'll get back to you," she lied, smiling.

He had his personal assistant, Miss Plum, make sure Remington Pictures still had option rights to *The Brain That Couldn't Think*, run copies of it, messenger one over to the Arbogast Agency, and read it herself—finally filling out the analysis/tracking form that accompanied every in-studio property. At last, Bernie was busy again.

He barely noticed the blueblack raven watching him through his office bay window and thought the chill that took a ride up his spine was just the air conditioning, known to over-amp on these hot summer days. The tic he'd developed when the bank had repo'd his Bentley had not subsided, and just now it was accompanied by furtive twitching and sweat-ing.

Why was that damn bird staring at him so? He ignored the twinge in his chest and lit a cigar, throwing his lighter at the window to startle the

Raven away; it startled him instead, flying from its' branch straight *into* the glass pane, nearly shattering it before bouncing off and falling out of sight.

Bernie jumped up and raced across the room, throwing open one of the French windows that flanked the large, trembling pane—he looked down into the courtyard two stories below but could see no bird, fallen or otherwise. What he did see made the back of his neck prickle like a cheap haircut; a blueblack cat slunk away from a spot directly beneath the window, *turning to hiss up at him before vanishing into the foliage...*

Eight days later Sandy called him back. "HBO and Showtime were flat out not interested—I guess you pissed somebody off at HBO a while back, according to my contact. That's why you wanted me to call—you fouled your nest there, didn't you?"

"What was Showtime's reason?" Bernie asked, turning off the speaker phone.

"They just said they were going to pass. That's all anybody says, usually."

"How 'bout basic cable?"

"Well, Bernie, it isn't all bad news."

"You can call me C.B."

"People call you that to your face—we're on the phone. Anyway, TNT was only interested in the project if the brain belonged to a famous Native American Indian or dead President, but Lifetime—and this is the good part—Lifetime offered scale-plus-ten... for the script."

"But I want to produce it! It's not just about money!"

"Your name is *not* to be associated with the project, and they want to put one of their writers on it—make it be about a *woman scientist* who keeps the brain of a lesbian athlete alive for the Special Olympics."

"Now you're putting me on, Sandy."

"No, actually I'm not—but Comedy Central thought I was putting *them* on."

"You tried to get backing from Comedy Central? Didn't you read it? *The Brain That Couldn't Think* is a horror-tragedy!"

"No offense, *Bernie*, but so is your career. As far as my involvement is concerned, I'm willing to close the Women's Channel deal for the standard ten percent as long as we keep it out of the trades..."

"Out of the trades?? what am I, a leper? What the hell is the 'Womens' Channel' deal? How much did *they* offer?" Bernie was sweating colors at this point.

"Lifetime is the 'Women's Channel,' and they don't want to be associated with the man who made *Love Tostada* and *Comes a Bimbo*... and frankly, beyond this point, Mr. Remington, neither do I!—Have a nice day."

"... Tell the Women's Channel they can blow me!" Bernie hurled back, ditching the phone before he heard the accursed *dial tone*, the sound of losers. In Hollywood, it's a constantly played game—trying to hang up first, that is. One can be in the warmest or most intimate of conversations, but as soon as it's clear the conversation is ending, both parties try to hang up first.

This could explain the continuing Tinseltown popularity of the Italian *"ciao"* as a one-syllable alternative to the equally brief, but lame "bye." "Later" has been cut down to "late." A complete "goodbye," or the more hip but three-syllable *"adios,"* will give the enemy time to beat you. Remember—one must always assume *they* have their finger poised over the hang-up button, just waiting for you to start that multi-syllabic salutation.

Hollywood is full of myriad horrors. But besides the mean-spiritedness, greed, selfishness, rage-addiction and colossal narcissism that abound, there are also darker underpinnings: depravity and corruption of a cosmic, ethereal form. Behind the boardrooms and brain-trusts, suits and charlatans, stars and star-makers, oftentimes lie nameless names—unspeakable powers that billow and eddy beneath the soft underbelly of show business, in grim synchronization with the careers that rise and fall above.

Something had been billowing and eddying inside Bernie all week, and nothing seemed to alleviate it. Besides the angina and twitching, he'd had a touch of dysentery—and now he was being watched by someone... or *something*. That raven, or crow, or whatever it was, kept coming back, and he'd seen the blue-black feline again, but never with the bird. It was as if he were victim of some curse, some demonic jinxing—other than the mercifully oblivious ignominy of simply being C.B. Remington, that is.

Chapter Two: A Man of Wealth and Taste

A few days later, Bernie and Miss Plum made the rounds of his former backers. Small video companies, sub-distributors, the European consortium... the answer was the same everywhere: money was tight, tied

up in post or coming in next quarter—take your pick. Production sched-
ules were either locked in or undecided, seemingly two opposites, but in
the bizarro lexicon of corporate Hollywood, both meant the same thing—
no.

Then they began weeding through secondary and tertiary
sources… like his angels. Bernie, fresh carnation in lapel and showing a
little silk, styled through a bevy of aging, palsied, Norma Desmond types
that would make Max Bialystock projectile vomit. He came up with just
enough to pay off one credit card and lease an S.U.V.—black with tinted
windows, of course.

He was back in the game, but he'd sold off nearly a third of *"Brain"*
to achieve it. Not exactly a shrewd deal, except that his standard ten-per-
cent-share contract had a clause reverting the rights back to him in the
event of the investor's death. Since all three of the widows he'd "closed"
were in their eighties, eventually, and soon, all the points he'd sold would
come back. Shrewd is as shrewd does.

He was on his way out the door to meet another octogenarian, a
man confined to the contemporary equivalent of an iron lung, when a
well-dressed gentleman in a gray topcoat and Homburg suddenly appeared at his door. Long dark hair, a neatly trimmed moustache and
vandike, along with the expensive apparel, lent an aristocratic air to this
curious stranger.

"Hello – C.B. Remington, I presume?" the man asked, a twinkle
in his eye. "May I come in?"

"I haven't answered your first question yet," Bernie drawled, giving his dapper visitor the fisheye. Without meaning to, he stepped back,
opening the door; the stranger entered, and looked around at the framed
one-sheets in the reception area.

"Don't worry, I'm not a process server. Ah—*Dog Men from Uranus!*
One of my favorites." The man removed his hat and overcoat and looked
Bernie in the eye, extending his hand, "B.L. Zebediah… executive pro-
ducer," he said.

Minutes later they were sitting in Bernie's office discussing *the deal*.
"… And the international market, while Remington Pictures would retain
fifty-one percent, plus domestic cable, video and sequel rights," Bernie
said, on a roll again. "We'll firm up the deal next week—lawyers, the whole
nine. How soon will the initial installment of the production budget come
through, for deposit, that is? How will you be handling that, Mr. Zebediah? Bank transfer? Cashier's check?"

"Call me 'B.L.' And I don't have the money—I *get* the money. Don't you want me to read the script?"

"... Oh," Bernie sighed, deflated, "sure... how did you hear about us again?"

"Your European friends. We've worked together before. They said you were looking for funding for another *brain* picture..." B.L Zebediah slowly opened a gold cigarette case.

Bernie smiled again. "You know my *brain* pictures?"

"Oh, yes—I know all your films, Mr. Remington," B.L. said, taking out a gold- trimmed cigarette. "That's why I want to help you, I think you are a great and misunderstood artist—got a light?

"Which one was your favorite?"

"Of the brain cycle, let's see..." The man reached for a table lighter and finding it without fuel, snapped his thumb and forefinger together. A yellow-blue flame appeared, hotly hovering over them. "... I guess I liked *Runaway Brain*, what with the luge chase and all the carny people. Of course, for technical innovation and pure genius, you can't beat *Citizen Brain*, arguably the greatest American brain movie of all time." B.L. puffed on his gold-trimmed cigarette, then blew on his fingers to put out the flame.

"How the hell did you do that?" Bernie's voice cracked, "And who the hell *are* you?"

The man smiled like a wreck on the freeway, exhaling a cloud of black smoke, "The answer to both of your questions is yes."

"Anybody ever tell ya, you look a little like Robert De Niro?"

"... You talkin' to me? Huh? Yep—All the time. Like Robert De Niro in *Angel Heart*, or Al Pacino in *Devil's Advocate*. Last week, somebody said I looked like Billy Crystal in *Deconstructing Harry!* Can you imagine that?" Bernie paused, taking it all in. Slowly he asked the obvious question, more worried about not getting funding for his movie than about confronting the Ultimate Evil Incarnate; if little else, at least he was a real producer.

"...Are you... are you the... you know, *him*? Are you the Devil?" Bernie stammered. The stranger cocked an eyebrow and burst out laughing.

"Don't be ridiculous, of course not... he doesn't do B-pictures anymore—he doesn't have to. B.L. Zebediah continued to laugh, as Bernie swallowed hard and squared his shoulders, sitting up straight behind his desk.

"Look, whoever you are, all my life I've made a living in B-pictures, some of them were even 'Z' pictures, they were so bad—and by the way, we call them independent films. However, this could be my last shot... the swan song of C.B. Remington, and if it takes my last drop of blood, or worse—*The Brain That Couldn't Think* is not going to be a B-movie!"

"*Worse* is what we were thinking of..." The stranger rocked his head from side to side, smiling exactly like Robert De Niro.

"We? ... Never mind. I don't want to know. You want my soul? Well, all right. Just see to it that I go out on top, and you can have it—like it's not already in hell-hock up to its ass for my sins." Bernie coolly pulled out a cigar and lit it, continuing, "I don't really believe you're... working for *him*, but if believing it helps you raise the money to produce my picture, then by all means, you're welcome to my soul, such as it is. But no tricks—this isn't a *Twilight Zone*, pal, just in case you are in league with the original Bad Boy. You can only take my soul if the movie gets made, gets released or aired, *and* is a critical and commercial success."

"Whoa, there, Bernie-Boy—if it's a miracle you want, maybe you should make a deal with the other team—we don't do miracles. We can get the movie made and released. It can even make a little money... but for you to have a critical success at this point in your career? Let's just say it'd be easier getting Manson paroled... Easier getting O.J. on Saturday Night Live... It'd even be easier keeping Alanis Morrisette from gasping between notes than to get the critics to actually *like* one of your pictures."

"Okay. I don't need your help to make a movie—or anybody else's for that matter. I've been doing it for thirty years. But I could use your help with the money. You'll get executive producer credit, the profit split we discussed and... my *soul*, as is, for 7.7 mil—that's the exact amount of the budget, and *my* lucky number."

"If you can make it for 7.7, then you can make it for 6.66 million—*my* lucky number," B.L. Zebediah replied. "If you run over, I can always get more money—it just means penalties, like when you work for the majors."

"What kind of penalties?" Bernie asked warily. The room seemed to distort at the corners, the walls bending slightly outward, like the view through a fish-eye lens. Tiny cool beadlets of true fear manifested themselves in the form of perspiration on his face and forehead, which suddenly felt fever hot. "Are you hypnotizing me or something, Mr.

Zebediah? What kind of a name for a... what you say you are, is 'Zebe-diah?' Isn't that Biblical?"

"Yes, I suppose it is... but so is 'Lucifer,' for that matter. Now, C.B.—you don't mind me calling you C.B., do you?"

"I prefer it." "Now, C.B., I think we should make that call on the man in the iron lung."

"How did you know about...? Hey! That's not bad—*"The Man in the Iron Lung!"* That could be our next picture—in fact, we can make a series of medical-themed *horror tearjerkers!* What else you got, Mr. Zebe-diah?"

"How about *Spleenless in Seattle?"* And you can call me B.L., or Zeb. Or, just plain *Bub."* The stranger smiled again, nodding and squinting, let-ting it sink in. Then he added, "Some folks even call me *Mr. Z."*

The man in the iron lung coughed up a half a mil, or agreed to, by the end of their meeting. B.L. had managed to convince him of the im-portance of his financial involvement in the project during the few mo-ments they'd been left alone. While Bernie went to call the man's nurse, B.L. terrorized the eighty-six-year-old invalid by shooting flames out of his eyes and fingertips right next to the oxygen supply.

On the drive back to the studio, which for twenty years had been on Seward Street, they passed through downtown Hollywood. In a cele-bratory mood, Bernie insisted that they stop for a drink at a favorite wa-tering hole he hadn't visited in years.

Chapter Three: The Liberation of Penelope Plum

"Just what I always wanted to do—have a drink with the Devil... "Shhh! Keep it down! And I told you, I'm not *him."* B.L. looked around to see if any of the pale young people dressed in black had heard them.

"What the hell is going on around here?" Bernie asked, "Did Alice Cooper die?"

"No... " the waitress said. She was a fuchsia blonde with the gloom of youth on her cheeks. "It's *Pub Portentous* night and the goths are arriving. What can I get you?"

"Goths?" Bernie asked, glancing sideways at B.L., "Sounds like you might get a few recruits if you stick around..." The waitress made a guttural sound, warning them to hurry up and order. "... I'll have a C.C.

with a splash of soda—and you, Mr. Z?" He turned to his new partner, smiling the we-just-scored-bigtime smile, "It's on me."

"… Perhaps some demon rum… on the rocks," B.L. said, taking out his gold cigarette case, "since we're celebrating."

"There's no smoking inside, sir, we have a patio out back…" the waitress said, moving away, "… I'll bring your drinks in a minute, I'm real busy right now…"

Discussing their $500,000 pledge, Bernie inquired about the old man's change of heart while he'd been out of the room, "… It was so sudden—what did you say to him?"

"Not much. I don't think it was what I said…" B.L. smirked, "as much as how I said it." He had been reading the script for *"Brain"* all afternoon in the car.

"Who do you have in mind for the scientist? Personally, I could see Ben Affleck in the role – or maybe even Liam Neeson, depending on the target demographic."

'Target demographic?" Bernie echoed. Whipping out his cell phone, he called the studio. "Miss Plum…? I want you to find out who handles Ben Affleck and Liam Neeson. Don't call anybody—wait for me to get back. Then I want you to go out to the storage bungalow and find my old mahogany desk and chair. Have Julio clean out the junk room and put 'em in there—that's going to be the new executive producer's office."

At her small but cheerfully appointed work station, Penelope Plum had been doing what she normally did between productions: entering all receipts from rentals—mostly international and military base bookings these days, and a few holdout drive-ins which still operated in the U.S. But there had been little to input this week and she was glad the phone had rung, especially since she was in love with Bernie, and had been since her start with Remington Pictures in 1980, as a P.A. on *Citizen Brain*.

"Julio doesn't work here anymore, C.B., remember? He went back to Mexico. His brother, Jose, works for us now…"

"Whatever—I'm bringing our new executive producer back from lunch…"

"Wonderful, can't wait to meet him. Could you please bring me back a sandwich? I've been stuck here all morn…"

"Yeah, sure, whatever… *Ciao.*" He said, cutting her off.

"Goodbye…" (too late – *dial tone…*) she muttered anyway, hanging up. They hadn't made love in almost three months, a record in their

nineteen years together. He always called her Miss Plum, though he usually referred to other women as *Ms.* He'd promised to marry her "when
things got better" several times over the years.

These last three months Bernie had been more depressed that
she'd ever seen him, but today he actually sounded happy again, she
thought. Maybe this new executive producer was the miracle she'd been
praying for.

As Bernie and Mr. Z were finishing their drinks, one of the black-
garbed twenty-somethings approached their horseshoe-shaped booth.
The man swept back a shock of dyed black hair and leaned over the table.
"Excuse me—Mr. De Niro?" He asked softly, "Can I have your autograph?"

B.L. shook his head tiredly, as though this happened a lot. Bernie
answered for him, "No, he's not Mr. De Niro—it's just an eerie resemblance—but I happen to be the real C.B. Remington."

The pale young man shook his head this time.

"Who?"

"... *C.B. Remington!* Bernie attested, "*Producer of Leather Werewolves*
and *Citizen Brain*, not to mention *Frankenstein Meets the Elephant Man?*"

"... Uh—that's great..."

"*Phlegm!* You must have seen that one—a giant infected lung attacks San Jose? In Mucuscope? How about *The Last Vampire Movie?* Or
The Last Vampire Movie II?" The twenty-something goth sidled away, crablike.

Bernie frowned, slamming down his empty glass. "This younger
generation really scares me—no sense of art or culture..."

"Come on, C.B., we've got a movie to make," Mr. Z said, "and I
can't wait to see my new office." Outside the bar, they walked to Bernie's
new, leased S.U.V. It was an overcast day on this side-street off the Boulevard of Broken Dreamers.

"Look!" Bernie stopped dead in his tracks at a sight that made his
surgically-tightened skin crawl: the blueblack cat was poised, staring at him
from a few feet away on the sidewalk, its yellow eyes glowing in the dif-
fused sunlight. "That thing has been following me for days—I thought it
was you!"

"Nope. It's not one of ours... I don't like this..."

The black cat loped around the building, ducking into a mid-block
alleyway, and leapt up, over the grating that closed the path to foot-traffic.

Bernie and B.L. hurried after the beast, only to be stopped by that iron barrier; through it they could see all the way down the sixty or seventy feet of the narrow plaster canyon, to its end beneath a Moorish arch. No creature but one could be seen in that space and it *wasn't* a cat.

It was, of course, the raven, and it was flying directly at them—or at the grate rather. At the last second it pulled upwards, screeching like a dive bomber, and flew straight up into the open air above the alleyway. "Christ!" Bernie muttered.

"… Try not to say that a whole lot around me, okay pal?" For the first time since their having met, B.L. Zebediah seemed less than cool—almost rattled. The Demon wiped the sweat from his forehead with a silk handkerchief and then rang it out, leaving little smoking holes in the concrete where the drops fell. Bernie tried not to notice at first, but as the pavement sizzled and belched tiny wisps of sulfur steam, he had to comment.

"… So what are you, anyway? The freakin' *Alien?*"

A mile or two south, as the crow flies—or *raven*, in this case, Penelope Plum sat looking at the mahogany desk-set in Remington Pictures' storage bungalow. While polishing the dark hardwood she'd been reminded of time spent taking letters and placing calls beside it. Once, Bernie had even had his way with her atop its burgundy grain—what she'd give for a repeat performance these days. It seemed that as the fire had gone out of his filmmaking, so had the lust faded from their *liaison*.

Wiping the dust from a deco moderne aluminum lamp, she heard a flutter from behind. As Penelope turned, a shadow fled across the wall beneath the window she'd opened and a black feather wafted to the floor. The storage bungalow had been musty, having been largely unused since the last feature had wrapped a year-and-a-half before. Now, among the dusty props and cobweb-covered scenery flats not ten feet away, she definitely heard the sound of *footsteps* in the room with her.

"Who's there?" Ms. Plum stammered, tripping as she stepped back instinctively, intending to inch toward the door but crashing into a suit of armor instead. She pulled it down as she hit the floor, gasping, "… H-hellppp!! Julio!—I mean *Jose!!*"

"Take it easy, Honey, I'm not gonna bite you…" A woman in black stepped out from behind a red-flocked, bordello flat. She had a reassuring voice for someone who might be a burglar, Penelope thought.

"What do you want? How long have you been here?" Ms. Plum rose up to her full five feet, four inches and squared her slender shoulders, pushing tortoise-shell glasses back up onto the bridge of her nose. "Well? We're not hiring right now... you're not an applicant, are you?"

"No. I've come here to help you, Penelope." The trespasser smiled reassuringly.

"Oh, Christ—a stalker..."

"... I'm not a stalker—and please don't swear around me—I've come to help you. Let's pretend I'm a genie and you have three wishes... you can call me Angela."

Penelope Plum's first reaction was to back off, humor this weirdo—after all, this was Hollywood, stalker central and fruitcake capitol of the world. But somehow, not that she was religious, her instincts told her she had nothing to fear. There was an aura around Angela that you could light a cigar from.

"A genie, huh? You sure don't look much like Barbara Eden," Penelope said.

"I tried that and got sued."

"Really? Barbara Eden sued you?"

"No," Angela replied, "a celebrity lookalike sued me—For restraint-of-trade, no less—what's the world coming to?"

"So, get back to the three wishes—I rubbed this art deco table lamp and you appeared from behind a scenery flat. Okay. I'm buying it if you can... pick up that suit of armor without touching it." Penelope crossed her arms and sat on the desktop, inadvertently recalling her afternoon delight with Bernie on that very spot.

"I'm not into parlor tricks, Honey, but if you'd like to get boffed on the old mahogany again, that I can arrange." Angela folded *her* arms, making the black leather jacket she was wearing rustle and squeak as only new leather can. She tossed her short-cropped blueblack hair and smiled like she knew how many pairs of panties were in Penelope's hamper and what color they were, as well as the secrets of the universe.

"You know you look a little like k.d.lang, Angela... I don't know if it's intentional. I'm not into girls, by the way—no offense."

Angela laughed and sat down across the desk from Penelope. "I look *exactly* like Margaret L. Kinney, who's a private investigator in Chicago. And I'm not into humans—no offense. I wasn't going to tell you just yet, but you know that movie, *Michael*, with John Travolta?"

"... Oh, my God! You're not a genie, you're my guardian angel!" Penelope laughed this time, saying, "I'd just about given up on you... this is too much. Wait a minute, if you're an angel, why did you try to look like a genie?"

"Because some people don't believe in angels—or even God, Penelope. Do you know why Bernie always calls you Miss Plum? Because it's shorter than Penelope."

"Yeah—well, I hate 'Penny,' Ms. Plum sneered, "so forget that one."

Angela smiled so warmly the air conditioner cycled on. "I think your new name should be... *Pen*. Pen Remington. That's a great name—for a *co-producer*."

"...You ever do any casting?" Pen asked, smiling.

Chapter Four: Yin-Yang, Walla-Walla Bing-Bang

When Bernie and Mr. Z got back to the office, they were greeted by the sight of a smaller, blonde maple desk and swivel chair being moved into the conference room. Bernie asked him what he was doing, but Jose could only say that Ms. Plum had told him to do it after moving the mahogany set into the storage room.

"You mean the new executive producer's office, Julio..." Bernie said, smiling.

"Julio, my brother—my name, Jose."

"Of course it is..." he replied, oblivious to the man's identity, other than as a pair of hands and a strong back. "Right this way, Mr. Z..." Bernie led the friend of the Devil into his new lair and B.L. smelled the toner and the rug potpourri, and it was good.

"C.B... I have to admit—this is a bit of a thrill..." The Demon said, laughing like a death rattle. "... I mean—I've felled empires, overthrown dynasties... but getting my own office like this—well, I'm kind of honored, in a way. Of course, I wouldn't be here if you didn't need money."

"You're an executive producer—it goes with the turf. And speaking of money, I hope you have a few leads, the man in the iron lung was my last gasp."

"... Okay... pack an overnight; we're flying to New York. I know a place where we can get the rest of the budget all at once," B.L. said, grinning like a toaster oven.

"Great!" Bernie exclaimed, "Now, where the hell is Miss Plum?" Reservations had to be made, travel needs had to be attended.

"Knock, knock, we're back," she said, letting the door swing slowly open.

"... Miss Plum? Is that *you*? What have you done to your... hair? Who's *we*?" Bernie stared through the doorway at this lovely creature, somehow more alive than he'd seen her in years—now looking like a page out of *Elle*, reborn from the ashes of the bookish Miss Plum.

"We went shopping—Angela wanted to see the Rodeo Collection, then I got 'Sassooned.' Did you remember my sandwich? *Huh*? I didn't think so. We had lunch at Morton's—I put it on the card we just paid off."

"*What*? Are you... *crazy*?—*Morton's*? I don't even get to go to Morton's! And you never got... *Sassooned* before either? What's the hell's going on around here? I go to lunch, and you lose your mind and start burning money? Who the hell is Angela??"

"Oh, this is... my *cousin*, Angela... our new casting director—I put her in the conference room..." The door opened wider, Angela smiled from the hallway.

"Miss Plum...?" Bernie stammered; he shook hands with Angela, grimacing. "Hang on a minute, please, B.L.—make yourself at home... Oh, this is Miss Plum... B.L. Zebediah, our new executive producer...". B.L. shook hands with Miss Plum.

"Call me B.L.," he said, "or, Mr. Z."

"I'm Pen. Pen Plum..." she said, shooting Bernie a look, adding, "for now." Bernie cringed. There was nothing left but for B.L. and Angela to shake as well, which ordinarily wouldn't be obligatory, but both were so reluctant, so hostile-looking, that their not shaking was conspicuously ominous. "Come on, Angela, don't be stuck-up..."

"You don't understand, Pen... it's like with—*Electricity!!!*" Angela screamed, as B.L. grabbed her hand and pumped it; he yelled, too—as their clasped hands *sizzled* and *sparked*, smoking.

Neither of the supernatural beings was able to break the hand-clasp, as Bernie and Pen watched, astonished. A crackling blue corona surrounded the vibrating pair, and when the other two tried to pull them apart, it surrounded them as well. Soon all four were hollering and pulsating, the intensity building, until finally—like a room full of popping champagne corks, they burst apart, caroming off the walls.

"I wanna see you in my office!" Bernie barked at Pen.

"… I don't understand what you're trying to do, "Bernie whined, moments later. "I'm not trying to do anything, Bernie—I *am* doing it. For years you've been promising to make an honest woman out of me…"

"I'll start taking out deductions and paying half your social security next quarter, I promise…"

"That's not what I mean! I'll help you make this picture, all the way. I've given the best years of my life to you and your studio, but now I need something from you: I need co-producer credit on this movie… and I want you to marry me. You know I love you, Bernie, and if you marry me I won't have to worry about getting screwed out of my points…"

"Points?" Bernie was turning gray—his face, not his hair. "Level with me, Miss Pl… *Pen*. Who's this Angela? I don't remember you having a Cousin Angela?"

"You wouldn't believe me…" she shrugged.

"Today I would. Honest. Try me."

"Okay… Angela is… my guardian angel…" Bernie laughed the nervous laugh of a man with his foot caught in a bear trap who heard and smelled bear.

"… Your *what*? I hope for both of our sakes that you're kidding! Do you know who that is in there? Let me put it this way… If Nixon was Satan—an' I'm not sayin' he wasn't—that would be Kissinger in there…"

"Look, Bernie, you're not changing the subject! If *The Brain That Couldn't Think* is going to get made at all, it's going to be a classy, non-sexist, non-exploitation film, and you're going to agree to my terms… otherwise, I'll stop inputting the bank deposits—hell, I'll screw up the computer program! If there's one thing you don't have a clue about, it's computers, especially the office program—I designed it. And I can make it crash like the friggin' Hindenburg!"

"Why are you doing this to me, Miss Plum? I thought you said you loved me, you call this love?"

"Your biggest problem, Bernie, is that you always think everything is about *you*! Well my life is not about you—it's about *me*! And I'm sick and tired of working my ass off around here for chump change and a bouquet of flowers on secretaries' day!"

In B.L.'s office, Angela said her goodbyes, "Sounds like the two lovebirds are working things out…"

"Just so there's no mistake, Angela, I don't want the girl, but don't waste your time on Bernie—or C.B., as he prefers to be called. He's mine.

All mine. Has been for a long time, but now I've got him under contract, so it's binding."

"Contracts were made to be broken," Angela replied, "that's what lawyers are for. But I don't need to tell *you* about lawyers. Fortunately for you, I loathe Bernie and wouldn't save him, even if I could. You stay out of my way and I'll stay out of yours—it'll be a paradoxically strange, but possibly fruitful alliance."

"Kind of like when Disney bought Miramax, back when they were distributing NC-17 Pedro Almodovar bondage films…"

"The yin and the yang… I hope it doesn't violate any *cosmic* union rules…" Angela mused, tossing her blueblack bangs."

"So are you the yin or the yang? More importantly, Angela, are you the cat-bird-thing that's been haunting my boy, Bernie, for a couple of weeks?" Mr. Z looked like Torquemada, grilling the paper boy for hitting the screen door.

"He's ruining my client's life…"

"Your *client?* It didn't take *you* long to go Hollywood," B.L. cracked.

"Look who's talking! You could take his soul right now, as is, and do us both a favor—but NO—you *want* to be the executive producer—you want to dabble in the movie business."

"You're the one who had lunch at Morton's…"

"*Dilettante!*" Angela hissed, jerking open the door. Bernie and Pen were on the other side smiling oddly; their hair was mussed, and Bernie had his shirt buttoned wrong. Pen was flushed and calmer than she'd been in three months.

"Are you two gonna get along, or are we gonna have to keep you apart like feuding dinner guests?" Bernie asked. "B.L.—would you mind, please…?"

"We need your office for about a half-hour," Pen said, smiling, "the desk, actually…"

Chapter Five: An Offer They Couldn't Refuse

It was a dark and stormy flight. They landed in Kennedy and took the Cross Island Parkway out to Long Island, then the Southern State Parkway up to Massapequa and the suburban home of the Acappella crime family.

Stella Acappella, wife of Big Al "Two Screws" Acappella, served drinks in the den as their two flesh-pierced, goth teenagers played "Chest-Burster" in the corner; Bernie and B.L. laid out their battle plan to Big Al and three of his gumbahs.

"It's a horror/tragedy, like *Forrest Gump meets Edward Scissorhands*, but with a *brain*," Bernie said, a little apprehensive his first time among the wise guys.

B.L. was more to the point, "Basically, we need 6.66 mil, no vig, no questions asked—by the end of next week, and repayable from the film's profits, let's say in... two years." Big Al reacted unemotionally: he turned to his wife and gestured "lose the kids" with his eyes. Stella vocalized his directive.

"Morella, Ambrose, you two scoot... Go on, now, do your homework."

"But, Mater—'*When Blenders and Lawnmowers Attack*!' is coming on," protested young Ambrose, "and you know I prefer to be called 'Scar.'"

"Get outta here, or they'll be callin' ya '*Bruise*,'" Big Al growled. After the pale, dark-clad pair left he turned to his visitors from the far coast and said, "See, my kids... they got metal stuck in their faces. Okay... not exactly my cup of tea, but it's all the rage today. The difference with them is, for one, they *wanted* it... For two, they had it done as *painlessly* as possible..."

All four gumbahs drew down, switchblades and straight-razors whooshing through the air like sound effects in a Hong Kong chop-socky flick. "We don't shoot in the house," Big Al smirked, "so you'll have to settle for metal stuck in your face... No *vig?!*"

As the wise guys moved in on them, Bernie ducked behind Mr. Z, who levitated the biggest goon and flew him through the wall. He gave the other two such an evil eye, they started waltzing with each other and speaking Chinese. Big Al tried to run for it, but the Demon turned the arched entrance to the living room into a sheet of blistering flame. Al screamed, and then smiled, remembering the insurance. His two kids re-entered the den, walking through the flames unhurt, admiring the hole in the wall with the snoring goon half-hanging out of it.

"The house is on fire," Morella purred, "cool..."

"I'll get the video camera," Scar said routinely.

"I can't give you six million dollars, it's not my money!" Big Al cried.

"That would fall under the category of *your problem*, Al," B.L. said stonily. "You know, there's a bar out in Hollywood where your two kids would fit right in… How would you like it if I switch their heads around? Do you think anyone would notice?" B.L. began gesturing at the two goth teens like a sorcerer, "Let's see…"

"Go ahead," Big Al said, "they're so screwed-up already, it might actually be an improvement…"

"Alphonse!" Stella whined, "These are your children. Who is this person? He looks like Robert De Niro in that movie with the egg."

"*Angel Heart.* I get it all the time," said B.L., "I think I'll play *Devil's Advocate* for a while."

With that, he began spinning in place, faster and faster, as if attempting to screw himself into the floor. His form and features became a dull blur, lost in a completely opaque, man-sized whirlwind. Then the Demon came to a stop.

"I don't understand why you're not more RECEPTIVE… to our offer," B.L. remarked, suddenly accenting the word "receptive" in a clumsy effort to vocally impersonate Al Pacino, whom he now resembled, dressed in a dignified-looking dark suit and tie, as the actor appeared in *The Devil's Advocate*. He gestured and emphasized words at random, moving through the smoky room, "Don't break my HEART, 'Two Screws,' you've been like a brother to me," B.L. continued, gesturing like Pacino.

"Holy shit… it's the Don, himself—Mic…"

"No, it's not!" Bernie interrupted, standing up to his full five-foot-two-inch height. "It's friggin' Be-EL-ze-bub," he said, accentuating the second syllable to ape B.L.'s lame imitation of the man who played Michael Corleone. "If you don't do what he says, he'll turn your wife and kids into trolls—not that that would be a big stretch—but YOU, he would probably turn into… Oh, I don't know…"

"A fire hydrant in a dog pound," B.L. mused, "or perhaps a malignant TUMOR!"

He stopped, poking Big Al's belly. Then he wheeled away, slicked back his hair, walked three steps and wheeled again to face the room. "Six-million, six-hundred and sixty THOUSAND… dollars, to be disbursed in a series of bank transfers, each, not to contain less than ten—no, twenty—percent of the total budget, at the rate of twenty-five percent interest, PER… payment, on the remaining principal." The Demon known as Mr. Z spiraled and stopped, threw his arms into the air, dropped them to his sides for effect, slicked back his hair, and grinned ironically. He was really getting into his new persona—as well as the Long Island mob pockets of Big Al "Two Screws" Acappella.

"I just got a couple of stipulations…" Big Al replied, more impressed with B.L and Bernie now that the former resembled someone also named "Al," who could make an offer he couldn't refuse. "You say this picture is like *Forrest Gump meets Edgar Scissorhead?*"

"*Scissor-hands…EDWARD Scissorhands.*" Bernie said.

"Whatever," Big Al replied, "But if we're investing all this dough in it, why couldn't it be more like… "*Rainman meets Goodfellas?*" Maybe you could even get Dustin Hoffman? You know, you got your retarded guy—the *Brain*—and you got your wise guys… Sounds much more exciting to me, already."

"We weren't planning on getting a major star to play the Brain Kid," Bernie said, "For most of the film, he's just a brain in a tank—anybody can loop the voice-over,"

"We need a star for the role of the doctor/scientist who keeps him ALIVE… on machines…" B.L. stated in Pacino-esque cadence, brushing back his dark locks and flashing his ivories like a Steinway in heat."

"Maybe you could get…"

"Maybe you could shut the fuck up and put your money where your mouth is," Bernie said, interrupting, emboldened by the Demon's new, mob-friendly *chutzpah*. "I mean, you're as bad as the 'suits' back in L.A! You know nothing about making movies—nothing about writing them, shooting them or marketing them, but that doesn't stop you from telling a seasoned professional with forty-five pictures under his belt, how to do his job! No wonder the Roman Empire collapsed—come to think of it, Julius Caesar was probably the first recorded mob hit…"

"… What movies have you made?" Big Al snorted, warming a bit to the whole idea, despite the tongue-lashing, "Anything I might have seen?"

"Well, *Frankenstein Meets the Elephant Man* is considered my biggest box office hit, but the brain pictures did well too—except for that stupid musical—especially *Citizen Brain*, remember that one?"

"Not really," Big Al said, shaking his head, "I don't go in for the horror stuff."

"… *Dope Titans of Little Italy?*" Bernie suggested, playing the urban crime card.

"… Huh?" Big Al said, startled, "that was a great movie! With Biff Halstrom and Serena What's-her-name."

"Serena Savage—I also used her in *MotorPsycho 'Ho'* and *Mono Lake Monsters*," Bernie declared, beaming; this wise guy knew his films, he thought, even his *stars*.

"I liked the scene in *Dope Titans* where Moe Digliani told the good cop he was takin' back the old neighborhood—makin' it safe for kids to run numbers, and mom-an'-pop stores to pay protection to the Families again… Great dialogue—four stars!"

C.B. REMINGTON'S
DOPE TITANS OF LITTLE ITALY

Starring
BIFF HALSTROM
LOIS LANFILL
MOE DIGLIANI
CREESE MASTERSON
And **SERENA SAVAGE** as "B.J."

Photography by VIKTOR ZILMOS   Produced by C.B. REMINGTON   Directed by LORENZO LOCO
Music by RAOUL CORNWIELDER   A Remington Pictures, Ltd., Release   RATED **R**

B.L. was perched on the back of the sofa next to the long-suffering Stella. Suddenly, he jumped up, whirling and gesturing anew, "We're getting off the TRACK... gentlemen. You—Big Al... I llllike that name—you make the first payment in cash, while we're here in town, no bullshit... We're gonna be partners in a very lucrative venture... Yeah, man—LUCRATIVE... lucrative as *hell!*" His Pacino impression slipped into Christopher Walken territory at times, but the look was perfect; and—he couldn't resist doing the trick where the flames shoot out of his eyes and fingertips.

Then, just for a second, he let everyone (Bernie included) see his favorite persona: curled horns, talons and fangs, jaundiced goat-eyes, and squamous, reptilian hide. The true Demon was bipedal, had two eyes, a nose and a mouth—but there, further resemblance to anything remotely human ceased. Even the morbidly preoccupied Morella and "Scar" ran screaming from the room as the leathery wings of Beelzebub rustled. Glistening, black tentacles that grew from his toadlike trunk, writhed in the smoky, burnt wallpaper-and-garlic ambiance of the Acappellos' trashed den.

Two hours later, the producers had their cash payment and were on the way back to the airport.

Chapter Six: Thanks for Coming In, We'll Call You...

Back in Tinsletown, the mice were at play. In the day-and-a-half that Bernie and B.L. were gone Pen and Angela had decided to rewrite the script as a romantic tragedy, and had changed the lead role of the doctor/scientist from a man to a woman. *And* they'd put their listing in the casting breakdowns—a service exclusive to agents and producers, in theory at least. Their *brain*storm was to sign a real handicapped actor to play "Timmy," the mentally challenged youth who winds up a brain in a tank. This would, ostensibly, curry favor with the politically correct media—even the good guys aren't above a little angling in Hollywood. Besides, what was so wrong with using a handicapped person to get free publicity, as long as it was for a good cause—like making money? A few days later they'd have a casting call for the doctor/scientist role, hopefully attracting A-list talent due to the publicity.

Since the boys had been gone, Angela had gotten a makeover too. Deciding on a softer, more *Cosmo* look, she was now the perfect image of Lou Ann Keighler, a Long Beach accountant that she'd noticed while waiting in line at the bank. She selected Ms. Keighler because she vaguely resembled Margaret Kinney, the mid-western P.I. whose appearance Angela had been *borrowing*. Margaret was the one who favored k.d. lang, but Ms. Keighler, while looking a bit like Margaret, also managed somehow *not* to look very much like the famous singer. Angela selected her "role-models" carefully, to avoid shocking people when she changed—unlike her spiritual *doppelganger*, the executive producer from hell.

Angela explained to Pen that ethereal beings needed a template to follow to appear realistically human: by copying a pre-existing series of aligned molecules, i.e., a human being, there was little room for error. If they just faked it—assumed *their idea* of a human form—they might turn out like living drawings or bad sculptures. Without a human pattern to follow, a spirit could end up looking like Gumby by Picasso.

"That's why this demon, Beelzebub, always affects the guise of a movie star—he has to pick *someone*, and he likes the attention. Besides, by picking men who've played the Devil, he adds that ironic, disturbing touch. Personally, I think he knows that impersonating movie stars who've portrayed The Dark One is as close as he's ever going to get to *being* number one. Now, me? I like to pick un-famous people who live in another city—that way, I'm never recognized. This "B.L.", or "Mr. Z" or whatever, is an egomaniac. His lust for recognition and adulation stems from low self-esteem—basically, from being Number Two, for... well, since before time began."

"That's oxymoronic, Angela, how can anything have occurred *before* time began? If something occurred—then time *began*. I thought you were supposed to know the secrets of the universe, being an angel and all."

"Are you kidding? I'm only a level three spiritual escort—there are nine levels before the board, and then there's The Boss. He knows the 'secrets of the universe,' but even the level niners, and the saints and prophets on the board can't get a meeting," Angela said. "Level threes don't know doodly, plus we feel pain and are even capable of committing *sin* while in mortal form. Let's work together on this movie—save your arguing for Bernie."

"Why do you have to be down on Bernie all the time? I don't know why you hate him so much," Pen sighed.

"He's a cheap, tasteless, no-talent who's spent his career denigrating women and purveying sex and violence. He treats you like his own personal doormat, and now he's selling his soul to the freaking *Devil!* Stop me when you've heard enough."

"Okay—Bernie leaves a little bit to be desired—but he's not a no-talent! You haven't seen all of his films," Pen said; then she sighed again. "And you don't know that for sure, about his soul… I guess angels and demons are just more-focused sorts of ghosts—but so much more complicated! How come you two don't look like you did when you were alive?"

"Mr. Z never *was* a person, and it's been over a thousand years for me—I can't even remember what I looked like as a human. Spirits who still resemble themselves either haven't been dead long enough for them to forget, or they were important enough to have likenesses made when they were alive."

"But, you're so serious and spiteful—*vindictive*, even. Not like in the movies and TV, where spirits are always floating amiably around, materializing or becoming invisible whenever it's funny, or inconvenient for the hauntee."

"You're another *Topper* kid, aren't you?" The angel sneered. "That show was the *Amos 'n' Andy* of the spirit world! Negative stereotypes and misinformation shrouded in a pall of bad taste… alcoholic dog-ghosts, indeed. Now, *Touched By an Angel*, on the other hand…"

"Yeah, I watched *Topper* in old re-runs," Pen replied, "so what? You know, Angela, you have absolutely *no* sense of humor. Lighten up a little! You're right about us working together, but tomorrow is the cattle call for the mentally challenged 'Timmy' role, and I don't want you scaring off any of these handicapped kids with your… *cosmic handle* on negativity.

"It's already going to take plenty of courage for them just to show up, subjecting themselves to ridicule and despair for daring to compete in a tough, dirty business in which even *normal* people consistently fail; and, after a childhood of being left out of everything from playing sports to teen romance, now, at best, they've got—*maybe*, one chance in a hundred of even getting a call-back to play a *retard* in three scenes, and dub the voice for a *rubber brain* in the rest of the movie… So don't piss on their party, okay Angela? Bernie and B.L. will be back tomorrow night, and team spirit is *de rigueur*." Almost to herself, Pen added, "I sure hope they come back with the budget."

That night, a day ahead of schedule, Bernie and B.L. stopped in Las Vegas to celebrate, where the former managed to win at craps for the first time in his life, due largely to the presence of the latter. This, like

every thing else Mr. Z had done for Bernie, was blood-writ in the Demon's Ledger of Souls, under "accounts receivable."

The next morning, seventy-five-hundred dollars richer, Bernie
pulled into the small parking lot at Remington Pictures, Ltd., to find it full
of cars and vans—all of them with handicapped parking stickers in their
windows. *All* of them. Every damn one. What the hell was going on, he
thought?

Inside, it was worse. There were at least sixty handicapped young
men in the office, between twelve and twenty-five years of age, sitting in
wheelchairs or on furniture, leaning on the walls or being coached by the
four-score of doting stage mothers accompanying the more helpless
hopefuls. One of the lads had a unique disorder, not unlike Tourette's
Syndrome, causing him to make a repetitive, apparently involuntary *bark-
ing* sound, even when he smiled at Angela, who was trying to get him to
stop. This was really freaking out the two seeing-eye dogs in the room and
pissing off most of the stage mothers. "Can't you make him stop bark-
ing?" One of them asked.

"He's a thirteen-year-old boy, not a cocker spaniel," the barker's
mom shot back, "What do you want me to do, hit him with a rolled-up
newspaper?"

Bernie tripped over somebody's aluminum leg-brace, and nearly
fell on an encephalitic teen, scaring him half out of his wits. Unfortunately,
it was the half that functioned; the lad bolted for the parking lot with his
mother in hot pursuit.

Face to face with Angela, whom of course, he didn't recognize in
her new persona, Bernie exploded, "What the hell is going on here?—
And who are *you*? Has everyone gone crazy?"

"No, C.B., I'm Angela Winger, remember? And these young men
aren't crazy—they're just handicapped, or have special learning disabili-
ties. They're here to read—sort of—for the part of Timmy the Brain Kid,
before the accident…"

"I've read the script; I know who *Timmy* is—but, you look different? Your hair is longer," Bernie questioned, squinting at her, "and you're
wearing different makeup or something—anyway, where's Miss Plum?"

"… *Pen* is in her office, evaluating the talent, and I'm rounding
them up and herding them in," Angela said. Reading from her checklist,
she turned to the pack of "Timmy" hopefuls, and hollered, "*Kevin Par-
TOO-ty?*"

"It'th pronounthed *Par-thoo-THAY*," a shy youth replied from a few seats away. Angela corrected herself.

"I'm sorry... Par-thoo-THAY," she said, accenting the last syllable as he had.

"No"—the boy argued, "*Par-thoo-THAY!*"

"That's what I just said," she argued back.

"I believe his name is pronounced Par-too-TAY," Bernie offered, "the boy obviously has a severe lisp." Turning to the youth now standing before him, he asked, "Your name is pronounced, 'Kevin PartooTAY,' isn't it, son?" The boy also had a serious retainer: it could have been a face-mask if the NFL allowed them to be made of steel and rubber bands.

"*Yeth*," the boy lisped through the chrome tangle that muzzled him.

"And you wanna be an actor?"

"Oh, *yeth*."

"Well, unfortunately, this picture is called *The Brain That Couldn't Think*, not *The Kid That Couldn't Talk*, so, don't quit your day job, Kevin.—Keep that paper route, and spend the money on a good vocal coach—or, you can stick a harmonica in that thing and get a tin cup." With that said, Bernie stormed off to find Pen, leaving Angela to show the crestfallen boy out.

"... I don't feel *tho* good no more—I think I'm gonna be *thick*... Who'*th* that *mean* man?" the boy asked, sniffling back the tears of rejection that come to all thespians at one time or another. Angela patted his head, aiming him out the door with kind words: "Oh... he's just the producer, Honey... but don't you worry—he's going to hell in a paper cup as soon as this thing wraps."

"So, just what the... is going on around here?" Bernie demanded, barging in on Pen and a prospective "Timmy" in the middle of a cold reading. The boy's mother jumped.

"C.B! I thought you weren't coming back till tonight?" Pen said, surprised.

"... Excuse me," the mother said to Bernie, "but my Hunter was just finding his character... How can we get the level of concentration we need with intrusions like this?"

"*We?*" Bernie exclaimed, eyebrows raised in feigned innocence, "What do you mean '*we?*' This ain't exactly *MacBeth*, lady... We don't need no friggin' witches, just an unknown teenager and a leading man."

The producer of *Night of the Dying Dead* was especially cocky since his recent easy victories in New York and Vegas, but B.L. Zebediah, his good luck charm and source of illicit power, had not yet arrived at the studio. Unaware that she was in the presence of the legendary C.B. Remington, the stage mom showed far less respect than the mini-mogul was used to receiving.

"… Are you… calling me a *witch*, you sawed-off, dickless little piece of crap?"

Bernie got a look on his face that spelled murder in seven different languages.

"Thanks for coming in," Pen said to the boy, "we'll call you."

"Oh… that's not fair—I only have six months to live! I need this part to keep my insurance through the union!" The youth, a pale, thin specimen, with dark circles under his eyes, was near tears. "Now, I won't be able to afford the operation," he sobbed, coughing. Bernie covered his mouth, fanning the germs away.

"Sorry, kid, but this part requires a *nine*-month commitment, off-and-on, what with re-shoots and the sound mix—dubbing, you know, then the publicity campaign…"

"No problem," The mother assured, "Hunter—show the rude man how good an actor you are." The boy coughed again, seeming quite ill; then, he straightened up and wiped the dark circles and pancake pallor away with his handkerchief. The sixteen-year-old faker leapt up on Pen's desk, balancing on his hands. Actually, it was Bernie's desk and office, but Bernie was too occupied with the events of the moment to notice. Hunter intruded on his saturnine thoughts.

"Being a physically fit, professional *ac-tor*, I can portray a mentally or physically challenged person better than one of *them*. For one thing, I'm intelligent, theatrically trained, and I can read and memorize quickly," the boy said, still stranding on his hands. Then, he did a back-flip off the desk, landing on his feet. "Plus, I'm not a spaz!"

"That's five things," Bernie quipped, "You can do everything but count. I hate precocious kids—so take your horse-faced WITCH of a mother and hit the road."

"You're the rudest man I ever met!" the mother exclaimed, dragging her little Olivier to the door, "You call this a studio? This is a pretentious *joke!*"

"No, lady, naming your kid 'Hunter' is a pretentious joke—I guess, all things considered, he got off lucky—since he don't look like *you.*" Bernie's crack made her slam the door so hard, several handicapped hopefuls jumped out of her path in terror.

At first, Bernie was upset with the idea of making the doctor/scientist a woman, but the pragmatic money-monger inside him realized that it wasn't such a bad idea after all. Especially the way Pen explained it to him.

"This way, it's still a medical-themed horror/tragedy, but with an added element that's sure-fire box-office gold—the 'love that cannot be' angle! By making the doctor a woman, we can have her fall in love with the Brain Kid after he's already a brain—talk about *a love that cannot be!*"

"But, Miss Pl... I mean, *Pen*—the kid's only thirteen!" Bernie protested, "That's a felony in every state but the one Jerry Lee Lewis comes from."

"We changed the Brain Kid to a sexually active nineteen-year-old and lowered the doctor/scientist's age to twenty-two," Pen explained.

"How sexually active can a mentally challenged youth be?" Bernie asked, "And what level of expertise can a scientist have at *twenty-two?*"

"To answer your first question: the Brain Kid's backstory has him getting raped in special ed., so he knows what sex is, and secondly; the 'love-that-cannot-be' between a tragic nineteen-year-old and a sexy nineteen-year-old *playing* twenty-two will bring in the teen money. Great 'love-that-cannot-be' movies are always successful, C.B., and the critics love 'em. "Think '*Gone With the Wind* meets *Dawson's Creek.*' Imagine '*Casablanca* meets *Buffy the Vampire Slayer.*' '*Titanic* meets *Scream3*'—But with a *brain!* We'll need armored cars to carry all the money to the bank!" Pen could be very persuasive, especially when she was right.

"*Titanic* made a hell of a lot of money..." Bernie said dreamily, completely sold.

"A registered letter came for you—I signed for it."

Chapter Seven: The Dork at the Top of the Stairs

That day, the filmmakers found their Timmy, a slender youth of twenty named Norman Ates. Norman wasn't mentally challenged like his character but the large square lenses in his horned-rimmed glasses were thick as bullet-proof glass. Surgery had repaired his congenitally crossed eyes, but his elbows and knees remained sharp things. He also had severe dyslexia and a stammer, but aside from all that, he was fairly non-challenged and reasonably good-looking.

Mr. Z pretty much stayed out of the casting process, but brought in one of his clients to do the special effects. "Berserker" Bob Gash was a mad genius of movie magic, famous for the "appetizing gore" movement in horror films—epitomized by his effects work in the *Corpse-Eater* series. Not unlike Bernie, he'd made quite a mark in the accounts receivable section of B.L.'s Ledger of Souls, as well.

In his late thirties now, Berserker Bob had gotten mixed up with Mr. Z a few years back. He'd wanted to be nominated for an "f/x" award so badly, he'd prayed for it—forgetting that he was an avowed atheist. His prayer was answered by the other side, and that year he got nominated for a "Nyiffy" for *Corpse-Eaters on Fire Island*, from the New York Independent Filmmakers Forum, but lost to Dale Hinder, f/x supervisor for the filmed version of the Broadway musical rehash of *My Dinner with Andre*, titled *Entrée de Deux!* Gash felt he was robbed: both by N.Y.I.F.F., and—the dark side.

Pen found the actress who was to portray Dr. Blair Chastewood, the medical professional who falls for the Brain. Her name was Kimberly Node, and she was from Lancaster, now living in Hollywood, beating the bricks with her resumes and head shots. She had one of those faces you see on autographed black-and-white glossies framed and mounted in Hollywood dry cleaners and pizzerias—and nowhere else. An equity waiver maven, Kimberly had trouble juggling her thespian career with her "day job" at a 24-hour pet beauty parlor/coffee house, where she hoped to meet the producer or director who would discover her. After all, she thought, a beautiful and talented actress like herself, who got the lead in her Lancaster high school play the last two years in a row, deserved to be a movie star.

Pen met Kimberly when she brought in her cat to be groomed at "The Insomniac Pet Salon." Noticing the cheerful groomer's signed photo on the wall, Pen asked if she were an actress. This led to discussion of the brain movie, and Kimberly's being invited to read for the part of Dr. Chastewood—a day *after* the general casting call. The cheerful groomer turned into a career-driven slut when she met The Producer, Bernie. Moments later Pen began to regret finding Kimberly, who, it seemed, was actually prepared to fuck her way to the bottom. When Bernie met her, he forgot about getting a star for his picture, later canceling the call-backs for the role.

"I see here on your resume, that you haven't done any movies or TV... Tell me, Ms. Node, why I should give you the lead in my picture?"

"Why Mr. Remington, I just love your movies—You know, you look really young for someone so famous and successful, it would be my pleasure to work... under you," she purred like Salome danced, "and it's pronounced No-*DAY*."

Bernie liked her, and so did B.L., who, to keep from driving everyone crazy, had reverted back to something closer to his *Angel Heart* look before returning to L.A. He had, however made quite an impression at the Vegas crap tables with Bernie while he was still doing his bad, if energetic, Pacino impression (*"Eight, the hard way—COME... to Papa!"*)

In the months that followed, the rest of the roles were cast, locations were selected, sets were built and most importantly, a *director* was hired. Not just any director either, but Carlton Tooms, a seasoned pro, famous for making popular, glossy soapers and tear-jerkers throughout the '80s and '90s, including a string of made-for-TV disease-of-the-week movies like; *Please Don't Let My Mother Die!*, *The Overlong Illness*, and *Not with My Dead Baby, You Don't!*—the latter a stinging indictment of alleged tax-funded medical experiments on alleged terminated fetuses.

Tooms was also widely recognized for his romantic melodramas—archaic and, for the most part, humorless attempts at replicating the style and substance of Douglas Sirk's '50s sudsers. *Autumn of Our Anguish*, *Rest-Home Hearts*, and *Year of the Bitter Corn* were but a few of Tooms' more lugubrious efforts. His career had already peaked, and then some; he was the perfect choice to direct *"Brain."* The aristocratic Brit wasn't thrilled about working for Bernie, but his agent demanded a quarter of a million bucks and got it—the producer had to pay him, unlike the original writer, Kip Lothar, whose letters and faxes Bernie had been avoiding.

"I could make three pictures for what you set me back, Tooms. No—*four.*"

"And, doubtless, they'd be abominable excursions into dreck, one and all," the sardonically effete director of *Malaise of Lust* replied.

Nothing salacious happened between Bernie and Kimberly, but the little tramp's flirtations gave Pen a great excuse for drawing lines in the sand. One day during rehearsal, Pen caught the 19-year-old vamp rubbing Bernie's neck and shoulders on set.

"Excuse me, Kimberly? I think there's a phone call for you," Pen said, hoping to get rid of the girl while avoiding a confrontation.

"Take a message," Kimberly snapped, not looking at her as she rubbed Bernie deeper and more sensuously.

"... A—excuse me? That's my... boyfriend you're kneading like pizza dough, why don't you go answer your own damn phone call that you don't have..." Pen was really pissed off and territorial, as well—Bernie might not have been much—but at least he was hers... wasn't he? They had an unspoken agreement, almost a verbal contract... didn't they? Bernie was being awfully quiet for Bernie, enjoying the moment and watching to see what else his Miss Plum would say or do.

"Well, well—a little jealous, aren't we? I don't hear C.B. complaining," the high school Jezebel taunted, "maybe he's got an itch that needs to be scratched?"

"Oh, yeah?" Pen shot back, serious as global warming, "Maybe, you've got a nose that needs to be broken?"

Just before principal photography commenced, Bernie and Pen got married in Vegas, but she'd insisted they go alone. Without their spiritual allies, Bernie dropped ten grand at the craps table and Pen almost had her honeymoon, a weekend at Lady Luck's Grotto of Love, ruined because of it.

Norman Ates and Kimberly Shayne (the studio made her lose the "Node") worked for scale, and the sets weren't too elaborate, except for Dr. Chastewood's high-tech Frankenstein laboratory, the Bosnian field hospital, and the full-size mock-ups for the dirigible chase. They shot most of the chase with models and computer generated effects, but what really ate up the budget were all the union base scales and their respective cost-overrun allocations: namely—overtime. Terms like "time-and-a-half" and "golden time" were relatively unknown to Bernie, who'd never made a completely union film in his life.

For a while, it seemed that the movie would get made without a serious hitch, except for Norman's dyslexia: it caused him to involuntarily transpose the words in his script whenever reading. He had less of a problem once he'd learned his lines, but in the read-throughs and blocking rehearsals, dialogue that was supposed to be coming from a mentally challenged individual in the first place now had the added spin of being read in jumbled, senseless order.

This would not have presented a problem once they were shooting because Ates could learn his lines all right—but the lines kept changing. Angela—yes, Angela—had acquired a mild amphetamine habit and was staying up night-after-night, endlessly rewriting the script on prescription speed, or diet pills, as the rich, famous, and overly optimistic like to say. This constant rewriting was hard on everyone, especially Norman/Timmy and the actors in his scenes.

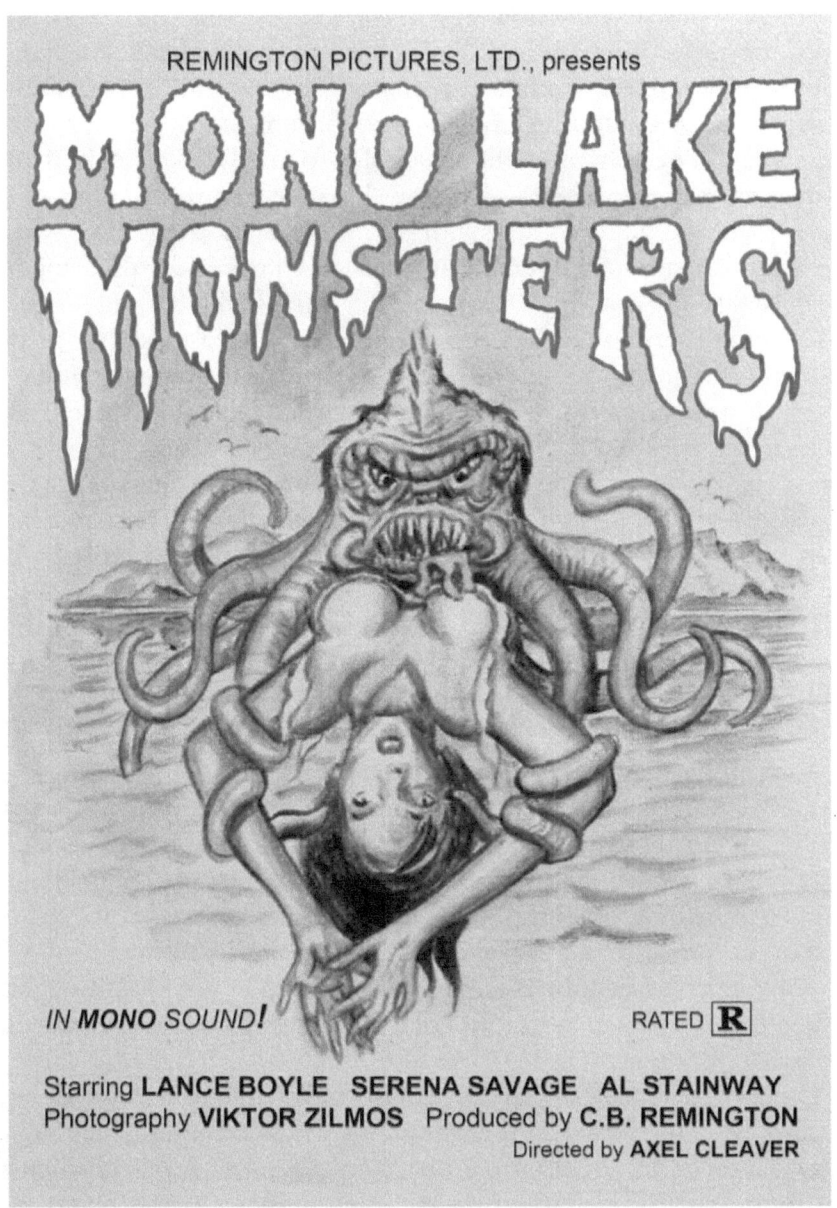

The whole cast and crew were counting the days till Timmy's accident scene was scheduled (none more-so than Tooms) so they could lose Norman's dyslexic, stuttering ass and start working with the prop brain. Even the sexually ambiguous set dresser and the weird intern wanted him gone. Norman had all the charisma of detergent. The director wouldn't need him again until the dubbing sessions, and that would be an entirely different kind of hell, two blissful months away.

Angela had rewritten the screenplay so that Dr. Chasewood meets Timmy before the accident—that way she'd have some memory of him as a *person* when falling in love with him as a brain. Meryl Streep would have been hard-pressed to create any illusion of desire for this rangy but inarticulate geek; Kimberly Shayne, on the other hand, despite her prowess as a high school drama-queen, was barely able to mask her copious hatred of him—it showed in the rushes of their brief scene together.

"Jesus, Kimberly, you look like you want to kill him," the British-born director declared loudly in the small screening room. "This is what they call the 'meet cute.' It's supposed to be charming and ironic. When you see him struggling in his leg-braces, accidentally knocking everything off of the counter in the fish-market, you're supposed to cross to him, pick up his trout and hand it to him gently, gazing into his eyes—you don't just *throw* it at him! Trout isn't very romantic... *Props!* Lose the trout—get a bouquet of flowers... He could drop caviar, but it might break."

"Roses—red roses!" Added Pen, who was covering line producer duties, allowing Bernie to come and go as he pleased.

Angela was in her trailer rewriting the Brain's confrontation with Father Time in the hallucinogenic dream sequence. In her final draft of that sequence, somebody slips LSD to the Brain in a Bosnian field hospital, and Timmy has a bad trip, dreaming that he's been transplanted into the skull of Noriega-like dictator, now operating in central Europe. We hear a poetic voice-over by Norman/Timmy, as his "point-of-thought" is displayed on the screen in riotous colors, courtesy of computer generated imagery.

Then, a voice-over by Dr. Chastewood cuts in and we discover that she's been hallucinating the whole Bosnian bad trip in a Malibu Starbucks—because an anti-abortion activist put LSD in her latte when she went to the rest room. We realize then that it *has* to be somebody else's fantasy—the Brain is much too lame to even know who Noriega is. Wearing sunglasses, sitting in the corner, talking to herself over that laced latte,

Dr. Chastewood is in her own world. The self-obsessed customers of Star-bucks-by-the-sea, jaded denizens of La-La Land, fail to even notice her in Angela's hip, culture-conscious rewrite of the script, anyway—color *her* Nora Ephron.

A few days later, Timmy's accident scene was shot—Norman was out and the Brain was in—but Ates refused to leave, his parents' ranch-style Brea home no longer offering an acceptable alternative to the glittering lights of a Hollywood movie set.

After two more days, he still insisted on reading the Brain's lines from off-screen to Ms. Shayne, on whom he'd developed a substantial crush, oblivious to her open abhorrence of him. A location shoot was scheduled that day, and it happened to be the very scene where Dr. Chastewood comes out of her Bosnian hallucination, realizing that she's in an American coffeehouse, whacked out of her skull on right-to-life acid. Part of the high concept of the 'love that cannot be' angle was to have the brain communicate telepathically with Dr. Chastewood whenever they're separated on screen...

A sampling of the morning's unedited soundtrack follows:

FIRST A.D: "Settle please... here we go... roll sound."
SOUNDMAN: "... Sound speed."
FIRST A.D: "Roll camera..."
CREW MEMBER: *(whispered in background)* "We're rolling... Cue the dork...

2nd CREW MEMBER: *"Shhhh!"*... *(tittering in background)*
FIRST A.D: "Quiet, please!"
FOCUS PULLER: "Camera speed... mark it." *(sound of slate clapping)*

DIRECTOR: *(softly)* "Ready...and... action."
DR. CHASTEWOOD: *(a beat)* "...Get the orphans into the heli-copter! *Now!* What do you mean, *there's not enough room?* We've got to go *now!* Here, take the last two orphans and this Brain in a jar—I'll stay be-hind... Wait a minute—*Where am I??* This isn't war-torn Bosnia, it's a *Starbucks in Malibu!* But I can still hear Timmy's voice, from halfway around the world... *(silence; several beats; impatiently)* ...But I can still hear Timmy's voice, from halfway around..."

TIMMY: *(interrupting)* "D-D-D-Doctor Wood-chase, I'm fartnot away—n-n-not FAR away *(coughs)* Find me, b-before tits oo'late—IT'S

TOO…late. (*Coughs, belches; breaks character*) S-S-Sorry—I just g-g-got these new p-p-p-pages… "

DR. CHASTEWOOD: (*angrily*) "… Timmy? Is that you, Honey? I see colors… and my tummy tingles—Could someone have put a powerful psychedelic drug, like L.S.D, in my café latte? Timmy… where are you? Don't fall asleep—you'll slip into a coma… I must have misplaced you, damn this American drug epidemic….Call out my name, so I can find where I left you…

TIMMY: (*BREAKS WIND; breaks character*) "I c-c-can't drink c-c-c-coffee… I have to go to the b-b-b-bathroom!"

DR. CHASTEWOOD: "*Goddammit!!* This is too much! Get a *grip* to read the fucking lines or I'm off this piece of shit! I mean it, Carlton—get this stuttering geek away from me! (*angry footsteps stomping off*) I'll be in my trailer till that idiot is gone—Jackie, get my agent on the phone…"

JACKIE: (*In background*) Right away, Ms. Shayne…"

TIMMY: I'm s-s-s-sorry, M-M-M-Miss Shay…

BERNIE: "Christ, he can't even *talk!* I might as well've hired the kid in the iron mask."

DIRECTOR: "Cut! (*softly*) Break for lunch…"

FIRST A.D: "*LUNCH – ONE HOUR!*" (*Norman/Timmy sobs in background.*)

In addition to Bernie's other problems, Kip Lothar, the disgruntled, and so far unpaid, original writer of "Brain" tried to crash the set, and was promptly kicked off the location in tears—after getting a noxious dose of Angela's unauthorized rewrite.

As bad as the dialogue and acting were turning out, the rubber Brain looked worse on camera. In the dailies it just laid there, looking rubber. "The Brain's gotta move or shimmy or do something," Bernie said, after watching another day's rushes with the executive staff, "It looks dead… lifeless."

"Lose the Brain Kid," said Angela, sweating and twitching in the corner, "Let's get James Earl Jones or somebody to dub his stupid voice—he's costing us a fortune in overtime!" Having spoken thusly, she'd managed to get the attention of the room—a situation which, then, made her *paranoid*. "I have to make a deposit," she mumbled, leaving quickly.

A harrowing thing happened at the bank immediately thereafter, when the real Lou Ann Keighler showed up. Angela had made it a point never to return to the places where her human templates had been spied—and copied—and this was the bank branch in which she'd discovered the unknowing woman originally, avoiding it, ever since. But she'd been up for three days on prescription go-*fast*, and that particular detail eluded her deluded mind.

Even though she'd lost ten pounds since the assumption of her new form, Angela was still a dead ringer for Ms. Keighler. To intensify the situation, unbeknownst to the strung-out angel, Lou Ann had been separated from a twin sister at birth, and had never been able to find her, despite years of searching and thousands of dollars wasted.

Needless to say, the woman had quite an emotional experience right there in the bank when she saw what she believed to be her grown-up twin. Angela's unwillingness to tell Lou Ann the truth was bad enough—though understandable—but her reluctance to stand still and talk to the poor woman, and especially her inability to look her in the eye were clear symptoms of amphetamine induced paranoia.

"My God! It *has* to be you!" Ms. Keighler exclaimed, "Lee Ann? Is your name *Lee Ann*? See, my name is Lou Ann—are you from Wichita, originally? My sister disappeared from the hospital—I've searched and searched—wait a minute, *don't go!!*"

"My name is An—Ann *Marie*," Angela said, backing out the door, "and, no… I'm from Florida." Lou Ann Keighler ran after her, her voice rising to a desperate, clinging shriek.

"But we look exactly alike—this *can't* be just a coincidence… *Wait, come back!* You could've been adopted by *Floridians!*—Wait!—*Please!!* Do you have a kidney-shaped birthmark *on your left butt-cheek???*"

"*No!*—Good luck!" Angela mumbled, dashing around the corner. She instantly changed into the blueblack raven, right in front of an old man in a wheelchair, just before Lou Ann rounded the corner behind her. The raven took wing, leaving Ms. Keighler scratching her head and the old man reaching for his inhaler. That had been a close one.

"…She turned into a… *a bird!* And *flew away!*" The man said to Lou Ann, gasping.

"… I don't think that's very funny," she said between sobs, "you probably know where your sister is!"

Just as surely as Angela was starting to unravel from the pressure, Pen Remington was holding up swimmingly, as if she were born to be a producer. There was little conflict between Pen and Bernie; they'd worked together on so many films that their relationship was symbiotic, no matter who was calling the shots.

B.L. Zebediah was in rare form as well, having taken to the movie-making process like a moth takes to flame. It was simply the most fun he'd had since the Inquisition. Back then, when Catholics were torturing and killing other Christians and Jews; and also, during the period of wholesale, ethno-religious Moslem purging called "The Crusades," he and The Dark One could take it easy in hell. There was not quite so much fun to be had there, as when they could sit back and watch all the "holy people" slaughtering each other in the name of The Boss.

History is written by the winners, and had it gone the other way— if Jaweh had fallen and Shatan remained in heaven, how then would history have been slanted? Would *The Bible* be the *Grimorian Verum?* And *vice versa*, pun intended? The concept that "one side is evil *for the sake of it*" is nearly always the argument of the other side, particularly if they're the winners. Countless millions of more people have been tortured and killed in the name of The Boss, than in the name of The Dark One. What is evil?

Chapter Eight: More Brains!

B.L. and Berserker Bob solved the Brain problem. It was simple… they used real brains. A local supply house for human body parts, which catered mainly to medical schools and research labs, had a shipping manager who'd racked up a debt in the unholy Ledger of one of B.L.'s demonic colleagues. After a little networking, getting *fresh* human brains proved much easier than getting a good performance out of either of the film's two leads.

Mr. Z had altered his appearance a bit; he still looked vaguely like the star of *Raging Bull* and *Ronin*, but the *Angel Heart* hair and beard were gone, replaced by a thin moustache and a shorter, more conservative hairstyle. He remodeled his physiognomy, too, giving himself a nose-job. Mr. Z loved Hollywood, and wanted people to ask for his autograph because he was B.L. Zebediah, not because they thought that he was a famous movie star. He lost the suits and went Tommy Hilfiger, and was never without his Ray-Bans and cell-phone. The last thing in the world that he wanted to do was to go back to hell.

He and Bob had come up with an innovative, if hybrid, Brain that was much more expressive on screen than the rubber prop seen in the first rushes. By utilizing computer-controlled, animatronic *eyes*, imbedded in a real human brain(!), they were able to give the thing some variety of expression, while achieving a disgusting degree of realism—*it was* a horror movie, after all.

The brain tissue began to decompose rapidly once removed from refrigeration. Freezing was no good—the brains had to be thawed to read right on camera; plus, it gave them freezer-burn and their little furrows lost their succulent definition. New brains had to be substituted nearly every day—sometimes several times a day—and each time the computer-controlled prosthetic eyes had to be "surgically" inserted into the new one. The body-part supply-house was running out of brains, but its shipping manager was wiping out his spiritual debt—and regaining his soul, while Bernie was *losing* his, hand over squamous, taloned fist, as the budget disappeared. That inevitable and rapidly approaching spiritual forfeiture was starting to eat at the producer, like a starving ferret, trapped in the jockey shorts of his mind.

They were on location at the Vasquez Rocks, an hour north of L.A., ready to shoot the finale. In Angela's demented draft, the Brain has been kidnapped by renegade Swiss terrorists intent on using it as a symbol of the ineffectiveness of their homeland's policy of neutrality in today's war-torn, post-Soviet Europe.

This last shoot required only a skeleton crew, besides the actors. Bernie and Pen were there; so were B.L. and Berserker Bob, using up brains in the hot summer sun like Bette Midler went through dress shields onstage. Tooms was there of course, his first A.D. taking the bulk of the duties from the manically depressed director of *Mommy Drunkest*.

That 1987 TV-movie portraying the horrors of a housewife's drinking problem sadly augured Carlton Tooms' own descent into alcoholism in the nineties, as he passed sixty and the offers dried up. Working for *C.B. Remington*, allowing the self-styled mogul to pick his cast and locations, even letting that "antidote to desire" – as he referred to Angela – trash a perfectly maudlin script (over which he had little editorial control), were all factors that helped push him over the edge.

He popped pills and drank Tanquery-and-tonic constantly. The sexually ambiguous set dresser had to refill his prescriptions and the weird intern was often dispatched on a run for more gin, tonic water, or fresh limes. All this drinking and pill-popping did Carlton Tooms no good— but only booze and drugs could mask the physical and mental pain of the British-born director, an American resident since the late '70s.

His educated, acerbic wit served him well, especially when he was insulting Bernie, whom he refused to call C.B.

On the day they were to shoot the finale, Tooms was in fine form, letting the first A.D. block and call the shots. He was watching a video feed in his trailer, barricaded against the world—a stiff double in a frosted mug his only insulation from the slings and arrows of outrageous fortune, particularly from the slings and arrows of Kimberly Shayne and Bernie— the latter, he absurdly imagined to be trying to sabotage the picture.

The demanding Ms. Shayne on the other hand, having disposed of her lovesick devotee, Norman Ates, had now fixated her withering abuse on the poor director. She had the nerve to blame Tooms for her dreadful line readings and numerous blown takes, the more inane of which were openly hooted by the crew, during video playbacks.

"All right!—I want to see my terrorists—up on the rocks—That's good!" the A.D. hollered through his bullhorn. It sounded more like, *"Rrr-rite!- ite!-ite! Wanseem-eye-tare-ists!-ists!-ists! Pontherox!-ox!-ox! Ts'good-ood-ood!!!"*

The actors playing the Swiss terrorists, called the Band of the Hour Hand in the movie, stood up on the famous jagged rocks and waved their automatic weapons at the camera below. It was an F-22 kind of day; blue sky, white tufts of clouds, and summer sun. The A.D. called action, commencing the first shot, *"Reddy!-eddy!-eddy! An!-an!-an! Akshun!-shun!- shun!"*

Kimberly/Dr. Chastewood stepped out from behind a rock, hold- ing an Uzi on the terrorists. "All right—throw down your guns and hand over the Brain," she said, actually making the awful dialogue more unbe- lievable with her stiff, high-school drama-queen delivery, "Be careful! Set him down, then back away! Drop Timmy and you're *Swiss cheese!*" From the shallow depths of her strident line readings to the hard-pretty face that became less attractive with each viewing, it would seem that miss Shayne had missed her true calling—performing in the hard-core adult video mar- ket.

"Here… vee leave it here, you come get it… American doctor *bitch,"* the head terrorist said, in the performance of his life. Setting down the Brain's cylindrical glass tank, which resembled a large Mason jar, he continued, " Da U.S. Government must help us… to convince our home- land of da suicidal dangers of political neutrality…"

"N-N-N-*NO!!*" the hooded, black-robed man shrieked, as he swung down a rope onto the tier of rock where the terrorists stood. He grabbed the Brain jar and scrambled back up the sandstone, climbing to his lofty pinnacle, unreachable from any other access. The man jeered the crowd like Quasimodo on the façade of Notre Dame, pulling off his hood to reveal—not surprisingly, the reddened, bespectacled face of Norman Ates. "I w-w-w-want Kimberly Sh-Shayne to c-c-c-come away with me…" he hollered, "I want t-t-ten-thousand dollars—and a *heli-c-c-copter!*"

"Stop following me around, you stupid little twerp!" Kimberly said, breaking her American doctor bitch character, behaving nothing like a doctor. Norman's bizarre appearance even got Carlton Tooms out of his trailer. The inebriated director watched, spellbound, with the cast and crew members who'd remained on location, as the stammering youth continued to terrorize the production.

"I m-m-m-mean it!" The despondent Ates cried, holding the Brain in its jar, high over his head, twenty feet up on the rocks. "Don't f-f-f-f—screw with me!"

The Euro actors playing the terrorists, roadshow Rutger Hauers all, were confused by Norman's sudden appearance. "Get out of da shot, you geek-head weasel," shouted their leader, a Teutonic-looking rogue named Sklar.

"Christ, B.L… uh, sorry—I mean, *shit*, B.L!" Berserker Bob said in the doorway of the special effects tent, "That's our *next*-to-next-to-last brain, and if he shatters those eyeballs, we're screwed—no back-up on the eyes." In a further bizarre twist, not twenty feet away both Bernie and the tipsy Tooms actually agreed on something. They kept the camera rolling and captured Norman's bizarre "hostage takeover" of the set.

"This is marvelous—a suitably surreal ending to what will turn out to be, without a doubt, the most unintentionally hilarious load of tripe with which I've ever been associated. No, Bernie," the British-accented Tooms said, suddenly shouting, *"KEEP R-R-R-ROLLING!"* at the camera operator. The crew howled at his aping of Ates, as the director continued, chuckling, "Thank God I'm in good stead with the Directors' Guild, because whether or not you like it, I'm taking my name *off* this piece of shit. You can release it as an *Alan Smithee* film."

"Is that a promise?" Bernie asked, "Don't worry, Tooms, the kid's under contract—so, technically, this is an *improvisation*. We'll re-dub it later with new dialogue. I'll get that pill-head Angela to write another surreal dream sequence around this footage…"

"It can be the Brain's fantasy," Pen suggested, "as he's being held hostage by the Swiss terrorists, you know—like, in *The Last Temptation of*

Christ when Christ is on the cross—but instead, the *Brain's* imagining, '*If only* I were a whole person again, this is what I'd do…'"

"What is this, a tent revival?" asked B.L., wiping the acid sweat from his brow as tiny droplets fell, sizzling, to the ground. "You people gotta watch it around me with that name!" The fire marshal and the state park ranger, both of whom were required to be on hand for the shoot (at the production's expense), approached Bernie about the rampaging Ates.

"What's with this guy? And, what's burning?" asked the fire marshal.

"Nothing," said B.L., smoothing out the tiny, smoldering holes in the dirt with his shoe. "No pyrotechnics today."

"What are you going to do about this stuttering guy?" Said the park ranger, "In regards to the production? Should we shut 'er down?"

"That's a wrap!" Bernie yelled, as if grateful.

"Nobody yells 'wrap' on my set, but me!—*KEEP ROLLING!*" Tooms called out, striding woozily over to the producers and authorities. "Why do you want to scuttle this picture, Mr. Small?"

"The name is Remington," Bernie said, not having heard his real surname uttered in years. "All right, Toomsy—keep rolling. I was just trying to comply with the ranger, here." To the uniformed pair, regarding Ates, Bernie added, "He's harmless—it's not like he's wavin' a gun around or anything."

Then, in a clear case of life imitating art, Norman began to deliver Timmy's voice-over lines, *in character as the Brain*, while holding the jar high above his head, "Dr. Ch-Ch-Chastewood? Can you f-f-feel my thoughts? C-C-Can you hear my phantom heart, as our t-t-two brains b-b-b-beat as one?"

"All right, Ates!" The first A.D. hollered through his bullhorn, *"Set down the Brain, carefully!"* but it came out sounding like, *"Ll'rite-ite-ite, Ates-Ates-Ates!—Siddown-tha Brain-ain-ain! Air-flee-flee-flee!"*

"Wh-What?" Norman said, confused. He would not be dissuaded, but he stopped reciting Timmy's voice-over lines, *talk-singing* his own demands instead, "J-J-J-Jam-it, Randy, I'm f-feelin' pain … A heli-c-c-copter and Kimberly Shayne… or I smash this jar, an' k-k-kill the Brain!!"

"What?—He's *rapping*, now?" Bernie asked.

"He's no Coolio, that's for sure," said Pen, "but he's better than Warren Beatty."

"They've got other Brains, dipshit!" Kimberly screeched at the distressed youth.

"You break my eyes, and I'll kill you!" yelled Berserker Bob.

"Oh, y-y-y-yeah?" Ates replied defiantly from his perch. There was a moment when time seemed to hang suspended—as Norman's hands, and the Brain that they held, reached zenith and remained poised there—a moment when everyone thought that things were going to be all right. And then, as if in slow motion, the youth's hands and their cerebral cargo began the slow, inevitable descent. "I got your b-b-b-brain," he screamed, *"right here!"*

As the big Mason-jar shattered on the rocks, razoring its soft, cerebral contents to shreds, the cast and crew let out a gasp that almost sounded staged. The terrorist-actors swarmed Ates, holding him till the ranger and fire marshal could properly subdue him.

Berserker Bob rushed the downed Brain, grunting like a mental case, examining his precious 'animatronic' eyes. Just as he gave the okay sign, another problem presented itself.

From the special effects tent, emerged the next-to-last brain—in the trembling, revenge-crazed hand of the film's real writer, Kip Lothar. In Lothar's other hand he held a revolver, which he proceeded to *wave around*, firing three times in the air.

Two sheriff's deputies were patrolling the area a half-mile away and heard the shots, which were nothing unusual for a movie company renting the Rocks, but the deputies headed over to watch, anyway.

Back at the location, the echoes died out and Lothar had everyone's attention.

"I want scale for my script," he said, "plus ten—no, *fifteen* percent, for my agent, Mr. Colt, here. You owe me two-and-a-half percent of the budget, Remington—and I want it now... *or the brain gets it!*" Lothar pointed the gun at the glistening back-up organ, which was quivering nakedly in his left palm, sans its customary, liquid-filled jar.

"Drop the brain, son—this isn't funny," said the park ranger.

"You mean drop the gun, don't you, Fred?" The fire marshal asked his colleague, "Who cares if he drops the brain?"

"I care!" screamed Berserker Bob, leaping down from the Rocks. "You mess with my brains—you mess with me, pilgrim!" He bounded across the location, nearly knocking over the D.P., stopping in his tracks only when Lothar put a round over his head.

"I'm gonna pay you, kid, don't worry!" Bernie said emphatically, "just don't shoot anybody!"

"The name is *Kip*—Kip Lothar, you… you… *despoilers of art!* How dare you rewrite my screenplay without paying me first? What's this bullshit about *Swiss terrorists?* Who's bright idea was it to make the doctor/scientist a *woman?* And that Starbucks scene?—There's nothing in my script about a Bosnian field-hospital *acid trip*, that takes place in the doctor's *mind* in a Malibu coffee shop?"

"… Coffee *house*," said the weird intern. "Starbucks is a coffee *house*—Denny's is a coffee shop."

"Shut the fuck *up!*" Lothar screamed, firing once into the dirt at the intern's feet.

"… I was jus' sayin', man… that's all," the weird intern said, standing open-mouthed and motionless, as usual, like a lobotomized deer in headlights.

"That's five shots—it's a six-shooter," Pen whispered to Bernie. "If we all rush him at once, he can only shoot one of us…"

"That's a terrible idea," Bernie told her, "besides, according to Bob, there's one more brain left after this one."

"Well, Remington," Lothar demanded, "You know, I wrote this screenplay as an homage to your brain pictures—now, that I hate you thoroughly, for ripping me off and mucking up my script, I figure I've got nothing to lose. You couldn't screw me like this if I had an agent—by denying me a *deal*, you've kept me from getting representation—well, guess what? Either I get my dough right now, or I blow the brain's brains out!"

"A…" Bernie mumbled, stalling, "… I must've left my checkbook in my other suit—if you drop by the office…"

"Bullshit!!" the writer exclaimed, firing the last bullet through the brain in his hand—*and*, unfortunately, through his hand as well; the slug being deflected by the brain tissue, causing it to arc downward, cutting a furrow through the patch of flesh between Lothar's left thumb and forefinger. "Aughhh! I'm shot! I'm actually bleeding!"

With that, Kip Lothar fainted dead-on-his-feet away, plopping face down in the dust with a dull thump. The second-to-last brain lay flattened on its side, oozing blood and clear fluid beside the noble, but fallen, scribe, whom the ranger promptly handcuffed.

Beyond caring about the loss of *two* of the three remaining brains, Carlton Tooms repaired to his trailer, gulped some more pills and poured a straight gin on the rocks, cackling madly. Within half an hour, the Sheriffs had Norman Ates in cuffs, as well, and were putting both of the self-styled terrorists in the back of a patrol car. "Watch your h-h-h-head," one of them said to Ates.

"You'll hear from my lawyer, Remington, *you shitbird!*" The writer yelled. "As soon as I get one. *Where's my ambulance?*—I'll sue the County, too! *I know my rights!!* My hand is *BLEEDING*, for God's sake! I *write* with this hand, and you're going to be very, very sorry, officers... very sorry, indeed."

"You shot *yourself,*" one of the deputies said, "and you're lucky you didn't really hurt anybody... or accidentally blow your dick off." Both cops cracked up.

"*K-K-K-Kimberly?*" Norman begged, as the black-and-white pulled away from the location. The hard-case drama queen from Lancaster flipped him the bird, spitting.

"That girl's got spunk," B.L. told Bernie, "she's not above cutting the occasional throat to further her career—plus, she has none of that cloying sentimentality most of *you people* like to wallow in."

"... She's just a touch colder than the last ice age," Bernie muttered. "And what do you mean by *you people?*' Is that some kind of group slur, or something?"

"No," B.L. said, "I meant, *you. People.* You know?—*Humans,* as opposed to cosmic, eternal life-forces... like me, for instance."

"Are you guys gonna be able to rig up another Brain here, before we lose our light? Viktor says we're gonna lose our light in a couple of hours..."

"Relax..." B.L. said, "Bob's got a man on it... Right, Bob?"

"... We're fucked," Berserker Bob whined, joining them, "That weird fucking intern—where'd we get that psycho-billy mouth-breather from? I told him to get the last brain ready while I fixed the eyes—I think they're going to work; the left one moves a little slower, but if we shoot the Brain from its good side it just might..."

"We can always call it *The Brain That Couldn't Think with the Lazy Eye,*" Bernie said. "Cut to the chase!"

"... So the weird intern set it outside on its mark before I put the eyes in—and without any sunblock! Now it looks like *The Lobster That Couldn't Think.*"

"I'll kill him." Bernie said. "Well, I guess that's a wrap..."

"You may have to kill him, C.B., if you want to finish this picture," Bob said.

"His family is dead. He lives alone, no girlfriend…and we need a brain…"

"No. B.L! We're not *really* going to kill him… are we?" Bernie asked.

"I'll do it," Bob said, breathing heavily.

"No—I'll take full responsibility… this won't go on either of your tabs," the executive producer from hell assured them. With Bob's soul in hell-hock, too, Bernie wasn't the only Faustian mortgagor on the set trying to keep a clean nose.

"Naw—the weird intern is *brainless*, what good would it do?" Bob said, raising his voice, building into a panic attack, "And, there's no more brains coming from Organs Overnight—they're fresh out! That *retard* you insisted on hiring smashed the 'hero' brain we were using… The fuckin' writer blew holy shit out of one back-up brain, and the weird, damn intern fried the other one. We have to be out of this location by tomorrow, and the rest of the crew—like me—are all booked on other shoots after today! We're *fucked*, man—we're in some real pretty shit now!!"

"Shut up! Just *shut up*," Bernie told him. "Stay frosty—we'll figure somethin' out… we've got two hours of sunlight…"

"*Bernie!*—I mean, C.B! *Come quickly!* Carlton Tooms is *dead!*" Pen gasped, as she ran up to the two men and their demon, "In his trailer…"

"He didn't shoot himself in the head, did he?" Bob asked.

"… No—he O.D.'d on booze and pills, at least that what it looks like," Pen replied, "Why…?"

"Where's Smoky an' Fire Marshal Bill? Do they know?" Bernie asked.

"No," she said, "since we're not shooting, they're playing liars' poker by the craft services table."

"Does anyone else know?" B.L. asked her.

"No—I found him, and locked him in his trailer."

"Good—don't tell anyone—*not a soul!*—No pun intended. Understand?" B.L. said. "There's no time to explain now, just keep Tooms' death a secret till an hour after we wrap, okay? I'll get rid of Smoky and the Fireman."

"Just what are you three up to?" Pen asked.

"Nothing…" B.L. said, smiling like a ribcage, "we just need to borrow his brain for a while, that's all. Get everybody in their places—and tell Randy that Tooms is *passed out*, and that he has to handle the last few set-ups. That'll keep him busy while we do a little… improvising—right, C.B?"

"You got to think on your feet in the picture business," Bernie said in a daze—stunned at the dark farce the Demon was prepared to carry out to finish the picture—and win his soul. "Can't you just make a brain appear—like the effects show you put on at that mobster's house in New York?"

"No, unfortunately. That was mass-hypnosis. You can't hypnotize a movie camera, C.B." Bernie took this in stride, swallowing. He decided to stall.

"Remember that time when we were shooting *Oath of the Blood Snails* in Boise, Pen? When the snail wrangler got shit-faced and left their tank open, and all the damn snails ran away? Well, they didn't exactly run, but they had a whole night's head start. They managed to crawl halfway across a Wal-mart parking lot before everybody pulled in to go to work the next morning… Talk about a *crunch?* Thank God we shot the carnage with three cameras—we had enough footage left over to make *Love Slugs…*"

"… *C.B?*—sorry to interrupt, Babe," Bob said, "but we're burnin' daylight…"

The four of them told no-one that the director had died. B.L. put a "whammy" on the ranger and the fire marshal that caused the pair to go on a burger run—to Tommy's at Rampart and Third—sixty miles away, in downtown L.A.

Berserker Bob did the deed right in Tooms' trailer, using the effects department's tool kit. With B.L.'s supernatural help, he managed to remove the top of Tooms' head without marring the brain inside.

The crew wrapped the last shots, and everybody but the guilty four did a walk-away. Bob and B.L. had time to put the brain back in the late director's head, long before Bernie and Pen called 911. Since Norman the "love terrorist" had been in the sheriffs' custody when Tooms died, as well as the gun-wielding Kip Lothar, they couldn't very well take the blame; yet, the *surgery* to remove and replace Tooms' brain had left evidence of trauma inconsistent with death-by-overdose. There was really only one way out—besides telling the truth, that is, which Bernie and B.L. nearly always avoided.

They decided to fake a shotgun suicide. That way, they could blow Tooms' brains—and their tampering evidence—right out the back of his head. Exploded pillows would explain why nobody heard the gunshot, and B.L. used his powers to roll back the body's time of death, like the mileage on a speedometer.

All of this worried Bernie a great deal, but despite his protests, the "shoot" within the shoot, as well as the cover-up, came off like an over-sized glove. B.L. put another "whammy" on the coroner's bag-men and investigating sheriff's deputies—even the homicide cops wrote it up as a suicide after the Demon finished with them.

"It's a damn good thing that Angela's in rehab right now, or she would definitely have screwed this whole thing up," B.L. said after Tooms' body had been taken away. "Boy, Penelope, you can sure pick 'em—who the hell else has a guardian angel that doubles as a speed-freak casting director/would-be screenwriter?"

"Bad would-be screenwriter!" Bernie said. Pen shot him a look; he softened his stance, adding,

"But, I love her off-the-wall approach."

"The effects in this picture are so much better than the dia-logue…" B.L. snorted.

"Thank you," Berserker Bob said, "I wasn't going to say any-thing—but, I mean, 'Throw down your guns and hand over the Brain'?? … It's not exactly *Shakespeare in Love*, is it?"

"My favorite line," Bernie said, "is when the Brain says, 'You gotta stop an' smell the roses—because some day, *you might not have a nose!*'"

Pen moved away, sniffling, as the other three laughed, releasing tension.

"What about right after the operation when Kimberly tells the Brain that she's surgically implanted his eyes into his frontal lobe?" B.L. offered, "'It's not much,' she says, 'but it's better than *being blind, too!*'" He and Berserker Bob howled like spider monkees, but Bernie shadowed Pen, who was now crying softly to herself.

Beneath the purple desert sky, in the blue shadows of the famous jagged peaks, Bernie caught up with her, and took her gently by the shoul-ders. "What's the matter," he asked. She fell into his arms, sobbing.

"It's just all been so much, Bernie… The pressure—I never real-ized it was so hard producing a movie. It seemed okay at first, but as soon as we had to start dealing with the… actors, things went to hell—pardon the expression. And that's another thing! I've never told you who you could have for friends, or business partners—even this devil-guy. He has his own peculiar charm, but Angela said you sold your *soul* to him."

"I've made a lot of stinkbombs, Baby, but none of 'em was bad enough to go to hell over!"

"What really happened to Carlton Tooms?"

"Penelope. Have I ever lied to you? Don't answer that—the man overdosed on gin and Prosac, or whatever he was takin'. All by himself. I swear to God."

"What? Are you playing both sides, now, Bernie? 'Cause I don't think God's going to care what you swear... Demons? Angels? *Dead bodies and human brains!?* Where did our love go wrong, Daddy?" she sobbed, crying into his shoulder, "I don't want to lose you for all eternity... over a lousy *brain* movie."

"Well, the deal is, that he only gets my soul if the movie gets *released*, and *makes money*—Why do you think I've let everybody and their speed-freak cousin from cloud nine screw this picture up, bigtime? Why do you think I've been calling 'wrap' before we get the shots all day? Do you think I don't know how to make movies any more?—That I just *forgot?*"

"I thought maybe you were letting me test my wings," Pen said, sniffling, "and that you were helping B.L. and Angela break into the business—I thought you enjoyed delegating!"

"I do," Bernie exclaimed, "but not the whole damn picture! A couple of weeks after the money came in, I decided that I didn't have anything to *fear* anymore—at least not with the film getting made. You know, I'm not used to millions of dollars to play with, or fall back on— and it's my nature to be ruled by fear—secretly, that is, irregardless of my enormous chutzpah and bravado...

"So I started to think about the future. *Our* future. And I realized that I was going to lose everything; my life, my studio, my new, leased S.U.V. with the tinted windows... and you, Miss Plum... my wife."

"So... so you let me help... in order to... *screw up* the movie— and thus, save your own soul? Is that what you're trying to tell me, Bernie?"

"... That sounds like a lose/lose question to me. Let me put it this way; the hardest part of trying to get my soul back has been letting this picture get turned into an unreleasable mess. You think I'm crazy? Listen to me? When have I ever made a picture without a star to draw to? Kimberely Shayne? Why in the hell do you think I allowed that ice cube-with-a-hole-in-it, who's got the career drive of Rasputin, to play the lead in an eight-million dollar movie?"

"I thought we were only half-a-mil over budget?" Pen said.

"Not anymore! This picture has to stink, Baby, 'cause if it turns one dime—I'm a dead duck."

"Don't worry, my love," Pen said reassuringly, "whatever didn't come out shitty the first time—we can always screw-up in post." They kissed in the moonlight, and she imagined that somewhere in the world, fireworks filled the night sky.

He imagined dinner.

Chapter Nine: All Wrapped Up and No Post to Go

Norman Ates was released into the custody of his parents the next day. Remington Pictures Ltd. didn't press charges because they got the best scene in the movie from Norman's *ad lib* takeover.

B.L. managed to get the untimely demise of Carlton Tooms officially ruled a suicide. The bloody, *alleged* shotgun death of the famous director fueled even more publicity around the film.

Kip Lothar was charged with possession of a loaded firearm, and for discharging it in a state park. He was released on bail, and after the publicity had no trouble getting an agent. He sent David Silverfield, from ICU, to get union scale-plus-fifteen percent from the little-studio-that-could. Bernie was broke at this point, but the agent was less than sympathetic—threatening to hold up *"Brain's"* release until Bernie signed the Guild signatory papers and Lothar's union contract, which the author hadn't signed yet either. Bernie had to capitulate—legally, Lothar still owned his original script—so B.L had to raise even *more* money—which he added to Bernie's tab in his Ledger of Souls.

Bernie and Pen released the story to the press—the love story, that is—of Norman and Kimberly. The media swallowed the "handicapped youth falls for small-town drama queen" angle. Then, Kimberly's nude spread in a popular mens' magazine landed her in the tabloids, destroying any perception of small-town innocence that may have been erroneously attributed to her. She hated Norman more than ever, but the fall cover boy for *Special Abilities Quarterly* was too busy doing daytime talk show and charity appearances to notice.

With Tooms dead and unable to remove his name from the film, Bernie's coveted *"Alan Smithee"* director's alias, a sure sign that the captain had chosen *not* to go down with the ship, was denied. Despite what would,

under normal circumstances, be favorable conditions for a successful release, the Remingtons worked as one to sabotage the watchable footage
they had.

Bernie knew the cheapest, sleaziest craft persons in Hollywood,
and now, with no money left for post-production, he *had* to use them.

Unable to continue paying their union rate, Bernie watched the
editor and first assistant walk. He hired "Shrapnel" Dick Hertz, an aging
rummy throwback whose war wound had earned him his *nick*name. A
non-union editor, Hertz had the shakes so bad when Bernie gave him the
reels, the producer said, "Here, take this advance and have a couple of
belts before you touch my film, okay?"

He got Vlad Aeschu-Gesundheidt, a deaf Romanian-German
composer, to do the music. Vlad worked with a sophisticated digital program that displayed musical notes on a video monitor as he played them—
that way he had a vague clue as to what the arrangement might sound like
to hearing people. His digitally produced, electronic score perfectly com-
plemented the dismal dynamics of the script and performances.

A few weeks later, the picture was ready for the press screening
and due to open in two days. Bernie and B.L. had a morning meeting set.

"Knock, knock," Angela said, sticking her head into Bernie's office, "I just came in to say goodbye?"

"Yeah, sure—but hurry up. I've got a meeting with B.L. in a few
minutes. You went blonde... it looks good."

"I thought I'd just change the style and color this time—instead
of the whole person. I looked up Lou Ann Keighler, the woman I copied
the last time..."

"The one from the bank who thought you were her long-lost
twin?" Bernie asked, laughing. "Send her a picture of you in a coffin—we
got a nice one in the warehouse."

"So I figured, what could it hurt if I told a 'white lie' and posed as
her sister—made her happy a couple of times a year?"

"*Please...* 'heartwarming' equals 'nauseating' in my book. Pen said
you were leavin'..."

"I am, Bernie. I'm opening Angela Winger's Guardian Agency—
strictly theatrical, no more futzing with scripts and writers... But I want
to confess something to you..." she said, looking out the window at a
crow perched on a telephone wire. "Back when you were a P.A., I was
your guardian angel—don't say anything, let me finish. I pulled some

strings to get you that director's gig on *Gourmet Vampires* back in '68..."

"No shit!?"

"Please—let me *finish*. I got in trouble over that one, and it didn't get much better for me when you used that big break to produce a string of sex-and-gore flicks that made Al Adamson look like Kurasawa—made Larry Buchanan look like Roman Polanski—made Ed Wood..."

"All right! You made your point..." Bernie said, scowling. "Penelope told me you were *her* guardian angel—do you have multiple assignments, or something?"

"Yes, but in your case, I got permission to be reassigned to Pen— her original spiritual escort got bumped-up to 'level-four haunting spirit.' I kept a skeptical eye on you over the years—hoping you would fail, and be swallowed forever by the dark pits of hell...thereby justifying my abandonment of you, which of course was unfair. So I owe you an amends— See in rehab, we have a..."

"*Please*—I'll puke—I swear to God!" Bernie looked up, as if in prayer, saying, "And this is my *guardian angel* talkin'—no wonder I'm not religious!"

"I'll still be assigned to Pen—you just won't see me when I come around..."

"Well then, stay outta the bedroom," he said. Angela turned into the blueblack raven, hopped up on his shoulder, gave Bernie a peck on the cheek and flew out the window.

"Knock, knock," said B.L., sticking his head in the door.

Chapter Ten: Bernie's Inferno

"You know, C.B., you're in such an extreme penalty situation with this movie, after that Lothar debacle, that you'll be lucky to hang onto your soul until it opens."

"I don't see how you can collect before the picture turns a profit?" Bernie said.

"That was the original deal, but you kept going over budget, needing more cash."

"Bullshit! We only went over-budget because I let *you* people handle critical responsibilities—You and that crazy Bob spent way too much money on brains, and I don't even want to think about how much Angela cost us..."

"Don't throw that Bible-humper in my face, Bernie, she was never part of our deal—I let you bring her in because of your weakness for Penelope..."

"Weakness?" Bernie said angrily, "Pen's my biggest strength! I should've married her a long time ago. Think of what I'll save on taxes alone. And you didn't *let* me bring anybody in—this is *my* studio." Bernie happened to be sitting behind his desk, in his office, where his power was strongest. "I've made a few decisions lately, B.L., and one of them is— that I want out of our contract."

B.L. actually looked hurt. He took off his Ray-Bans and cocked his head to one side, like a cocker spaniel. "Haven't I given you everything you've asked for? Haven't I let you make the calls, be the leader? I don't believe this... *Et tu Bernie*," he muttered to himself. Looking *down*, he asked rhetorically, "Why do they always want to break it off in my ass, Lord?" Then, turning to Bernie, he threw up his hands, whining, "I thought you were my friend? I've got a lot invested in you, you know... it's just not fair!"

"*Fair?*" Bernie said, "You work for the *Devil!* I'm not saying we can't co-produce any more, I just don't particularly feel like burning in eternal flames right now."

"Do you see me burning in eternal flames? Have you ever seen me so much as scorched? The slightest bit toasted? *No*—Because the fire thing's a bum rap, that's why."

"I don't see you in a big hurry to go back right now, either," Bernie said.

"Well—of course not! I've got a picture opening... What if I extend your contract?" The Demon offered. "You know, C.B., in this town, everything's negotiable—besides, if this thing bombs, I've got to let you off the hook. And if it doesn't, I might give you another six-month lease, anyway... with just one catch..."

"Oh, yeah, there's always a catch with you devil-guys," Bernie said cynically.

"You believe everything you see in the movies—the flaming pit, steaming rock walls, naked people being whipped—Oh, sure, we've got our B&D wing, but lots of folks never even see it..."

"Folks?" Bernie asked disapprovingly, "You make it sound like Branson."

"Funny you should say that, believe it or not..."

"I don't wanna know. I'm just not a 'hell' kind of guy... What's the catch?"

"You don't want to spend eternity a bachelor, do you, C.B? ...Leave your little wife here, all alone? She'd want to be with you, right?"

"You son-of-a-bitch! *No way!* Damn you for even asking... Her soul is *hers!*—Besides, she's too good for *you people!*"

"... Okay, Bernie... if that's the way you want to play it. Not a 'hell' kind of guy, huh? I think you need a little sneak preview..."

"No!" Bernie screamed—but it was too late. The room had begun to spin.

Desks and lamps and file cabinets swirled around them, floating in a sea of rolling, ectoplasmic gelatinous goo. The walls became vertical walls of boiling water—not falling—just being there, two stories high—Churning. Steaming. Misting on them. Bernie felt the tiny drops sting, blistering him instantly. Feeling himself dropping down, he screamed louder; the wet sound around him rushed into a roaring blackness. B.L. laughed, as an evil, yellow light defined his grinning features from beneath.

The walls had become the rocky sides of a vertical shaft as the pair continued to fall—*down—down.* B.L.'s carved features took on actual *demonic* proportions, gradually, as the light in the underground chimney strobed off-and-on. By the time they'd floated down to the bottom of the shaft, B.L. had completely become Beelzebub, *the True Demon.* Not unlike the way he appeared to the New York mob family, he had horns and eyes—*many of them*—as well as wriggling tentacles, but was not necessarily humanoid.

Bernie looked around at the bizarre scene before him.

Like a huge carnival, set up in a ten-story-high cavern, this underground world looked friendly—riddled with small-town Americana—at first glance. Then the brightly colored structures, fashioned in a variety of shapes and styles, came into hallucinagenic focus, revealing shadowy figures darting in and out of their dark doorways.

A line of death-camp-thin, wraith-people, their bones showing through stretched, yellowed skin, stood in line before the "Guess Your Weight" booth.

"Who are they?" Bernie asked.

"People who sent their food back in restaurants for petty reasons. Still others who ignored the sick and hungry—some of them, especially the children, were people who continually neglected to clean their plates at mealtime. Food wasters—now *they're* all wasted!"

Bernie noticed that he and the Demon were gliding along without moving their feet—the ground was covered with a dry-ice-like fog, swirling in two-foot-high drifts. "Are we on a people-mover, or something?" He said, looking down.

"Something. How do you like the fog effect—it's based on the movies. We've got to compete with the Other Place, and they've got some real P.R. flacks workin' overtime—let me tell you: Socrates, Solzhenitsyn, Shakespeare—not to mention both Lennon and Marx—*John and Groucho,* that is—they all write promo spots for the Happy Camp.

"Spirits who were prolific creative types in life, usually contribute their talents in the afterlife—you should hear the orchestra they've got up there!" The Demon said with deepening voice; twisted horns crowned his misshapen head, a bank of yellow goat-eyes stared straight through Bernie's soul.

"But we've got a hell of a rock band down *here!*"

"You're scaring me, B.L."

"This is your new neighborhood, Mr. Small, here—we turn left at Short Eyes Lane, see how honest the folks are around here?"

"Folks... there's that 'folks' again. What's with the sandwich boards? Oh, my @#$%!!!" Bernie said, watching in horror as his voice cut out at the word "God," which, of course, cannot be uttered in the Underworld; watching in horror, because black, wavy typewriter character-symbols actually floated out of his mouth. "@#$%-damn motherfucking shit!!" He yelled. Once again, black, undulating type-symbols floated out of his mouth, but only in place of the name of the Deity—swear-words could be spoken without engaging the automatic word-blocking program, apparently.

The thing that made Bernie swear in shock was the realization that all of the residents of *this* micro-neighborhood, *contained somehow* inside one of the dark carnival booths, were former child molesters. Huge sign-boards proclaiming just *that*, to one and all, hung front and back on each "neighbor," each wearing a colorful clown costume."

The children who passed in safety among them, were, upon closer inspection, revealed to be tiny old people—elderly children, or so they looked to be. "@#$%, B.L.,—the children are aged and wrinkled, walking on canes—and the little boys are bald-headed! What did they do?"

"They are the ones, who in their later years on Earth, could not appreciate the wisdom they could have accumulated, or the good they could have accomplished. Rather, they envied, held-back or cheated *the young*, bitter because they could not regain their own youth. Here, they are the wretched, aged children of a Hood made up entirely of 'outed' kiddie-humpers... but they're too weak to do anything. Watch the fun..."

"I can't take it anymore!" yelled one of the molesters, whose signs read, *"I like to do it with little girls—lock up your daughters!"*

"I can't take it anymore, either!" "Neither can I!" "Grab her!" "Hoo-Mama!" Yelled several more, ripping off their sign-boards and clown togs, surrounding a particularly frail, old-lady-girl of about six, going on a-hundred-and-sixty. They wrestled her to the ground, tearing off layers of lace and gingham.

"These perverts lose their starch at the sight of her naked, nubile—but, *wrinkled, sagging* flesh, and run away," Beelzebub declared, "because, of course, they can only be aroused by youth—that which their victims both desire and jealously hate—but can never possess." The child-woman cried out in frustration after her attackers, "You bastards can never get it up! It's the same thing over-and-over—I haven't gotten *laid in a hundred years!"*

"This is getting kind of heavy..." Bernie said, hurrying out of that booth to the next attraction. Beelzebub followed, rumbling in the lowest tones ever heard by mortal man, "It's hell, Buddy—what can I tell ya?"

Entering the next enclosed booth, they were somehow, again, in an outdoor neighborhood, facing a fenced-in backyard. The Demon covered Bernie's eyes and pushed him inside the high, redwood gate; Bernie could hear screaming, weeping and the gnashing of teeth—and the gate closing behind them.

"Holy shit!" Bernie hissed, as B.L. uncovered his eyes. He flattened out, his back against the inside of the gate. In this large backyard that was contained, in some way, *inside* one of the ten-by-twelve-foot carnival-booth structures, growling, slavering pit bulls, rottweilers, and junk-yard German shepherds leapt, ripped and tore at various men, women— *and* children, who tried in vain to climb over barbed razor-wire, coiled in great, slicing loops atop the vertical redwood slats. Hands were torn and bloody, chunks of flesh were ripped from legs and thighs, one elderly woman had fallen and she couldn't get up—and, a particularly stubborn pit bull had locked its jaws over her screaming face. Two other hounds each had an arm, and were playing tug-of-war with her. Blood was everywhere.

"These people are punished *especially* hard... for being cruel to their pets, or animals in general. That old lady on the ground has been in that precarious position for over thirty years, and she never bleeds to death—she ran an alleged animal shelter, which, in actuality, funneled the poor beasts to an unlicensed medical experimentation lab—which specialized in vivisection among other tortures... Even I hate these shitballs. Incidentally, the dogs are hypno-phantasmic holograms, no actual animals are harmed—or even *present*, in hell. Hell requires cognizant intent. Hell requires man."

"This is really frightening, B.L., but what does it have to do with me? Where are the producers who simply made bad movies stashed. Do they have to watch *Manos, Hands of Fate* and *Showgirls* over and over? I haven't died, or anything—so don't get any ideas about me staying here! In fact, I want to *leave!!*" Suddenly, they were back on the midway, continuing to glide along without walking, their feet and ankles lost in the low, swirling cloud bank.

"Bernie! Would *I* trick you?" said the Demon, morphing back into his handsome, De Niro-like human form. "Here, Sailor... have a beverage. It's on the house." A mint julep appeared in Bernie's hand—he dropped it, and it bounced back up out of the fog and lodged in his hand again.

"See that gingerbread cottage in the town square?"

"The one with the seven midgets playing on the swing-set in the front yard, and the satellite dish on the peaked roof?" asked Bernie.

"The same," replied B.L. "These are your servants: Nappy, Vicious, Sleazy, Fearful, Groggy, Junkie and Jock. They never do any work, never shut up, and basically make your life a living hell. You only get one TV channel—the menu—so you can see what you're missing; you get one sports video—Superbowl XIII—the Steelers win, in case you missed it, and one movie video—"North." Meals are frozen TV dinners three times a day, every day—not heated up—served frozen..."

"Stop! That's enough! You can't make me stay here!"

"Hel-lo, C.B! We live to serve you!" A trio of the diminutive domestics sang in three-part chipmonk-pitched harmony. *"The movie tonight is..."* they paused, opening a big, round film can and pulling out the print inside, unspooling it as they wrapped it around each other and the swing set. *"...Frankenstein Meets..."* the trio sang, cutting the film in two with oversize shears, *"...The Elephant Man."*

"Hey, Elephant Man?" The trio chimed.

"Hey, Elephant Man?" The other four midgets taunted, joining in, aping the "Hey, *Culligan* Man?" soft-water radio jingle. Two of them

tossed the round, metal film-can halves back-and-forth, Frisbee-like. Then, they sailed them through the cottage's two front windows, shattering the glass. The tiny pair giggled, tittering, as the other five repeated the tweaked jingle: *"Hey, Elephant man? Hey, Elephant Man?"*

"This is a pepperoni pizza nightmare. It has to be. I'm actually asleep at home," Bernie said, half to himself, "Hell is doing your taxes, being in jail, having your heart broken or losing any amount of money, at all, on a sporting event. It's not having midgets sing, 'Hey, Elephant Man' to the tune of a radio jingle! This is totally nuts!"

"Hey, Elephant Man? Hey, Elephant Man?" sang the midgets.

"I'm not gonna have to live here, 'cause *The Brain That Couldn't Think* is gonna bomb worse than fucking &%$#@'s Gate—except, nobody's gonna notice!"

"It is not!" B.L. said.

"It is so!"

"Is not!"

"Is SO!"

"IS *NOT!!*

"It's gonna bomb, bomb, bomb!" Bernie said. "If there's one thing I know how to do, it's make a bad movie."

"Okay—I'll go you one better! If the movie *does* bomb, that is to say, in the parlance of the trade, that if it doesn't make it's money back on the initial run... I'll not only relinquish your soul, but I'll *come back to hell*, and stay here for the rest of *your* life, which I will not terminate or diminish in any fucking way—okay, *Bernie?* Happy now?"

"Fine... Can we go now?"

"Let me check my mail and we're outta here."

"Huhaaa! Augghh! Not midgets... not midgets... I wanna thank all the... the little people—*Wha??*" Bernie muttered incoherently, waking up next to Pen in their bed at home. He shook his head and rubbed his eyes.

"What's the matter, Bernie?" she asked, sitting up.

"Oh, nothing... I just dreamed I was in hell, that's all."

"Are you worried that the movie might be a hit?"

"Oh, *no*—are you *kidding?* I'm just glad I always cleaned my plate, loved dogs, an' never boinked any underage broads..." Penelope rolled over, pulling up the covers.

"... So am I, Honey..." she sighed, "now, go back to sleep."

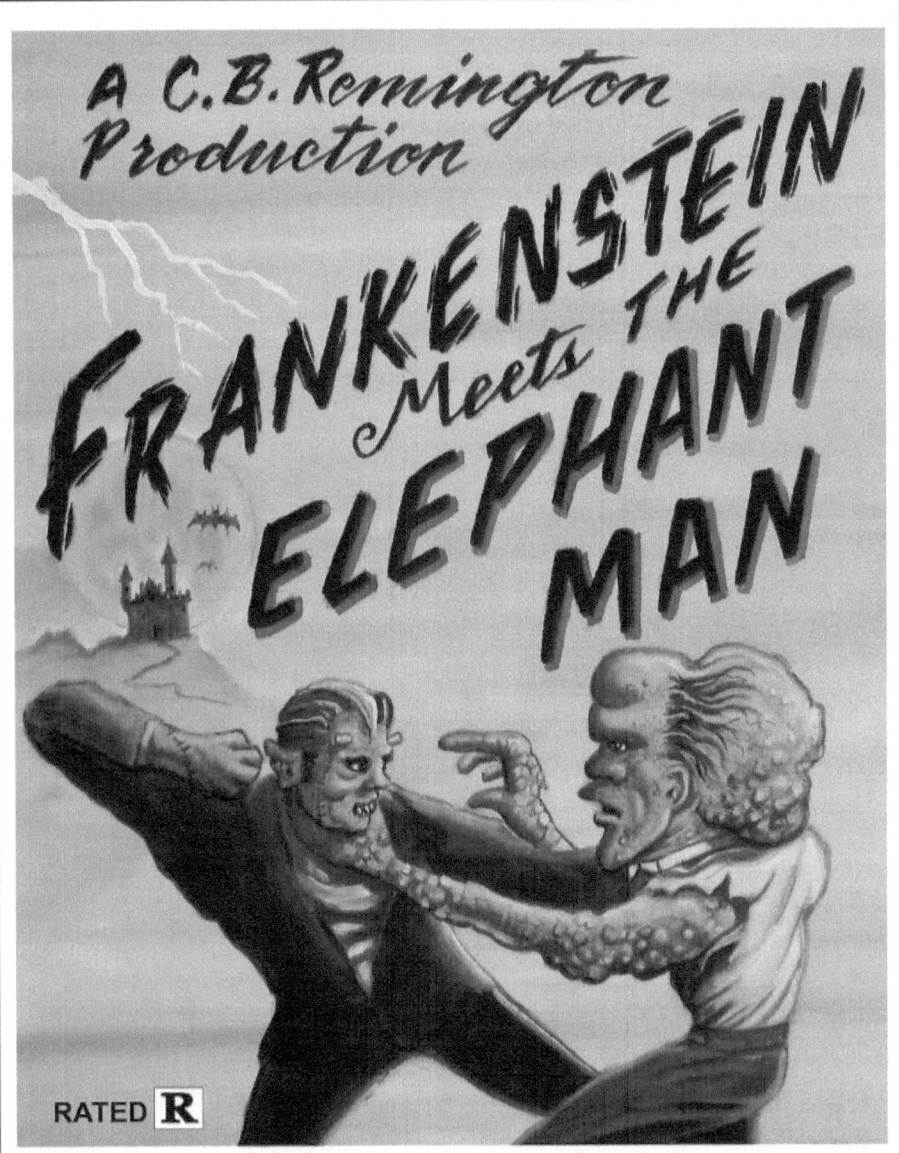

Chapter Eleven: MIDNIGHT "BRAIN" SCARES UP B.O. $$

TRUART THEATRE, WEST L.A. – *The Brain That Couldn't Think*, an indie flick from Remington Pictures, Ltd., has beat *Pink Flamingos, Eraserhead*, and all other bookings at that venue for midnight attendance, in its sixteenth week. Seems $10 million bomb has finally found its audience after disastrous initial attempt at platform release, and—some of the worst reviews in movie history. So dreadful were reviews, a sampling of which follow, that executive producer B.L. Zebediah went into hiding, and has not been seen or heard from since flick was pulled from first-run situations. Even though *hit* status in the art house run is only expected to return 3 – 5 % of film's budget, producers and studio heads, C.B. and Pen Remington, are hard at work on a straight-ahead horror flick, tentatively titled, *"Interview with the Demon."*
– *Hurd Floy, Daily Variegated*

"'Brain' is Reprehensible! ... Worst possible taste—offensive on every level!"
— *Bud Sludge, CLIT MAGAZINE*

"Frivolous portrayal of the handicapped—unnecessarily cruel... A mean-spirited tearjerker... Brainless!"
— *Allison Brackish, PROSTHETIC APPLIANCE SPOTLIGHT*

"A blasphemous obscenity! Performances so dreadful you'll wish YOU were a brain in a tank..."
Joe L. Cygiel, GOOD MORMON AMERICA

*"Rarely does one find a textbook example of how **NOT** to make a film as cannily, lovingly, and expertly executed as Remington Pictures' 'Brain That Couldn't Think.' Absolutely wonderful, if you're looking for the worst possible filmgoing experience..."*
Leo Nerd-Maltoni

"Remington does it again—Worse than his *'Leper Babies!'* A performance by Kimberly Shayne to rival that of the snow in *'Fargo.'* Much-hyped 'special' newcomer Ates stinks on ice—Can't act?—C-C-C-Can't *speak!* Hardly any cool underwater scenes... not a cephalopod in sight..."

Ed Plankton, MARINE BIOLOGIST QUARTERLY

"Irresponsible filmmaking with a vengeance... What were they thinking?? So bad, you may never go to the movies again... Pretentious, preposterous, prosecutable...So wretched an experience, I quit my job!"
— *Mitchell Medavoy,* REACTIONARY DIGEST

"... A bungled 'Brain' movie so bad, the director blew HIS brains out!"
Egbert Rogers, EGBERT ROGERS GOES TO THE PICTURE SHOW

"I loved it."
— Reid Rexton

AFTERWORD

I began this as a novel, spoofing the title, "The Brain That Couldn't Die," but felt that 23,000 words were enough to tell the story, and stopped there. Comedy is funnier when it's faster, and the old saw, "Always leave 'em wanting more," works better for me than "Thank God that thing is finally over!" I thought this also might have made a good movie ten years ago, when the actors whose features are de-scribed were young enough to reprise their devilish characterizations.

From the moment I wrote the line "tell the Women's Channel they can blow me!" I visualized Danny DeVito as Bernie. "C.B. Reming-ton" was the nom de plume I assumed as director of the 1980 direct-to-video feature, "Leather Persuasion." Not quite "Leather Were-wolves," but close.

I have no trouble reveling in political incorrectness – like describ-ing the casting call of handicapped youths who want to break into show business, or some of the punishments of hell. Just describing hell as a bad amusement park was worth writing the whole thing – and I love Berserker Bob, the SFX supervisor in hock to The Dark One. While he may have some traits in common with actual SFX men in this town, they are not specific to any one particular asshole.

Of all the things in the world to parody, to lampoon, eviscerate, and deride shamelessly, "show-biz" has to be the most enjoyable – at least for me. I was born in Hollywood, and I've seen 'em come and go. Also, though it doesn't relate to this story – or even to this book very much – I find there is nothing easier to ridicule than someone who takes himself too seriously.

Casting Call of Cthulhu

"L. J. Dopp, I am absolutely in awe of your *'Casting Call of Cthulhu.'* October of this year (2001) will mark the 75th year that I have been reading science fiction and fantasy stories. Your tale of Lovecraft, Smith, Cooper, Delgado and Kong is the most fascinating short narrative I have ever read. You are a genius."

Most sincerely,
Forrest J Ackerman

[NOTE: The above letter from Forry Ackerman is absolutely real – it arrived in July, 2001 – the rest of this epistolary narrative, perhaps less-so – LJD.]

The following letter was written by this author in the Spring of 2001 to Robert M. Price, publisher of the long running pulp journal, "Crypt of Cthulhu," and frequent editor of anthologies pertaining to the Cthulhu Mythos of H.P. Lovecraft.

Dear Mr. Price,

Having recently purchased your excellent Chaosium, Inc. anthology, *"The Cthulhu Cycle,"* and having subsequently read your comprehensive introduction to that volume, I felt compelled to submit to you the following arrangement of letters, memos, telegrams, and news clippings – bridged by paragraphs of narrative (speculation?) in my own voice – which combine to describe a series of historical events *barely hinted at* in your introduction.

My narrative interruptions, offset in italics, will usually be employed when two or more physical records illuminate the same data, or when no specific paperwork exists to support an obvious conclusion. Also, the seemingly endless prattle of the separated lovebirds, Jennings and Phipps, has been frequently, mercifully, edited and paraphrased.

I found the documents in the early 1970s, stuffed in an army ammunition tin, hidden in the crawlspace above a closet in my Atwater Village home, near Griffith Park in Los Angeles. Research confirmed that

Arthur Jason Phipps had owned the house at 4632 Angeles Street from June, 1936, until his death in the spring of 1952. No record exists of his or Amanda Jennings' employment at RKO-Radio Studios at that time – however, the in-house studio memorandums in their possession, and the unabashed descriptions of their appropriation, would seem to contradict independent records of the period, extant.

        The existence of the cache of documents in the ammunition tin, including photocopies of previously unpublished (and apparently unknown) correspondence between H.P. Lovecraft and Clark Ashton Smith (c.1932), would seem to substantiate the events described herein, and explain Phipps' and Jennings' preoccupation with them. This spiking interest evidently caused one of them to write, or possibly even to personally contact, Smith (more likely him than Lovecraft), eventually persuading that writer-artist to relinquish said photocopies into their care. Perhaps Phipps and Jennings had a story of their own in mind. He died unpublished after a twenty-year career in real estate; she survived him by eleven years.

        Although a fan of *King Kong* since childhood, I had not yet discovered the sub-genre of fantasy fiction called "The Cthulhu Mythos" at the

time I came upon the documents in question, although I'd read other stories written by H.P. Lovecraft.

The tin and its odd contents subsequently gathered dust for three
decades until the fall of 1998, when I was researching a horror screenplay
and finally read Lovecraft's 1928 story, "The Call of Cthulhu." That trig-
gered memories of the cache of letters, so I dug the ammunition tin out
of storage, but still hadn't the resolve to organize its contents into a co-
herent format for publication.

It was the following comment in your *Cthulhu Cycle* introduction
(regarding the final third of "Call of Cthulhu," titled, "The Madness from
the Sea") that caused me to finally proceed with this project. You wrote,
and I quote:

"... Lovecraft has made Great Cthulhu far too concrete in 'The
Call of Cthulhu,' more like *King Kong*. In fact, there are several startling
similarities between 'The Madness from the Sea' and *King Kong*..."

When confronted with your statement, and realizing I was not
alone in noticing striking similarities between these two seminal works of
fiction – however prejudiced I may have been by being privy to the contents of the box *before* having read Lovecraft's story – I proceeded to trun-
cate and carefully arrange the data into the manuscript form before you.
Hopefully, you'll find the result entertaining, if not in all aspects convincing, and will forgive my humble attempt at playing historian.

Very truly yours,
L.J. Dopp
Valley Village, California

*Personal letter from Arthur K. Phipps, RKO-Pathe Studios, Culver City, to
Amanda Jennings, RKO Radio Studios, Melrose Avenue, Hollywood, dated July 14,
1931:*

Dear Amanda,

I miss you terribly – yet I'm excited about my promotion and
transfer to the settings department, even though it means having to take
this bungalow in Culver City near the Pathe lot, and be apart from you.
I'd never make the call time, travelling from town each morning. I miss
the gang down on Gower, though – especially Mr. O'Brien and his production team – but most of all, seeing you every day.

I hope you like this little clay tile, with its ancient-looking glyphs
and queer "craven image:" some sort of Polynesian squid-god, I was told.

I hope you can find a spot for it in your eclectic menagerie of white elephants. There are all sorts of quaint little "shoppes" in Venice not too far from my new digs, many of them run by Bohemian/artist types like yourself. You'll feel right at home, there. I bought this piece from a Gypsy in a shop overlooking the canals — which have real gondolas!

This Sunday, take the red car down Venice Boulevard and I'll come up and meet you at Helms Bakery, around 10:00 a.m. — crullers and coffee on me. The beach and its piers are nearby, and the air is swell over here, compared to Hollywood.

Amore,
Arthur

Reply from Amanda Jennings, RKO-Radio Studios, Hollywood, dated July 17, 1931:

Dear Arthur,

Wherever did you find such a horrid thing? — tentacles and wings! What curious writing beneath the effigy; I simply love it. How kind of you to post it to the studio and surprise me. I've not taken it home — it's currently on my desk as a paperweight, you see. Even your Mr. O'Brien has noticed it and the girls in the steno pool are jealous of me.

I am it seems, in charge of the script pages — such as they are — for Mr. O'Brien and Mr. Hoyt's *"Creation"* picture: mostly notes of scenes requiring trick photography, they are not even numbered yet. I am keeping them beneath your grotesque ceramic, the better to keep prying eyes away. Everyone seems somewhat secretive about this project — the first thing they're going to film is a shipwreck.

I cannot meet you this Sunday, darling, as I am expected to work through the weekend. Sorry, but this is what happens when they put one on salary, it seems. I have been given the following weekend off in advance, so I will be sure to meet you Sunday a week, 10:00 a.m., at Helms Bakery on Venice Boulevard.

All my love,
Amanda

The Canals of Venice, California.

Phipps' reply, written the following Saturday, is of little consequence, other than to confirm that he had previously been employed at the (RKO) Hollywood studio as an assistant to the property department. It would seem that both he and Ms. Jennings were new to RKO, and to the movie business in general; he refers to her family in Arizona.

It is in her next missive, dated June 24, 1931, that the pattern of preternatural, supernatural, or possibly even extra-terrestrial, origin begins to unfold like a black orchid, blooming in a blaze of midnight.

Dear Arthur,

I'm so looking forward to this Sunday, and can use a couple of days away from this place. The strangest thing has happened – or, at least I think it has. It began when OBie – Mr. O'Brien insists that I call him OBie, now – expressed a desire to borrow the uniquely disturbing tile you sent me week-before-last. Fascinated with the octopus-dragon image, he had the piece photographed, and plans on incorporating the motif in the pagan temple set that has been added to *"Creation."* OBie is keeping the script pages beneath your curious tile as I was doing – except on his desk instead of mine.

The strange thing I mentioned is that *the script pages have changed!* Practically overnight, they formed themselves into a story of a sort; the ship wrecks on an island – but the island *rises* from the Pacific Ocean, now. The new temple is surrounded by a great wall, with an immense carved door – OBie is very specific about the art direction here. Yesterday, I heard him arguing about shooting the island rising. He promises he will return the tile to me when the stars come right again – whatever that means. I told him to stop eating in the commissary if he doesn't like their attitude... I expect movie stars to act like movie stars, don't you?

Willis O'Brien

Ms. Jennings goes on about the time she met Clark Gable at the Plaza Hotel, and what a gentleman he was, etc., etc. Her salutation is particularly annoying this time out. She also admits to sneaking into the Gower studio's Ozalid darkroom to copy the following letter from Harry O. Hoyt to Willis O'Brien, dated July 26, 1931.

Dear OBie,
        While I appreciate the fact that the best scripts are rewritten many times over, I thought we had agreed to tackle the plot-lines and dialogue together on *Creation?* I understand that shooting the island rising from the

sea, instead of stationary – even though it's being shot in miniature – has caused problems in your technical department. Mr. Gibson has informed me that the glass comprising the tank has shattered thrice, with a thicker pane being substituted each time. Now I hear that the glass is so thick, you are having trouble shooting through it! Also, while I somewhat reluctantly okayed your idea of a pagan temple miniature, I never said anything about a full-scale set! What's this about you trying to get Le Baron to appropriate part of De Mille's *King of Kings* set for re-dressing? Please consult with me regarding such dynamic changes in budget and design. Returning from New York August 6.

Best regards,
Harry

To catch you up on the back-story, first of all, Creation was the brainchild of legendary stop-motion animation pioneer, Willis O'Brien, and Harry O. Hoyt. Stop-motion animation is creating the effect of movement by moving a small model's limbs and facial expressions ever-so-slightly between exposures of only one frame of film at a time. Creation, a telling of the same from Genesis, was green-lighted by William Le Baron, then vice president in charge of production at RKO. It was the project that brought OBie, as Willis O'Brien was called by those close to him, and his team of master craftsmen to RKO. With expert model-maker and sculptor, Marcel Delgado, they had made The Lost World in 1925 (which Hoyt had directed), for First National Pictures. E.B. Gibson and Orville Goldner were part of OBie's team at RKO.

The following is a memo from O'Brien to Delgado, also dated July 26, 1931.

Marcel,

Please note the unique design of this Figure. While the clay tile It is embossed on is an obvious reproduction, I believe that the Image of the Deity, itself – and the exotic-looking characters under the Idol – date from Biblical times. See if you can design an armature that will allow us to animate tentacles (see drawings with specs).

This could be the greatest horror show of all! I've had several vivid dreams of this Entity – even of Its marine habitat – and I know that it is our destiny to bring It to the screen. Please get cracking post haste – I want something to show Harry when he gets back from N.Y. in two weeks.

As per my sketches, this Deity – named *"Kutullu"* – should have a tentacled head, like a squid or octopus – and a roughly bipedal body covered with dragon scales and leathery, bat-like wings. Should scare the bejeezus out of 'em.

OBie

Sadly, the sketches alluded to by Willis O'Brien were not in evidence among the papers. During the months of August and September, 1931, however, a series of events occurred that would forever change the future of motion pictures: due to mounting financial problems and pressure from the New York stockholders, William Le Baron left RKO for Paramount. His replacement was none other than David O. Selznick, himself, and one of Selznick's first acts was to hire Merian C. Cooper as his assistant.

Merian C. Cooper

Merian C. Cooper, known affectionately as "Coop," and Ernest B. Shoedsack (whom Cooper would bring to RKO after our story ends) had made three jungle pictures on location together after meeting in the military during WWI. They would eventually direct the picture that came to be known as, "King Kong." Eight years later, Selznick would make Gone with the Wind at MGM.

Two Ozalid photocopies of in-studio memos from Selznick issued during Sep-tember, 1931, are pertinent; the first is a general greeting, dated September 12:

To all department heads and administrative personnel,

It is with the greatest pleasure and anticipation of success that I hereby assume the duties of vice president of production at RKO-Radio Pictures.

I do not bring a host of sweeping changes, nor do I plan a reduction in personnel. In fact, it is not my intention to scuttle any projects currently in production, or even in pre-production. Moreover, it is in the keenest interests of my job to watch and learn from all of you – and most especially – to keep this great and growing motion picture studio at the forefront of the field, creatively, productively, and financially.

Very truly yours,
David O. Selznick
Vice President of Production

Then, two days later, this memo is issued to the newly-hired Cooper:

Dear Mr. Cooper,

Among your first duties as my assistant are to screen the footage of films currently in production and assess their financial viability – with special attention given to adherence to *budget*. I intend to cut twenty percent of the administrative staff by October 31, and to slash salaries of those who remain, accordingly. You are to do basically the same thing in regards to production. Some of these directors have to go. I'm all for bringing in writers and directors from the New York stage; we need to create a better quality of dialogue if we're to compete with Paramount, Warners, and the rest.

Make yourself available for a Friday a.m. meeting, and plan on bringing all data regarding your decisions on which films to cut. This is why we're here, in case you were wondering.

S.

Basically, after one week at RKO, Cooper advises Selznick to cut Creation and Luther Reed's Babes in Toyland from the production schedule. There is an out-raged memo from OBie to Selznick which remains unprintable in anything other than a merchant marine's memoir, or a magazine with at least three "Xs" on the cover.

Of more pertinence is a letter from Ms. Jennings to Phipps dated October 30, 1931, and a memo from Cooper to Willis O'Brien, dated November 3, 1931.

Dearest Arthur,

The situation around here gets worse by the day. OBie is obsessed with your tile! He has had Marcel build an articulated model of the hideous creature thereon, and I cannot describe its loathsomeness! One of the steno girls fainted dead away upon walking onto the miniature stage while OBie and his assistants had it out. The sad thing is*,* *Creation* has been bumped from the schedule and OBie is still working on it. Something else is going on around here: Mr. Cooper and OBie have been taking meetings in the technical department, unbeknownst to Mr. Selznick, I believe.

What have you done, Arthur, in sending your simple gift to me? Please, return to the shop where you found the ceramic tile and inquire as to its origins. I sincerely believe the thing to be haunted. Everyone but his staff is terrified of OBie these days, and I'm told his bellowing can be heard next door at Paramount, right through the walls. Even so, he's never been anything but a sweet old dear to me and the other girls. It's the boys who scramble when he barks. I do hope he isn't sacked like so many others have been over here; you're lucky you got out when you did.

I must work through the next two weekends, at least, but my heart will be at the beach with you, my love.

Again, I have spared you Jennings' syrupy salutation. Now, see what Cooper offers to OBie; it seems everyone at RKO had a personal obsession that year:

Dear Mr. O'Brien,

I cannot tell you what a heartbreak dropping *Creation* from the schedule has been for me. I tried to reason with Mr. Selznick, but New York wants heads – and pictures – cut, apparently. I've had an idea for several years that might serve to incorporate a lot of the wonderful dinosaur models and prehistoric sets your department has created; we may even be able to use some of the expensive footage you've shot. With barely a fifth of *Creation* done, costs are already above the $100,000 mark; for twice that we can get an "A" feature. *Creation* was looking to cost over a million, by completion.

Take lunch with me tomorrow. I'll describe what I have in mind.

Merian C. Cooper

What Cooper had in mind was a giant gorilla. What OBie had in mind was animating his dinosaurs and this new, "Kutullu," creature. From the letters of Jennings, particularly, we are given a sense that the two men agreed to work together; OBie could have his octopus-god, huge wall and carved door, if he would also bring to the screen Cooper's obsession — a fifty-foot gorilla. It is unclear from the hearsay of Ms. Jennings just who was humoring whom, and which mythic creature would have the title role in RKO Production 601 — now, as 1931 came to a close, tentatively titled, "The Beast." Cooper got permission from Selznick to keep OBie's department on the lot to shoot a test reel for his giant gorilla movie. He realized he needed OBie, and was prepared to humor Hollywood's reigning master of special effects... to an extent.

Among the new writers brought in by Selznick in December, 1931, was Edgar Wallace, a popular British author. Cooper quickly snagged Wallace to write The Beast, largely featuring his giant gorilla, and hopefully, relegating the "Kutullu" character to the level of the island's ancillary horrors. This memo from Cooper to the newly-hired Wallace would seem to confirm that hypothesis:

Dear Edgar,

It is both a thrill and an honor to have you assigned to my production, *The Beast*. If you have seen *The Lost World* you know how invaluable is the technical virtuosity of Willis O'Brien; likewise, with that of his entire effects department — including his illustrators, Larrinaga and Crabbe. We need them, Edgar. And for that reason, I am asking you to allow two versions of the script to be created.

The studio version will retain O'Brien's *Creation* remnants — including his morbid octopus-dragon creature, which will eventually go in the ravine sequence with the other models they have devised that are too *outré* for a prehistoric jungle.

Off the lot, you and I will meet to discuss the "real" script: the one beginning on the island but concluding atop the Empire State Building in New York City. The sequence where the terrified sailors run screaming for their lives from The Beast will remain. That part seems soundly motivated and potentially exciting to the audience, as is the idea of chanting natives sacrificing someone to their pagan god in a dark ritual.

Sincerely,
Coop

Storyboard by Mario Larrinaga depicting the ravine sequence of "King Kong"

Another letter from Ms. Jennings, dated December 21, 1931, confirms that the goings-on were becoming even stranger by year's end:

Dearest Arthur,

I must tell you how much good last weekend at the beach did for me. Remembering the days when we worked together on the lot here is akin to remembering another life. Yesterday, the door to OBie's office was ajar, and I discovered all of them chanting, as if mesmerized. They didn't hear me knock, and neither did they seem to notice me, nor acknowledge my presence. The words were of a strange language – and, I fear it may be the language of the ancient-looking characters on your accursed tile! I distinctly heard the phrase, "Aye-yay, aye-yay, Ku-tullu fatagon," as they were praying to the image on the tile! The hideous, tentacled model was on OBie's desk – and *I swear it moved all by itself!*

I believe you now, Arthur, regarding the vanished shop. I have never seen you so upset as when we came to the place above the canal where you claimed it had stood. The vacant lot which you say now inhabits its space is far too overgrown with weeds and the like to have accommodated any recent structure, so clearly you were given the tile while under a state of hypnotism; perhaps, by the Gypsy man you described.

Surely, this was *no accident*. As to your coming on the Gower lot, I should have to advise you against it. Conditions are not as friendly as when you were here.

I shall write you again this week, my darling.

All my love,

Amanda

The following piece appeared in the major industry trades on December 29, 1931:

RKO ANNOUNCES SUPER HORROR FILM

HOLLYWOOD – RKO-Radio Pictures has announced the commencement of production on The Beast, a South Sea island adventure to star Robert Armstrong and Fay Wray. Produced and directed by Merian C. Cooper, film's screenplay is to be provided by noted English author, Edgar Wallace. Plot is top secret – but, sources say the story involves a ship landing on a mysterious island, where the presence of a giant gorilla, among prehistoric creatures, is discovered. A studio press release states that it will be, *"The most terrifying horror of all time – the Eighth Wonder of the World!"*

It was this anonymously placed advertisement in the little known Show Business Gazette, however, which caught the eye of a young, Los Angeles-based correspondent of Clark Ashton Smith, who was a charter member in H.P. Lovecraft's writer's circle:

SUPER HORROR PICTURE BEGINS PRODUCTION

HOLLYWOOD, CALIFORNIA – Announcing the start of "The Beast," the most terrifying horror ever to be seen on a motion picture screen! Coming to audiences in 1933, courtesy of RKO-Radio Pictures and the creative team behind The Lost World. Unveiling, for all the world to see – *Kutullu*, tentacled god from the fabulous sunken city of R'lyeh – in the miracle of stop-motion animation!

A very faded photocopy of the following brief letter from Smith to H.P. Lovecraft, dated January 13, 1932, was enclosed in an envelope with the news clippings:

Dear Howard,

The enclosed clipping, from the obscure Hollywood entertainment monthly, *Show Business Gazette*, was sent to me by Ronald Atkins, a fan of our circle, and an avid reader of the magazines in which our fanciful tales appear. It would seem that the publisher of your "Call of Cthulhu" story has either sold the copyright to RKO-Radio Pictures Corporation, or – that some person, or persons, employed by said studio have outright stolen the idea, including at the very least, the names of Cthulhu – here, obviously disguised as "Kutullu" – and that of the Isle of R'lyeh!

Might I suggest writing to your solicitor – or to Farnsworth Wright, himself – and, initiating litigation against this motion picture studio? If I can be of help in any way regarding the righting of what seems a heinous and lamentable act of plagiarism, you know you have only to ask. I quite liked "Whisperer in the Darkness," by the way.

With highest regards; yrs. very truly,
Clark Ashton Smith

Copies of Smith's second letter and Lovecraft's reply were also contained in the envelope within the tin, and will be presented later in this account.

Arthur Phipps' letters, at this point, began to express a desultory transposition of denial and overwhelming guilt regarding his culpability in the events unfolding at RKO. They tend to ramble self-indulgently, and will be omitted from the remainder of this account, for the most part. Jennings is the better writer of the two, in any event. Her next letter is dated February 6, 1932.

Dearest Arthur,

You must stop blaming yourself. I am sorry now that I urged you to return to that phantom shop; things will aright themselves. It pains me greatly to hear you so depressed. I've had a few of the dreams as well, and they are terrifying. Mr. Cooper and Mr. Wallace had taken to working on their script at Mr. Wallace's house, but now, they have both become quite ill. Pneumonia, the doctor says, according to Mr. Cooper's assistant, Zoe. He has been hospitalized, but Mr. Wallace insists on staying at home.

Meanwhile, OBie's department has been stalling on the giant gorilla model. He had Marcel create one with a human-looking face, which

Mr. Cooper didn't like much at all. This was before Mr. Cooper went into Cedars of Lebanon for the pneumonia.

She makes plans for their next weekend tryst. Blah, blah, blah... The following obituary notice appeared on February 11, 1932, in the trades, and was echoed shortly thereafter by every major English-language newspaper in the world:

Edgar Wallace

Noted Author Edgar Wallace Dies

HOLLYWOOD – English born writer Edgar Wallace, author of nearly 200 books, including the popular novels, *"Sanders of the River,"* and *"Dark Eyes of London,"* has expired here, apparently of pneumonia complicated by diabetes. Hired by RKO-Radio Pictures last December to pen original scenarios, Wallace had just completed a first draft of *Death Watch,* and had been assigned to script the Merian C. Cooper super-horror production, *"The Beast."* Wallace was 57.

This does not escape the attention of Clark Ashton Smith, who by that point was reading all the Hollywood trades he could get in his Auburn, California, home. He fires off another letter to Lovecraft, dated February 13, 1932:

Dear Howard,

Now someone connected to your unauthorized "Cthulhu movie" has gone and died (see enclosed obituary notice). It was the writer-to-be; how appropriate a coincidence, considering the absence of true justice in a chaos-ruled universe. I know that you are quite busy, and may well be traveling as this letter arrives, but perhaps you could find the time to reply. In any event, I should surely like to know if you have indeed initiated proceedings against this motion picture studio, or if our Mr. Wright has done so. Irrespective of your intentions, I remain your friend and greatest admirer.

With highest regards; sincerely,
Clark Ashton Smith

The next day, Lovecraft replies thusly (wish I had the original):

Dear Klarkash-Ton (a pet nickname),

So alarmed am I by these events of which you speak, that I have undertaken to book passage west on Union Pacific Railroad, to which I will transfer via the train from Providence to Boston; the latter is a local line, with which I am not at all unfamiliar. According to my estimated arrival time, I am scheduled to disembark in Los Angeles at Union Station, 1:00 p.m., on Thursday, February 21. Since your kind letter included an offer of further advocacy, it is my privileged duty to accept, having great need of your personal assistance in the righting of a terrible virulence – if indeed that is intense enough a word to describe the meretricious, and potentially calamitous, debacle now unfolding in your accursed, sun-vanquished state.

I should very much desire your company at Union Station, and for the rest of the afternoon of February 21, during which time we shall pay a visit to RKO-Radio Pictures Studio, on Gower Street in Hollywood, for the purpose of retrieving my personal property. Your agreement to assist me in this matter, and your speedy reply of confirmation thereof, would find me forever in your debt. For one thing, this errand would provide a chance for us to finally meet in the flesh. Absolute discretion must be maintained, however, Klarkash-Ton, for all is not as it seems with this Cthulhu affair. My story, "The Call of Cthulhu," which appeared in *Weird Tales*, was based on existing Pan-Asian mythic beliefs; Cthulhu, himself, may well be this *"Kutullu"* of which your enclosed article speaks. In actuality, he may have been – or perhaps, more correctly, may still be – *quite real.* I based his appearance on an image I'd discovered embossed in a clay tile, along with characters of an apparently antediluvian language – which I believe, constitute the phrasing of an occult spell, or attestation of devotion; that tile in question, *also described in my story*, is alleged to be a reproduction of a larger stone found in Polynesia that is said to represent an ancient god of the sea (Dagon?)

Author H. P. Lovecraft

The tile was stolen from my home last May, and although a window latch was broken during the intrusion (for which I was not at home, fortunately), not a single other item, valuable, or paper in my house was molested – much less removed – by the unknown intruder. What gives me ominous pause, and causes sanguinary rhythms to pound in my ears like the clangorous tolling of Poe's bells, is the existence of one curious

and foreboding detail: left on the floor and carpet in the wake of the intruder were *puddles of sea water, along with a strand of salt-water kelp*. I might
think this business a practical joke – but no-one knew of the tile's existence; I had acquired it at a curio shop in Boston shortly before the bur-
glary. The reason I believe the theft of the tile to be connected with this
business on the West Coast, is – that I *dreamt* about it – on two lamentably
successive and most assuredly horrid, nights! These were not the seemingly opiate-induced phantasms which entertained my slumbers whilst the
tile was in my possession – *even causing the text of my story to appear, quite
clearly, to me in the mornings following those haunted reveries*. There are mysterious
and nefarious powers afoot, Klarkash-Ton, and do not doubt my veracity
should I insist to you that the world, as *homo sapiens* has known it for mil-
lenia, may very well find itself in the grip of tenebrous perils untold. If this
Cthulhu – or R'lyeh – cult indeed exists, and should become an affair of
widespread proportions, quite possibly the Ancient Ones, or Great Old
Ones, may find ingress to return and once again rule the world!

So expeditious must be our action in this regard, that I very nearly
sent you a telegram regarding my imminent arrival; however, as you may
know, I find the things terribly limiting in the quality of message one is
allowed to transmit, no matter what amount of money is spent. It's bad
enough that the telegraph company charges by the word, but they make
no provision whatsoever for marks of punctuation!, – a simple period,
e.g., is represented by the word "STOP." Have you ever heard of such a
maddeningly idiotic system? No provision at all is made for semi-colon
use! To paraphrase a cliché from the current, if vulgar, American vernac-
ular: "What indeed is the world coming to?" I await your reply and look
forward, as much as I can under the circumstances, to meeting you on
February 21, in Los Angeles. Thank you for your kind words re: "Whisperer in the Darkness."

Yrs. most cordially and sincerely,
H.P. Lovecraft

A portion of one of Phipps' missives is pertinent: letter dated February 18, 1932:

... I got to see the drawings for the great wall and huge, carved
door set we are to create. Actually, we're to re-dress the Council House
exterior from *King of Kings,* adding carved-looking characters – like hiero-
glyphs – and hanging vines. Instead of one huge door, we're going to build
two, with a great wooden bolt and an enormous gong.

(Upper Left) Council House exterior from King of Kings *(1929); (Right) re-used in* King Kong (1933)*; (Bottom) The glyphs are more obvious in* She *(1935).*

While the thought that these document copies might be fakes teases at the back of my mind, independent research has borne out the validity of many events described herein. According to the excellent volume, "The Making of King Kong" (Orville Gold-ner, George E. Turner), the above excerpt describes exactly how the huge doors and wall eventually seen in that movie classic were created.

A final letter from Ms. Jennings, dated February 23, 1932, brings this chap-ter in the making of "The Film That Would Be Kong," as well as our story, to a close:

Arthur, My Love,
    It is with the greatest degree of relief imaginable that I can finally say things are getting back to normal around here. On Thursday, two men

found their way past the main gate and managed to enter Obie's office while his team was on the miniature stage. They did not give their names, but both were tall; the younger-looking one, a handsome gent dressed to the nines, seemed to be accompanying the taller one. That one never smiled – his face may as well have been cut from stone.

Stone-face came out of Obie's office holding your disturbing-looking tile – the root of all this corruption – high above his head. He made a bombastic statement that went something like this: "I shall never permit anything bearing my signature to be banalized and vulgarized into the flat, infantile twaddle that passes for 'horror tales' amongst radio and cinema audiences!" Then he whispered to the tile! It sounded like he said, "You've been very, very naughty..." and, he placed it in his valise.

Just as abruptly as they had arrived, the two men left. It's a good thing OBie wasn't around, or there would've been fireworks. The weirdest thing is – as soon as the tile was gone, OBie forget all about it, and began hard-pressing Marcel to get the gorilla model right for Mr. Cooper, who returned to work today, about ten pounds thinner. Thank God, the whole eldritch taint in the air around here is gone; I swear, that tile was haunted, Arthur!

It's too bad about Mr. Wallace, but Zoe said he was diabetic; the pneumonia was just too much for him, I guess. Working title of RKO Production 601 is now, *"The Eighth Wonder of the World,"* and Mr. Cooper's old partner, Ernest B. Shoedsack, is coming over to help out. You're going to be very busy over there at the Pathe lot, Arthur. They are planning on shooting *The Most Dangerous Game* simultaneously with *"Eighth Wonder of the World"* on your Stage 11. You fellows will have to build an indoor full-scale jungle, and I can't wait to see it.

Her steamy salutation led directly to Arthur Phipps' next letter, which is almost completely devoted to a proposal of marriage. He did get to work on the jungle set, but Ms. Jennings was finally discovered in the Ozalid copy room, making duplicates of in-studio, administrative memorandums – and was let go.

From what I could ascertain from the documents in the tin, the pair got married, entered the real estate business, and lived happily ever after – at least until Phipps died twenty years later. How they obtained the copies of Smith and Lovecraft's correspondence is not explained, however several hard facts exist to corroborate at least part of this account:

In King Kong, there is dialogue that speaks directly to the Mythos of Lovecraft; regarding the great wall that separates the tip of the island from the dense, mountainous jungle, Robert Armstrong's character suggests that it was built long ago. So long, in fact, that the natives who inhabit the island have forgotten the higher civilization that built it. Later, when viewing the massive, (Cyclopean?) structure, the captain regards it as colossal, noting the almost Egyptian architectural design.

Jungle set used for King Kong *and* The Most Dangerous Game

According to the aforementioned non-fiction book, "The Making of King Kong," there was a scene filmed in miniature for OBie and Harry Hoyt's Creation *project, in which an island rises from the sea; the glass sides of the tank kept shattering and really were replaced with successively thicker glass which proved difficult to shoot through.*

Also, Edgar Wallace did contract pneumonia along with Merian C. Cooper, and unfortunately, Wallace really died – on February 10, 1932.

Finally, The Making of King Kong *describes the original footage of Kong shaking the terrified sailors off of the fallen tree bridge. In the test reel for what was then called "The Eighth Wonder of the World," the sailors plunge into the ravine, only*

to be attacked by giant spiders and insects on the bottom, as well as an out-of-water octopus creature! A storyboard illustration by Mario Larrinaga printed in that book clearly shows a fallen sailor being pulled into the side of the ravine's bottom — by huge, writhing, suckered tentacles!!

"King Kong" *is the copyrighted material of Warner Bros. Pictures, Inc.;* "Call of Cthulhu" *is a registered trademark of Chaosium, Inc.;* "Weird Tales" *is a registered trademark of Weird Tales, Limited.* "The Making of King Kong" was published in 1975 by *A.S. Barnes & Co., Inc., Cranbury, New Jersey / Tantivy Press, London, England, and is available at Amazon.com.*

Tommy Amos of Mars

Tommy Amos kissed his mother and stepped back from the shuttle door. "No dancing-in-the-dunes till you've done your homework," she said. "There's dinner in the KC – I programmed a vegeplate."

"I'll graze with Rwen and Omar after we bounce. Where's the tour, tonight?"

"We're doing Valles Marineris," said his father. "Client pick-up is in Wellsville."

"You know, I really wish you'd eat before you go out, Tommy – in case you get busy and forget."

"He's old enough to eat with his friends, Az – as long as he earns his own spending money – right, son?" Mrs. Amos shot her husband a look as he released the steam-locks that secured the *Silver Tern* to its berth. They'd agreed not to disagree in front of Tommy, and had usually managed to maintain that directive throughout their son's twelve years – all of which had been spent on his birth planet, Mars.

There were seven American cities on the Red Planet in 2067, and nine others under foreign jurisdiction, but most featured diverse ethnicity and lay in the terraformed or *wesafe* areas. A few still stood apart – like domed oases, solitary islands of refuge in the thin air of the outzone, or "barrens." Including residents of the vast tundra-camps that dotted the polar ice caps, and the nomadic tribal dwellers of the deserts, the population of Mars numbered well over a million by the Summer of Love Centennial.

"I'll be home before you guys come back in," Tommy said, grinning. "Fly fast and take chances." He darted off the platform as the steel door slid shut, leapt down the diamond-plate stairs as the jets belched steam and smoke, and turned to watch as the shuttle lifted off – squinting as it sped away, rockets blasting into red-sun corona.

I can still get my homework done before they come back in, Tommy thought. *Algebra is boring no matter when I do it, but there's no time like sunset for bouncing.*

Yes, they studied algebra in the seventh grade on Mars in 2067. What did you think? – That the human race was in decline at the beginning of the new millennium? Maybe cynics who read the newspapers of the early 21st Century believed that, but the fact is, people just kept getting smarter and nicer to each other as time wore on, and as conventional warfare was replaced by the threat of mass *neutronization.*

Once the neutron ray had been perfected and implemented, whole armies could be destroyed instantly. Due to the ubiquity of human greed, weaponry that only destroyed people had been made available to any warlord with money. Certainly, each of the nuclear powers on Earth had neutronic capability: the same powers that were colonizing space. This gave the jingoists pause; eventually they were all "paused" permanently by their own devices. New science had replaced old politics, religion was optional – completely separated from all government – and, the designated hitter rule had finally been struck.

But, heaven had not come to Earth – rather, Earth had gone to the heavens.

Tommy sent a wrist-mail to his girlfriend, Rwen. She was an AfricAmerican-Marsling, too, and was taking a pre-flight-training course at the McCauliffe Institute after school and on Saturdays. Rwen (pronounced "Ren") wanted to be a pilot, like Tommy's dad, Horatio. She got Tommy's message and sent one back, gently speaking it into her wrist-pilot: "Sounds good to me – I'll meet you at the Outworld. Bring back my Repulsa VDR, you thief... of my heart."

Rwen was being pretty romantic for her usually pragmatic self, but girls matured faster than boys on Mars, just like everywhere else.

She was suited-up for bouncing when Tommy arrived at the Outworld Drive-In in his new, state-of-the-art "Leggers," or L.G.R.S. (light gravity recreational suit). Leggers was a brand name turned generic – but Marslings usually called the things "bouncers."

"You're gonna kick my butt again, Tommy – that new bouncer can fly circles around me."

"Shut-up an' bounce, baby – I can fly circles around you in my old one. I thought Omar was gonna come, too."

"I called his dock, left a message." Rwen rolled over, touching the dome of her pod-suit to his for a more personal communication. An L.G.R.S. looked like a steel barrel, capped by a clear, Duraplex dome. "Do you really care if he shows up?" she asked, batting a thousand with her eyelashes.

"You want me all to yourself, huh? Maybe we should come to this drive-in on Saturday night in my dad's 'Vette.'" He set his controls for initial lift-off. Bouncers couldn't actually fly but they were equipped with computerized hydraulic shocks in their massive legs, which ended in big, round rubber pads. The pads shifted to a vertical, wheel-like position for ground travel, but the bouncing action needed a primer blast of *thrust* to begin.

Further in-flight blasts could change the bouncer's course and prolong the kinetic rebounding indefinitely in the light gravity of the Martian outzone, a mere 38% of Earth's planetary pull. Bouncers had telescopic "waldos" – robotic arms controlled by human ones, which could be used for gripping, balance, and airfoil.

"Who's gonna drive your dad's 'Vette' Saturday night? Last time I looked, you were twelve and I was thirteen."

"Details, woman. Mere details." Rwen laughed at his bravado, wondering in her heart if he really cared for her. She *would* like to deep-out with him sometime – to lie beside him, whispering – like at a slumber party, and maybe make out a little. She'd dated older guys who'd tried to get in her jumpsuit, but Tommy was different. He was special: he respected her. Or, he wasn't really interested – but she didn't want to think about that.

Her mind whirled, screening possible scenarios for Saturday night – eyes scanning the empty parking bays… imagining. "You're blushing, Rwen!" Tommy said. Embarrassed, she fumbled with her controls, priming her hydros for lift-off. The Outworld Drive-In was a throwback to the outdoor movie theatres of the 20th century because most Marslings had all-terrain vehicles, usually equipped with oxy pumping through their pressurized cabins; and, they loved to cruise around in them.

But, only bouncers could *bounce*.

"I'm ready when you are, Red Leader," Rwen said, feeling every bit of her thirteen-and-a-half years. She could see him inside his bubble, resetting the power-pulse of his N.A.P.S. (nuclear auxiliary power stores), probably to give her a break.

"Bouncy, bouncy," he teased. In the reduced Martian gravity, a good bounce could feel like rocket lift-off, bungee jumping, and a roller-coaster ride all at the same time. Like off-roaders on Earth, Marslings liked to "do it in the dirt" enough that bouncing had become a teen craze. Bouncing-in-the-barrens... or, dancing-in-the-dunes.

"Whenever we leave the wesafe zone, Tom, say a prayer like I do." The wesafe zones had oxygenated air, or *prana*, and automatic pressure and climate control: insulation from the extreme temperatures of the Red Planet. Domes and dustwalls shielded the wesafe cities and their environs from sudden, ravaging dust-storms.

"Better pray you can catch me, girl – that ol' bucket'll never keep up. Here we go!" Tommy yelled, kicking up sand and rocks as he blasted off. Rwen followed, ducking under him, still on her ascend as he came down for his first bounce.

"Show-off,' she muttered, following him into the deep desert between Bradbury, where they lived, and the nearest wesafe town, Ben-Al-Amin. They bounced and glided, speaking freely; each bouncer had its own sophisticated, voice-activated com-system, plus vibra-quad speakers. The reinforced bubble surrounding the rider's head was tinted, and a small computer screen mid-front displayed all specific data and temp stats, as well as optional, 3-D holographic geo-maps and exterior views.

"Link me up-top, Rwen," Tommy barked. She may well have been a pilot in training, but Tommy was the born leader. Their metal barrels clunked, touching for a second, a hundred feet high in thin air. In that moment, Tommy was holding up a VDR labeled, *"Repulsa's Greatest Hits,"*– the album Rwen had asked him to return. "'Time Enough for Time' is entirely wet!" he said, grinning.

"I know – play it! That's why I bought it in the first place." Rwen heard the song begin in her speakers: besides the suits' com-systems, their vibration disc recorders were integrated as well. She hit the VDR button on her view-screen, allowing 3-D images of Repulsa to appear in place of the geo-map grid. The notorious singer romped on-screen with her chorus boys in the award-winning "vibe" of the song:

"*...In the great uncharted – ocean of your mind... thinking is believing, feeling is divine...*"

Rwen became completely absorbed, watching – and feeling – the vibe.

"Look-out, Rwen! – rock tower at 12 o'clock!"

"Copy that, Red Leader – I saw the damn rock, Tommy."

"*...If you have no hunger – for roses dipped in wine... I've no time for you – but, time enough for time...*"

"After we round *Notre Dame*, I'll race you back to Bradbury – at half-pulse."

"Why are you so competitive, Mr. Amos? I think you should be a pilot, too."

"You fly, Mz. Robynn – an' I'll solve the crimes."

"What crimes, Tommy?" she asked, aware of his fascination with the great sleuths of literature and history. "What good is Sherlock Holmes, without Professor Moriarty? Or Gaston Flambert... without Mal de Morte?"

One of her hydros whined like an old dog who missed his nuts. "I think I need to grease my shocks," Rwen said. The old dog smelled like burning rubber, now. They bounced out, retroed down, and greased up.

A few minutes later, Tommy had lubed Rwen's left hydro with his waldos; both bouncers tucked under a sandstone arch, cooling down for the return bounce. "We've never been in this little box canyon, before, Tom."

"There're a lot of digs we've never seen, Rwen. This is a big desert, on a big planet. It took until 2043 to terraform enough of the surface to connect the first Mars-stations – which grew into the first three cities..."

"New Moscow, Xiou-Xan, and New New York were founded simultaneously, by waves of ethnically diverse settlers in the great migration of '45," Rwen continued. "I had to memorize the *Profunda*, from Devlin's *Brief History of Mars*, too – remember?"

Now, twenty-two years later, great domes rose from the dusky shadows of red-rock cathedrals – from which sandstone spires towered, splintering off into space like fingers of nimbus. It was better to build in the shelter of any kind of hill or mountain, due to the violent, unpredictable dust storms. TexarCanada had been built around the base of *Olympus Mons*, the largest extinct volcano on the planet. Elevation – 15 miles! The biggest off-worlder trap on Mars, what could one say about a city with a tourism slogan like, "Y'all come back now, *eh?*"

Ben Al-Amin was one of the outzone cities, and Tommy and Rwen could see its minarets and onion domes up ahead as they bounced around the mountain peak they'd named after a real Earthworld cathedral. On the way back to Bradbury they bounced into Omar 79Brown, a fifteen-year-old flight-trainee, also enrolled at McCauliffe.

Doing loop-the-loops and barrel-rolls, the three young people danced-in-the-dunes, hop-scotching all the way home; blood-red sunset glinting off metallic shells – sounds of post-hip-hop, neo-flip-flop, and native *redrock* music drowning out the creaks, whooshes, and bangs of their infernal machines. It was about the most fun a Marsling kid could have, and seemed the perfect ending to a perfect day.

But, elsewhere on the Red Planet, things were less than so.

Bouncing-in-the-Barrens

2.

An hour past sundown, Tommy Amos got back to his dock. His parents S.U.M.V. wasn't in the flyway, but Mz. Goldstein, the Amoses' next-door neighbor was, along with her son, Moshe – and the cops.

"What's goin' on? Where are my parents, Mz. G?"

"Are you Thomas V. Amos?" the short cop asked him.

"Of course he is," Mz. Goldstein told the policeman. "Tommy – come inside and sit down."

"What the hell's goin' on?! Has somethin' happened to my folks?" Tommy said, raising his voice, not believing the answer in his heart.

"There's been an accident, son," the older cop said.

"Are they all right? *Answer me?* Mz. Goldstein? *Somebody answer me!!!*" Moshe said something to his mother in Hebrew – she shook her head, then she cleared her throat and put an arm around Tommy, which he shook off. *"Where are my mom and dad??!!"* Tommy screamed. Other neighbors came out and stood in their flyways and yards, watching the boy's life unravel like kite-string in a Kansas wind.

"… I'm afraid your parents… aren't coming back. They didn't make it, Tommy. I'm so sorry. So very, *very* sorry," Mz. Goldstein said. He buried his face in her chest, exploding in tears. Idaho Goldstein held Tommy, tried to comfort him as he cried, having known him since his terrible twos when the Amoses had moved-in next door. "The shuttle went down in the east end of Valles Marineris, Tommy… they said there's nothing left." The boy wiped his face and stood up straight.

"I'm going out there," he spat, pushing through the policemen to get back to his bouncer. "I wanna see my *parents!*" One of them gently took him by the arm.

"The crash area is a crime scene, Thomas – we found some contraband…"

"What are you sayin'?"

"A case of knock-off Blue Dreamers and vials of liquid overdrive got thrown clear before the explosion," the short cop said. "Looks like your parents were…"

"This is no time to go into that!" Mz. Goldstein said, cutting him off.

"My parents *didn't* traffic drugs! They didn't even use script drugs, let alone illegal meds or overdrive," yelled Tommy. "*Overdrive?* Are you people *crazy?*"

"We're just telling you now, so you don't have to find out on the news," the older cop said, like he was doing this crooked family a big favor.

"The news?? My parents are not drug smugglers! You're *wrong!* Dead wrong – an' I'm gonna prove it!"

That night, Tommy Amos chose to do-the-deeps in his own bed, in his own dock, alone. He knew he was going to cry himself to sleep, and didn't want anyone to hear him. The frost-dust howled like banshees that night. Rusty, roiling clouds of angry particles sandblasted the thick dome high above Bradbury, keeping half his neighborhood awake... but, even the storm couldn't drown out the sound of Tommy's heart breaking.

3.

The next day Rwen dropped by the Amos dock. "*God,* Tommy, I'm so sorry," she said, hugging him, reining in tears. He seemed cold – indifferent to her. "I saw it on the news... *Tommy?* Are you all right? Can I get you something?"

"The District Consul says I have to relocate to Earth, unless my uncle Armstrong moves his whole family up here and takes me in – which ain't too likely."

"Oh, no!"

"Oh, *yes.*"

"What're you gonna do?" New tears, from a deeper well in Rwen's soul, brimmed over, carving salty trenches in her pretty face. "I know we're barely teenagers, Tom, but I also know that I... that I... really *like* you. You know how I feel. Maybe you can stay with us – my dad's doin' A-okay at the bank."

"The Goldsteins offered me the same deal, but the Consul's office said the law was specific. At least one parent, relative, or District-appointed guardian is required for a minor to maintain residence on Mars."

"Maybe my mom and dad could adopt you?"

"Yeah, an' maybe they'll buy us bunk beds to deep in – I don't *think* so. The worst part is, if I have to go, I won't be able to catch the stiffs who did this to my family."

"What stiffs?" she asked.

"Whoever put those drugs aboard the *Silver Tern* – you believe my folks were innocent, don't you, Rwen?"

"Of course I do," she said. "How long till they send you to Earth?"

"Two weeks."

"*Two weeks?* What about finishing the semester?"

"They said something about the District assigning me a 'guardian' so I could stay longer, but I checked out the available 'nannies' on my VIP. ...Hacked into the District mainframe. ...Nothing to send home about, there – all 'bots or droids. Wanna see my potential candidates for babysitter? Here, look," he said, bringing up the file.

"Okay… just don't snap at me, I'm on your side."

"I mean – look at these robo-derby rejects!" Tommy said, indicating the District-approved guardian selection that came up on his vibration-imaging personal computer. "Look at that bot, girl – I wouldn't let that pile of chips baby-sit a sand dune, much less me."

He indicated a dark, glowering, neo-classic humandroid, with a humped back and long, pendulous arms. It was about as state-of-the-art as a pair of roller skates, and about as useful on Mars, with its tank-like tread-belts that couldn't hop a boulder. Even old-time "froggers" from back in the early 2000s had been designed to hop across rocky terrain.

"Oh, my God!" Rwen said, looking at the selection.

"Don't swear so much."

"… I'm sorry – it's just unbelievable that they wouldn't let you stay with our family…" Tommy flipped to the next page. "Instead of with *that!*" she said, referring to a matronly droid with ample bosom and rosy cheeks who smiled frighteningly from the screen. The mini-bio said her name was "Hermoine."

"It's 'Body Electric' time, but you don't hear me singin'."

"What about that one?" she asked, pointing at a conservative-looking male android. Pale, thin, and bookish, that District guardian was a kitchen droid, experienced in food service and filing, according to the mini-bio. He resembled an elegant vampire butler – immaculately dressed, and white as the polar ice caps.

"He looks pretty stiff," Tommy said, "and so *pale!* What a dorkmeister."

"I thought it was up to the District, which one you got?"

"It is, but I'll tolerate anything to stay here and clear my folks' name." He saw the lights dim in her brown eyes. "… *And,* stay here with you, pretty girl. I'm just not myself today, Rwen… don't take it personally."

"…Who could blame you? Wanna bounce a little?"

"Naw... I'm through with that stuff."

"Tommy?"

"I mean it, Rwen – from now on, I'll go to school. I'll get up in the morning and go to bed at night. I'll do my job. I'll eat when it's time, and I'll obey their laws…"

"I don't wanna hear you talking like this – like you've lost hope!"

"No way – hope is getting me through this. But, I'm not wastin' my time doing *anything* that doesn't directly relate to finding my folks' killers and clearing their names – if those District assheads don't kick me off this red rock, first."

"Now who's swearing? I don't think they were smuggling drugs, but your parents crashed in Valles Marineris in a *dust storm*, according to the news. They're calling it accidental." Tommy caught on her words and hung there a moment.

"Yeah – right. If the ship exploded on impact, how could the cops find vials of overdrive? They would've broken – vials are glass, right?"

"I think they're made of glass."

"See – somethin' ain't right!" That cop said the drugs were 'thrown clear.'"

"I don't know. How would I know – I don't *use*, remember?"

"That's why you're with me, Baby – I don't like mush-heads. They fall asleep in the movies, or keep you up all night yakkin'."

"Speaking of the movies, can we at least go to the drive-in Saturday night? My dad said I could take the Rover, and use my sister's old I.D. – I can pass for Janet." Tommy looked at her with a soft sadness that said "no." He could take no pleasure in his life, right now. *She'll understand,* Tommy thought. *If she really loves me, she will understand.* Just then, the doorbell chimed. He looked out the make-hole and opened the door, sighing, "Oh, *no!*"

"Hello," said the pale, thin man at the door, "my name is Eldon 46-T, and I am your District-appointed guardian droid… that is, if you're Master Thomas V. Amos?"

"Oh, no, Rwen – it's that pasty-faced droid from the District nanny file!" Turning back to his visitor, he said, "And, knock off that 'Master Thomas' shit – this ain't no old-time space movie from the flat era. My friends call me Tommy – or Tom, but no 'Master,' okay? I'm not your master. I'm just a kid who's parents got *killed* yesterday. I know you don't understand that, being basically a mannequin stuffed with wires and circuits, but it happened, and now I gotta deal with *your* insensitive ass, too."

A big wet tear spilled out of Eldon 46-T's silicon eye and rolled down his foam-latex cheek – followed by another. "I'm sorry Mas... I mean... *Tom-my*. At the District personnel office, they told me your parents moved Earthworld and left you here, all alone – but, they were really *killed?* How *horrible,"* the android sobbed, wiping his eyes with a silk pocket handkerchief, "you must be devastated. I'm so sorry! Of course, being a droid, I never had a family of my own – but, still, I'm programmed for... programmed for..." He blew his nose, honking, into the handkerchief, "... *Emotional response!"*

"That must be why they lied to me at the personnel office – they know I'm a sentimental old wreck. May I come in, please?" Tommy opened the door wider, and Eldon 46-T entered with his suitcases, looking around. "Hmm... perhaps you would like to play a game of chess, Tom-my? When your homework is completed, that is." Eldon 46-T smiled like a tin idiot.

"You better go, Rwen. I've got a feeling this is going to be a *long* night."

4.

The funeral was held the next day. There were no remains, but Tommy scoured the crash site anyway, looking for any evidence he could find – anything that might lead him to the real smugglers. There was no reason why anyone should want to kill or discredit Horatio and AzDoran Amos; they were standup citizens. Horatio had even been a decorated N.A.S.A. pilot before settling on Mars. He'd met his future wife where she worked, at the District com-center in Vasquez, near the Sagan Space Academy.

Horatio had taught briefly at the Academy in the early '50s. After he and AzDoran married, the young couple started their own shuttle business; when there were no tourists, his father had hauled freight and his mother had booked the flights. Then, Tommy was born. They'd scrimped and saved and worked side jobs to raise him in comfort, and now Tommy was going to pay them back.

He'd applied to the esteemed Pinkerton Detective College of Social Anthropology in New New York, and one of his teachers, a retired detective named, "Casper Wyoming," had written a letter of recommendation for him, but so far, no response had come. College age could be as young as thirteen, as in Rwen's case, and Tommy was only three months away from being an official teenager. It was Mr. Wyoming to whom he had come to finagle official access to the crash site; the former detective still had powerful friends on the force.

Returning empty-handed from Valles Marineris, Tommy stopped at the municipal skyport where his folks berthed their shuttle. "Thanks, Mr. Delany – I'll bring 'em back when I'm done," the boy said, pocketing a stack of plain-wrap VDRs.

"That's all right, Tommy, nobody will miss a few security-cam discs. How's that guardian droid working out for you?"

"You have to ask?" Tommy smirked, shaking his head. "Thanks for coming to the services for my mom and dad." Sam Delany had been a watchman at the Bradbury municipal "Launch 'n' Park" skyport for ten years; the Amoses had leased a berth there for nearly that long, and Sam knew Horatio well. He didn't believe the drug smuggler paint-job the news had given Tommy's folks, especially having seen them load and unload the *Silver Tern* a thousand times, never showing a hint of apprehension or guilt. Lending Tommy the security-cam discs from the weeks prior to the *Tern's* final flight seemed the least he could do.

A tourist couple, the Landrys, had gone down with the Amoses. Tommy was in his room, hacking into their travel accommodations, to see if they had any connection to the pharmaceutical trade – or, if either Brian or Celeste Landry had a prior criminal record. They were from Detroit: *Earth* Detroit – a nightmare on wheels. Although there was no more war on Mother Earth in 2067, and very little crime on Mars – there was still a helluva lot of crime on Earth, because the only people still stuck there were the poor.

"Okay, Brian Landry, have you ever been arrested?" Tommy said. The computer rapidly displayed all available background information on Landry – which wasn't very much. *This guy looks like he just fell out of the sky. These records must be stiff – there's nothing further back than two years.*

"Knock, knock?" said Eldon 46-T, poking his pale face in the crack of the door.

"You're supposed to actually *knock* on the door – not open it and just *say*, "knock, knock," Tommy said, instantly dumping the government file from his VIP-screen. "That defeats the whole purpose of knocking."

"You are finishing your homework, yes?" Eldon said.

"Yes, I'm doin' my homework – is that all you're here for? Get off the *homework*, okay, Circuit Boy?"

"Then why did you have the District's visa/spaceport information up when I came in? Do you have a school assignment that requires such research?

"No, I don't have a...."

"Perhaps I can help you – I know most of the passwords to District information files, as well as those to Earthworld records, from my last job..."

"No, you just clean the dock – *Wait a minute?* You know the passwords? – what a great idea, Eldon – you helpin' me with my homework, that is. How about criminal records? See, this assignment is about how criminals can't get on Mars because of the extreme screening process for immigrants. So, I'm just randomly checking travelers."

"Then, why did you have the Landrys' file up? – Didn't they die in the crash along with... along with..." the droid's voice started to break.

"Damn – you've got some eyes. And don't start cryin' again, Eldon – this is hard enough to go through without you rustin' out your servos every time I mention my folks. You never even met 'em, and I'm looking for clues to find their killers – do you *mind?*"

"Of course not, Tom-my. I hope you know that I'll do all I can to help you. That is my assignment. Do homework... Eat well... Dress warm... Those are my directives for your care. Plus, your new one – 'find killers.'"

"But, you work for the District."

"*Incorrect.* I worked for the District. Now, I work for you."

"Oh, you work for me, huh?"

"Yes, I work for you, Tom-my Am-os. Give me directives!" Tommy thought about it for a second, then, tested his new guardian's independence.

"Okay, Eldon. Hack into this file for me and then finish my algebra homework." Eldon took over the keyboard and begin typing-in the password.

"I was in records, doing computer filing when I first came to Mars..." Suddenly, an alarm began to blare from the speaker in Eldon's throat; his eyes strobed bright red. "Oh, dear... *the override chip.* I forgot about that," he said, deleting the file. "Perhaps you have another directive for me, Tom-my?"

"Yeah – beat it. Lose yourself... *go away.*"

"Very well, it will be my pleasure... as soon as you have completed your Algebra. If $a + b = x$, perhaps I can help you in a purely... *theoretical* capacity, with the unknown quotient, x. ...Hypothetically speaking, of course." Eldon paused, cringing, waiting for the override chip to kick in the alarm. Nothing happened and Eldon smiled.

"Okay, Circuit Boy," Tommy said dryly, "'X' – equals '*shut-up*.'"

5.

It took nearly a week before Tommy even accepted Eldon 46-T as a housekeeper, much less as an authority figure – and he refused to socialize with the droid. He put in his four-hour school days then went to his job on Tuesday and Thursday afternoons at the District environmental control center. The rest of the time he spent collecting reference materials and potential evidence.

By Monday, the inside of the Amos dock looked like headquarters for the Lunabomber task force. Walls were covered with maps of the entire Red Planet, with every dead sea, canal, and crater represented. Pinned up among the maps were architectural blueprints of the sixteen Martian cities, including dome and dustwall diagrams.

"If the police came here for a visit, Tom-my, they would think you are a terrorist," Eldon said, wiping down the coffee table. Then, he replaced the stacks of print-outs and file folders on it, shaking his head. "You keep going over the same information and finding nothing – how long will you continue?"

"...Till I find something! I can almost get into this D.A.A. file – it's got the flight plans filed by every tour and delivery service on Mars, for the last year – you sure you can't help me with the password?"

"I will try, Tom-my, but I cannot prevent the override chip from stopping me. Every time I have tried to do something illegal or improper, to help you – I have been obstructed. Unless...?"

"Unless what?"

"Unless... you disconnect it. The chip is implanted behind my left ear."

"Show me." Eldon did just that, without saying a word – and, flipped back the hinged tip of his right index finger, extending a long, slender computer jack, which he fitted into a port on Tommy's VIP. The droid's internal schematics began to flash across the screen. When the detailed plans of Eldon's head came up, Tommy saw a way to disconnect the chip.

He shut-down the droid and peeled back a couple of inches of foam-latex flesh from his occipital region. *There it is – under that little plate...*

Tommy removed the Allen screws holding the plate; then, very carefully, snipped out the override chip, replaced the plate, and closed.

It would take a while for Eldon to power back up, so Tommy waited. After ten minutes, he was starting to panic. "Come on, Eldon – come on, *wake up!* What have I done, now? Just boot up again – I don't care if you bug me about my homework. Did I mention you're a great cook? I don't wanna have to go to Earth – I need to find out who killed my parents! You have to help me – you promised!! Wake up, Eldon! *Please, wake up!!*"

As a last resort, Tommy decided to shut Eldon down again and re-open his skull. When the Allen wrench found its first screw, Eldon said, "Just a little off the top, this time."

"*Whoa!* – Jeez, Eldon, you scared the *stiff* out of me! I thought I broke you."

"I was playing possum – to use an old Earth expres…"

"I read books; you don't have to explain the damn language to me."

"It is considered vulgar to swear, Tom-my. You say 'damn' entirely too much."

"Shut the flock *up!* Why were you playing possum?"

"Because… I let you remove the override chip, but am still responsible for using good judgement. I wanted to observe your reaction – and true *feelings* – regarding responsibility. Now, the chip is out, and I am free to subvert District guidelines to help you find your parents' killers. But first, I must finish your algebra homework."

The operation had been a smashing success. Tommy Amos grinned hugely for the first time in six days, and it was good. On the seventh day, he bounced.

6.

With Eldon's help, Tommy was able to obtain some very interesting information regarding Brian and Celeste Landry. "Look at this!" Tommy said out loud. "The Landrys booked six flights to wesafe cities this year; each time departing from Wellsville, and stopping briefly in Ben Al-Amin – but they had six different destinations. They only flew with my folks that one time, to Vasquez."

Strange music was coming from the guest room – now, Eldon's room. Tommy hadn't had the heart to do anything with his parents' bedroom, but leave it exactly as it was. Once in a while, he'd go in there to talk to them.

"Eldon? What the stiff is that thing?" Tommy said, pushing open the door to the droid's room.

"It's a CD player from the early '20s – before home entertainment technology went vibration and 3-D holographic," the droid said.

"CD? You mean like the old CD-Rom games they've got in the Bradbury Museum? Who's that singing?"

"For every cyber-circuit in his bent and broken frame – he stood a day without no oil, or lubricant to claim… Till the union bosses dragged him, well-dressed in their shame – down to Oleson's slag heap, Big Tin Riley was his name…"

"That's the great protest singer, 'Leviticus Spartacus.com.' He used to get arrested all the time, back in the '20s, for protesting injustice. Leviticus helped abolish the fossil-fuel engine in favor of nuclear power, but his greatest claim to fame was in the '30s – as a champion of *robots' rights.*" A dull whining instrument took a solo.

"What's that he's playin' now?" Tommy said, cringing at the recording.

"That was called a harmonica, Tommy."

"Sure glad it's gone.

"You should have heard the accordion."

"All alone against the tide, his courage never strayed – give the androids in the mine, a chance for equal pay… A steel and copper sentry, Tin Riley blocked the way – until the strike was settled, on that first 'Robots Day.'"

"He's singing about a real event: twenty-eight years ago on Earth, a labor droid named Tin Riley stood in front of a mine entrance without any lubricating fluids for forty-nine days, protesting the working conditions and pay scale for the droid miners."

"What did they do to him?" Tommy asked.

"They melted him down into ash trays – but that incident sparked the famous 'Robot Riots,' which began on the first *Robots Day,* March 15th, 2039. After our rights were recognized, science and government created the override chip, so we'd never turn on our owners again."

"So, just because I took that chip out of your iron skull, don't be getting any ideas about bossin' me around," Tommy said. "I *let* you feed me, and tell me to dress warm, but I'm glad we finally got that homework thing straight. Oh, and I got invited to the Goldsteins' to graze tonight, so you don't have to cook."

"Pass the potatoes, Moshe," Idaho Goldstein said, and indicated their guest. "Moshe brings me the best vegetables in town from his job in the greenhouse district, Tommy."

"This is great, Mz. G. – it's nice of you to have me over again."

"So – why you never bring your friend along? ...Your guardian?"

"I dunno," Tommy said, reaching for the zucchini. "It never came up."

"Look, Momma – he's standing outside, on the curbwalk." Through the window Tommy could see Eldon out in front, watching the Goldsteins' dock intently. ...Almost wistfully.

"Oh, no – I'm sorry, Mz. Goldstein, he follows me around like a dog-bot."

"Well, invite him in, Tommy – your parents didn't raise you to be rude!

Tommy got up and opened the front door. "Hey, Circuit Boy – you hungry, or what? Get your pasty ol' butt in here!"

"So, after teaching at the *Cordon Bleu* for ten years, I was employed in the palace of King Oscar of Denmark. It was my job getting all those little sardines in the tins..." The Goldsteins howled, as Eldon worked the room.

"Your friend is so funny, Tommy – you have to bring him back next week!" Ida said, wiping her eyes.

"Sure," said Tommy, "he's never that funny at home." *You ready to lift, Eldon? I want to go over all that new info about the Landrys with you, before I deep out.*" Two weeks had passed since the crash, and still, Tommy could think of nothing but his task. *As long as I've got the investigation, I'll be all right,* he thought. *But then, what am I going to do...?*

7.
"So, is this solid evidence, Mr. Wyoming?"

"Well, Tommy... it's evidence that the Landrys took frequent excursions around Valles Marineris and the American cities. The fact that they always stopped-off in Ben Al-Amin bears scrutiny – especially since knock-off drugs were involved."

"I thought Ben Al-Amin was a Muslim city? …Drug and alcohol free?"

"It is," Casper Wyoming said, stroking his yellow-white beard. "But Devil's Graveyard is right next door... in the 'Neutral Zone.' Ever heard of it?"

"No," said Tommy.

"It's an unincorporated area – District free, because it's on for- eign-owned soil, and in the outzone. There isn't a more grisly collection of cutthroats, pirates, and thieves anywhere on Mars – not to mention *grifters!*"

"I thought Mars was 98% crime-free," Tommy said.

"It is – especially in the District-run, wesafe cities. But get outside the dustwalls and that other "2%" can kill you dead as digital. If the Land- rys were muling mush out of the Neutral Zone, then it all makes sense. See, Tommy, the District heat knows about the thugs in Devil's Grave- yard, but it's next door to Ben Al-Amin, which has its own government and police. District heat can't just barge into a neutral area, dazers blasting, right next to another sovereign city – it would be seen as a brazen act of aggression. We have to wait for those bottom-feeders to come out in the open."

"What about the deep desert? Can you arrest them in the bar- rens?"

"Yes, anywhere outside the Neutral Zone," Casper said, tapping out his pipe.

"Think I'm gonna pay a visit to Ben Al-Amin…"

"Well, look up my friend, Ruben California, if you do. He's a P.I. in the Baghdad Building and he'll help you back-track the Landrys' trail, if it's not too cold. As to the king of the dope traffickers, that would be a fellow named Jack Churchill – they call him 'Freeze' Churchill, because he's been busted so frequently. We've crossed dazer beams a few times over the years, but I've never gotten a collar on him, and – oh, yes – be sure and wear a pressure suit under your robes! Dress like a desert nomad – you can pass for Muslim. Your folks were Christian, weren't they, Tommy?"

"Yeah. But, they raised me to believe what I want to believe – and I'm not sure what that is."

"What do you mean?"

"I don't know what I mean, Mr. Wyoming. Do you believe there's a God?"

"Oh, I think there has to be, Tommy. Otherwise – whom have I been praying to for all these years?"

8.

"You haven't gone bouncing with Tommy, lately. What's the matter, Rwen?" her mother asked. "He never comes over anymore, since the accident."

"He's consumed with finding out what really happened to his parents, Mama. I talked to him yesterday – he'll come around. It was a horrible tragedy for a kid his age to go through – Tommy's only *twelve*, you know."

"And you're an older woman of thirteen?"

"What if you and Dad got killed? And then got smeared as mush smugglers? Would you want me to just buy it, and go dancing-in-the-dunes like nothing happened? Well... would you?"

"No, Baby – come here." Georgia Robbyn put her arms around her daughter and squeezed – as if by holding the girl tightly, she could keep her from growing up so fast. "You've really got it bad for that boy, haven't you, Rwen? I just don't want to see you get hurt, that's all. You're so young."

"All I know is – when he hurts, I hurt, too. Is that love, Mama?" Georgia kissed her daughter as a story came on the news that grabbed their attention. A picture of Tommy's late parents filled the big, living room VIP screen, as the newscaster spoke in voice-over:

"In a noble, but desperately futile attempt to clear his parents name, twelve-year-old Thomas Amos, a hopeful future detective of social anthropology – call him a Gaston Flambert in the making – is conducting a one-man investigation of his own..."

At that same time, fifty miles across the dusty red desert, watching the same newscast from the safety of the Neutral Zone, Jack Freeze Churchill and his cadre took careful notice of the story. Just then, Tommy's picture splashed across the screen.

"...Retired interplanetary detective, Casper Wyoming, the Amos boy's teacher at Ray Walston High School, has pulled in some favors to help out. Amos believes that his parents, who operated a shuttle service out of Bradbury, were framed by a deep desert mush-ring and were not trafficking in counterfeit pharmaceuticals as accused..."

"Ya 'ear that, Charlie Bones? 'At old dust-buzzard, Casper Wy-omin', 'as been after me arse fer nearly thi'ty years." Churchill stroked the white Persian cat-bot in his lap. "Now 'e's 'elpin' that witness *you* left alive!"

"No witness, Squire," the slight man called Charlie Bones replied. "They was jus' the two of 'em – like bookends, they was. Jus' the pair, Squire – the bloke an' 'is missus... As God is me witness."

"Well, Charlie... I'd leave God out o' it if I was you. I got another job... y'see that Amos lad on the vippy?"

"That I did, squire."

"He needs to disappear, too. Take Vegas with you, Charlie – an' the next time I see that kid on the news, 'e better be dead or missin'! Got that, you rummy wanker?"

"Beggin' your pardon, sir – I do, indeed."

"It was bad enough you losin' the cargo like that, Charlie Bones, but if you screw up this time, they'll 'ang you for *murder*... if I don't toss your arse in a volcano, first."

9.

Three weeks from the crash date, Tommy was ready to bounce over to Ben Al-Amin. He polished the metallic-green shell of his Leggers in the Amos family's service bay, as Rwen and Omar kept him company.

"Hand me that buffer, Omar," he said. None of them noticed a rustling in the artificial bushes across the curbwalk.

"So, if I can't talk you out of this, can't I at least come with you to Ben Al-Amin?" Rwen asked.

"Not a good idea – I'll have enough on my hands without watching out for you."

"Maybe it'd be *me*, watching out for you, Tom." Rwen argued.

"*Maybe* doesn't cut it this time. I'm not just bouncing-in-the-barrens tomorrow, Rwen, this is a dangerous recon mission. If I take anybody it'll be Eldon, cause he's exo-pressurized, strong as hell... and more expendable than real people."

"Lunch is ready, Tommy!" Eldon called from the back porch, pretending he hadn't heard what the boy had just said. "And, bring your friends... I made blintzes."

"What're blintzes?" Omar asked.

"I don't know, but he's a really good cook. He hardly ever programs anything," Tommy said, heading indoors as Phobos rose pink in the western sky.

When the three of them had been inside for about five minutes and he was sure they weren't coming right back, Charlie Bones crept out of the faux foliage, tiptoed across the astro-turf, and ducked into the Amoses' service bay. With a penlight, a wrench, and his greasy little hands, Charlie did what he'd come to do. After a few minutes he slipped back into the night like a dark thought.

Omar left, and Tommy walked Rwen to her aero-scooter as Phobos was already in half-phase, overhead. "Don't worry about me, Baby. You just be here when I get back."

"You know I'd do anything for you, Tommy."

"Hold that thought for four or five years," he said, and kissed her on the forehead. Then, he turned and walked up onto the porch, to his front door.

Look back. Please, look back. If he looks back, he likes me, Rwen thought, holding her breath. *He* did *look back – entirely wet! He really likes me!*

Tommy smiled, and went inside his dock.

Rwen rode home two feet off the ground. ...Literally.

"I really hope we find what you're looking for, I can't wait to go bouncing," said Eldon. "I will try not to be expendable." Tommy shot him a look.

"I've got the "Boomer" charging overnight. It'll hold up fine, Eldon, it doesn't have as wet a VDR system as the Leggers does – but, don't worry – I won't leave you in the dust."

"Goodnight, Tommy. Thanks for letting me be a part of your quest," the slender droid said. "We'll find out who killed your... killed your..."

"I guess you're not so bad... for a white robot. And I don't mean *Caucasian* white – I mean refrigerator-door *white!*"

"I am a forty-five-year-old kitchen model – I was *designed* to complement refrigerators and blenders," Eldon said, defensively.

"You *redefine* white."

"The 46-T originally came in sunflower yellow and avocado, as well."

"Well, that would be an improvement." Tommy teased, "I mean – how would you like to be *me*, an' get stuck with some... albino droid from the graze channel?"

"Graze channel…? I would be very good on a cooking program…"

"Yes, you would… but your face would read a little *hot* under the lights – *Makeup!"* Tommy hollered.

"I know you are joking, Tommy, but perhaps makeup of some sort would be appropriate for my visit to Ben Al-Amin?"

"Not a bad idea, Eldon. I hear they got some serious brothers in Ben Al-Amin.

"And, looking like this, I would stand out?"

"Like a mad dog in a flea circus… *Goodnight."*

After Eldon retired to his room, Tommy looked out the window and watched Phobos, in its final crescent phase – in the eastern sky, now – a scant three hours after it had risen. *I hope Rwen stays home tomorrow, he thought, but I kind of hope she shows up, too…just so I can send her home again. Now, why do I want that? I'm not a hero type, or insecure… just… just tired, I guess. Get some deeps, T – tomorrow's a big day.*

10.

Sunrise spread a coral quilt over the parched ground, as Tommy and Eldon rolled their bouncers past the Outland Drive-In, the last structure before open desert. They wheeled through the dustwall portal and prepped their hydros for bouncing commencement, adjusting the pressure in their cabins.

"You never bounced in one of these before, eh, Eldon?"

"No, Tommy – but I am exo-pressurized, strong as hell, and more expendable than… *real* people, so I am ready for anything."

"Oh… you heard me say that last night, didn't you? I'm sorry, Eldon – I didn't mean you were expendable – I just said that to let Wren down easy. She wanted to come along, and it's just too dangerous for a girl."

"It is all right. I fail to keep my place sometimes. Getting away from the District offices and living with you has been the happiest assignment I can remember, and sometimes I forget that I am only a temporary domestic, and not a… family member."

"You're family, Eldon – try to hit the brake when you come down, and release it just before impact, or you'll hobble the rebound – *Yeah,* you're family, Circuit Boy – we just keep you in the toolshed, that's all."

Bradbury

Tommy confined his bouncing to long, forward-moving strides, this time. Eldon was keeping up in the Boomer, and they were halfway to Notre Dame rock, when another bouncer dropped down out of the sun.

"Rwen Robbyn! I told you to stay home, today!" Tommy said angrily.

"You're not the boss of me, Tommy Amos," Rwen said, gliding past his bubble.

"Women!"

Less than a mile away, Charlie Bones and Reno Vegas heard every word on their Sand Crawler's signal scanner. Charlie had also sound-surveilled Tommy's house, so he knew what the boy planned to do in Ben Al-Amin, and had given Jack Freeze Churchill a heads-up call. Then, the thugs heard a loud metal "bang" over the scanner.

"What the hell?" Tommy exclaimed. "I just blew a leg cylinder – lost one of my hydros. My left leg is stuck *extended*, and I'm comin' down fast!"

"Tommy! What can I do?" Rwen cried.

"I told you – stay home!"

"Fire your retro-thrusters, Tommy," Eldon said.

"What do you think I'm doing? Oh, Jeez – *this is it – lookout!!*"

Bones and Vegas grinned, anticipating a big crash and wishing they could be there to see it. Being a school day, there were no other bouncers in the area.

Rwen and Eldon held their breath (figuratively, in the droid's case), staying out of the way. Tommy's bouncer hit the ground hard, and flipped sideways on impact. "Hyaaah! – *shit!*" Tommy yelled. The barrel-shaped machine landed on its side, rolling into a redrock column, breaking off one of its waldo-arms. By the time it came to rest, Rwen and Eldon had landed and watched as Tommy's hull breached, buckling-in from the lower air pressure of the outzone. They could hear Tommy screaming, inside.

"Tommy! Jesus, Tommy – are you all right?" Rwen hollered. "Say something!! Are you okay?" Eldon jumped out of the Boomer and rushed over to Tommy's bouncer; he ripped the metal hull away, tearing latex flesh from his own steel-framed hands, calling, "Tommy! *Tommy?*"

Taking advantage of the low grav, Tommy leapt straight up from the steaming wreck, floating down to land on top of it, his coffee-colored robes blowing in the dusty wind, an Arab headdress flapping at his shoulders. A snorkel-like nose-tube pumped oxy into his clear, contoured face-mask, and the pressure suit beneath his robes kept him from imploding. *Thank you Casper Wyoming!* Tommy thought, glad his teacher insisted he wear the thing.

To Rwen, he looked like a mocha-colored *Lawrence of Arabia*, straight out of that old movie from the flat era. Tommy stretched out his arms, palms up and open in the *Prana* intake yoga position. *Somebody tampered with my bouncer – they tried to kill me, but they failed.* He turned 360 degrees, hollering through his mask speaker as loudly as anyone ever had on that desert planet, his voice echoing across the dunes: "You failed! *I still live!* I'll not only *clear* my parents' name – *I WILL AVENGE THEM!!!*

Inside their Sand Crawler a mile away, Charlie Bones and Reno Vegas heard Tommy's words over their signal scanner, and it chilled them to their rotten cores. "Lucky fer us th' lit'le bugger's only twelve, eh, mate?"

"It's best this way, trust me – I am more expendable than Rwen Robbyn. I will run to Ben Al-Amin, right beside you in the Boomer. I can run very fast…"

"No, Eldon – Tommy can take my bouncer so you two can continue – I'll wrist-mail an emergency pickup from one of the training flights out of McCauliffe. There should be a mini-cruiser in the area, and I know all the instructor-pilots."

"Rwen, you'll *implode* and your eyes will pop out!"

"Tommy's right, Rwen – you are not wearing a pressurized suit like he is. You had better go home, or we'll have to abort the mission." Sadly, Rwen agreed, and made her good-byes, rolling her bouncer rather than hopping it, back towards Bradbury.

"*Abort the mission?* Listen to Circuit Boy." Tommy got in the Boomer, re-pressurized the cabin, and bounced off to Ben Al-Amin with Eldon running beside him, dragging a long shadow toward the low, morning sun.

Rwen watched the Sand Crawler get closer and closer in her viewscreen, until she was sure it was pursuing her. As the bulky, steel-plated vehicle pulled alongside, she blasted off into a series of bounces.

"Stiff me!" Charlie Bones cried, "We almost 'ad 'er, mate."

"Use za magnet, Bones – ve haven't got all day vis zis young vooman. Here – let me show how ve do it in New Moscow," Vegas said. He crossed to the other side of the Crawler and entered the code that released the electro-magnetic towing winch. When Rwen bounced down the next time, Charlie swerved in front of her and Reno engaged the magnet; the pull yanked Rwen's bouncer right out of its rebounding pattern, locking her onto the back bumper of the Sand Crawler against her strident protests. Then, Charlie turned the Crawler around and sped off toward Ben Al-Amin… and the *Neutral Zone*.

11.

As they neared the foreign-ruled city, Tommy decided that Eldon needed a makeover. Abandoned vehicles dotted the sand dunes, and they found a ratty burnoose and a tin of Groovelube in an abandoned Sand-Samurai which had apparently rolled in a duststorm. After Tommy had finished with Eldon, the droid made a passable, if greasy, nomad.

"Try not to talk much, El-don, and if you must, please refer to me as… let's see… *Hey!* Remember when we first met, and you wanted to call me 'Master?' Now's your chance. You will be my servant, *'El-dondo,'* and I am, 'Master T.'"

"*Master T'* – I understand, Tommy. With disguises and false names we will be harder to target. Not unlike practitioners of guerilla warfare on planet Earth…"

"And, that's a negatory. No more know-it-all yakkin' – *dummy up*, Circuit Boy!"

The history of Ben Al-Amin was portrayed in multi-colored mosaics and bas-reliefs, beginning at the huge, Moorish arch that hooded the city gates, and extending into a great open-air courtyard. This agora, or bazar, contained every type of green-housed vegetable and synthetic meat-flavored dish known to Mars. Masked, robed merchants and servants scurried between eroded sandstone buildings, and even some of the legless beggars wore pressurized suits under their rags.

Tommy stared through the bug-eyed goggles in his face-mask, entirely fascinated by the exotic array of characters and substances that existed here, barely fifty miles from his suburban, *American* dock. Having known mostly AfricAmericans born on Mars, Tommy was now confronted with black people who had a more direct connection to Mother Africa – even if she was 100 million miles away. He hadn't seen many Arabic Muslims before, either; their women wore opaque masks.

Ben Al-Amin was only partially terraformed, but still qualified as a wesafe area. Better air and pressure made it livable, but nearly everyone outdoors wore suits and masks, anyway. The buildings had *prana* pumping, and a good deal of oxy spilled out of the minarets, 24-7. Natural Martian low-grav kept things light, so lead-soled *heavy boots* were always in style.

Arabic flutes coaxed lilting, robotic cobras; timbales rapped a hypnotic pattern behind them, as strange aromas filtered in around Tommy's breather. Martian air wasn't poisonous — mostly carbon dioxide, so he could smell traces of incense, spices, and synthetic camel-scent. There was not enough water on Mars yet to support anything but robotic animal life — but, Tommy could even smell danger in the thin, pink air.

After confusing directions led them through arches and alleyways for at least an hour, the disguised pair found themselves in front of the Baghdad Building. A transparent bubble of an exterior elevator whisked them to the 9th floor at the mere mention of the name, "Ruben California."

Ben Al-Amin

"Casper dropped me a line, told me you were coming," said the man in the Ray-Bans. His Hawaiian shirt made the snub-nosed dazer in his shoulder-holster look like a toy. It wasn't. A sawbuck said the shirt was louder than the gun. It was.

He had his feet on the desk, but there were no holes in his lead shoes, nor half-empty bottle of rye keeping a shot glass company on the desk. The gold-leaf letters on his pebble-glass door read, "Ruben California, Private Investigations," but the little holographic "L" decal by the brass doorknob meant that wildcat lotto sniffers could be had there, too.

"R.C.," as his friends liked to call him, was full of contradictions. And, he was also Casper Wyoming's good and trusted friend. "Casper said you were investigating that shuttle crash in Marineris last month, and that I should help you – *Tommy*, is it?"

"Yeah, but my name can get me killed; somebody tried to discorporate me on the way over here, so, *dig*… on the street, I'm "Master T.""

"Dig your own reality, man." Looking at Eldon's greasy face, the P.I. said, "If you wanna clean up a little, Pally, there's a sink behind that curtain."

"That's a disguise," Tommy said.

"Oh. It could have fooled me. Now, as to the people you call the Landrys – did the bag-boys recover four bodies in the wreckage?"

"No. I went out there after the fingerprint team and the coroner. They didn't find any *remains* intact – that's how they put it – and, neither did I. Plus, it happened right in the middle of a dust storm, so the evidence blew all over the place.

"I found this," Tommy said, holding up half of a charred N.A.S.A. Medal of Honor. "This was my Dad's. That's how I know he's really dead – he never took this off… not even in the shower."

"I just asked if they found four bodies – I don't need your life's story, kid." Turning to Eldon, the detective asked, "Does he always run-off at the air-hole like this? You'd both better come with me."

The inside of the Ben Al-Amin jail smelled exactly like you'd think it would. Breathing masks went back on as Ruben guided Tommy and Eldon through the narrow, winding tunnels. The walls were lined with cells containing the worst that this desert metropolis and its neighboring cesspool, the Neutral Zone, had to offer.

Ruben stopped in front of a filthy, barred cubicle that housed a man and a woman. "Meet the Lowreys – alias, *the Landrys*," he said, "also known as Klaus and Eva Von Braun, Julius and Ethyl Rosen-Mertz, and, more recently, The Fabulous Continis." Despite the bad dye-jobs and the circus costumes, they looked a lot like the Landrys.

"It is them! – What did you do to my parents?"

"Hey, the kid from the news, Fred," the woman said. "Any of you got change for a thousand? I need a pack of Placebos, and the machine doesn't…"

"*Did you hear me?*" Tommy yelled. "What happened to my *parents?* How did you bail before their shuttle crashed?"

"Yes, I was wondering that, myself," Eldon said. "And what are your *real* names?"

"… Well, we're booked under Fred and Ginger Lowrey, will that do?" the man in the cell said. "And we got off, *here*, the afternoon that shuttle crashed in Valles Marineris – right here, in Bel Al-Amin."

"We were never on board with the bootleg mush," Ginger said, "two other guys carried it on when we got off – an' that's the last we saw of 'em, *and* your folks."

"Do we get out if we give up the two guys?"

"I'm not with the police department, Mr. Lowrey, I'm just private heat for hire, and once an' a while I work one for a friend – on the house. *Comprende?*"

"Who were the two guys?" Tommy demanded.

"Get us out of here, and we'll tell you." Fred said.

"Let me see your manacles," Tommy whispered, glancing up at the security-cam. Eldon blocked the view, grinning into the lens, even though Ruben had bribed the captain of the guard with a virtual-drinking game. Acting like he was going to unlock Fred's wrists, the boy yanked them through the bars instead, and quick as light-speed, pulled out an old-style stunner, which he held against Lowrey's crotch. "Seriously, Mr. Landrey – or *Lowrey* – you need to tell me the names of the two men who brought that mush aboard my parents shuttle… and *murdered them!!*

Tommy hissed the last two words, keeping eye contact while he shoved the stunner into Fred's sack and pulled the trigger.

"*Yaaaahhhhaaaahhhh!!!!*" Lowrey screamed, as a flickering band of blue lightning arced into his balls. "*Okay!! OKAY!!*" Tommy relaxed the trigger and the crackling ceased as Fred slumped, gasping and flopping.

"Wow, that thing stiffed him up good – do it again," Ginger said.

"Okay, watch this!" Tommy said.

"NO!!!" screamed Fred. "It was Charlie Bones — and that other guy who works for Churchill — the big guy — oh, what's-his-name?"

"Let me jog your memory."

"Yaaaahhhhaaaahhhh!!!! — *OKAY!!"* Fred screamed, *'McGurk!* — Darwin McGurk! *Turn it off!!!*

12.

Half an hour later, they were ready to enter the portal in the great wall that lead to the Neutral Zone. Ruben California knew the sentries, who were more concerned with people entering from the Zone than with those leaving Ben Al-Amin.

"Now, you're gonna see some serious depravity," he said, "as opposed to those hired beggars in the marketplace."

"What do you mean, *hired?*" Tommy asked.

"I mean those dudes with no pins? The geeks with no gams? They're veterans and ex-stunt men — the city pays 'em a salary to add color and authenticity to the Mid-east Earthworld motif."

"Get off the planet!" Eldon said. "You're serious? They pay people to *pretend* to ask for money?"

"Pretend? A good pitchline will get one of them forty, fifty grand in one afternoon. Now hold on to your breakfasts..." Ruben led them through several layers of hanging plastic strips until they came out in another agora — this one, clearly, a thieves market.

Mutants and congenital freaks passed among "cadre" types with slicked-back hair and zippered, leather pressure suits. Black Market mush was everywhere: pill-poppers buying jars of brightly-colored caps and drums, while overdrivers ran in place, sweating through their masks. Hookahs pumped purple clouds of spent, opiated brain-cells skyward as the Blue Dreamer "deepers" stumbled blindly, their heavy-lidded eyes a pupil-less, robin-egg blue.

This frontier Martian outpost was the wildest thing Tommy had ever seen, and the most impressive building in sight was an old hotel with a cockeyed vertical sign that flashed, *"Devil's Graveyard,"* in red neon. Downstairs housed a tattoo parlor and a bar.

A faux-ivy-covered trellis blocked their view from the parched ground, as Jack Freeze Churchill, Charlie Bones, and a few other crusty types watched from the hotel balcony. Tommy, Eldon, and Ruben California approached, below.

Off to the left, Tommy saw the bartender from the Crimson Dunes Tavern drag a drunken patron out and throw him down one of two slanted, aluminum tunnels in the ground. The drunk screamed from below, as he whisked away in the dark.

"What are those?" asked Tommy.

"Ejector tubes – for eighty-sixing people no longer wanted in the Neutral Zone." The man in the Hawaiian shirt checked his dazer, setting it on fry. "That tube on the right will drop you outside the main gates to Ben Al-Amin, the one on the left that *he* just went down – that one drops you out the back way, right into the landfill. Gotta watch out for dust-crawlers and maggocites, back there. You could get the heebie-jeebies, or worse, kid, so stay outta that left tube, unless you like the idea of un-killable parasites eating away the insides of your eyelids!"

"Hold it right zere!" Reno Vegas said, stepping out on the hotel balcony. "Trow down your dazors an' come in za lobby!"

"I got some bones to pick!" Tommy yelled back. "*Charlie Bones*, as a matter of fact!"

"Nobody gets my gat, Boris, but you guys can come down if you want," Ruben said. "I'll be at the bar." He strolled right in the front door, followed by Tommy and Eldon. Inside the lobby, they crossed to the adjoining bar which was in the wall between hotel and pub, and the detective ordered his drink. "*Cuervo Rojas*, light-speed, *por favor.*"

The button lit up, and the old-fashioned needle atop the elevator doors panned left as the elevator began its drop from the second floor. Little bells chimed somewhere as the needle passed the mezzanine mark, and the green-tattooed barmaid set down Ruben's shooter and took his fifty-dollar bill. Tommy and Eldon looked at each other, and Tommy realized he'd really had no plan *but to get them there.*

Little bells chimed louder as the elevator stopped. Ruben downed his shot glass and slammed it on the bar, drawing his dazer; he aimed it right between the doors as they started to open – and, *Rwen* stepped out!

"Don't shoot! – It's *Rwen!* Damn it, girl – I told you to stay home!" Tommy yelled.

"Drop the dazer, mate, or th' gal gets a second mouf," said Jack Churchill, stepping out from behind Wren, who had Charlie Bones' knife at her throat.

"Shoot 'em anyway, whoever you are! A District mini-cruiser is on the way to mop up – these mooks were too dumb to take my wrist-pilot," Rwen said, waving it in her captors' faces. "They can't court-martial *cadets* for coming here."

"Nice job, o' bluffin,' Sweetie," said Churchill. "but, that's just an ol' micro-VIP. They're a grand-a-dozen down in Vasquez." Just then, Rwen's wrist-pilot kicked in with an audio transmission:

"Cadet Rwen Robbyn, this is Cadet Crew Leader 79Brown – I copy your send, Cadet! Ditto your position, locking on now – unable to send mini-cruiser, so we're neuting the site with no-fault M.A.B.s – get the hell outta there! Repeat: evacuate Neutral Zone! It's about to be neutronized – with the blessing of the Ben Al-Amin government."

Bones peeked around Rwen's head and got Churchill's attention. "Do that mean wha' I think it do, Squire?"

"Crimony – I was gonna trade 'er off in Port au Pills, along wif the rest o' me dungeon! Oh, well – somebody *get me 'elicar. Ev'ry man for himself!"*

"No! Nobody's goin' anywhere till I find out how Charlie Bones killed my parents!" Tommy yelled, as the little bells chimed again.

"You want Charlie Bones – *take 'im* – I'll keep the girl," Churchill said, grabbing Rwen and pushing Bones out as the doors closed.

"Rwen! *No!!"* Tommy screamed. The needle above the elevator panned one-eighty; the car was headed for the seventh floor – and the roof.

"What did you do with the kid's parents, you scum-squirting pustule!" Ruben said, shoving the muzzle of his dazer into Bones' face.

"Nothin'! I got on the shuttle next door, wit' Darwin McGurk. Your dad didn't take to us – no sir, 'specially since Darwin couldn't wait. He started to do some o' the overdrive in the cabin, an' your dad tried to stop 'im. Your ma was flyin' an' what with the dust storm an' all, I jumped out with spring boots an' a case o' the mush. Lost it on the way down, I did. Couldn't see in the dust – a few seconds later I 'eard the crash – saw the ball o' flames. It was my mush what the coppers found – I'm sorry your folks got the rap... your dead folks, that is – truly, I am, young Squire."

"Oh, screw you, Charlie Bones – I'll deal with you later! *Eldon – to the roof!"*

"I'll hang on to Bones," Ruben said.

"The elevator is taking too long to return, Tom – I mean, 'Master T,' so we'd..."

"Better take the stairs..."

"I'll carry you," Eldon said, scooping up Tommy and running up the circular stairwell, one, two, three, four, five, six, seven dizzying, cork-screw flights of it – in about twelve seconds. The droid burst through the door and onto the roof, and Tommy erupted off to the side.

"Hup-ralphhh!... You can run, all right."

"'Ow intimidatin'...." Churchill said, as his helicar swooped over the edge of the roof to pick him up. It hovered; smoked bubble lifting, hinged at the T-bar; masked driver inside, smoking a thick cigar.

"Bones told me what happened – leave Rwen an' go – we'll take our chances with the neutron missiles," Tommy said.

"I don't think so. I can always use a bit o' insurance, plus they'll really like 'er down in the mush-factories o' Port au Pills. Come on, Sweetie," Churchill said, waving a big, nickel-plated dazer at them as he pulled Rwen into the car.

"Vat about me, Boss – vere do I sit?"

"Where'd an unlucky bastard like you get a name like 'Reno Vegas?'"

"I buy it at Ellison Island Space Station, like everyvun else, vat you tink?"

"I think your a dumb ox, mate – enjoy the last thi'ty seconds o' your life." Churchill smiled as the bubble closed. Rwen yelled something Tommy couldn't hear.

"No!!" Tommy screamed, as the helicar whooshed away. Vegas scratched his head, watching it whoosh.

"We must hurry to get you away from the neutronization effect," Eldon said, scooping up Tommy again.

"The ejector tubes! Get me in the *tubes,* down there – on the ground!" Tommy hollered. Eldon raced to the edge of the building, the metal armature of his hands exposed, digging into Tommy's suit as they leapt. Eldon didn't give it a thought – it had to be done.

They landed in a crush of metal and tearing foam; having no pain sensors, Eldon failed to notice the foot-long shard of steel infra-structure poking out of his right leg – right through his burnoose. His speech was slightly slurred, and his servos were humming badly, but he got to his feet. And, Tommy was A-okay.

"Do homehomehome-work, eat w-w-well, dresssss warmmmm... *find killers!"* the droid said, limping quickly over to the two big holes in the rocky ground.

"We want the right one," said Tommy.

"The l-l-l-left one is the r-r-r-right one, because w-w-we're fac-inggggg the other way, now." Eldon said, leaping into the ejector tube, his arms wrapped around the boy. Ruben California came out on the hotel porch, his hand cuffed to Charlie Bones.

"You can't arrest me – this is the Neutral Zone!"

"I'm not a cop – I can do what I like! You can stay here, pally— but, the Neutral Zone is about to become the *Neutron Zone.*"

13.

Tommy and Eldon came spitting out of the hole in the ground like millequarters shooting out of a paying slot in a TexarCanada gaming palace. One could almost hear the bells going off. Actually, Eldon did hear ringing in his microphones, as he staggered to his feet. Tommy revved his bouncer's retros as Churchill's Nexus became a black spec over the hori-zon. "I'm goin' after Rwen!" he yelled, bounding off in great, long strides toward the vanishing dot.

Right then, a District mini-cruiser, all 180 feet of her, flew over the high wall surrounding the Neutral Zone. She hovered over the cracked and dusty yard as a loudspeaker voice called out: *"Cadet Rwen Robbyn, this is Cadet Crew Leader 79Brown. Just kidding about that neutron strike – Gotcha!" Come on out! ...Lowering landing basket, now."*

California heard them as he pulled Charlie Bones through the ver-tical strips of plastic, traversing the portal back into Ben Al-Amin. "Hey *Flyboy!*" he called up, while dragging his prisoner back out into the sunlit yard. Ruben gazed up up at the softly humming cruiser through his Ray-Bans. "She went that-away! In a Nexus stretch-helicar. *Follow 'em!*" Charlie slipped his cuff and started to sidle away, crablike. "Not so fast, *bloke,*" Ruben said. "You're still comin' with me. If you're real nice, I'll buy you a tequila before you start your 20-year stretch for kidnapping a minor on Mars, fraud, mush-smuggling, and *murdering* the English language."

As Tommy bounced across the rusty plain, Eldon followed at a run, feet smoking. His servos were vibrating him apart; he was a kitchen model, and not used to jumping off buildings, much less being shot at. They were closing on the Nexus, and Jack Freeze Churchill was firing his rear machine-guns at the boy and his droid.

Tommy was able to duck and roll, but Eldon took a direct hit – which blew off the droid's left arm. Tommy couldn't communicate with him because Eldon wasn't interfaced with the bouncers' sound and com systems. "Lookout, Eldon!" He yelled, just before he hit ground and sprung up again. A burst of explosive pellets sped toward him as he braked, mid-air, letting it whiz by overhead.

"Damn these foreign jobs – where's me Bently when I needs it? "'E's gainin' on me in that bucket... I've mind to turn 'round an' give 'im what for."

"You'd better let me go, or my boyfriend is gonna kick your ass," Rwen said.

"Oh, yeah – 'e scares me, 'e does." Churchill nudged his driver, and the Nexus banked, turning around.

"Look out, Tommy," Rwen said into her wrist-pilot, "he's got heat-seekers up front – *look out!!*"

"Gimme that thing," the drug lord said, ripping the device off of her arm. Talking into it, Churchill said, "Say goodbye to your girlfriend, 'ero... *adios!*" Then, the cockney drug lord of Mars released a heat-seeking Terracuda air-to-air missile. It roared through the thin atmosphere straight at Tommy, who was coming out of a bounce, right up into it. Braking would do no good – he was soya-toast.

Then Eldon, burnoose shredded and latex exo-skin in tatters, without a care for what was left of him, leapt straight and true into the path of that deadly projectile, and just to make sure that it took *him* out and not his charge, pushed his body temp to max, closed his eyes for the last time, and thought-sang Leviticus Spartacus.com's lyrics:

"For every shattered circuit in his ruptured, dying frame – he bore no ill against them, forgave them for their blame... First no-one would stand with him, then many robots came – lest old acquaintance be forgot, Tin Riley was his n..."

"Eldon – *noooooo!!!*" Tommy screamed. The droid's body blocked out the flashpoint, but Tommy refused to spin away; he took the second-ary brunt of the powerful explosion, which shattered the bubble on his Boomer. Tommy flipped his breathing mask down, instantly, still scream-ing the droid's name. A rain of bullets scoured Tommy's hull as Church-ill's helicar made a final pass over the scene.

Tommy scrambled out and ran to Eldon's side – what was left of his side, that is. The missile had blown the kitchen droid apart, scattering bits of white latex and chromed steel over hundreds of feet of desert. Tommy cradled the shell of Eldon's head in his gloved hands, as the droid hemorrhaged foamy blue liquid, which hissed, bubbling around his mouth and severed neck.

"Eldon! *Eldon!* Say something!" Tommy begged. *"Circuit Boy...?"* From up in the sky he heard the District mini-cruiser's loudspeaker voice order the Nexus down. He watched through a blur, his mask fogging-up as Churchill's long black craft ducked, dropping down to the ground between the cruiser's bracketing sheets of roaring liquid flame. The bubble flipped up, and out came the driver with his hands high. The flame-sheets dwindled to flickering dazer-beams as the mini-cruiser floated, hovering.

Rwen came out of the helicar next, followed by Churchill, who had his dazer tucked between the girl's ribs. "I don't wanna 'ave to scorch 'er, Mate – tell this cruiser ta bug off, an' I'll let 'er go." The mini-cruiser lowered a ramp down to the cracked desert ground. First out of the gate was the captain, Cadet Omar 79Brown.

"Sharpshooters! Sorry, Rwen, mandatory directive..." Six uniformed, long-range DazerKnights stepped up in the cruiser doorway, three on each side of Omar, each aiming at the mush king's head. Tommy sneaked around behind Churchill and got out his stunner, just as the thug caved in and dropped his nickel-plated sidearm.

Then, the sharpshooters parted, and a familiar face – behind mask and goggles – appeared beside Omar. "Freeze, Churchill! – I arrest you in the name of the District of the United States of America, Mars, for crimes too numerous mention into in this miserable, stinking atmosphere. Cuff 'em, Cadets."

"Mr. Wyoming!" Tommy yelled, pulling Rwen from Churchill.

"I was just runnin' 'er 'ome," said the drug lord.

"Tommy!" said Rwen, falling into his arms.

"Hang on a minute, woman – there's somethin' I gotta do first." Tommy held back the troopers-in-training, then lunged at Jack Freeze Churchill's crotch with the stunner.

"Yaaaahhhhaaaahhhh!!!!" the thug screamed.

"That's for gettin' my parents killed." Tommy lunged again.

"Yaaaahhhhaaaahhhh!!!!"

"An' that's for Eldon! Take him away Cadets." Tommy looked at his teacher, who was proud to have a collar on Churchill, at last. "Eldon's finished, Mr. Wyoming. I've lost everything – everyone who loves me, dies."

"That's not true! I love you, and I'm not dead," Rwen said.

"Yeah, but you almost got dead, if it wasn't for this cruiser showin' up."

"I told you I called it in – I *rate* at McCauliffe, buddy. These cadets are the astro-pilots and sky-troopers of tomorrow. And I don't mean sometime in the future – I mean *tomorrow*. Omar's class graduates tomorrow. After summer break, they go away for two years active training."

"Radar says there's a dust storm comin'," Omar said, "we'd better lift."

"C'mon, get in," said Casper Wyoming. Just then, a class-3 skyvan flew up and alighted, right beside the cruiser. Jose California stuck his masked head out; custom tinted goggles suggested his Ray-Bans.

"Glad I caught up. Look what I found in Churchill's drug factory!" He slid the door back, revealing his masked cargo. "Bones gave 'em up, so I had to let him go."

"Mom? *Dad!!???* – You're *alive?*" Tommy yelled, running to the skyvan door. He leapt into his father's arms as his mother hugged them both.

"We jumped out of the shuttle, wrangling with a mush-head named McGurk, right before it exploded," AzDoran Amos said.

"We passed-out in the dust storm, and woke up in a locked transport, headed for the Neutral Zone," Horatio continued.

"Churchill kept us in his dungeon – along with a lot of pissed-off tourists his men had captured," said his mother. "He was going to trade us to the drug-mine lords to cook overdrive all day and night – we were even in a training program for it – and you know how I hate to cook."

"This is incredible! I wanted to believe you were still alive – I never stopped looking. And Eldon helped me – come here, Dad – you gotta meet Eldon! *Mom!* Come on – he's lying over here in the sand. You can meet his head, anyway..." They all walked over to the spot where Eldon's head lay, spewing its turquoise ichor, shuddering in its death throes. There was little human about the thing, now – clearly, it was a machine past its usefulness. It rattled and coughed and whistled and tried to speak, all at the same time.

"*D-d-do h-h-homeworkwork, eat-t-t-t well, dressss warmmmm-mmmm….. f-f-find k-k-ki-ki-killers-s-s-s…f-f-f-find p-p-p-parentssssssssssssssssssssssssssssssss…*"

14.

A month later, the Amos family had a big party at their dock. Music, a barbecue, and tales of Tommy's adventure were entirely wet, but the cause for celebration? The return of Horatio and AzDoran from their unlawful imprisonment was most of it, but so was Tommy's acceptance by the Pinkerton Detective College of Social Anthropology. When they heard about Tommy's heroism, they even gave him a scholarship.

"I must admit, it was fun getting back in the game," Casper Wyoming said. He stroked his beard and tapped out his pipe. "Things have been a little stagnant at Walston High, so next semester I'm going to be teaching a class at Pinkerton, too. Maybe do a little consulting for the District boys, when they get stuck on a case."

"Go get 'em Casper," Ruben California said. He was wearing a bright orange and green luau shirt with a straw snap-brim – and, of course, his Ray-Bans. "It's nice to walk around in crepe soles again, thanks for inviting me over to Bradbury, Horatio, where gravity is not B.Y.O."

"Thanks for breaking us out of Churchill's dungeon, Ruben! They didn't even have a public sandbath in that place, much less hot, running gray-water."

"And they've only got forty-three channels – some prisoners had to share VIPs, two or three to a screen!"

"That's brutal, Mz. Amos," said Rwen. "Did they fight over what they watched?"

"To the death. …Who hasn't had any of the tempura tofu-shrimp?"

"Where's Tommy?" Rwen asked. "I haven't seen him for a while."

"Yeah, where is Tommy," said Omar 79Brown. "A friend of mine wants to meet the hero." But, Tommy was in his room, sitting on his bed… alone.

"You all right, son?" Horatio said, entering quietly. "Omar's here and the tofu T-bones are going on the grill any minute."

"Thanks Dad, I'm okay. I'll be right out. I was just thinking about Eldon."

"You really miss him, don't you, son? …Even if he was only a machine."

"Can a machine make the decision to destroy itself to save a human being? Can a machine care about somebody's feelings? Eldon was more than a machine, Dad – he was more than a friend, too – he was *family*. All the family I had while you and Mom were gone."

"Knock, knock," said Casper, sticking his head in the door, "hope I'm not interrupting anything too important."

"…No, we're coming out," Tommy said, remembering the time that Eldon had done just that. "How's the cauliflower surprise, Dad?"

"Your mother does the best she can, son. Considering that *she* made it – it's fantastic." They moved through the crowded dock, spilling out the back door, where a dance floor had been set up in the service bay. Ruben was downing tequila shooters and hitting on Rwen's flight instructor, as Idaho Goldstein and Moshe entered with a basket of vegetables. Even Sam Delaney was there with a couple of the other skyport customers who knew the Amoses. Friends, neighbors, and Tommy's classmates filled the dock and its small yard.

"The only thing that isn't clear to me," Tommy said, "is how my story got on the news in the first place?" Casper Wyoming cleared his throat.

"... I guess I'm to blame for that," he said. "I planted the news story to smoke out the bottom-feeders, but it almost got you done-in as well."

"Besides trying to kill me in the barrens, Charlie Bones had a knife at Rwen's throat," Tommy said. "And, he knew Mom and Dad were alive *all along*... I wish I knew where he is tonight."

"You don't want to know," said Ruben. "Freeze Churchill was deported to Earth. He's the stiff who came up with the kidnapping idea. Besides shipping mush to the wesafe cities, he was grabbing tourists and rogue flyers to sell back to the mush-makers, to work their factory mines."

Tommy drifted over to Horatio and said, "Dad, I have some unfinished business out in the barrens tomorrow. I'll be gone early." His father smiled and put his arm around Tommy's shoulder.

The next day, the sun rose pink in the morning sky, and Tommy stood in the little box canyon under the sandstone arch he and Wren had found a childhood ago, his bouncer parked nearby. The young detective had collected as much of Eldon's metal and latex that he could find, and buried it here under a pile of stones, with a marker of sorts chained around a tall rock at the grave's head.

"Well, Circuit Boy," that's pretty much it. You know I'll never forget your titanium ass. I swear, you were so white eggs looked gray in your hands. You were so..."

Tommy broke, sobbing into his breathing mask as he took a final look at the marker – a round metal memorial plate he'd found in Eldon's suitcase. The plate was copper, and had a dazer-chiseled message beneath a raised effigy of Tin Riley blocking the mine entrance on First Robots

Day. Tommy had written in marker across the top of the plate, **"HERE LIES ELDON T-46 – A BETTER MAN THAN YOU."**

The engraved writing beneath Tin Riley was a famous quote from Leviticus Spartacus.com's testimony at the notorious House Un-human Activities Committee hearings of 2047: **"It's what's inside a person that counts – even when they're not a real person."**

Dedicated to Robert A. Heinlein

AFTERWORD

George Clayton Johnson said this story reminded him of Robert A. Heinlein's juvenile space adventures with some Robert Sheckley-style social satire thrown in. He also said that at one point it moved him to tears. The character of Casper Wyoming *is* George, in fact, who was born in Cheyenne, Wyoming, but lived in Casper for a while.

The bouncing in the story was inspired by the lunar, floating-on-wings ride attraction in Heinlein's, *"The Menace from Earth,"* also a young adult, sci-fi romance story, which intrigued me in high school. "Discorporate" is his synonym for the word, "die," from the 1960 novel, *"Stranger in a Strange Land."*

The idea of pilgrims from Earth having names that reflect their origins on the home planet – like Idaho Goldstein and Ruben California – is not unique. The lifestyle of the future immigrants and "Marslings" (humans born on Mars) here is based on an *L.A. Times Magazine* projection of what Martian colonization would require, published in the early 2000s. It included an essay by Ray Bradbury, whose name bedecks the town where Tommy Amos lives. Story elements like jobs in the greenhouse district or recycling center, and gravitational weight, were detailed in the article and adhered to.

Daughter of Depravity

NOTE: *This is the only story in the book that parodies bad writing (intentionally). It's dedicated to the great and the near-great who have carved out a niche in the "horror genre."*

Prologue

"It was *A Dark and Stormy Knight* that garnered her first award."

"But it *was The Best of Times & the Worst of Times Cookbook* that first made the best-seller list," said I.M. Grisly, from his seat at the signing table.

"Romance novels and cookbooks don't count," said the blonde. "Between you and I, we're talking 'big' in the horror genre, I.M., not the mainstream."

"Call me Ishmael," he said. "And, the preposition 'between' takes an objective case pronoun. 'Between you and me' is correct, because it is a prepositional phrase, and the pronouns are objects of that preposition. You want to be a writer, Drusilla? Learn the language."

"So guess whose day job is teaching middle school? What I meant is that it's her vampire character, Juliana Jestiny, for which Karisma will always be remembered. In horror, it all started for her with *Daughter of Depravity*, Juliana's debut; and, Rex Stevens at *Boneyard Stomp* agrees with me!"

A tall drink of water joined the group. "You were just talking about me," she gurgled, taking her seat. "I saw your lips moving while you stared. How's the crowd?"

Blueblack hair in a Cleopatra cut tucked under, just touching porcelain shoulders. Bettie Page bangs kissed the tops of perfect eyebrows, as long lashes framed piercing eyes. Those violet eyes, that had cut their teeth burrowing into the souls of men, seemed to glow. Karisma St. Shatan had arrived.

1.

An hour earlier someone else had come to the multiple-author book signing; it was being held at the Morbid Opus on Ventura Boulevard in Encino. The someone else was named Earl Ray Kimball, and by all rights he was a monster, but one concealed in the body of a young man. *I'm a monster*, he thought to himself, *concealed in the body of a young man*. He had no family since his mother had died and left him the castle. And, he had no life beyond his computer games, his beloved gerbils, and the vampire novels of Karisma St. Shatan.

Earl Ray Kimble circled his prey like a shopping cart with a bad wheel. A charcoal blazer hung on his gaunt frame like a cleaning bag on a cheap suit, and even though he was a spineless, cruel, undeserving sociopath, he'd made sure his socks matched his turtleneck sweater, which was a glaring shade of safety orange that day. Kimble's obsessive-compulsive disorder was actually an asset in the planning of his unholy crimes.

Karisma had already signed and dedicated his copy of *Platelets of Love*, her fifth Juliana book, so she wasn't aware he was watching her. And even though Kimble's badges and buttons did make him look frighteningly like a sci-fi fan, she still paid him little mind.

"I liked your crack-head vampire story in *Boneyard Stomp*, Karisma," the blonde said, "but your clumps of exposition irritate me no end. And, those Chandler-esque metaphors? – Sometimes two in a row! Dump the derivative short stories, darling – thank goodness you have another Juliana book out."

The blonde was Drusilla Slye, a twice-divorced, failed vampire author whose contract had not been renewed. She was bitter over it, and needling Karisma provided some remove from the melancholy debris of her life. Not the first envious mediocrity Karisma had encountered on her rise to success, Drusilla started again, but her target spoke first.

"From one vampire author to another, Dru – bite me." A rangy young man offered the successful author a glass of wine.

"Burgundy from a box in a plastic champagne glass – how can I refuse?"

"They don't spare on the glamour around here," the tall man said.

"Here's to success," she said, raising her glass and burying Slye with a sideways look of distain.

"I'm Todd Raventhorpe. I love your Juliana novels, Ms. St. Shatan – can you please…?" He smiled, air-signing to finish the sentence. When he set his open copy of *"Platelets"* in front of her, they locked eyes. "I hear

Daughter of Depravity went into its seventeenth printing last month – congratulations!"

"Thanks! You really keep tabs on my career – what about you?"

"Just got my second tale picked-up by *Eerie Yarns*," and I'm writing a novel."

"I think I've heard of you..."

Earl Ray Kimble, still circling Karisma, eyed the handsome young man flirting with his obsession; he moved closer to hear their words. *Rats,* he thought, *this guy could ruin my plans! Now she's getting up... she's cruising him – SHIT!! ... It's hot in here... Did I pay the power bill? Yeah, I think so.*

"What ever happened to Rhonda Macabra?" I.M. asked, signing one of his books for a reader. Someone told me she dropped out – another told me she killed herself. She's been gone at least a year, and there's no phone or e-address listed under that name, I searched."

"*Mutant Love* showed the beginnings of greatness," Todd said. "It's too bad she quit the game."

"Thanks, Mister Grisly," the reader said, moving on.

"She just couldn't handle winning the Bloch Award, and then getting cut by Rune Morgue Books," Drusilla said. "The irony killed her. She burned-off her prints with acid and did a razor-blade walk-away – or, she reverted to using her real name, and now, nobody knows who she is."

"A fate worse than death," I.M. said.

"How come *she* knows so much about Rhonda's disappearance?" Todd asked. "...You don't mind if I call you Karisma?" He stood very close to her and gazed into her violet eyes. *Naw... she couldn't be,* Todd thought. *It's daytime, but she could be wearing sunblock. She does write some pretty convincing vampire stories.* Karisma smiled, revealing normal, if perfect, canine teeth.

"Drusilla held the razor blade," she said. "Besides, Dru, at least Rhonda didn't get dropped by a print-on-demand publisher. What does that feel like, anyway?"

"...God, you're a bitch."

"Praying won't save you."

"I'll hold your coats," I.M. said. The group laughed, as Karisma nestled against Todd, breathing-in his cologne and man-scent, getting a little wet. He brushed her hair with his lips. They hadn't kissed, but the burning inevitability of that was rapidly becoming a tangible thing: like a child created by their lust, crying to be fed.

Somebody throw a sheet over those two, Kimble thought.

"I liked Rhonda's straight-forward style," Todd said. "She es-chewed the cliché of using pregnant metaphors, while avoiding clumps of exposition that plug-up the narrative… unlike some writers.' Drusilla laughed this time.

Karisma shot Todd a look and asked, "Are you two in league or something?" Right then Karisma got a mental picture of Todd fondling her. *Naughty girl*, she thought… *Unless… Could Todd be psychic, too? …Or, telepathic?*

A *"yes"* seemed to pop into her mind. *I'm imagining this – wishful thinking.*

"No," said Todd. Then he silently projected, *I'm sending you thoughts. Are you one of us?* Her mental image of a romantic embrace changed – and Todd was mounting her from behind.

Are you asking me questions psychically, Todd? She projected a thought at him: *more specifically, are you some sort of supernatural being?* As they stared at each other in eerie silence, the Gordon Lightfoot song, "If You Could Read My Mind," began playing on the bookstore's sound system and the clock on the wall read five-fifteen.

I really just want to go back to my hotel – for tonight, anyway, Todd. There'll be time enough for us, soon. You're the first guy in ages I can really communicate with. Call me after the weekend; I'm in the book.

Okay, he thought back. *If you're sure you're too busy tonight?* He stared deeper into her eyes, hoping she would relent.

How do I know it's really you projecting these messages? It might be someone else, throwing their thoughts at me. Give me a sign that it's really you.

What? Are you crazy? I'm standing right in front of you!

Tell me what you're wearing, so I'll know you.

…Then, Todd smiled.

Gotcha! she thought, grinning back.

Quite the staring contest," Drusilla said. "Like a bad moment from one of your novels, Karisma, where you reveal the thoughts of two or more characters in the same scene – usually offset in italics – but con-fusing to the reader." Karisma smiled back.

"Confusing to the dull and ignorant, perhaps – I think they have some large-print books in the back, Drusilla… for those who move their lips while reading.

She better look at me pretty soon, Kimble thought, watching closely, *or I might just have to kill everybody. I was expecting a lot of attention today!*

"You really do have a love-hate obsession with Karisma's writing, don't you, Dru?" said the man who called himself 'I.M. Grisly.' "Let me take you away from all this. The signing's about over – what say we repair to that restaurant across the street. It has a bar, and we're *writers*, after all. We are, therefore we drink."

2.

Karisma finally convinced Todd that tonight wasn't going to happen for them, so he took off and she settled with the store's owner on the day's take. By the time she left the Morbid Opus it was sundown, and Earl Ray Kimball was waiting for her. He lurked, thinking, *what souvenirs I'll get tonight!*

The St. Shatan shrine in his bedroom at home boasted Juliana dolls – and, usually a life-size cutout of her, eerily posed. Behind her altar, the wall bore a collage of photos, blown-up and reduced to different sizes. By altering the variations in his obsessive-compulsive way, Kimball had created a Karisma wallpaper motif. On the altar, red and black candles flanked an unspeakable thing.

As she walked to her Lexus, the author didn't notice the dark green van parked next to her, but after unlocking her car with a loud BEEP!, she heard a familiar voice.

"Excuse me, Ms. St. Shatan? Can I get you to sign this, please? It's too big to bring into the store. I liked it when you killed-off Lordvark, by the way – who cares what the critics think... and, that's a pretty dress you're wearing." *I can't wait to rip it off!* he thought.

How would you feel if you were a "public figure" and discovered a fan had a life-size cutout of you that you didn't know existed? Especially if that fan was wearing loud orange socks and sweater, and was waiting for you in a van with no windows that he'd backed-in next to your car? If you are a normal horror writer at an out-of-town event, you might be frightened or flattered, but if you're Karisma St. Shatan you actually get in the van.

"Uh – okay – but, let's make it quick. I have to get back to my hotel. Where did you get this?" she asked, sitting inside the van's open side door. The huge cutout's stand was awkwardly wedged beneath the rear seat; Karisma leaned in a bit more to sign it, uncapping her Sharpie.

"You want it personalized, don't you?" *What a weirdo – what's that smell? …Doctor's office? Glad this dude is no telepath – I wouldn't want him inside my head!*

"Yes, of course," Earl said, barely concealing his glee. *That's it – lean in a little more… Damn, you're beautiful! You said you loved me in writing – what's the problem?*

"Well?" *…Bad dresser, slow on the uptake… What's your NAME, dufus?*

"Well, what?"… *Jesus!! She HAS to know my name! How can she love me if she doesn't even know my NAME?*

"I'm sorry. I forgot your name… I mean – there were so many people…" Karisma faltered as she caught the blood in his eye. *Now, I've done it…* She tried to jump out, but was off-balance and hit her head on the van's door frame. "Oww – don't touch me!"

"Liar!" the fan hissed, hooking an arm around her throat and pulling her down. Karisma tried to scream, but was muffled by an ether-soaked rag. *Who says drugs can't help you score on a date? I thought there'd be more of a struggle. Good. And, there's no-one around.* He shut the door, secured her, and drove away.

Earl's father, a television executive, had remodeled their hilltop home into a castle with a faux-stone façade, mock turrets, and a scalloped roofline: a familiar sight to cruisers of Mulholland Drive, the blacktop spine of the Hollywood Hills. Duke Kimble had died at fifty, leaving the castle and its grounds to his widow, Carlotta. She lasted another three years, before meeting her demise in the basement – a room since converted to Earl's "play-pit."

Soon, the loudly-attired kidnapper turned the van quietly into the castle's garage. When Karisma began to stir he gave her the rag again.

3.

"Where am I? Who the hell are...? Oh – it's *you*." Karisma said gasping, as she recognized Earl – or, "that guy in the orange sweater," as she'd thought of him that afternoon. The Fan. He was wearing a dark hooded robe now, over what looked like a black latex unitard. Feeling drugged, she scanned her new surroundings, images fading in-and-out of focus. She was lying on her back, her wrists and ankles manacled, outstretched. *This guy is really bughouse!* she thought, taking a deep breath. *The worst thing I can do now is panic.*

"You forgot my name," Earl said, screwing up his face like he was going to cry.

"Yeah – well, I do that. Think you could untie me now, please?" Karisma noticed the high ceiling and purple-gray stucco walls, painted with ghostly shapes that formed a ring around her. The shapes had narrow slits for eyes, and looked-down on the slab to which she was bound. This wacko – whoever he was – had recreated the dungeon motif from 1961's *Pit and the Pendulum*, minus the pendulum. A dark wooden staircase led upstairs, and in the corner sat an iron maiden, like the one Barbara Steele got locked in.

"Listen, Pally, I got bad circulation from smoking and this overhead striation is killing me, so untie me and I'll sign your little dick if you want."

"Oh, don't worry – you'll get your chance. I thought you said you loved me! How could you rub up against that stranger in the bookstore? LOVE?? 'To Earl, with love, Karisma St. Shatan,' you wrote – LIAR!! Did he infect you with his seed yet?"

"Infect me with his...? I fail to see how that's any of your concern. Have you been watching me?" She held him off with words, while trying to send a telepathic message to Todd – a brain-mail, if you will –

since this seemed an excellent time to explore their unique link. *Hopefully, Todd is within my psychic range, and hasn't picked-up another floozy yet. Boy, I really kind of blew him off back at the old bookstore – oh, well. Todd! Todd Raventhorpe! Wonder if that's his real name... Come in, Todd! Karisma to Todd! ...Mayday! ...MAYDAY!!*

Kimble pulled-up the hood on his black robe, trying to look as much like Vincent Price as possible, which wasn't much really, considering Price was a tall man. Crazy Kimble, as the neighborhood kids called Earl, was just five-five and weighed but twenty pounds more than his captive. The wolverine is not a particularly large animal, but it's the only one that kills for pleasure, besides twisted men like Earl Ray Kimble.

"My name is Earl, and I've built a shrine to you, upstairs in my room."

"Really?" The author of *Drink Me, Drink You* perked up. "That room wouldn't happen to be your bedroom, would it – *Earl?* Take me to your bedroom," she hissed through wet, red lips, trying to turn him on.

Her pale limbs struggled, as Karisma's teacup breasts spilled out of their silk prison; the tight, low-cut black mini-dress was held up by spider-web straps climbing to a choker. Black webbed stockings and red spike heels completed the illusion that Vampirella had just taken down Frederick's of Hollywood with a platinum card.

Unfortunately she was spread-eagled on a marble slab in the basement dungeon of a loony-tunes Poe freak. *All dressed-up and no place to go*, she thought. Karisma was no helpless femme. A degree from the University of Chicago informed her writing, and she was tough in the clinch, but right now she felt she couldn't breathe in this dank basement.

"I gave you something to help you breathe... slower," Earl Ray said. "And now, I have to kill you. I lied when I said you were right to kill off Lordvark in *Blood Brunch!* I just wanted to please you, to lure you here – but you had to ruin everything.

"Oh—I had it all planned: dinner and a movie. We would marry in the name of The Dark One, make passionate love till dawn – and *then* I'd kill you. But, you don't love me – you don't even know my name! After all those times we've been together – after all those book signings! 'To Earl, with love' ...BULLSHIT!! What kind of a monster are you?" He began to sob like a child.

"...Dinner and a movie?" Karisma asked sweetly, trying to charm him. "What movie are we gonna watch? Of course – *Pit and the Pendulum.*

Is that your favorite movie, Earl?" I *have to get out of this basement*, she screamed in her mind.

"No..." he said, selecting a large knife from the dozen horrific edged weapons in a handy wall-rack. He drug the blade softly along her breastbone, and then down, past her navel. Slowly, breathing wine and cheddar in her face, he hooked the tip of the knife under her hemline and pulled it up, ripping fabric. His muggy breath came faster, now.

He's getting turned-on — I can use that. Fortunately, one of Karisma's early jobs had been as a phone sex operator. Besides, she was a talented writer, a spinner of gossamer tales.

"*The Collector* is," he finally said, letting it sink in.

"Is what?" she asked, intent on the blade as it hooked under her black lace brassiere. "Careful there, Earl."

"...Is my favorite movie." *Go on — react!*

"Oh," she mumbled, thinking, *doesn't the girl die in The Collector?*

Then, Karisma began spinning a web of words, using characters and events from her Juliana Jestiny stories as bait, finally getting the slavering man-beast to bring her up to his bedroom, to the St. Shatan shrine, but not before getting another dose of the ether first. As Karisma faded-out she sent another brain-mail to Todd, and dreamed he faintly answered.

4.

When she awoke, she was laying on her back again, looking up at the stars. She could see the Hyades, in Taurus. Karisma knew the stars and could navigate by them, if necessary; they stood out in the big, moonless skylight. A bay window in the north wall framed the twinkling lights of the San Fernando Valley; they looked like jewels, spilled across a velvet carpet.

Her dress and undergarments were gone, this time she was spread-eagled to the four posts of a large bed, completely naked, and her abductor was standing over her. He was au natural, as well, and she could not help looking down. Looking down, she could not help but laugh, so he slapped her, amidst clumsily trying to mount her, and his lower body lost all interest.

"Damn you, woman! Juliana would never laugh at her lover. How can your books seem so real, while you're such a phony? I thought you were a real vampire, like me!" Earl slid off her and ran to a cabinet, poured something from a flask and turned back.

"This is real blood, watch me!" he said, quickly downing a goblet of what looked exactly like blood – then, promptly vomiting it into a wastebasket.

"Sexy move, Lord of the Dark..." Suddenly, Todd was in her mind, speaking in the language of her thoughts.

Where are you Karisma? Where can I find you?

She did a one-eighty in attitude, playing up to the freak again as he wiped his face. "Uh... what's the address here, Earl?"

"Why do you want to know?" He asked. "It's 6720 Broken Tortoise Drive, not that you'll live to tell anyone."

"I might send you a Halloween card – since you're such a Vincent Price fan."

She sent the brain-mail, and Todd would rescue her soon. He would prevent the otherwise, inevitable, grisly murder, and later they would write a story about it. Not afraid of this psycho – especially since she'd gotten out of that claustrophobic basement – Karisma remained calm as "Crazy" Kimble began to mount her again, his breath rank from puking.

"Only your Juliana books are real to me, my love," he said. "Please, do the scene from *Blood Brunch* with me? The one where...*Uhhh!* ...Lordvark seduces Juliana in the vestibule of Hades?" He maneuvered into a better position atop her. "I'll be Lordvark, okay? *Uhhh! —* 'Lie still, hussy from the Isle of Sirens, and surrender what's left of thy maidenhead to me!'"

The son-of-a-bitch is actually going to do it — Hell's bells, Karisma thought. What's taking so long tonight? Where's the damn..? … Ahhhh! Here it comes now… AHHHH!! …Better than an orgasm, opium, or any drug… the sweet, soft, caressing MOONLIGHT.

It filtered down from the skylight, from the now-visible edge of the full moon, its enchanted, nocturnal rays finding her, vulcanizing her, *immortalizing* her.

Dark hairs sprung from tiny pores; nails grew, twisted, and curled. He wasn't looking at her just then; like so many men, his face was buried in the pillow — beside that other, rippling, changing face. Too bad for Earl the author hadn't made it back to her hotel room as planned; be careful what you wish for.

He raised-up to look at her — they were both panting now — and, as the moonlight washed over her pale breasts, they too, sprouted course black hairs, as did her lengthening snout.

"What the f…?" He said, as she grinned dog-like, blowing that dog-breath all canines have into his predatory face. *What the hell is happening to her? Am I dreaming? Wake up! Wake the fuck up!!* Karisma's hands and feet ripped themselves from the bedposts as they twisted into huge, grotesque paws. Then, she flipped her abductor over, pinning him to his own bed. As the worm turns, so turns the worm.

"Let me go! NO! Your face…? *Noooooo…..!!!"* Her eyes turned yellow; their pupils narrowing to vertical slits, as fangs burst from blackened gums. A low growl began to build in the back of Karisma's throat as she bared those jagged daggers of bone, drooling ropy strands of spittle. *Not the face!* he thought.

She bit hard, hooking his lip — stretching it till it snapped free, like a rubber band, spraying red. Then, she took several bites from his jack-o-lantern face, but left his eyes so he could watch her chew. She let gravity provide the resistance, like a big dog getting a whole can of food in one bite, dropping it inside the mouth with an upward jerk to better chew. Karisma also left Earl's throat intact so he could keep SCREAMING. It was sweet music to her pointed, furry ears after having heard his psycho-babble all night.

He watched horrified as the dreadful visage slowly dragged itself down his body, leaving a river of blood and saliva. His view was hindered by the crimson fountain, pumping where his nose used to be – but, Earl could feel her going down past his belly button. Down…

5.

"Pass the blunt," said Kevin. The neighborhood kids often sat on the rocks outside Crazy Kimble's castle just to hear the screams of the hookers he liked to beat.

"Here – keep it down. If my mom catches us…" Another blood-curdling scream split the night – only tonight it was not a hooker being abused. Whispering, Mike said, "What's he doing up there, anyway?"

"Shit! … Just *listen* to that!"

"Dude!!

"I *know!*"

They heard the sound of something crashing out a window on the other side of the stone wall surrounding Kimble's castle. …Something big.

Suddenly, a great gray she-wolf leapt over that wall and landed right in front of the stoned pair. Her jaws ran red, and shaking her huge head, she tossed something bloody to the ground, growled at the youths, and bounded across Mulholland into the tree-line.

"Did you see that, Kevin?"

"Prolly a coyote… we get 'em up here all the time."

"That was no coyote – that was a fucking *wolf!*"

"Look, Mike – over here! It dropped something… looks like a bloody hot dog."

"No way – it's a chicken neck – see!" Mike flashed his Mini-Mag-lite on the ground.

"…A *circumcised* chicken neck," said Kevin.

Epilogue

His breath came in bursts as he ran up the hillside. They had barely met, and she was so beautiful! …So special. They shared a unique bond, and Todd wanted her like no other. But right now his only concern was getting to her in time: according to the message she'd sent, this was a matter of dire consequence.

Karisma stepped out into the narrow trail – on all four feet. Todd stopped dead, thinking her name, *Karisma?* He approached cautiously; she growled low and sexy.

Todd? she said, telepathically.

The Griffith Observatory

Yeah, Baby. You look great. Brushing against her sleek fur, his wet nose eventually found her crotch. She did the same, but more demurely. *Am I too late?* he thought.

Slightly.

He's dead, then?

Very.

So, you've already eaten. I was hoping we could grab a bite later.

I'll be hungry again after we mate all night, rolling in the cool California grass, basking in this glorious, golden MOONLIGHT.

Howling, they ran side-by-side, crashing through the lunar-lit chaparral, cresting Mount Hollywood past the Griffith Observatory, crossing over to the city side of the Hills. They ran west, where an endless sea of light-grids – blinking red, gold, and periwinkle blue – stretched all the way to San Pedro and the Pacific Ocean.

After tearing a pack of coyotes to shreds just for drill, they finally stopped at the Hollywood Sign, and made sweet, undead, lupine love in the shadow of the big "W." With the hyper senses of the Eternal Wolf they could smell the steaks grilling at The Derby down on Franklin Avenue, and see the landing lights at LAX, miles and miles away.

Very… cinematic. …Did he really love you, my sweet?

I sincerely doubt it.

Why?

I wasn't this yo-yo's first rodeo.

How do you know that?

Well, for one thing, he had Rhonda's ROTTING, FRIGGIN' HEAD ON MY ALTAR.

…Humans! thought Todd, scratching at a flea.

AFTERWORD

This is the least popular story in the collection, having been rejected in its original form by two magazines in 2000, and criticized by several horror writers, including the late, Gary "The Howling" Brandner. I asked Mr. Brandner for a blurb on the story, and he was only too kind to give me the backhanded compliment, "Any story with sex and violence and creatures of the night can't be all bad."

In his letter, he also said I had a "good touch for dialogue, and the milieu of pretentious goth horror writers is ripe for satire… but…" He thought my including a book signing or mentioning fanzines was asking too much of the reader's knowledge – and, I completely disagree. He also felt I had chosen to write in a difficult genre, combining humor and horror – but, that's WHAT I DO! Mr. Brandner's insight did help me with the re-write, and I wish to thank him here.

Yes, I bash hell out of the black-clad, pretentious "horror" personalities with their ridiculous, made-up monikers. I mean, how insecure in one's abilities does one have to be to fabricate a *horror* name to succeed in the *horror* market? What are they going to do if they decide to spread out to other genres some day? H.P. Lovecraft and Algernon Blackwood were damn lucky to be born with those names – they almost had to become fantasy writers.

On the plus side, I love the romantic ending – hope you did, too. *Woof!*

In The Day

Chapter One: The Past Perfect

"Tear out the front page."

"What?"

"Tear out the front page – lose everything above the fold."

"It's nine o'clock already, Bart. ...Okay – you're the editor," Ted Bayliss said, looking at his watch, "but let's get it into typesetting, ASAP." Ted was art director and production manager of the *L.A. Free Voice*, and the new owners had made clear their dislike of having to pay the tiny production staff to work late, just because the editor preferred to wait until the rest of the paper was finished to write his own column.

"*The Froice*," as it was affectionately called, had been the first underground paper in the country. Thus, it was highly respected, and Terry Dorn was proud to be an artist on the staff. He moved closer to editor, Bart Gunkin, and his boss, wordlessly watching.

"This is different, Ted. I wrote my column last night, had it set this morning, the front page has been done since six. Now *tear it out* – you're not gonna believe this – it's still coming in over the wire from the "*Post*." Burglars were caught bugging the Democratic headquarters in the Watergate Hotel, and two of them had Howard Hunt's phone number in their wallets – Hunt's an ex-spook who works for Charles Colson!"

*The actual Los Angeles Free Press offices, next to the World Theater
with its bargain matinees, circa 1974*

*Artist Tom Nikosey, L. J. Dopp, and Tina Saddington, in the real L.A. Free
Press city room during the press conference called by Joanna Harcourt-Smith, the day
after her husband, Timothy Leary, was arrested in Afghanistan (1972).
Photo by Shary Bowman*

"So, who's Charles Colson?" asked Kip Van Nuys, music editor.

"Special counsel to the president..." Bart said, not looking at him.

"Nixon's mouthpiece?" Terry asked, butting in.

"Yeah, guys. Nixon's lawyer. Who else would bug the Democrats but the Republicans? You think the Panthers would do this? Or the Weathermen? There may be hope for this election yet."

"Stinkin' Republicans..." Terry muttered, begging acceptance.

A few weeks later, Terry turned his Rambler off Franklin and drove down Gower to Hollywood Boulevard, taking his usual route to work. The World Theatre marquee displayed its bargain double-bill in battered, red plastic letters: "LAST HOUSE ON LEFT, and BRAINMAKER."

Terry turned into the driveway next door, parked in the back lot, and entered the one-story *Free Voice* building. He walked down the few steps that passed the receptionist's cubicle, pausing to say hi.

"Morning, Terry," Laurie said, grinning. "How was Big Sur?"

"Incredible." Terry watched her breasts jiggle as she typed – there probably weren't two bras in the whole *Free Voice* office in the summer of 1972; Madras dresses – or halter tops and cut-offs – comprised the "girls'" wardrobe for the most part, and Laurie liked to wear the most outrageous skimpy halters and see-through blouses in the entire hippie headquarters, which was saying quite a lot.

"...Rough night?" Terry asked, staring blatantly, now.

"We dropped last night – and hiked up to the Hollywood sign." Leaning over to reach the switchboard, she gave him the whole show. "*Free Voice*," she said into her headset. "Yeah, Jesse's in – I'll put you through..." One of her breasts popped out for a second as she leaned back again; its nipple taunting him.

"Laurie, your boobs are as perfect as the ones I draw for the massage parlor ads."

"Don's in Venice all day – we can have lunch at my place... if you feel like drawing on your lunch hour..."

"I'd rather draw on you."

"We've got body paints... God, Terry, you're blushing!" She checked out the little red-painted heart on her cheek in his mirrored shades.

"Shh!" he hissed. "No, I fell asleep in front of the sunlamp again. Gimme a rain check, Laurie. Sharon insists on balling the shit out of me every morning before I come to work – 'specially since that party at Lynda's where everyone was skinny-dipping in the pool. She doesn't trust me with you girls... undrained."

"Sharon's smart. Bring her, too – *Free Voice*," she said again, "I think he's in, you wanna hold an' I'll put you through?" This time as she leaned forward she demurely covered her cleavage, giving him the *I-can-see-you-trying-to-look-at-my-tits-you-male-chauvinist-pig* look; hell hath no fury like a woman scorned.

Terry clocked in and headed for the art department. He was the third one in.

"... Morning," he said, sitting at his table. There was a memo taped to its sloping, rubber-coated surface. It was addressed to Ted from Bart: "Need a Nixon cartoon to go with this quote." Clipped to the memo was a Nixon comment from a few years before: "Any president who can't bring about peace in four years should not be given another chance." *Hang him with his own rope*, Terry thought, *right on!*

A couple of months away from the November '72 election, the *Free Voice*, *The Berkeley Bomb*, *The Surrealist*, and New York's *Village Vanguard*, were hammering away at the incumbent president, using lead coverage of what became known as "The Watergate scandal" provided by *The Washington Post* as the basis of their attacks. The rest of the mainstream media was definitely slow, probably reluctant, and possibly afraid to join the anti-Nixon throng.

Next to the art department were the writers' desks. Rob Ribenhauser – a self-proclaimed Marxist, and easily the most radical of the lefty scribes – was pontificating.

"Nixon actually dragged out the conclusion of the Vietnam War until right before the election – at a cost of thousands of more lives – just to look good to the voters for calling 'our boys' back home. By ending the war, he also ripped off the Democrats' greatest rallying point without giving them time to find another one! By January, all U.S. troops are supposed to be out of Vietnam, leaving the South Vietnamese holding the bag – but, so what? The great fascist, *Nixon*, will begin his second term – brilliant, unless you have a conscience! Who cares if a bunch of third world dirt-farmers are dog food for the Viet Cong? Kennedy did the same thing at the Bay of Pigs – ran, and didn't look back. Capitalism just doesn't work, no matter who has the reins of power..."

"Put a lid on it, Ribenhauser – you lay a 'pinko' twist on everything," Terry said.

About that time, the least respected writer on the staff, the mad poet, Henry Pukowsky, arrived, dropping off his "Scribblings of a Perverted Dipsomaniac" column at the assistant editor's desk.

"You're early this week, Hank," Dick Dawber said.

"I need to pay my tab," Pukowsky mumbled, heading for the administrative office where he'd pick up his check. Then, he'd cash it at the East Hollywood liquor store that floated him week-to-week, return home, drink all afternoon and get bombed, fight with his girlfriend if he had one at the time, pass out, wake up, vomit copiously, and repeat the procedure till he ran out of cash and credit. Then, necessity being the mother of intervention, Henry Pukowsky, without a hint of pretension, would churn out another fascinating and hilarious – if occasionally vulgar – prose elegy to the tragi-comic alcoholic horseplayer, while metaphorically chronicling the extinction of the "beat generation iconoclast" in early '70s, American blue-collar culture.

"Puke is early this week – at least no plug," Stefan, a Czech-born artist said, smiling. Stefan was nearly always smiling because he was fucking glad he didn't have to live in a communist country any more.

"Yeah," Terry said. Stefan was referring to the occasional production night when Bart would get *the phone call*, turn to the room and announce, "Run the plug, guys, Pukowsky's on a binge again." And, the production team would do just that – paste a wax-encrusted stat on the page, reading:

"There will be no 'Scribblings of a Perverted Dipsomaniac' column this week – Mr. Pukowsky is on a binge."

You could call him "Puke," and his friends called him, "Hank," but if you called him "Mr. Pukowsky" – in those days he'd probably have run, thinking you were a bill collector or something.

"I hope the whole country figures out what crooks the Republicans are," said Ribbenhauser, "after this Watergate scandal."

"On that I agree." Terry said, squaring and taping a fresh sheet of drawing paper to his table. "So another Nixon cartoon, great – where's Ted?"

"In Bart's office," Stefan said, cracking up. "You're so stoned when you come in, man – you have to wear those glasses for an hour, you're eyes are so red."

"… Am not – I just have sensitive eyes. Plus, I got fried by the sunlamp again." Terry removed his mirrored aviators, revealing the white, mask-shaped area around his eyes left by the sunlamp goggles.

"Those are pretty big pupils, Terry," Glenda said. "And, you look like a negative racoon." She and Johnny Nakota were the other artists on the staff, five in all with Stefan – including Ted, their boss.

"You guys comin' to the gig?" Johnny asked.

"Where is it again?"

"The Bitter End on Santa Monica…" Glenda said.

"You mean that gay bar?" Terry said, laughing. "You guys should be a big hit."

"His band is cuter than your band, Terry – except for you, of course."

"Yeah – 'Firefox' should burn down the house, Glenda – like it's not flaming enough already." *They're playing a gay bar!* Terry Thought. *Thank God, we haven't had to do that yet.*

"The Bitter End has a lot of straight customers…"

"… They follow you straight into the bathroom," Stefan said, grinning.

"I'll go before I leave the house," Terry said. He noticed Sandra the bookkeeper trying to get his attention from across the busy room, which housed sales, editorial, and production. He signaled back, excusing himself from the art department; but, halfway through the writers – whose typewriters *clack-clacked* like machine-guns – he was collared again by Ribenhauser.

"Did you hear? Hunt, Liddy and the five burglars were indicted on federal charges today?"

"That's great, Rob – excuse me a minute…"

"Come here, Terry," Sandra said, pulling him into the dumpy little lounge outside the women's restroom. After making sure there was no-one inside to hear her secret, she sat him on the dingy sofa and whispered intently.

"It's Andre! Since you've been gone to Big Sur – just in this last week – it's like he's become a completely different person!"

"What do you mean?"

"I mean he's different!" she said, her eyes tearing up. "He's cold… emotionless. Like a… a… Republican! He eats different food, doesn't remember his own filing system – for a controller, he's totally out of control but cool as ice about it."

Nixon admits aides attempted to hide Watergate involvement
Caulfield says clemency offer came from Dean

"Take it easy, San. You didn't happen to drop acid with Laurie and Don last night, did you?" She looked at him, shaking her head, wiping tears.

"No – I didn't. I'm not on anything. Andre is different, that's all. Watch him, Terry."

"I hardly ever see him – you guys work in the other room, with the brass…"

"I'd better get back, before he notices I'm gone."

She left, and Terry started out the door. Suddenly, intent hands grabbed him, pushing him back into the women's lounge – tanned, supple hands belonging to Dana Kaczinski, a Polish-born ad salesman who was always after him. At twenty-four, Dana was still a mysterious older woman to Terry; her European attitudes and sexual frankness scared him.

"So why can't I fuck you?" she said in her thick accent, pushing him down on the sofa, sitting on his lap. Dana was wearing a transparent silk blouse with long puffed sleeves, that day. Twin breast pockets provided a second gauzy layer and some stitching, at least, to hold her impudent nipples in check. "You can keep your girlfriend, I don't care – I just want to fuck."

Her left breast rubbed his cheek. Warm, it jostled against him puppy-like, while her perfume shrieked like the sirens' wail. He jerked his head back from her as droplets of sweat began to roll down his back. "*Here?* You can't be serious!"

"You don't want to fuck here? We can go to apartment."

Laurie entered the lounge suddenly. "Whoa!" she said. "Sorry if I'm interrupting anything, but, I have to pee – *Jesus!*" She nearly tripped over Terry's deerskin boots, hidden as they were by his voluminous bell-bottoms. The receptionist stared ceremonial daggers at him as she entered the can. SLAM! went the door behind her.

Hell hath no fury... well, you know. Terry jumped to his feet, dumping Dana on the floor.

"So – you like it rough?" Dana said, laughing. Her accent oddly reminded him of Natasha from Rocky and Bullwinkle. He headed back to the art department, flattered, but determined not to be cornered again by the Warsaw Bombshell.

What if Sharon had somehow walked in on us instead of Laurie? he thought, *like if she'd just shown up at the office to meet for lunch and had to use the can? Girlfriends do that kind of stuff... Or what if I WAS balling Laurie on the side, Laurie caught me with Dana – and she ratted me out to Sharon for revenge!* He took his seat again. *That doobie on the way in is making me paranoid – lunch isn't for two more hours yet so that scenario couldn't have happened.*

A good-looking young dude had to be careful, even in the day. *The day* in this case was one of free love – or, free sex – before the day when the mere act and its variations would carry the price tag of potential death. The day was one of German beer, gin-and-tonics and grass, and not the day of cirrhosis, mutant prostates and emphysema.

Terry re-read Bart Gunkin's memo and started sketching – a reference photo wasn't necessary for him to draw Nixon; he started by roughing out the ovals of the figure with an oversize head and tiny body. I'll make his mouth look like an asshole...

The following Saturday, sunbeams streaked Terry's bedroom, making Sharon's long hair glisten red-gold when caught in one particular diagonal ray that angled across the waterbed. That beam was multi-colored, piercing the pane right where a faux stained-glass, vinyl butterfly applique had been positioned, and it caught Sharon's hair and pale breasts as she rocked forward, bouncing astride Terry, making love in the afternoon.

"*Ohh... Ohhhhh!... Oh, God – Oh, GOD!! – Ohhhhhh GODDDDDDD!!!*"

"... The neighbors definitely heard that one – unless they're deaf." Reaching for her bouncing B-cups Terry happened to look up – but it was Dana Kaczinski's face that leered down at him. *Gaaaak!"* he screamed, as Sharon melted, her orgasmic energy spent. He let go of her chest puppies like they were hot potatoes, rolling out from under her, sweaty and trembling with guilt.

"I think I just had one of those flashbacks they're always promising us."

"Well, *slam-bam*..." Sharon said, a little hurt by his abruptness.

"Sorry – I'd love to cuddle, but we've gotta get ready for the party. I'm supposed to play a few songs with Johnny."

"I guess if I'm going to live with a musician, I'd better get used to coming second."

"...You came first that time."

"That's not what I meant," she said, smiling slightly.

That night there were no spaces on Primrose, so Terry and Sharon parked on a sloping side street and walked back to Bart's. The eclectic editor had a rambling old, two-story stucco in the Hollywood Hills a couple of canyons over from the famous sign. Members of the staff and their significant others were conversing – drinks and a few joints in hand – milling around Bart's yard and throughout the big, comfortable house.

"Terry and Sharon!" Ted called from the den, "the bar's over here."

"You read my mind..." Terry's voice trailed at the sight of Laurie approaching in a completely see-through dress.

"A... hi, Laurie..." He tried not to stare.

"Terry and... *Sherry*, is it?" Laurie said, needling.

"Sharon." Terry's girlfriend said, trying not to glare at Laurie. Then, she shot Terry one of those sideways, "are-you-fucking-this-cheap-slut-behind-my-back?" looks, and they were sucked into a cloud of pot-smoke and patchouli, swallowed by the tide of revelers.

A little later, disappointed that the guitar jam with Johnny Nakota had been called off, Terry found himself pulled into the pantry by Carol, Johnny's girlfriend. Carol had a Brooklyn accent like Johnny and the rest of his band, and she was really upset.

"Does Johnny seem different to you tonight, Terry?"

"What do you mean, different?" An alarm bell went off in Terry's mind. He flashed on Kevin McCarthy in the 1956 *Invasion of the Body Snatchers*. Playing Dr. Miles Bennell, he had experienced the same complaints from his fellow townsfolk – after returning from a road trip *just like Terry had*.

"He's not Johnny! – He din' even remember I'm a vegetarian! And in the bedroom… well, it's kinda personal – but, he's changed, believe me! He tol' you he couldn't jam with you 'cause he sprained his finger – but that's bullshit! I don't think this Johnny can even play the guitar. He ain't even touched it for three days – they had to cancel the gig at the Bitter End – Terry, he even *talks different!*" She sobbed, falling against his chest in the shadows of the little room off the kitchen. Suddenly, Johnny walked in, smiling sardonically.

"So, Terry – making time with my old lady, huh? Come on Carol, we should be getting home – it's late." Johnny peeled the trembling girl off of Terry and led her away.

He does sound different – his accent has changed.

Back in the den, the writers were gathered around the bar, spirits guiding their voices to greater heights. "I think Nixon is probably innocent of this Watergate business," Rob Ribenhauser said, knocking back a brewski. "And, anyway, the Republicans have an obligation to keep track of what the liberals are up to – it's from the left that we can fear internal collapse, from runaway spending and coddling the unemployed with handouts."

"From the left we can fear internal collapse?" Bart Gunkin said in shock, the whites of his eyes brightening the room. "This is the same Rob Ribenhauser that was denouncing Nixon and capitalism in general three days ago?"

"Yeah," Terry said. "The big Marxist turns pro-Republican? What gives, Rob?"

"I never said I was a Marxist – I said I liked the Marx *Brothers* – there's a difference."

A difference! Terry thought. *Is this what Sandra and Carol were talking about?*

"Hey, Terry – you want to take a run up to Bronson Cave and see the movie set?" Johnny asked. Rob echoed the invitation.

"Yeah, man, you gotta see this spaceship they built – it's right out of *"Close Encounters!"* Johnny elbowed Ron, shaking his head, no.

"Close *what…*?" Terry looked at Sharon. "You wanna go for a ride, cutie?"

"Think I'll stay here," she said, "I feel a little buzzed to be riding around right now." Right then, Terry noticed Barry Krautman, the sales director, circling her like a shark.

"Maybe some other time, guys... I'm staying here with my lady." Terry watched the predator migrate into the kitchen, looking for un-guarded prey. He wasn't insecure – just not overly stupid, and kissed Sha-ron on the cheek to mark his territory.

"Totally whipped," Johnny smirked. Off in the corner, Carol was drinking doubles, watching Johnny through a mask of horror.

A few weeks later Nixon and Agnew were re-elected by over 60% of the popular vote. Somewhat dismayed, the liberal/radical underground press valiantly continued the struggle to dethrone their tyrant. More in-dictments came down that lead, like a trail of rancid bread crumbs, straight to the White House.

But something else was happening in the underground press; other artists and writers were jumping the fence and creating pro-Nixon articles and cartoons! *The Village Vanguard* ran an editorial urging the rad-ical left to cool it on Watergate, and Saul Krasnick of *The Surrealist* even spoke of Nixon's great statesmanship regarding *future* trade talks with China.

And, at *The Froice*, more staffers were turning conservative. Mili-tant "Afro-American" writer, Ellswood Garth, went soft on the right wing and so did assistant editor Dick Dawber. Meanwhile, Johnny Nakota's whole drawing style had changed since Bart's party, and editor Gunkin had twice refused to run his pro-Nixon panels.

Laurie and Dana stopped wearing see-through fabrics – and worse – they stopped hitting on Terry. Dana mysteriously managed to lose her Polish accent, and once Terry overheard her talking about how much she missed her personal computer! The only computer he had ever seen was the big, refrigerator-sized blue tower in the production department that housed the IBM typesetting "brain."

Other *Froice* staffers tried to get Terry to go see the movie space-ship. One day after lunch, Barry Krautman drove Terry up to Bronson Canyon. The cartoonist had downed a couple of Martinis and didn't want to hike up the huge dirt embankment that led to the caves. Besides, he was afraid: this almost *had* to be connected with the "differences" in his friends and co-workers... didn't it?

"What's the big deal?" he asked Barry. "Why does everyone want me to see this spaceship or whatever it is? It's just like that airplane in the fake snow they had up here for the *Lost Horizon* remake. That one hasn't come out yet, has it?"

Bronson Caves

"Quit changing the subject, old son," Barry said. "Let's go."

After testing Barry with a half-dozen details of their past that only the real Barry could know, Terry and *The Froice* sales director finally reached the famous, blasted-out caves that have graced the screen in hundreds of B-thrillers and westerns.

A large spacecraft set that vaguely resembled a Mixmaster stood at the entrance, where a security guard led a couple of hippie chicks out, through the temporary barricade. Terry recognized Sandra the bookkeeper and Glenda from the art department as they came closer.

"What's in the cave, San?"

"Everything's all right, now, Terry. With Andre, I mean – I don't know what I was thinking. Hurry up – you won't believe the special effects inside." She rummaged through her purse and said, "Have you got a cigarette, Glenda?"

Sandra always smokes cigars! Terry thought, panicking. He tried to turn around, but Barry blocked his path; then, the guard had him by the arm.

"Bring him inside," Ted Bayliss said, standing in the mouth of the cave. Barry grabbed Terry's other arm, as the artist's screams echoed off the hills.

"No! Not me! I don't wanna turn into a… a…*Republican!* I don't wanna lose my emotions, and not care about the sick and the poor and cute little animals, anymore!"

"What do you mean?" Ted said. "We love cute little animals… It's just the sick and the poor that we don't give a shit about!" Everybody but Terry laughed like B-movie villains and the three men drug him into the cave.

"It's not so bad, Terry," Glenda said as she and Sandra turned to leave. "You won't feel a thing… for *anybody.*"

A long, tunnel-like portion of the spaceship set extended far into one of the twin rocky caverns that branched off Bronson Cave's main entrance; tubes of purple and red light lined chrome extrusions that, like an armadillo's plates, overlapped each other along the tunnel's sides. Clear plex windows were set in the top half of the extrusions, so that whatever occurred on the inside could be viewed.

"Let me go! I won't tell anybody! *Barry?* Don't tell me you're one of them? You can't be! You remembered watching that Steelers game at The Bagpipe, and the time we saw Samantha Eggar at The Source!"

"No, I'm not one of the 'transposed' ones, Terry – but, I'm a 'mutual.'"

"…A *'mutual?'*"

"Those of us who are chosen to serve the Vulgarians – the new masters of Earth – but, still keep our own souls," Barry explained.

"There are six ambassadors from the planet Vulgaria on our world right now, and they hold the key to time travel, among other handy scientific advances," said Ted. "Unlike Barry, I am one of the transposed ones. The mind and soul of Ted Bayliss exists 29 years in the future – in my real body. Allow me to introduce myself: I'm actually the mind and soul of Brent Timberlane, from the year 2001, currently inhabiting the body of Ted Bayliss in your year, 1972."

"So, you're a… a… *Republican from the future?"* Terry said, shaking off his Martini buzz, looking around for a way out. Suddenly, he could hear screaming; it was Stefan, the Czech artist, and two 'mutuals' from circulation were pushing him into the neon-lit tunnel through a door at the far end. His cries were somewhat muted by the enclosure.

"Let me go!" *Please!* – I don't do nothing! – why you put me in here?"

"Behold, the Vulgarian ambassador to Hollywood, Bhleau-jhabb the *Unbeatable!*" Ted said, or rather, Brent-inhabiting-Ted's-body said.

"*Blow-job* the Unbeat...?"

"*NO, NO, YOU PUNY LIBERAL...!*" said a deep, tremulous voice from the rock. "The name is Bhleau-jhabb... the Unbeatable." The wall of Bronson Cave melted open, parting just enough to allow a huge, rugose cone-shaped creature to emerge.

Terry couldn't believe his eyes – and neither could poor Stefan in the tunnel. The Vulgarian ambassador looked like a giant conical hedgehog. Its tiny head and great, sloping body were covered in pointy spines like a porcupine. A ring of lavendar tentacles writhed around its neck, and movie dry-ice smoke lolled over the ground, wafting out from the vestibule in the rock where Bhleau-jhabb the Unbeatable lived – or, at least where it was staying while in Tinseltown.

"Why are you doing this?" Terry screamed.

"What a cliché," rumbled the alien creature, as it reached out with one of its four backwards-bending arms and threw a big electrical switch on the cavern wall. A blue corona surged from the switch-plate, flickering down the wall and across the dirt floor, following the conduit. When the blue lightning hit the transformer box on the outside of the structure, the interior began to pulsate with an eerie, cobalt glow and a droning hum. Stefan's body shrieked mindlessly – as his *mind* was literally jerked out of it and flew wraith-like down the length of the chrome corridor.

A similar mind-spirit passed through Stefan's going in the other direction, both specters screeching at the moment of overlap; then, Stefan's wraith disappeared into the ship, and the other spirit flew into Stefan's body – which suddenly stood upright, cleared its throat, and looked around.

"What the hell are you doing? Why *us*? Why the underground press?" Terry yelled, as Krautman and Brent-inhabiting-Ted's-body dragged him down to the end of the tunnel.

"Stop struggling!" Barry shouted. "There... that's better. You should be happy you get to see the future – you're a cartoonist. I don't get to be *transposed*, 'cause I'm just an ad salesman. The Vulgarians say we don't influence people's minds enough, but accounting got to go – and *Dana!* – That 'Warsaw Bombshell' fucked her way to the future!"

Brent-inhabiting-Ted's-body cleared his throat. "The hippie art-ists and writers of the underground press are being 'transposed' with the mind-spirits of Republican volunteers from 2001 – to stop the wave of negative Watergate coverage that will spread to the mainstream media and eventually... cause President Nixon to resign."

"Nixon resigns in the future?" Terry mused, "Right on."

"Not if we can change history," Brent/Ted said. The door at the tunnel's end opened, and the new Stefan emerged.

"And we *can*," said the Republican-from-the-future-inhabiting-Stefan's-body.

"*No!!* – I won't go! I'll *tell* in the future. I'll blow the whistle on what you're doing up here," Terry hollered, struggling again.

"On what we *will have done*, you mean," Brent/Ted smirked, "be-cause this will all have happened 29 years in the past. No-one will believe you anyway, and Richard Nixon will have been honored all those years for having been a great president – or, rather, the Vulgarian ambassador to Washington who's inhabiting his body will be honored..."

"'Sneau-jhabb the Prevaricator' – my brother-in-law," said the Vulgarian, picking its nose with a lavender tentacle.

"You've... *transposed* the mind and soul of Richard Nixon? And, a space-alien – like this – is running the free world? Then, where is the soul of the real Tricky Dick?"

"In the body of Sharmayne DuValle, in the San Fernando Valley of 2001," Brent/Ted said, laughing.

"But, if you're Republicans, how can you do that to Nixon?"

"*We're* not doing it – the Vulgarians are. They're taking over the world anyway, and they've assured us it'll be for the 'greater good.' Better that Nixon be *remembered* for having been great, than for him to actually have been great. And besides – our world will be much better off, when run by... conservatives from outer space!"

Brent/Ted opened the door to the chrome tunnel. Barry and the new Stefan pushed Terry into the structure and Brent/Ted locked the door.

"But if you're not... 'transposed,' Barry – then why are you help-ing them? What are you getting out of all this? And, why did the city let 'em occupy Bronson Cave?"

"Well, old son, they promised to let us 'mutuals' help 'em rule the world, take other people's property and... women – stuff like that. So, we pulled permits for the location, just like a movie company."

"Who's going to inhabit my body while I'm gone? More importantly, who's gonna be doin' my old lady??"

"Your body's going to be owned and operated by a 'Log Cabin' Republican from 2001... who's queer as a three-dollar bill."

"No!!" cried Terry as Bhleau-jhabb the Unbeatable threw the big switch on the cavern wall.

"Yesss!" said Barry Krautman, "and I get to move in on Sharon."

"NoooooooooooOOOOOOOOOO!!!!!!!!!" screamed Terry's mind-spirit as it was ripped from his slender frame, and flew hurtling, hurtling, down a tunnel 29 years long.

Chapter Two: The Future Present

Terry stood up and brushed himself off. Looking around the cave, he saw a smaller, cheaper version of the chrome tunnel, made out of inflated plastic like the sides of a doughboy pool.

"Barry? ... Ted? Or, whatever your Republican name is..." He ran his hand through his long hair – which was gone! "What th...? I'm fuckin' bald! They gave me a damn crew-cut! He looked down and gasped at the wrinkled skin on his tanned arms. Terry was wearing a sleeveless sweatshirt with bare-midriff, short cut-offs, some kind of fancy tennis shoes – with rolled-down apricot socks! "Christ! I'm dressed like a *fruit*! I've got a purse around my waist!"

Terry felt his face – it was wrinkled, too. He took a few steps and got dizzy – walking had never been this hard before! It was as if he were in heavier gravity.

I feel like I'm twenty years older!

"*Bry-ice?*" a wispy voice echoed, stretching the name into two syllables. "Are you in here!?" The owner of the voice entered Bronson Cave; he was whisper-thin, middle-aged, and dressed like Terry's host body.

"There you are!" he said, approaching. "What's the matter, Bryce?" The man touched Terry/Bryce affectionately.

"Hey! – watch it, pal – no *hands!* And my name is Terry. Terry Dorn. What in hell is going on around here? Who are you? And who is this *Bryce* that you keep calling me?"

"Stop it, you're scaring me."

"I'm serious!"

"You know I hate it when you do this. You're so mean to me. Where's Antoine?"

"You think *you* don't know what's going on?"

"*Okay!* – I'll go wait in the car. You said you had to meet Antoine at Bronson Cave. You said to wait twenty minutes and then come get you."

"I don't even know you! I've never met you in my life! Where is the big spaceship set? And, Barry Krautman? – That bird-dogging S.O.B! He's trying to nail my girlfriend back in 1972! It's all coming back to me now. It must be true, then. This must be the future, and I'm in somebody else's body!!" The other man was making tracks, hands over his ears, jamming Terry's transmission with baby-talk gibberish.

"I'm not listening – na-na-na-na-na-na…"

"Shut up and talk to me!!"

"Na-na-na-na-na-na…"

"Goddamn it!" Terry yelled in his host-body's voice, running stiffly after his apparent friend. "Listen to me!" He grabbed the smaller man, spinning him face-to-face.

"Aiiiiiiieeeee! I love it when you get butch – there's no-one around." The other man scanned the cavern. "Take me right here, you animal…"

"Listen, for God's sake! I'm not this Bryce guy – okay? Let me guess. He's a – what was it? Oh, yeah – a '*Log Cabin*' Republican, right? Well, his mind and spirit went willingly back in time to inhabit my body and save President Nixon – except he's not the *real* Nixon – and my mind and spirit came here, against my will – *see?*"

"… I don't like this game, Bryce. You're making me very uncomfortable."

"Didn't he tell you? See, I'm not him – I'm just inside his body. It's not so… it's not so hard to… Oh, for God's sake, don't *cry!*"

After awhile, Terry/Bryce managed to get from "David" that Bryce had advised him not to panic if the latter seemed different upon returning from the famous cave. But the 21st Century '*Log Cabin*' Republican had said nothing to his Libertarian partner about switching bodies via the transposing! Terry-in-Bryce's-body asked David all about life in the year 2001, marveling at the new cars – particularly the S.U.V.s, which he called space-Jeeps.

David was humoring his weird-acting partner, thinking it was merely a bizarre game Bryce – apparently the dominant one of the pair – was playing. David even drove down Hollywood Boulevard to humor him, past the old *Free Voice* office – which was now, however, just another blank, empty-looking building on the once-bustling street.

"I don't believe it! The Broadway's gone – and Aldo's Coffee Shop! The Haunted House is a peep show, all the regular theatres are closed except The Vine, and the big neon Coca-Cola sign is gone!" They rolled on, past Wilcox, past Las Palmas, toward Highland, and Terry shed a borrowed tear.

"…The bars are all gone… and Dugally's – both of 'em. And, Magoo's is gone! Where are all the long-hairs and the head shops? …The Gemini? …The Scented Gift Garden? All gone. …*Gone forever!!*"

Terry wept through Bryce, then: deep, racking, Liza-with-a-'Z' sobs that drowned his last hopes for a lost generation. *This "David" must be the Ghost of Christmas Future, he thought, and that diminutive wino, spouting prose over a hand-lettered star on the Walk of Fame, oblivious to all but the wine bottle in his hand, looks like…   God! It looks like an older, rummy version of that sci-fi guy who writes – or, wrote – a column for* The Froice! *What's his name? I've forgotten already.*

It was an eerie scene. Thunder cracked and rumbled high above the Hills, and a cloud shaped like Mickey Mouse's head cast a purple shadow over the concrete landscape. The sensitive pair continued on, passing La Brea.

When they got to Bryce and David's apartment in West Hollywood, there was an envelope addressed to *"Terry"* stuck in the door. David got it first, but Terry snatched it away with Bryce's trembling hand. It read:

"Dear Mr. Dorn,
If you would like to meet others like yourself, be at the Hollywood
Presbyterian Church on Highland tomorrow at 2:00 p.m. Come
alone.
A friend from the past"

"You see?? It's for me – 'Mr. Dorn.' *Terry* Dorn – like I told you!"

"Okay, Bryce. What's going on? If you want to break up, just say so! You don't have to screw with my mind and leave little notes all over the place. I do not appreciate this…" David paused, gasping dramatically. "… It's Antoine, isn't it?"

"I want to clean out my bank account…"

"*Aiiieee!!!* – I knew it!"

"I mean – where's my bank account, David? I can't remember."
Terry smiled with Bryce's perfect white teeth. David's eyes quavered side-
to-side, and he relented.

"I don't know why I put up with you… *sigh* …Wells Fargo."

"…Thank you. That wasn't so hard, now was it?"

Amazed at seeing money come out of a machine for the people
ahead of him in line, Terry was hoping to grab some walking around cash
from the Republican who'd stolen his life – and his youth – 29 years ago.
He put Bryce's card in the ATM slot.

"Well?" he said.

"Don't look at me, *Martin Guerre*, I don't know your PIN number."

"… Oh, no – you mean there's some kind of secret code?"

"Are we having a problem, here?" a security cop said, muscling
over to them.

"No, officer, we just forgot our PIN number…"

"A – excuse me, who ordered pork?" the Terry in Bryce said.

"What did you say?" demanded the guard.

"I said, who ordered pork? *Oink, oink!*" It was after four pm and
there were few customers around right then. The security cop, who
looked like a big fan of contact sports, grinned sardonically.

"Get out of here, you faggots – or I'll bust your heads."

David gasped, tugging Terry/Bryce's arm. "Hey, Porky," the
transposed hippie shot back, "don't take it out on us, just 'cause you're
too dumb to be a real cop."

"What did you *say?*"

"You say that a *lot*, don't ya, bacon-ass?"

"Let's go before he hits us," David said. Then, over his shoulder
he bravely added, "and watch who you're calling a faggot!" The security
cop pushed him. Terry bristled, getting Bryce's body between the two.

"Security guard brutality?" He smirked. The rent-a-cop swung on
him, Terry ducked. "Off the pig!" he said, head-butting the guard mid-
section, knocking him down.

"Come on! – are you crazy? *Beat those feet, girlfriend!*" David yelped.
He grabbed Terry by the hand again, jerking him out onto the sidewalk;
they'd run halfway down the block by the time the rent-a-cop got to his
feet.

"*FAGGOTS!!!*" he hollered at the top of his lungs. People all over the parking lot stopped and stared at him. "Never mind," he muttered, putting his shades back on.

Back at their apartment, they discussed the incident.

"So I don't see what the big deal is? So he called us 'fags' – it's not like he said we're 'queers,' or anything."

"If what you're saying has an ounce of truth to it, times have certainly changed since 1972. 'Faggot' is the worst thing they can say, now – 'queer' is sort of *in* – like Queer Nation."

"You got that from 'Woodstock Nation' – from us, back in the '60s."

"'Faggot' is as nasty to us as the 'N'-word is to black people..."

"The *'N'-word?* What the fuck? You're afraid to say the word, even in analytical conversation? Even here in your own home? It's just a word, David – not that I use it, or anything – I'm not a racist."

"People in polite society don't use such language. It's politically incorrect, and simply crude. Besides – you never know when it might slip out and offend someone. And, you don't have to use the 'F'-word about it, either."

"The *'F'-word?* – Jesus Christ! *Whoops!* – Call the language police. I just used the 'J' word and the 'C'-word."

"That's not the 'C-word,' Honey, don't even go there."

"Go where? What are you talking about? What ever happened to free speech? ...To everything we fought for in the '60s and '70s? I could sure use a drink and a joint right about now! *'F'*-word, my fucking ass..."

After an accelerated relaxing session they went back out, and Terry sold some of Bryce's jewelry. He was amazed at how much he got – until he bought a Coke. He became more accustomed to being in Bryce's body, and explained the "transposing" more carefully to David, convincing him that he had to help if he wanted to get the real Bryce back, whose body Terry was only temporarily occupying. David went along skeptically, his last refuge sarcasm.

"But if you're here in Bryce's body, and my Bryce is back in 1972 – and he's *definitely* gay – why are you worried about him doing your girl-friend, *girlfriend?*"

"Stop calling me 'girlfriend.' And, I'm not worried about Bryce balling Sharon – he's in my body, so it would be okay – *sort-of.*"

"God, you're weird. It's that bad ecstasy from last Halloween —
it's lodged in your brain."

"I'm worried about Barry Krautman, the sales director; all he does
is chase pussy — mostly other guys' pussy — and he said he was going to
'move in on Sharon,' damn it!"

"Let's say you are telling the truth. By some weird Quantum Leap time
warp, you really are a hippie cartoonist from 1972 named Terry Dorn,
inhabiting Bryce's body… That means that a very promiscuous homo-
sexual man is inhabiting your body in 1972, pre-A.I.D.S. Hollywood. So,
it's lose-lose for you, too!"

"Oh, no…" Terry cried with Bryce's sibilant, 42-year-old voice.
"It just gets worse! Do you think he really would?"

"Honey. Would a bird eat a worm?"

David, despite his skepticism, managed to hip-up Terry to living
in the 21st Century. Political correctness, A.I.D.S., computers, cruising
the internet, premium cable — even VCRs, were all new to the cartoonist's
1972 consciousness. The next day, Terry couldn't wait for 2:00 p.m. to
arrive. After promising David he'd return, he went to the famous Hollywood church used in *War of the Worlds,* arrived early, and found a small
group of conservative-looking types milling around the steps.

"Hello? Are you the people who left me the note?"

"Who are you?"

"I asked you first."

"Then… we're not the people who left you the note."

Terry weighed his options. "Okay. I'm Terry Dorn — in the body
of Bryce Balaban."

"… Terry?" a sexy brunette asked, looking him over. "Your host-
body is older — like Ted's."

"Hi, Terry… it's me, Ted," said a gray-haired septuagenarian. My
host-body belongs to a senior from Orange County who voted for Pat
Buchanan in the last election."

"Who's Pat Buchanan?"

"A contemporary arch-conservative," said the brunette. "Worse
than Nixon — who resigned in '74, despite the best efforts of the Vulgarians. Their plan must have failed, because obviously they're not ruling the
world, now. Some type of space-time conundrum — we don't know."

First Methodist Church, Hollywood, Ca.

"Who are *you*?" Terry asked, twisting Bryce's features into a scowl.

"Oh… sorry, I'm Sandra," the brunette said.

"I should have known from the cigar."

The rest of the group introduced themselves. Rob Ribenhauser was in the body of a thirty-three-year-old yuppie ad copywriter from Encino named "Roy Silver," and Johnny Nakota was in a twenty-two-year-old cartoonist named "The Claw" from the *L.A. Freakly*. Johnny was kind of digging the whole transposition/exchange thing, except he missed Carol.

Dana the Warsaw Bombshell and Stefan the Czechoslovakian artist had managed to end up in *identical twin sisters* at a Republican analysis firm, and they were knockouts. Stefan wasn't too crazy about the whole thing, but at least his accent matched Dana's – sort of. Except, Dana kept hitting on men, and they'd play slap-and-tickle in return, often mistaking poor Stephan-inhabiting-Sara, in his/her 36-24-36" identical twin's body, for the transposed Dana.

Most of those transposed had been there for a while, except for Sandra/Robin, Glenda/Dale, and Stefan/Sara who'd arrived in the future just before Terry. Dana/Cara, the other half of the twins (who were straw-berry blonde, by the way), had arrived a week before, at the same time as Laurie, the racy *"Froice"* receptionist. Those that seemed "different" ear-lier, back in 1972 – like Andre and Johnny – had jumped into the future earlier.

The free-wheeling Laurie, who could give a eunuch a hard-on, had been transposed into the body of a forty-eight-year-old Sister of the Bloody Gauntlet, an obscure, largely mute, Roman Catholic order re-nowned for self-flagellation and calligraphy.

"But, how did you all get together?"

"Jesus, Terry, you look really gay!"

"Shut-up, Glenda – or *Dale* – or whoever you are."

"We escaped the enclosure the Vulgarians prepared for us," Old Ted said. "…Up in the hills! And, we found their chart of the names and addresses of the transposed from both time periods, in a cave they'd dug out behind the Hollywood Dam."

"They must like caves," Stefan said, jiggling.

"They don't want us to run into our older, 2001 selves," Laurie the nun said.

"You just blew your vow of silence, Sister."

"That's not all she blew, Rob," said Dana/Cara, in her Euro ac-cent. "So, Terry…you want to fuck, now? …Now, that your girlfriend is fifty, and lives with aging construction worker?" The last few comments hit Terry like a bobsled full of bricks.

"Sharon? Here? *Omigod!* – I'm alive here too, somewhere!! An-other of me! …In my own body. Let's see… I'd be fifty now, too. Where do I live? How do I find me? …The *phone book!!*"

"We already checked you out, Terry," said Rob/Roy.

"Yeah," said Ted. "On the internet."

"Oh, yeah… David showed me that on his Big Mac…"

"I-Mac," said Rob. "You just type in the name and you can find out anything about anybody! For instance, I found out Ronald Reagan became president in 1980; sadly, the Berlin Wall came down and the So-viet Union broke up less than ten years later. Communism didn't work, Europe's in a worse mess because it didn't – and there's a more dangerous Republican in the White House now than Nixon!"

"Yep," said Terry, "that's the old Rob talking. But, what did you find out about me?"

"Well, you're alive, and that's better than I'm doing," said Andre/Judy.

"Yeah," said Sandra/Robin, "Andre died in 1986…"

"So, we've got no idea where my Republican's spirit ended-up…"

"Terry," Sandra/Robin continued, "you're single, childless, a recovering alcoholic, and over thirty grand in debt. You don't even drive any more."

"Am I a famous recording artist?" Terry asked. For the first time since he'd arrived in the future, he thought about his rock band back home, Mythical Deities. *What do they think of the new me? I hope to God Bryce isn't hitting on them in my body…*

"Not exactly a recording artist," said Sandra.

"So, I'm a famous illustrator? A bitter underground cartoonist, struggling in some garret to put out my own brilliant line of comics?"

"No," said Ted, "you're a commercial artist and a struggling writer, trying to sell comedic stories and screenplays. One could pretty much say obscurity has not been kind. You live in North Hollywood!"

"*North* Hollywood!? …I didn't marry Sharon?" Terry protested, as pigeons fluttered at their feet. The traffic was picking up; rush hour on Highland had begun.

"Sharon dumped you in '74," Sandra told him, "…Left you for that Jock guy who used to hang around your house. I met him at one of your parties."

"*Jock!?*" Terry shouted. "But, he's a terrible musician! He can barely keep time."

"Yeah, but he didn't gain 50 pounds and turn into an every night, blackout drunk. You've had two drunk-driving arrests."

"Oh, my God," Terry said, sitting down on the stone steps. "I've got to get to me and warn myself. *NO!* – It's too late!" He jumped to his feet again, almost knocking over Glenda/Dale. "We've got to get back to 1972 and change things! We can learn from our mistakes – and I'll be different this time!"

"We think we can overpower Bhelch-fharrt the Malodorous if he returns… the Vulgarian ambassador to the future – or, the present, I mean. He's responsible for all the transposing in 2001, for lining up the Republicans *here* who took over our bodies back then."

"But, Rob? If the Vulgarians control time travel, why didn't they just take over the world in 2001, and leave us alone back there in '72?"

"Because, Terry, their plan was to control the world through its most powerful man, and the leader of the free world is the American President. They discovered that Richard Nixon was the most corruptible president in modern history."

"More corruptible than Bill Clinton?" asked Sister Laurie. "I'd like to get him in *my* oval office…"

"Knock it off, Sister," said Rob. "This new guy, we call him "W," can't be taken over by alien beings, because he's already being controlled by big business, the multi-nationals, the military-industrial complex, oh – and the FUCKING OIL COMPANIES, MAN – like, this *W* can't even take a shit without oil coming out!"

"So, why didn't these Vulgarians use the spirits of Republicans living back in '72 instead of coming all the way into the future for 'em?"

"Because the Republicans from '72 weren't nearly ruthless and venal enough; they came here for the Neo-cons."

"The *what?*" Terry asked. "If Nixon's here, I want to talk to him, Rob!"

"Nixon's in the body of a hooker out in the Valley," Ted said. "Probably working Sepulveda right now, since it's Friday night," "On Monday mornings she goes to court-ordered meetings at Colfax House. …Bad crack habit."

"Crack?" Terry asked, scratching his graying crew cut.

"A cocaine bi-product," said Rob.

"But, cocaine's not addictive – all drugs should be legalized, right, guys? Off the pig! Up against the wall, mother-fucker!" Terry shouted, waving his arms and singing, "Power to the people, right on!" The traffic rolled on by, and a sad couple with long, matted hair pushed a shopping cart with everything they had in the world aboard. Their dog's ribs stuck way out, and the sky was gray as a tombstone.

"You've got a lot to learn about the future, Terry," Andre said. "I may be dead now, but I know enough to admit that I was wrong back then – we all were. Go to some AA and NA meetings – you'll find Jesse and Will-the-typesetter at Colfax house, too. And they didn't come through any Vulgarian time warp, they aged naturally. They're recovering alcoholics and dopers, whose lives were shattered like a glass… bong."

"Old hippies have bad teeth – no dental plans, no IRA accounts," Rob added.

"The term, 'drug casualty of the '60s,' has become a sad cliché, Terry." Sandra put an adopted arm around the transposed artist.

"You said IRA accounts?" Terry asked. "What does the Irish Republican Army have to do with this? Don't tell me they've become Nixonian Republicans in the future?"

"Lighten up, Terry," Johnny/The Claw said. "You wanna talk to Nixon? How about *fucking* him – actually fucking him – in this black hooker's body, I mean. It only costs forty bucks – we do it all the time."

"Wha-a-a-t...?"

"Johnny!" Sandra said, scolding him. "He means the guys do it all the time, Terry. I've never actually met Nixon – or *Sharmayne* – or whatever Nixon's shared host body is called."

"This is another shameless exploitation of the black woman by the white male!" said a well-fed, white Republican – with the soul of Ellswood Garth inside. "I think we should take all the money out of our conservative hosts' bank accounts, and give it away to the poor in Watts, and on skid row!"

"That's mighty white o' you, Ellswood," Johnny said. "I'll help you do it – as soon as you figure out our PIN numbers!"

"Come on, Terry – you too, Ted. We can take my Republican's S.U.V. They're all the rage in the future y'know." Johnny leered lasciviously with the borrowed features of The Claw. "Let's go screw Richard Nixon in a cheap motel room in the San Fernando Valley!"

Chapter Three: Meanwhile, Back at the Past

"He's different, Mom," Sharon said. "Terry never touches his guitar – let alone me. He started listening to Broadway musicals – *you know* – show tunes: *'Gypsy?'* ... *'Meet Me in St. Louis?'* Yesterday, he re-arranged the kitchen utensils and dishes in the cupboards – said they weren't fully functional the way they were."

She watched their black cat cross the hardwood floor and twirled the phone cord, while her mother, a pushy Englishwoman, ranted on the other end.

"I know... I'll get a job and move out. I don't want to marry him, Mom, I'm just biding my time till I can trade up – you know. It's gonna be soon, if this keeps up. Yesterday, he ordered opera tickets and wanted to go *antiquing*, whatever that is. Yuck!"

The doorbell rang, Sharon was rescued. She begged off the phone and went to the door, where Barry Krautman stood.

"Hi, Sharon," he said through the screen. "Terry said he was going to a bar in West Hollywood after work, so I thought maybe you could use some company."

"Listen, Barry. I like you and everything... but I'm Terry's girl-friend – at least for now – and you're supposed to be his friend. So, I really don't think we should get involved."

"I just thought, now that Terry's a queer, maybe you could use a real man."

"Hmnn..." she said, thinking it over. "Maybe I could... Too bad there isn't one around." Then, she shut the door in his face and went to fry a ganzer egg.

It was Tuesday night at the office: production night. The now-conservative, oddly-behaving staff had left. Editor Bart Gunkin, the last liberal-minded employee of *The L.A. Free Voice*, would stay behind, and slowly, working alone till dawn, would replace nearly every pro-Nixon piece of art and copy – exactly as he had been doing since the Vulgarian corruption had begun.

"...Not gonna get me to go see that damn spaceship. I read *The Puppet Masters* twenty years ago. Let *The Bomb* and *The Vanguard* print their reactionary propaganda – I know what's going on. It's a far-reaching, right-wing conspiracy! Somebody has to print the whole truth and nothing but the truth."

His eyes wandered over the flats, coming to rest on Saul Kras-nick's "Mind Smegma" column on page eight. "So help me... they got to Krasnick, too," Gunkin said, shaking his head, as he tore the contributor's galleys from the page.

"At least Pukowsky hasn't been turned." He scanned the drunk-enly apolitical "Scribbles..." column, with its cartoon heading by Nakota. Although the Vulgarians had tried transplanting Republicans from the future into the then, relatively unknown mad poet, they couldn't take all the vomiting from Pukowsky's drinking, so had retreated back up the time-line.

There had been talk amongst the transposed of kidnapping the forty-five-year-old editor and dragging him up to Bronson Cave – or do-ing worse. They'd let him have his way this one last Tuesday, but it had been decided: Bart Gunkin would not be screwing up their new, conserva-tive *L.A. Free Voice* next week.

Chapter Four: The Once and Future President

"That's her – over there!" said Johnny/The Claw, pointing at the African-American woman in red mini-skirt and matching pumps, strolling back-and-forth on the corner of Sepulveda and Roscoe.

"Hey, Sharmayne!" Old Ted hollered, his host-body's seventy-four years no hindrance when it came to boning the transposed Nixon. Unlike the other transpositions, with the 2001 right-wingers' mind-spirits having been sent back to inhabit the transposed hippies' bodies in 1972 – Sharmayne had remained *in* her body while it also hosted the former President from Whittier, California. Meanwhile, the Vulgarian named "Sneaujhabb the Prevaricator" occupied Nixon's body in 1972 Washington, while *its* body remained unoccupied, in suspended animation on one of their ships.

"Yeah – you know ah gots it, Honey!"

"We want to know if you've seen Tricky Dick?"

"You the one they call 'Johnny,' ain't ya? Tricks an' dicks is all ah sees, Johnny," she said laughing. "All day long – tricks an' dicks, tricks an' dicks."

"Come on, girl – climb in – we'll get a motel."

"You gots to pay me triple, for all three o' y'all.

"No sweat, dollface," Johnny said. Sharmayne got in the S.U.V.

"It can't be true – Nixon couldn't possibly be in the body of this… crack whore?" Terry/Bryce said. Then the strangest thing happened. Sharmayne's natural voice became intermittently interrupted by a familiar, middle-aged, male voice. Kind of adenoidal, deep and throaty, it sounded exactly like that of Eisenhower's unpopular VP, better known as the 37th president of the United States.

"Ah likes the pipe – don't get me wrong, Honey – but I ain't 'xactly no crack 'ho'… *The American people deserve to know that their president…* Ah mean, ah gets up an' ah goes to work, don't ah? Pull in right there… *That their president is not a crook…* The Lazy-Ass Bitch Motel – that's what ah calls it… *And, I am not a cr… cr… crack whore!* …Shut-up! You ol' white mutha-fuckah inside me, or ah'll eats a bowl o' that fi'-star chili again, an' y'all goin' shit fire, an' regret what you been sayin' 'bout black folks."

"This is amazing," said Terry, "it's really him." Johnny pulled the Explorer into the parking lot of the Lazy S Beach Motel.

"You wouldn't believe the racist bullshit that come out o' his mouth!" Sharmayne said in her real voice. C'mon, you ol' white devil! –

then, Nixon's voice added, *"The Mexicans, unlike the Negroes, have some sense of family, at least...* He say that on the tapes. That Watergate thang fuck' him *all* up."

"Did you just make him say that?" Terry asked. Johnny got out of the S.U.V.

"I can make him tell the truth – whadda 'bout that? It my damn body, ain't it? Go on, Tricky... *I... I... I am not a cr... cr... crack whore!"* Nixon's voice said. "'Ho!'" Sharmayne corrected. *"Ho,'"* the president inside her pronounced, complying.

"Hey you guys?" Ted said, "I thought we were going to rent a room, and..."

"...Bang this schizzy wench," finished Johnny. At that, the others got out, too.

"Mr. President? I'm addressing you," Terry said. "Don't you want to go back to 1972 and be in your own body again – so you can take responsibility for your part in the Watergate scandal and cover-up? After a pause, Terry added, "Go on, Sharmayne – make him answer truthfully!"

"Ah'ight. You heard the man, Tricky, you mean ol' racist prick. Tell the truth, now… *I… am not a cr – I mean, YES! I want to go back*," Sharmayne said, in the former president's voice. "*…Just not responsible for… not responsible for Watergate, it's a bum rap!*"

"A bum rap?" Ted exclaimed. "Fuck *him!*"

"No! – he be tellin' the truth – them V'garians from outer space swapped bodies on him right befo' the break-in! He din't start that cover-up neither – ah know it. Ah know ever'thing in his evil sewer of a mind! So, '*Negroes*' got no sense of fam'ly, huh? – well, take this, Tricky Dicky!"

With that, Sharmayne began pummeling herself about the face and chest, and crying out in Nixon's voice. "*Oww! – stop hitting myself, now, goddammit – Owww! Stop it – please!*" The three transposed hippies stepped back in shock. Sharmayne continued Nixon's self-beating and rant: "*Why does everyone hate Nixon?— what did I do to them? I'm not so bad… Oww! I like some Sidney Poitier movies… and Sammy! Who doesn't love – OWW! – Sammy?*"

A screech of tires signaled the arrival of Ellswood Garth in his white conservative host-body. He jumped out of his Republican's Cadillac and wrapped a coat around Sharmayne. "Come with me, now, and I'll get you a nice room and a hot bath – you've been degraded by your lifestyle – not to mention the white man – long enough!"

"Get lost, mutha-fuckah – ah gots me three tricks at once, you dumb-ass, white-bread honky! Ah can retire fo' the ev'ning – what th' hell make you so special, anyhow?" Then Nixon's voice said, "*I… am not a crack… 'ho'. How was that?* …Better," she answered as herself. Ellswood Garth took two steps back.

"If you really have Richard Nixon in there, then you should have no trouble believing that I'm actually a famous Afro-American writer trapped in this white b…"

"*Afro*-American? What planet you from, Honey? *Afro?* – I ain't heard that one fo' awhile. So, where you Afro at? – I don't see no Afro on yo' haid? If you a black writer, ah'm a rocket scien'ist!" While Ted and Johnny were watching Ellswood's host crumbling from her attack, Terry jumped in the S.U.V. and fired up the engine. Johnny jerked his head around.

"Terry? What are you doing?"

"I'm going to North Hollywood – to find myself!" He lisped, roaring out into the traffic.

"Noooo, Terrrrry!!!" Ted screamed. "You can't come within a hundred feet of your 2001 self, or you'll *de-raid the angels of Molly Cools, an' some of Tommy Maverick over you no worse!"* At least that's what it sounded like to Terry over the Explorer's engine and the horns honking at him.

He took Burbank east, away from the setting sun. At Lankershim he turned right, heading south – into the heart of NoHo. He didn't notice the red and blue lights in his mirror but heard the siren. Traffic stopped around him and a few people cried out. As he pulled over, the flashing lights rose up, out-of-sight.

Terry leaned Bryce's head out the window and looked up.

The vehicle hovering above him was not a police car, and the flashing lights were red, turquoise, and another color Terry had never seen before. The turquoise light beamed down on him, and his S.U.V. began to rise.

"Oh, shit!" he muttered, trying the door – it was frozen shut. The last thing he remembered from his ascension was the look on the face of a Latina woman on the ground. She was smiling broadly, no fear in her face, and Terry could see the silver-work in her teeth as everything went turquoise.

Chapter Five: Pulled Over by the Time Police for Unsafe Frame Change

"So, are you a couple of slimy *'mutuals,'* working for disgusting Vulgarians?" Terry said, looking around the inside of the boxy ship. He could see the Earth below through an elliptical window as they streaked up, beyond the stratosphere. Finally, they leveled off.

"You really know how to make friends, Terry. I cannot impress upon you too strongly how critical it is that a person travelling in time DOES NOT GO NEAR THEIR OLDER OR YOUNGER SELF! – understand?" the navigator said. The other man, piloting the alien-looking craft, explained.

"Yeah. Ya don't wanna do dat, no – you'll degrade de arrangement o' molecules in da sub-atomic fabric of da universe!"

"That sounds oddly familiar…"

"It's a frequently implemented concept in science fiction – that just happens to be true," said the navigator. "And, it's our job to make sure it never happens."

"We got a way of cleanin' this mess up... puttin' everything back da way it was before da Vulgarians transposed Nixon into Ms. Sharmayne DuValle."

"You from Chicago?"

"It's da accent, huh? – no foolin' dis jumper, is dere, Alf?"

"No, Bud – he's a smart one."

"So..." Terry mumbled, taking a deep breath, "you guys can put me back in my real body, back in 1972?"

"Oh, yeah – piece o' cake," said Bud.

"We can put everybody back – even Richard Nixon. The Vulgarians took over his body just in time for the Watergate scandal to draw more heat than their ambassador-in-the-body-of-Nixon could withstand. But when we put him back he'll be on his own, as far as the cover-up goes."

"We just gotta go back a few steps in da temporal frame – sorta like de edit feature on your computer, when you click da 'undo' button a couple o' times."

"I don't have a computer. I live in 1972."

"He's a hippie, Bud – he doesn't know jack about anything."

"But, I have so many questions! How did you know this was happening? Where are you from?"

"We're from a hundred years up the line from you, Terry," said the navigator, taking out a small, metal skull-cap. "I happen to live on Mars in 2072 – in Wellsville, as a matter of fact." He placed the cap on Terry's head, and a propeller emerged from its crown. Tiny fiber-optic strands trailed down, blinking on either side of Terry's face, and the propeller began to spin, slowly at first.

"What is this thing?" Terry asked, trembling with anticipation.

"You wouldn't understand."

"It's a friggin' hat – okay, pal? – It'll do da job."

"I just asked," Terry sighed. "At least I know how my life will turn out – we all do, now. And it's our duty to make sure that the dreams of a generation won't die of abandonment – or drug overdoses! What warnings from the future we'll bring back..."

"Time travel was discovered in 2069, but we're still perfecting it..."

"Mars... people living on Mars in the future...?"

"Earth is a hell-hole *when* we come from. Everybody useful is on Mars or Io."

"But what about the Vulgarians?" Terry asked, watching the Earth loom larger on their descent. His propeller spun faster and faster.

"We'll ship them back to their galaxy by intersecting their temporal frame before they came here – and merely lengthening it," said Alf.

"So, they'll still come – eventually?"

"Kid… there will always be Vulgarians trying to drag the human race down to their level. But not all conservatives are vulgarians; I happen to be a Republican, and believe me, you *need* the two-party system in your day. So, in the future, try to get both sides of things before you go off half-cocked, okay?"

"You mean 'in da past,' doncha, Alf?"

"Yeah – did I say 'in the *future?*' What's the difference, anyway?"

"Yeah – what's da difference? It ain't like he's gonna remember nothin'."

Terry panned his gaze back-and-forth between the two temporal peace officers.

"How can he remember what hasn't happened yet, Bud? – or might not happen at all?" The world was rushing up at them through the window, now. Terry broke a sweat. The propeller on his cap gyrated like sixty – enough to almost pull him from his seat.

"What do you mean, *I'm not gonna remember anything?* Why not? I've earned this information and the right to use it! For all I know, back in 1972, my real body's a West Hollywood pincushion, and my girlfriend's getting drilled by a gin-swilling ad jockey – just look at this haircut! I mean, HOW MUCH MORE DO I HAVE TO FUCKING SUFFER??

"I've gotta warn the past about the future… about *drugs* – and *A.I.D.S!!* Not to mention, political correctness! Gotta tell 'em that gays are just like us, really, and all discrimination is wrong. *HELL!!!* – I DEMAND MY RIGHTS AS AN AMERICAN CITIZEN!!!"

"Here, kid. Take a whiff o' dis…"

Past Prologue: "Doomed to Repeat It" Department

"Well? What's the verdict?" Ted Bayliss said as Bart Gunkin read the thin strip of paper printing off the wire. The stoic editor pushed his horned-rim glasses back up the bridge of his nose and stroked his goatee.

"They all entered guilty pleas – except for Liddy and McCord. I didn't expect Liddy to cop out, did you, Ted?"

"No – the guy ate a rat… he'll do the time."

"Stinkin' Republicans," said Terry Dorn, affecting the popular stance, clutched in the arrogant grip of youth, knowing everything and knowing nothing at the same time.

AFTERWORD

This story is based on my two years as an artist for editor, Art Kunkin, and New Way Enterprises at *The Los Angeles Free Press* during the Watergate scandal (1972-74). "Bart Gunkin's" words at the beginning are accurate; I was working production the night the story of the Watergate Hotel break-in came in over the wire from *The Washington Post*.

My cartoon of Richard Nixon, holding a flag-colored bomb behind his back while flashing the "V" sign, made the *Freep* cover in 1972. It was on bumper stickers in L.A., posters for the McGovern campaign in the East, and helped land me on President Nixon's White House enemies list. At a reunion party in '78 I found out that during the Watergate scandal the FBI had created files for all of us artists, writers, and editors at the *L.A. Free Press* – as well as for those at *The Washington Post, Berkeley Barb, Village Voice*, et al.

President Nixon's dialogue is partly based on actual statements he made on his own surveillance tapes; the statement about "Negroes" and "Mexicans" really came out of his mouth! I did make up the line where he says he's not a crack whore. As far as I know, Nixon never denied that.

Some of the staffers depicted here are based on real people but black activist, Ellswood Garth, was completely fabricated for the story. You would have to have worked there to recognize anyone, though; except for, maybe, the thinly veiled Charles Bukowski, whose weekly column, "Notes of a Dirty Old Man," was the main inspiration for my beginning creative writing at all.

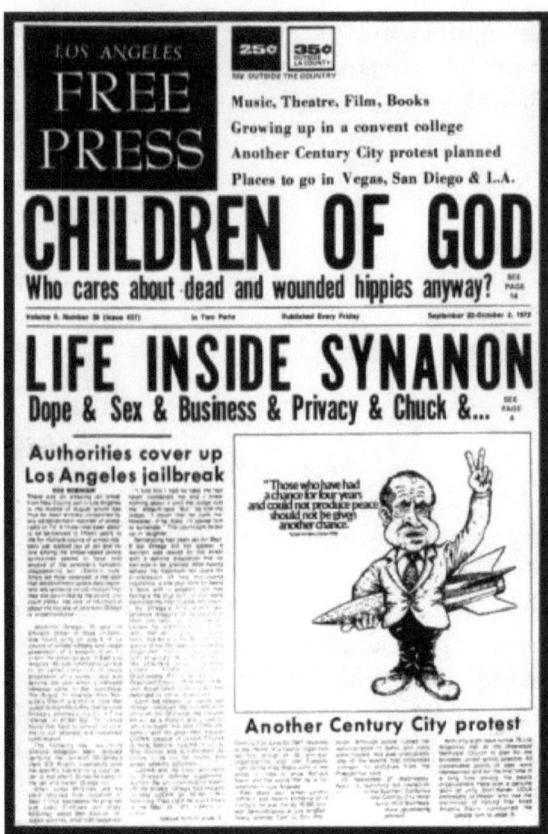

I drew a lot of massage parlor ads at *The Freep*. That's where I learned to render women; in high school I had drawn mostly superheroes. So many details here are real – like getting burned by my sunlamp, or wearing shades for the first hour at work to hide my red eyes. The lunch treks up to Bronson Cave really happened, as did the editor's house party.

As to Terry's sudden conversion to gay "activist?" You should never judge a man till you've walked a mile in his shoes. For one thing, by then you're a mile away... and he has no shoes.

A Conversation with George Clayton Johnson

This interview, originally published in early 2000 on the Subterranean Press website, was commissioned and paid for by William K. Schafer, in order to detail and underscore Mr. Johnson's 465-page, hardcover career retrospective, "All of Us Are Dying and Other Stories" (Subterranean Press, ed. W.K. Schafer). *It was conducted over the phone Thursday, October 28, 1999. Updated and re-edited for several websites over the years, it remains one of the most fascinating, informative, and important pieces of writing I have ever been associated with. I love writing, and if you do too and would like a lesson from a true master - a Jedi Knight of the written word - then read on.*

Besides illuminating a wonderful book, this dialogue hopes to enlighten, describing the "between the lines" process that a great writer undergoes in order to present us, the readers, with these tightly humming short stories, teleplays and story outlines. The book also includes essays on writing and a complete screenplay by Johnson.

Making things look (and read) easy is where the true craftsmanship comes in, as you will see. The book, "All of Us Are Dying and Other Stories," *also includes a wonderful introduction and a stirring afterward, by Christopher Conlon and Dennis Etchison, respectively. The book is sold out, but might be available on-line, and it wouldn't hurt to contact Subterranean Press regarding reprinting it, or to inquire there about other books by Mr. Johnson.*

When did you begin writing?

GCJ: *(he confers with Lola, his wife of nearly fifty years)* … Forty-five years ago (1954).

You have a Burt Shonberg illustration on the dust jacket of All of Us Are Dying and Other Stories – *was he a friend of yours? (Note: Shonberg did the paintings seen in Roger Corman's Poe pictures, among many other famous works.)*

GCJ: Damned right. A very, very good friend, back in the fifties… I bought a lot of his paintings, I have paintings of his in my home; I own that illustration. He was a very, very intimate friend, one of the most talented men that I knew. He was a comer – I knew he was going to be an important person, and we remained friends until the day he died.

Tell us about The Creature's Blood, *your Frankenstein-based TV series treatment…*

GCJ: I was hired by Universal Pictures, who said, we want to do a series about the Frankenstein Creature. Come over and look at all of our movies and tell us what you think, and I told them. And they said, all right, write the story as a pilot, and I wrote it and turned it in – only by that time the producer had been changed. The new producer was Gene Coon, who would soon be producing *Star Trek,* and when he started to ask me to change the script around the way he wanted it done, I figured he was just an utter jerk, and said no, because it seemed silly… He wanted to modernize the Frankenstein series and make it take place in New York City… I thought… I see a guy like the Frankenstein Monster on the street in New York City – I think he's a war vet or something… I don't think that he's a creature from hell or anything like that, he just looks like a poor *victim* in modern times, but back in that gothic world, he's an ominous and frightening figure.

You have a lot of treatments in here… outlines for TV and the movies. Ocean's Eleven? *I have to ask – it's not in the book, but it's a seminal work of yours*
…

GCJ: It's the first thing I ever wrote… The beginning of the book started in 1954, when Jack Russell and I sat around a kitchen table trying to write what started out as a novel. But later on, when a director friend-of-a-friend saw the pages, he said this would make a fine movie, so I started to rewrite it as a movie… But that was the first thing I ever sold, and I spent five years after that, with that one thing sold and never sold anything else. Because during those five years the movie wasn't made, and as far as I knew I'd sold it to a couple of guys in a closet and the minute I took their little money, that was the end of them as far as I knew. I never heard from them again – I had no idea in the world it would go to Sinatra… but I knew the Lawfords had bought it, because the check was signed by Patricia Kennedy.

Did Charles Beaumont introduce you to Rod Serling, and wasn't the story for "The Four of Us Are Dying," *your first sale to Rod?*

GCJ: I met Rod Serling for the first time at a party at Chuck's house – nobody needed to introduce you to Rod Serling, everybody knew who Rod Serling was... I introduced myself to him. Later on, I submitted the story to an agent, and the agent was Jay Richards at Famous Artists Agency. Jay Richards read this story; he didn't like the title – the title at that time was, *"All of Us Are Dying."* He drew a line through it with a ballpoint pen. He scrubbed out the title and he wrote, in printing, *"Rubberface."* And I thought, ooh, how obvious and how awkward, and how stupid a title that is... *"Rubberface!"* But then, he offered to submit it to *The Twilight Zone*, which he did, and then they subsequently bought it. Rod saw the original title, *"All of Us Are Dying,"* and he used the title, *"The Four of Us Are Dying,"* because at the end of the show, the "all of us" are really only four people.

One of my favorites came next, I believe. You sold the story for "Execution," *that featured Albert Salmi and Russell Johnson (no relation). Then what?*

GCJ: After *"Execution," "A Penny for Your Thoughts."* But in between... there was another show called *"Sea Change."* I submitted it to the *Twilight Zone* offices. By then, I knew who they were and they knew who I was, so I had a meeting with them, and they bought it. And then – about a week later I got a call from Rod, saying that his sponsor was General Foods, and that the idea of chopping a man's hand off over the dinner table didn't appeal to them when they're trying to sell food, so they didn't want to use it – a case of censorship. Rod called me to ask if I'd buy it back – and I did. And then, he felt somewhat obligated to me, so I offered him the fourth story a few weeks or months later, *"A Penny for Your Thoughts."*

"A Penny for Your Thoughts" *was the first one you wrote the teleplay for, right?*

GCJ: ...He wanted to buy it, and I then held him up. They call it "breaking into television" – well, I held him up and said no, not unless I get a chance to write a first draft. It looked like the sale was off for two weeks, and I sat around the house thinking I'd blown it – because here I was, collaborating with the greatest TV writer of all, and now, over a silly thing like this, I was telling him I had to write the first draft. But then I got a call from a lawyer who represented Cayuga Productions, who said

they were going to buy it. He called me into his office and he had a contract… in which they would buy the story and then they would option the
rights from me to write a first draft of the script. He had a check there for
the both the story and the option on the first draft. I went home and wrote
the first draft – and then they filmed it… exactly as written, with no
changes.

The Twilight Zone was famous for that, for not toying too much with the
writers' work, isn't that correct?

GCJ: Yes. There was some rewriting; I rewrote on several scripts
– just a question of making them better, but in this particular case, there
was no need for that rewriting, because they liked it the way it was.

Could I ask which of your *Twilight Zone* stories you like the best?

GCJ: *"Nothing in the Dark"* is the one that I think is the best… But
I think *"A Penny for Your Thoughts"* is right in there, because comedy is very
hard to write.

Of the *Twilight Zones* that you didn't write, do you have a favorite episode?

GCJ: I have a lot of favorites… *"Walking Distance,"* by Rod Serling;
"The Howling Man" and *"Shadowplay,"* by Charles Beaumont; and *"The
Hunt,"* by Earl Hamner, Jr. I thought those were exceptionally fine shows.
There were a number of others that I liked an awful lot…

Although the main purpose of this interview is to discuss the book, "All of
Us Are Dying and Other Stories," I have a couple of questions that aren't about
the book; you mentioned "Sea Change" – that's in your own underground comic
book, "Deepest Dimensions." Do you have a favorite comic book artist of all time?
… Prose writer? … Pulp magazine?

GCJ: Not of all time, no, but if you want to talk about the great
comic book artists of the past… people like Hal Foster, Burne Hogarth,
of course… But, as to today, I'd say the underground comic artists, Robert Crumb, S. Clay Wilson, Robert Williams… And as for favorite prose
writers – Ray Bradbury for the lyrical part of it; Alfred Bester, a science
fiction writer, for excitement – I think he's really, really good. I have tons

and tons of prose writers that I think are wonderful. And, as far as pulp magazines, no. No favorite – except perhaps *Famous Fantastic Mysteries*, a big pulp quarterly.

Were you a fan of Weird Tales?

GCJ: Not much. *Famous Fantastic Mysteries* featured writers like A. Merritt. I would say that of all the old pulp magazines, the one that I looked for the most was *Famous Fantastic Mysteries*.

You were interviewed in the Oct. - Jan. 2000 issue of Filmfax, *were you not?*

GCJ: They did a major interview with me, and several others...

There's an article about Charles Beaumont's Group and one by (the late) Beaumont, himself...

GCJ: Yes, there's an article about the Group by Chris Conlon, taken in part from his introductions to my book and the California Sorcery anthology. I was interviewed by Matthew R. Bradley, as were Richard Matheson and Jerry Sohl, in that same issue.

Do you want to talk about the E! Entertainment show?

GCJ: I was interviewed for their Rod Serling documentary.

You mentioned the other night that you were watching Buffy the Vampire Slayer, *are you a fan of* "Buffy...?"

GCJ: No. But I like to keep up with what's going down... that's part of the reason I watch *"Buffy..."*

It's nice to see horror making a comeback on TV with some quality shows, "Buffy's..." got a spinoff now, and the Sci-Fi Channel has a lot...

GCJ: Do you like those shows?

I like to see the genre kept alive – I don't watch them...

GCJ: Yeah, well, see – there you are, I don't watch them either, usually... My wife watches them a lot. When you called I was watching ("*Buffy*").

Actually, I have all the Outer Limits *from Showtime in my library, as well as all the X-Files. What the Buffy-type shows may do is prompt kids that are bright and want more, to go find books. If having things on television that attract the interest of young people causes them to read – even comic books – then, that's probably a good thing.*

As to writing: according to "All of Us Are Dying..." you write on a typewriter, rewrite extensively, listen to TV and radio in the background, and sometimes put it off when you don't know what to do. Frank Yerby was quoted as saying, "I quit writing if I feel inspired because I know I'll have to throw it away. Writing a novel is like building a wall brick by brick; only amateurs believe in inspiration." Would you advise other writers to abandon inspiration in favor of discipline and consistency?

GCJ: The thing is, when we look at Frank Yerby, we could just as well be looking at Danielle Steele, or one of those current people who write these, what's the word...? There's no attempt there to try and write anything in the way of serious literature, but I've read Frank, and he's an excellent writer *(Frank Yerby, an African-American author, wrote the novels, "Foxes of Harrow" and "The Saracen Blade" in the forties, both of which were made into motion pictures).*

Now, when he's saying, "...Believe in inspiration," yeah, some writers do. Like your "Daughter of Depravity" was an inspiration, wasn't it? You had an idea – you'd probably been cooking the idea for a long time about trying to use these gothic writers. But now, suddenly, you had a concept, or an idea, and you went for it – you made a rough draft...

What kicked it off were the phonies at that other signing...

GCJ: ... So that's pretty much the way it works. The idea of inspiration comes with the idea – when an idea occurs to you, when you suddenly realize you've got a good story here, that's the inspiration part of it. But, when it comes to working on things, it is pretty dogged. Most of the people that I know, who are professionals, who write every day and make a profession of turning out words, they don't – none of them – seem to talk about inspiration. I've talked with Robert Silverberg a lot. Robert

Silverberg is a disciplined guy; he goes in his office, he works a certain number of hours, he turns out a certain number of pages, then he leaves. And he does that every day, every day – if he had to depend upon inspiration, he'd be doomed. Look at William Faulkner. William Faulkner didn't believe in inspiration either, he was a worker. He sat down and he built his books, and so do most people. This idea that you sit down, an idea suddenly occurs to you, and you write a great novel – it doesn't work that way, it takes months and months – it might take years, to write a novel. I have to re-write everything.

What's the ratio of your rewrite pages to final draft pages?

GCJ: *(He mentions an average half-hour teleplay)* ...   The files on it measure about three inches thick; it's about four or five manila folders filled with notes, typing, drawings, pages, diagrams, synopses, dialogue and other things... And it reduces down to less than a quarter-of-an-inch in terms of a final draft. When I look at almost every story that I've written, I've got that same situation of looking at a huge, huge pile – a great big folder, and then out of it, you pluck out the story itself – it's maybe eight pages. So it is a case of building it, an inch at a time.

Well, and then you've got Harlan Ellison (R), who likes to write them in bookstores.

GCJ: ... Those stories that he writes in the bookstores, he doesn't just turn around and sell them. He writes them in bookstores to show that he can write them, and then he puts them in his files, and maybe ten years later, he sells them – after he's thought of what the hell is wrong with the middle. That's the way it works... Most of the writing I've done in the last ten years is still in my workroom.

I have a major opera... a musical drama that I think is like *Phantom of the Opera, Man of La Mancha* or *Westside Story*... It's music and it's drama, and it's the whole story of the death of Emile Zola, and it fills a file box with folders, *jammed* folders *("Madame Zola")*. And it's not finished yet, it's about half-finished. All the music is written. All the lyrics are written. I've got various drafts of the drama itself, but in terms of turning it into a screenplay...? The story itself is basically a love story between Emile Zola and his wife, Alexandrine, and this is all taking place during the Dreyfuss affair, when Zola's life is being threatened because he's dared to accuse the general staff of the Army of France of taking part in a conspiracy – in a cover-up. Now, if someone said to me, "What about this thing? It was dramatized in the year 2005, when did you write it?" Well, I've been writing it for over ten years, in bits and pieces, when I get off of the work that I do for a living, when I've got time to work on things like that. I've got half of the sequel to *Logan's Run* written, called, *"Logan's Run: Lastday."* Nobody has seen any of it... I've written a lot of stories that I've never sold. Some of the stories in *"All of Us Are Dying..."* were never sold, some really quite fine stories. But I never found a magazine or a publisher that was at all interested... for that purpose. So, when they're sold, when they're written – there's no connection whatsoever.

(I'd originally tried to correlate the writing of his stories and scripts with their publication dates – not a good idea, I found out. As to gaps between appearances of his work, George was most particular about how that's all about not selling, as opposed to not writing) ...What happens when the producers who like and buy your work don't have anything going, do you make new inroads?

GCJ: Or, you go write a short story, or you go write an article, or *you don't sell anything* – you just keep writing stuff, and nobody buys it. That's the life of a writer... Eventually you have a trunk full of it, and somebody comes along and says, "How 'bout we publish a book of yours?" And you say, fine, and you whip out all this previously written stuff, and you show it to them, and they think it's all brand-new. Some of the stuff that looks the newest is the oldest.

I was really impressed with "A Bicycle Like a Flame." *I had an intense emotional reaction at a certain point in that beautiful story... I don't want to give anything away.*

GCJ: That story is really quite a true one. *"A Bicycle Like a Flame"* is not all made-up, there really was an Abraham and George. And they were really good friends.

It's a great story; to be in touch with that kind of emotion that isn't artificial or calculated...

GCJ: The same thing about "The Ring of Truth." That's a true story also – except that it's all made up... *(I laugh)* ... I'm trying to be honest, here. I knew Captain Ed, sure. I know all those guys very well.

I've been to Deadhead concerts, but I'm not a Deadhead. But I'm very interested in psychedelica in all of its aspects. And so, I go to these conventions... You know, I could've written this at a science-fiction convention just as easily as at a Grateful Dead concert, but because of the feelings I had about the story, and the environment and everything, I ended up writing it that way... It's really a made-up story, but it's made up out of truthful things. That's why it has the ring of truth – that's why I call it "The Ring of Truth," because you can't tell what is real, and what is not real in it because I talk about them both in exactly the same tone of voice, which is, I think, part of the power of the story, that you totally don't expect the ending...

You don't expect it if you know YOU... (I laugh again) First impressions and all that, but you never know...

GCJ: Or, how 'bout yourself? If you were in a position where you really thought your life was threatened, do you think you might drop a lot of your old code systems and go to work with a shovel or something?

Lord of the Flies. We're all animals at heart, and there's a tremendous sense of self-preservation in most people, so I think that, sure, in a given situation, anybody could... I have a story, too – a long one – called, "Snake in the Grass," about two kids in Iowa in 1960 that has a similar bent to it. It sort of goes from Huckleberry Finn *to* Something Wicked This Way Comes, *to* Deliverance. *It has a lot of truth in it because a lot of it really happened, and it's about real places and real incidents. I just jammed a lot of them together and made up some things to bridge the gaps...*

GCJ: That's sort of the way I function as well. There are a lot of little things that happen to you, and you know that they're material for a story, even though you don't have a story for them. For example, the guy coming up to me and saying, "I used to be a serial killer...?"

Yeah...?

GCJ: That happened. And I was pretty chilled by the damn thing too, thinking my God, I don't want this guy to follow me home. But, I walked away. I never had a second meeting with him, I made that part up.

*It's inevitable that we change subjects abruptly, considering how many, truly different elements are included in the "*All of Us Are Dying*" volume – it must have been tough to edit. There's also a complete teleplay from* The Law and Mr. Jones, *an hour-long drama from 1962 starring James Whitmore, produced about the same time you were selling the Twilight Zone half-hours?*

GCJ: Here's the way that worked… I had this agent. This agent knew that I was writing these things for *The Twilight Zone*, and he wanted to broaden my base. He didn't want me to be stuck with the fact that I could write these kinds of things, but what happens when there's no more *Twilight Zone?* So he sent me out to the show, *Mr. Novak…* And he sent me out to this show, *The Law and Mr. Jones."* He also sent me out to *Dobie Gillis.* The *Dobie Gillis* guys, they had a premise – an idea. They said, if you can turn this into a story, we'd like to hear about it, but I never could quite figure out just exactly what they wanted, so nothing came of that. The Mr. Novak people? I went back for endless meetings – endless, endless… I must have taken seven months of meetings and talks with these people before I got a commitment to write their show. When I went to see *The Law and Mr. Jones*, their situation was, they had shows to write and their theme was the first ten amendments to the Constitution; the Bill of Rights. They said, choose one of these ten, so – *the right to dissent*, the idea that you could stand up and say no, and that that was a power, is the one that I chose to do. And that's how I got *The Law and Mr. Jones* gig. I worked quite closely with the producer and with James Whitmore on the development of it.

Okay. Great answers, George. People who read this on the internet and want to pick up a copy of All of Us Are Dying and Other Stories *(out-of-print) will now have a better understanding of just what it contains.*
I asked Ray Bradbury about you, and he said you were a wonderful short story writer, and that you should write more short stories.

GCJ: … I tend to talk my stories a lot – Ray says, don't talk. I tend to think a lot when I'm writing – Ray says, don't think, just go in, vomit it out onto the page, send it out. Don't ask is it any good or not? Let the editors worry about that – if nobody buys it, well, too bad – it's their mistake. You're a great writer, keep on writing, go write… I can't function that way. For me, unless a thing is really good, I don't want it published.

Maybe he doesn't understand that…

GCJ: The point is, he's a different person than I am; he's had a different experience than I have. My ambition is, not to do a lot of things, most of which are crap. I would like to do a lot of things, all of which are good. Whether or not I've done that is another question for people to answer, but that's my motive, and I don't really like to let anything out of my workroom until I'm ready to stand up in front of it because I don't want someone to read one or two of my stories and decide I'm a lousy writer, just because they happened to pick up the two worst things I ever wrote.

See, now we're getting to the heart of it, because this is how you give that impression of being a great writer – as I said in the introduction, "A world-class writer," and it's because you're not a hack, you're not out there cranking out these novels, you're not trying to be a millionaire. I don't want to name names… They write into tape recorders, some of them…And some other poor bastard has to make sense out of their gibberish. But when people read something of yours, they don't realize it's been crafted. It's been rewritten and personally retyped and retyped and polished and put away, and you come back six months or a year later and read it and say, that's what's wrong with it!

GCJ: Of course the truth is – Ray Bradbury does that too. Ray Bradbury writes and rewrites and rewrites, that's exactly why his work is so hot. Maybe he doesn't have to do as much of that recently as he used to when he was younger. But one of the things that he was always talking to me about was *rewriting*. I learned something from Ray that I think is one of the most valuable lessons I ever learned; it's a very simple word: *cutting*. How to take sixteen pages, turn it into twelve pages, and not lose anything, not take anything out of it. Just get rid of four pages somehow – a half a line, here… a word there. Compress these three paragraphs into one paragraph – cut, cut, *cut*. And I find that every time I do cut, it sharpens the piece; the work starts to take on a lean quality. It starts becoming less commonplace. And learning how to spot the crap in your work is the hard one. You have to develop a very good detector; it's very easy in someone else's writing, to find the weak stuff – you know, I don't like this, or this second act doesn't work or I don't believe this premise... But try and do that to your own work, and it's really very difficult.

I need time. I need time from when it's first written to come back to it, and come back to it – things that seem really heavy, two weeks later you think, what was I thinking of?

GCJ: I'm still the same way – there are certain things that I look at, and I see that nobody else gets it, but it works for *me*... now I've got to figure out what it is that I'm putting into it when I read it, that isn't on the page. Some thought or memory that *I* have, and I'm unaware, completely, that I just haven't put it in yet...

I know, that's tricky. When it's in your mind, and you automatically know that element, but another person doesn't have that element to work with...

GCJ: They say well, how long has she known him? And you realize that's a very interesting thing to know – in the story.

We could discuss the elements of writing endlessly, particularly of short stories... But there are going to be quite a few stories, etc., that we won't have time or space to address, here... What about that complete screenplay, right in the middle of your 465-page book? Do you want to talk about The Edge of the World?

GCJ: I'm very, very ambitious to see that screenplay actually made. See, I think that today, a story about the '60s, kind of lampooning and exaggerating the '60s would make for a very good movie. Perhaps it would be better today, than when it was written. When it was written, the decade of the '60s was fairly fresh and many people were still wandering around in a daze from it. But now, in retrospect, I think *The Edge of the World* would make a very fine film. Of course, it's a first draft – I wrote *The Edge of the World* for Sid and Marty Krofft, and they were going to do it for Columbia, and Columbia, after reading the script, decided that they didn't want to do it, and that killed the deal. And so, *The Edge of the World*, though everyone was paid, never got made. Now, the question is how to get *The Edge of the World* made, because in order to do it properly, it requires a rewrite.

Well, you should get Terry Gilliam interested, your opening is like something he'd do; I mean, Columbus and his three sailing ships go over Niagara Falls and wind up in the '60s, getting rescued by a warship, and escaping into New York City, dressed as 15th century sailors? ...Anyway, plunging on – You were telling me that you have 42 filing boxes full of manuscripts in your house?

GCJ: I have 42 filing boxes full of manuscripts, full of folders – plus, a full file cabinet. And that represents work done over the last forty-five years. Most of that stuff has never seen the daylight. Much of it has never ever been submitted or even discussed. Nobody knows about this little story, "The Guilt in the World," and one of the reasons that I may end up finishing it is because I was talking with Steve Bloom, who is the editor of *High Times Magazine*, and I asked him, do you guys ever publish fiction? I don't notice any. And he said, "In your case, we'd make an exception." So, I thought I'd better do this little story about Captain Ed and his doper tale. *(The late Captain Ed, a peripheral character in George's story, "Ring of Truth," founded and operated a prominent Van Nuys, California, head shop since the mid-sixties. And, it's still open.)*

You know the part of "All of Us Are Dying" that I've been dying to ask about, the outline for the movie, "Lovecraft, Man of Mythos?"

GCJ: Some guy came to me and he had this theory that the town of Providence, in celebrating H.P. Lovecraft, one of their favorite sons, might end up financing a movie if the movie was done in Providence. I thought it was a bad idea, but the guy offered me a thousand dollars to tell him *where was the story* in H.P. Lovecraft. So, I went and read all of Lovecraft's material. I read everything I could get my hands on, including the novels. And I read the short stories, and then I read about his life, and I read biographies and even his fanzine – he published one of the first fanzines – it was called *The Conservative*, and they've got seven or eight copies of it at Cal State Northridge in their Lovecraft file. But, I took the thousand dollars, I read all of Lovecraft's stuff, and I tried to figure out, where *is* the story? Do you try to do a Lovecraft novel? No, I didn't think so because most of them, when you get down to it, are really more terri-fyingly *described* than in terms of what you might actually see if you were there. He's always seeing things that would freeze him into helplessness, the narrator character in his stories, that is...

Which was basically him…

GCJ: Which was basically him, but several of his stories are really quite him, because he identifies with his character, Randolph (Carter). So, I ended up writing that little outline for how to go about making the movie about the death of H.P. Lovecraft, and encompassing a lot of his material in the movie without necessarily trying to dramatize a particular novel or a short story of his.

As Lovecraft is dying in the hospital, we see flashbacks of his life – from his friends and family, gathered outside his hospital room, as well as creatures and super-natural elements from his stories in the form of his own dreams and nightmares…A "Finnegan's Wake" with tentacled monstrosities lurking in its subconscious… It's a great idea – and one way of getting all those things in…

GCJ: Yeah, that's what I thought. They were unable to get it off the ground, so now it's all reverted back to me. Nevertheless, that's sort of how one's life goes on its way… You asked about *The Strange Case of Charles Dexter Ward?*

That's something we discussed the other day, Charles Beaumont's screenplay for Roger Corman's "The Haunted Palace," *actually an adaptation of the Lovecraft novel,* "The Case of Charles Dexter Ward," *disguised as an Edgar Allan Poe movie. I don't know if Beaumont wrote it for Sam Arkoff, Roger Corman, or if he had already written it – but it's one of my favorites in that cycle…*

GCJ: It was something that he had when I met him. He had made attempts to sell it – all of us have several scripts we've tried to sell; he sold *The Queen of Outer Space,* but he couldn't sell *The Strange Case of Charles Dexter Ward.* Until finally, Roger Corman came along, but Corman came along much later. By that time, Beaumont was a well-established author.

You have a lot of short stories in "All of Us Are Dying…" *Were they written with eventual dramatization in mind, since you were "writing for the tube," as one of your essays, contained herein, is titled?*

GCJ: Each of these short stories was written to be a specific story, for an attempt mainly just to continue to make a living at selling stories. And I would send them out to the various magazines and get them back.

I was never very, very successful at short stories, so when Ray tells me to go ahead and write more short stories... Now that I've got an established reputation, I could probably sell almost anything I wrote that was any good. But I wrote some things that were absolutely wonderful, and never, ever got them sold.

I read about Lovecraft getting rejected, too. From the editor of Weird Tales, *Farnsworth Wright? He would stamp "A Farnsworth Wright reject" across the top of the first page before returning them, and Lovecraft would send them straight off to Harry Bates at Strange Tales like that.*

GCJ: Where did you read that?

In an interview with Hugh B. Cave in Cemetery Dance *(#29; with Darrell Schweitzer).*

GCJ: And Harry Bates rejected them, too. I think Lovecraft's stories were mostly published in *Weird Tales*, and only about a dozen, all in all; most of his work was never published in his lifetime. Many of the novels, like *At the Mountains of Madness*, were never even typed up, although they were all fully written. After his death they were dug out, but typing was such a difficult task for him that until he knew he would have a sale for them, he just left them in manuscript form. He was, during his lifetime, fairly unknown. He became much more famous afterwards.

Look at Robert E. Howard, and look what's been done with the bits and pieces and scraps of his story ideas by L. Sprague DeCamp and Lin Carter... They made a cottage industry out of exhausting every possible idea in Robert E. Howard's files...

GCJ: ...And Roy Thomas is continuing the work in the comics, with the young Conan.

I think Howard would be pleased...

GCJ: Yeah, sure, Conan is an interesting character, especially since he represents Robert E. Howard's attitude.

Back to your book again: Star Trek: "Rock-a-Bye Baby – Or Die!" *Is that the one that was never produced?*

GCJ: That was the Star Trek story that never got filmed.

And it has something to do with the ship, itself, taking on a life? An idea which was later used in Nightflyers *and more recently, in* Event Horizon, *but back then, it was a pretty original concept...*

GCJ: Oh, it was. It was an original idea, yeah. They were absolutely happy to have the idea, the only problem was, their producer wanted to change it, and he and I got into a fight, and I bought it back.

That was Gene Coon, again?

GCJ: Yes.

And the script they did buy? Wasn't that the first Star Trek *episode aired?*

GCJ: Yes, it was. It's called "The Mantrap."

Going back to the fifties, for a minute – you came out of the army into the beat generation, and you mentioned your interest in psychedelia, the Merry Pranksters and the '60. But before that, there was the beat generation, which kind of morphed into the hippie thing about ten years later. You seem to have taken your image from, and were forged more as a personality by, the late '60s – early '70s, than by the '50s. If I had to guess by looking at you, I would say, this is a man of the '60s. A lot of people of your generation are more rooted in the '50s, do you know what I mean? They have crew cuts...

GCJ: Yeah, it's true... The late '50s is when that beatnik thing was really going well. And that's when I started hanging out in Laurel Canyon, trying to become a writer. I spent a lot of time arrogantly flaunting my poverty; sandals, no shirt... a windbreaker, pair of dungarees – that was my idea of dress-up. And of course – to let oneself go to seed, so to speak. There was a lot of wine and partying, bongo drums and marijuana... Stuff like that was going on amongst the so-called beatniks. I was very much caught up with the whole beat generation idea. The Jack Kerouac thing, I could identify with an awful lot of that. As you say, it sort of morphed into this other thing when The Beatles came along, and added that element of color, and the exotic aspect...

And rebellion. The element of revolution – the cultural revolution in which, like most cultural revolutions, the advanced guard were the college students. So, unlike the beat generation, where everything was kind of a really delicious secret to those special few that chose to live on this wavelength – all of a sudden, there was a cultural revolution, and it became very popular to live on this "expanded" wavelength.

GCJ: That's right. I really had roots in that, and knew the others – the Allen Ginsburgs of the world and people like that – I knew those guys.

You had a column in The Staff? *Who was the editor, Brian Kirby?*

GCJ: Yes, and before that I wrote for *The Freep (The Los Angles Free Press),* for Art Kunkin.

Well, that's where I started out – my first real job, selling cartoons and comic strips, working for Art Kunkin at the Free Press. Harlan Ellison (R) had a column there, too, then ("The Glass Teat"), and so did Charles Bukowski ("Notes of a Dirty Old Man"), who hadn't really become famous yet, nationally. Back then, he drove a beat-up Volkswagon. Occasionally, on production night, Art would come off the phone and say, "No column this week, – Bukowski's on a binge again," so we'd run a plug that said exactly that.

GCJ: I remember it was a very grubby scene. We worked at a coffee house – the Third Estate. He had offices downstairs, Art Kunkin did, and I'd go there and hang out with him. That was on Sunset.

It was a great time, and I'm glad to have been a part of it. I'm very proud to have worked for a newspaper that was on Nixon's White House enemies list. I believe you had a comment for the close of this interview?

GCJ: Yes... I could make another entire book, like *All of Us Are Dying,* out of just what's in my files.

Then we could do another interview...

Afterword

By Paul Jeffrey Davids

I met L. J. Dopp at the Thai Plaza restaurant in Hollywood in 2006 at a birthday party for our mutual mentor, Forrest J Ackerman (Forry), who had just turned 90. My film, *"The Sci-Fi Boys,"* which extolled the contribution of Forry to all things science fiction, had come out that spring, and L. J got a copy of the DVD of the film that day and quickly embraced it at a true fanboy level of exuberance. The nitty gritty and ragged edges of early sci-fi films had always spoken to L. J. in a personal and intimate level.

Our paths were fated to cross again three years later when I bought one of his paintings at the estate sale of the late Forrest J Ackerman in 2009. It's known as the *"Blue Forry"* painting, which either coincidentally or by some act of providence predicted the exact time of Mr. Ackerman's death four years in advance. There is a clock in the painting that inexplicably shows the time-of-death that was yet to occur, and there is also a raven, a wonderful Poe symbol of the "Nevermore."

That painting became the basis of the DVD cover of my film, *The Life After Death Project* in 2010. Three years later, it was used again as the key art for the cover of a book I co-wrote with Dr. Gary Schwartz: *An Atheist in Heaven: The Ultimate Evidence for Live After Death?*

L. J. is a filmmaker and director in his own right noted for *The Boneyard Collection,* hosted by Forrest J Ackerman, which has seven Oscar-nominated guest stars, one Oscar winner and two Golden Globe winners. He is also known for *Crustacean* (writer/director); his original music for that cult film received significant recognition. However, at first I knew L. J. mainly for his paintings. I knew him and admired him as an artist, because he is certainly a painter with an obsession I share. He has primarily dedicated himself to preserving the 1950's and 1960's science-fiction and horror films by rendering their leading men and leading ladies, their spaceships and their monsters. As cover artist for Vincent Price Presents comics, L. J. has painted Vincent Price more times than any other fantasy genre artist. I consider that a distinguished accomplishment. All the moreso because almost every time I would visit L.J. and admire the depth and scope of his collection of his own works, I would depart with one of those paintings. Can I even count the number of Vincent Price paintings I have added to my own collection of original L. J. Dopp works?

I love his paintings and bought many different ones he created as speculative works, including his *"Bettie Page"* and *"Marilyn Monroe."* I also commissioned paintings of my family, and I soon enlisted several of my friends to commission his work as well.

Throughout the years of giving meticulous attention to L. J.'s art, which I consider brilliant, never did he breathe a word to me about his short stories. Or if he did breathe a word, I wasn't listening carefully enough. Finally he brought forth some of his stories for me.

You have now read them, and I hope you share my opinion that they are not only very good, they are unique, splendid, entertaining, gifted in conception, witty in execution, full of surprises and generally unforgettable. That is a long-winded way of saying that I love them, and I hope you have loved them too. My short assessment is this: L. J. Dopp is an entirely brilliant writer. He is an undiscovered treasure as a writer. What a treat your friends will have in store when you tell them about this book you stumbled upon, or which fate tossed into your life. While reading L. J.'s stories, I have laughed, gasped and been bewitched and filled with wonder. His wit and sarcasm truly cut like a very sharp knife. I especially appreciate the way he absolutely mercilessly skewers the world of low-budget independent filmmaking, as well as Hollywood itself. How natural that he should be the one to lift and heave the heavy hatchet to strike some hefty blows, because he is a Hollywood-born filmmaker. From his younger years, he learned where the rats make their nests, and where the maggots convene. If you are like me, you have marveled at the fate and fetishes of the various fictional characters who populate his pages.

I have asked myself many times, how can a writer who is this good have kept his talents secret from the world for so long? The answer is partially that the stories were often rejected. His submissions to various magazines often met with little interest from editors who must have thought he didn't have a big enough name. (Well, L. J. Dopp IS a very short name!) Seriously, though, many are the writers who have had to wait for recognition, including H. P. Lovecraft and even Franz Kafka (who wanted all his works, all unpublished, burned after his death, but his heirs did not agree). This is not to compare Dopp with Lovecraft and Kafka, though perhaps his blood has had a few literary transfusions from theirs. I think of Dopp as a Benchley-esque Terry Southern reincarnation with a shake of salt from Edgar Allan Poe and a pinch of pepper from Bram Stoker… and even a dash of spice from humorist par excellence Mark Twain.

I'd be remiss if I didn't mention that in 2016, L. J. Dopp was associate producer of my film *"Marilyn Monroe Declassified,"* and not only does he also appear in the film, but he painted the beautiful rendering of Marilyn as the key art that appears on the DVD cover and poster.

As for *"The Brain That Couldn't Think,"* I want to emphasize that it seems to be very appropriate that this book began with his story *"The Man Who Was Severely Edited,"* because if there is any better short story about a writer's ultimate, perfect, clever and stupendous act of revenge, I do not know of it. And this particular revenge is not even violent, which makes the punishment fit the crime just perfectly. And it is fitting that this book ends with his extensive interview with one of the writers he admires most, George Clayton Johnson, because it is a sort of ultimate intimate lesson on a writer's lot in life. Must it always be a fact of life that for most writers, a dozen stories (sometimes half-finished) gather dust in a drawer for every one that sees the light of day?

I feel that every hour of helping L. J. to prepare this book for publication was worth it, because you have had the opportunity to experience the same delight that I did when I discovered for the first time the fabulous literary talent of a writer who is also one of my favorite painters: L. J. Dopp.

So now you can turn your cell-phone back on and make your first call to some friends to tell them about *"The Brain That Couldn't Think!"* That is, if your brain can still think, after the literary roller coaster that you, as a reader, have just experienced. Never mind if you suffered brain damage - you will recover, and you will live to think another day.

Paul Jeffrey Davids
Los Angeles, January, 2017

About the Author

Artist-filmmaker L.J. Dopp was raised by his grandfather, a pianist from the jazz age, who was a very successful Hollywood music copyist/librarian by the '50s-'60s. He sometimes took the boy to work with him on Saturdays—often, to rehearsals or tapings of TV programs like *The Chevy Show* at NBC, *or The Danny Kaye Show* at CBS. They also visited museums, amusement parks, and the movies. Dopp had his first art lessons as a child from his cousin, famous Catholic artist Corita Kent—but it was an early '60s TV show on Saturday mornings, *"Learn to Draw with Jon Gnagy,"* that taught him light and shadow, horizon line, and perspective.

He was attracted to the comics during the silver age, and while in high school, his spy-parody comic strip in the school paper caught the eye of a student who introduced him to official comic-collecting and the Los Angeles Science Fantasy Society. Dopp's first published works were covers and illustrations for fanzines. To this day, his greatest influences remain the work of the E.C. comic book artists and writers, including the "usual gang of idiots" who put out *Mad* Magazine.

Accepted by Chouinard/Cal Arts, Dopp took life drawing classes there after high school, but instead enrolled in the renowned Los Angeles City College Theatre Arts Department as a full-time acting and voice major. He dropped drawing 101 because he disliked the teacher, but by his second year at L.A.C.C., was staff artist of the Theatre Dept., designing posters and playbills for a small salary. His scene shop class led to a later work as a scenic artist and eventual production designer. Dopp switched his major to directing, co-wrote and directed an original play, and wrote-directed a student film in the Cinema Dept., *"Fangs for the Memories."*

At 22, Dopp got hired as a cartoonist at The Los Angeles Free Press, back when artists Ron Cobb, Gilbert Shelton, and R. Crumb were published, along with columns by Harlan Ellison (R) and Charles Bukowski. He rose to his first position as art director and had his own sci-fi comic strip running briefly. Dopp continued working in the Hollywood publishing field throughout the '80s, writing and drawing for newspapers, as well as being art director for David F. Friedman's pioneer home video company. He co-wrote a big budget adult film, *"Lust on the Orient Express,"* under a pseudonym, that also played the drive-in circuit with a "R" rating. Dopp picked-up as much freelance work as possible in the '90s, including weapons design for *"Spawn the Movie,"* storyboards for director, Herb Freed *("Graduation Day"),* and designs for Disneyland's new Tomorrow-land and Rocket Video on La Brea, with its 3-D Flash Gordon rocket-ship and planets in a 60' mural. He began writing sci-fi comedy spec scripts at night in '95, hoping to get one made so he could possibly bring his art and music skills to bear, as well.

In the winter of 1998, his comedy screenplay at Trimark Pictures stalled out and the studio asked if he had any "dark horror" scripts lying around, so he decided to write one. A horror fan who'd cut his fangs on *Famous Monsters of Filmland* (starting with issue #15), this was fate! While still providing art services, Dopp started reading Lovecraft again, as well as *Weird Tales* and *Cemetery Dance*, and sending out short stories (some of which are in this book). When Trimark passed on his horror treatment, he finished the script anyway and dedicated his life to the horror-fantasy genre, soon getting his non-fiction published in *Cemetery Dance*.

After doing some movie art for producer Edward L. Plumb, Dopp began co-producing a couple of faux horror comedy trailers with him in the early 2000s—this time doing complete production design, writing some gags, and composing music. The trailers came out pretty good, so they decided to create an anthology feature to house them *("The Bone-yard Collection;"* 2012; Green Apple, DVD and downloads. Re-released by Echo Bridge in 2016 in a package DVD titled, *"Paranormal Encounters").* Dopp got friend, Forrest J Ackerman, to host it as Dr. Acula, co-writing his scenes and designing an entire crypt set for him. The two producers continued making the anthology's segments for several years.

Dopp also scored half the comedy feature's 100-minute running time and wrote-directed the 28-minute *"Cry of the Mummy"* segment with Plumb directing the rest of the film. Guest stars in the feature who ac-company Ackerman include Brad Dourif, George Kennedy, Susan Tyr-rell, Ken Foree, William Smith, Robert Loggia, Kevin McCarthy, Tippi Hedren, Candy Clark, Budd Friedman, and Barbara Steele.

Brad Linaweaver—a sci-fi author of some note and publisher of Mondo Cult Magazine—got Dopp a sculpting gig for Dragon Con's pres-tigious Futura Award in 2003, based on the Ultimate Futura Robatrix from Metropolis; first recipients were Forrest J Ackerman and Ray Brad-bury. Linaweaver regularly published Dopp in his magazine (now an ezine, mondocult.com), commissions unique paintings that often become iconic, and co-executive produced Dopp's horror comedy, *"Crustacean,"* (2010; DVD).

Dopp's oil portrait of close friend, George Clayton Johnson, has become rather iconic, but it was the depiction of a clock in *Dopp's "Blue Forty"* acrylic portrait—given to Ackerman as a gift in 2004—that eerily predicted the exact minute of his death four years later. This caused it to be published in *Fate* Magazine (Sept.-Oct. 2009) in an article by producer Paul Davids *(Roswell, The Sci-Fi Boys)* who had acquired the painting. A weird typo from Davids' printer, that had seemed enough of a posthumous message from the recently deceased Ackerman to warrant writing the article, occurred again in Fate Magazine—in the middle of Dopp's name!

In 2008, Dopp was co-nominated for A Rondo Award for Best Magazine Cover for *Mondo Cult #2*, and in January of 2011, became a cover artist for *Vincent Price Presents* comics. In 2013, Dopp received a Rondo Awards Honorable Mention for Best Magazine Cover of 2012, for Mondo Cult #3. After that, the films, and four years as a featured artist at Monsterpalooza, he's starting to get known in the genre.

"Call me a late bloomer," Dopp says. "Although humor has graced my work since the *Free Press* days, concentrating mainly on the horror-fantasy genre didn't happen till the '90s, and I didn't really start painting oil-on-canvas every day till the 2000s. That's made all the difference—both in my own happiness, and in finding a niche. I like to combine a photo-realistic image taken from a still or publicity shot with a drawn, original background. But should my drawing hand continue to deteriorate, I see the future as being more 'drawn' to writing. I sold two short stories in the last year, and now, thanks to Paul Jeffrey Davids, I have this book out that you are holding in your hands. If you enjoyed reading it half as much as I did writing it, then I still had twice as much fun as you. Cheers, and thanks for reading!"

WEBSITE: LJDopp.com
FACEBOOK
https://www.facebook.com/profile.php?id=1248890287
CRUSTACEAN THE MOVIE: crustaceanthemovie.com

www.ingramcontent.com/pod-product-compliance
Lightning Source LLC
Chambersburg PA
CBHW030515020726
47494CB00004B/1109